JON CLEARY

Dilemma

HarperCollins*Publishers*

HarperCollins*Publishers*
77–85 Fulham Palace Road,
Hammersmith, London W6 8JB

The HarperCollins website address is:
www.**fire**and**water**.com

This paperback edition 2000
1 3 5 7 9 8 6 4 2

First published in Great Britain by
HarperCollins*Publishers* 1999

Copyright © Jon Cleary 1999

Jon Cleary asserts the moral right to
be identified as the author of this work

ISBN 0 00 651345 X

Set in Times by Palimpsest Book Production Limited,
Polmont, Stirlingshire

Printed in Great Britain by
Omnia Books Limited, Glasgow

For

Natascia and Vanessa

Part One

March 1994

Chapter One

1

Malone pulled up his car in the Erskineville street where he had been born, got out and waited for the memories to flood back. He had been doing this for the past six months, but now the memories were only a trickle; drought, the bane of farmers and sentimentalists, had set in. One side of the street had lost its row of workmen's cottages; they had been replaced by a row of town houses or, as the estate agents now called them, villas. On the side where Malone stood, *his* side, the terrace houses had been gentrified. All had been painted: pale cream but with different-coloured doors: red, yellow, blue, green; all with ornate knockers, like suddenly proclaimed coats of arms. Some of the narrow verandahs that opened right on to the pavement had planter boxes behind their painted iron railings. All of them had security grilles on the windows; some had security doors. Only on the very end of the terrace was the rebel, the memory anchor.

Painted cream like the others, yes; but the door was brown, the plain knocker was black, there was no security grille. A youth had broken into the house a couple of years ago and Con Malone had met him with one of Malone's old cricket bats and beaten him senseless. The kid had wanted to charge Con with assault and the two young cops who had been called by Brigid Malone had had to hold Con back from assaulting him further.

Con Malone was sitting on a kitchen chair on the verandah, soaking up the hour's sun that the front of the house managed. He was reading the morning's newspaper, a ritual that took him from the front pages, through the obituaries to the sports pages, read in sequence like a book. Malone paused a few steps from the front gate and looked at his father. The old man, like the memories, was fading. The tree-trunk body was thinner and smaller, there was now a hunch to the once-straight back. He suddenly felt an immense affection for his father.

Con looked up as Malone stepped in the front gate. 'G'day.'

'G'day. You're still reading the *Herald*.'

'Nothing but bloody opinionated columnists.'

'The *Daily Worker* was *all* opinion.'

'It was an honest paper, knew what was going on.' He folded the paper carefully. If he had believed in butlers and could have afforded one, he would have had the butler iron the paper before bringing it to him. He had read that British aristocrats did that, the only thing he admired them for. 'Bloody country's going to the dogs.'

The bloody world, which didn't really interest Con,

4

was going to the dogs. The IRA had just attacked Heathrow airport in London; Bosnia was trying to go back to pre-1914; in the US the Whitewater scandal was overflowing its banks. At home things were slightly better: the economy was breaking into a gallop, condoms were being urged in schools to protect sexually rabid teenagers against HIV. The Chippendales were on tour, always promising but never actually doing the full monty, whatever that was. And down in Canberra, the Prime Minister, as all PMs before him and to come after him, was attacking those who criticized him and his politics. The world spun in monotonous circles.

'Look at 'em!' said Con in disgust. Two women had passed by on the other side of the road: Arab women in *chadors*, though their faces were uncovered. 'Wogs, slant-eyes . . . When you were a kid growing up, this street was *ours*.'

'Grow up, Dad. That was the nineteenth century. Mum inside?'

'She's down at the church. Putting the holy water in the fridge, case it goes off. You know what she's like. Bloody churches, they've gone to the dogs, too. You been away?'

'Up to Noosa, just Lisa and me.' He had told his mother and father about the planned trip; but their memories, like themselves, were fading. 'A second honeymoon, I think they call it.'

'You've been lucky. Both of us, you and me. Mum'n I've been happy. Just like you and Lisa. That ain't common, not these days. I read in this –' holding up the

5

paper '– two blokes married. *Blokes*! You think they'll be happy like we been?'

Malone shrugged. 'They could be.'

'Bloody poofters. Wogs, slant-eyes – I'm in a foreign country. You back at work?' Con Malone, then working on the wharves, hadn't been able to hold his head up when his only child had become a cop. The union had doubled his dues for three months. 'That last job must of wore you out. Two women poofters killing one of them's husband.'

'They're called lesbians, Dad. Or dykes.'

It was Con's turn to shrug. 'Who cares? The cases get you down sometimes?'

'Sometimes.'

'What d'you do then? Hand 'em on to someone else?'

'It doesn't work like that. Not like on the wharves.' He grinned when he said it; he'd better or his father would be on his feet, two fists up. The wharves had been Con's parish, the union his religion.

'So you've never walked away from a case?'

'Not so far. But . . .'

'Here comes Mum. Pious as hell. She's just been talking to God or the Pope.'

Brigid Malone smiled as she approached, but she didn't put out her hand or turn her cheek to be kissed. She kept that sort of affection for her grandchildren; she too belonged to the nineteenth century. A long while ago she had been a handsome woman, maybe even close to a beauty; but that, too, somehow seemed as distant as the

6

nineteenth century. Like Con, she had shrunk over the past six months. Lately she had begun to talk of Ireland, of her girlhood: but only to her grandchildren. To talk like that to Scobie, her son, would be too difficult. With him she was still trapped in the tight corset of her earlier feelings. She loved him, he knew that, but if she shed tears for him he had never seen them.

'How are Lisa and the children?'

'Fine. How's the Pope?'

'I'll ask him next time he writes. You coming in for a cuppa tea? I've made some scones.'

'Date scones?'

'What else?'

He followed them into the house. The safe house, where they had protected him as securely as he tried to do with his own children. Where crime, when it entered, could be handled with the simple logic of a cricket bat.

2

Ron Glaze had gone to the house, *their* house, but she had not been there. It was a Housing Commission home, built in the 1960s, improved by the garden he had built around it. Brick veneer, tiled roof, three bedrooms, one bathroom, living and dining rooms combined; three years ago, when things had been going well for them and between them, they had taken out a mortgage and bought it. They had grown up in this area, they were both Westies, and they had felt comfortable with it as a starting point. They occasionally dreamed of a house in one of the seaside suburbs, on a northern beach, say Collaroy or Narrabeen; but that was for the future, when they would have more money, even have kids. The future that had never come within coo-ee of them.

The light had been on in the hallway and he had pressed the doorbell. There had been no answer and after the second ringing of the bell he had taken out his key and let himself in. He had kept the key in his pocket, prepared to let her ask him in, not just barge in as if he owned the place. Which he still did – or anyway, half of it.

She had not been there. He had gone slowly through the house, as if looking for reminders of her and himself. He had been gone three months, but now it seemed like only yesterday. He was not a reader, but somewhere he had read a proverb or something: *What was hard to bear was sweet to remember*. Wrong: like so many proverbs. The last fight with her, when she had thrown him out of the house, had been hard to bear; there was no sweetness in remembering it. That fight had been right here, in the kitchen. He had been standing there, in his hand a Coke that he had taken from the fridge. He had looked around, then put down the Coke and walked out of the kitchen quickly, as if she were chasing him again, throwing things at him. He had walked into the bedroom, their passion pit, and lain down on the bed, *his* side, put his hands behind his head and stared at the

8

ceiling, wondering if the effort to reconcile with her was going to be worthwhile.

He was of medium height, with thinning blond hair (a major worry) and a round cheerful face that hovered, like an image in water, between good-looking and plain, depending on the light. What appealed to women was his smile, wide and white. But he was not smiling now. He tried to remember the passion here in this bed, but it was just cold ashes. The gap between them had been growing over the past year; he had seen it widening and been unable to stop it. Maybe it had been his fault (the women) or maybe it had been hers (the ambition). He was not a chauvinist (so he thought), but women undoubtedly didn't understand men. But he would not tell her that, not tonight.

He had lain there for almost an hour, waiting for her to come home. But she hadn't, and then he had got up and gone looking for her, knowing for certain where he would find her.

They had been members for ten years of the Golden West Club; it was there they had met. It had been one of the first of the clubs that had sprouted in the western suburbs and it had grown and grown. It now had 60,000 members, all of whom, fortunately, did not attend on the same night; it had 1000 poker machines, all of which were genuflected to by the congregation each night. It had four restaurants and put on floor shows almost every night. It could afford overseas performers: Tom Jones had done his best to dislocate his hips here and John Denver had sung songs of places far away from the flat plain of the western suburbs. The Chippendales had performed here on Ladies Night Only; orgasms had erupted like an epidemic of wind. The women went home and sexually attacked their husbands. Those lucky men, more K-Mart than Chippendale, hadn't been able to believe their luck.

Now they were sitting at a table in the club, as stiff with each other as on a first date.

'Ron, it's no use. It's all over. Finished. What was it you used to say about the politicians and the union officials, you used to laugh about? At this point in time. That's it, Ron. At this point in time it's all over.'

Norma Glaze was thirty-one, a year younger than her husband. She had been a hairdresser ever since she had left school; even doctors did not need the ear and tongue that successful hairdressers had to have. Buzz words and phrases came and went like hairstyles; *mode* was the latest, but she had heard them all. Her clients picked them up from their husbands and boyfriends, though she could see none of them on a *level playing field*. Ron, a car salesman, had the tongue but not the ear; the latter was not necessary in the motor trade, he had often told her. At any point in time, on a level playing field or wherever. Talk was action . . .

'Don't you miss the fucking we had?'

'Don't start talking dirty, Ron. It's not gunna get you anywhere.'

'Okay, okay.' He had three feet tonight, kept putting the wrong one forward. Selling himself to her had never been easy; maybe that was why he had sold himself so

10

easily to other women. A Holden Caprice with low mileage: that was how he had sold himself and the women had laughed and bought him, if only for a demonstration run. 'Miss you, hon. Really. Not just the sex bit . . .'

She looked around, glad they were at an isolated table; she had chosen it and led him to it as soon as he had walked in the door. They were a fair distance from the long bar, but close to the nearest bank of poker machines. Players were at the machines, but their backs were to the Glazes; their eyes, minds, every sense concentrated on the bright faces of the machines. This was Monday night, always a slow night. Two hundred people maximum, she thought, every one of the bastards looking at us out of the corners of their eyes or through the back of their heads. A hairdresser, she knew that gossip hung in the air like legionnaire's disease.

She was attractive, too heavy in the jaw to be beautiful; she had large dark blue eyes and a mouth enlarged by careful makeup. Her black hair was cut in a bob with a fringe; a ninety-year-old customer had told her she looked like Louise Brooks, whoever the hell she was. She was as tall as Ron, with a good figure that needed careful dieting and two sessions a week at aerobics. All that was exterior: the interior, not even Ron had come close to knowing. Though, to tell the truth, she was not even sure she knew herself.

'Ron, try and get it through your head –' She shook her own head; the black hair moved, throwing off lights

11

like a black mirror. The way he had always loved it . . . 'We're incompatible –'

'Oh, for Crissakes! Jesus, hon, how can you say that?' He sat back, looked round the huge room as if about to appeal to the gamblers at the poker machines, to the two barmen and the barmaid, to the drinkers at the other tables. But they were all ignoring him; or so it seemed. He looked back at her: 'Norma, don't start sounding like a fucking psychiatrist – You're not going to one, are you?'

'Don't be silly.' She toyed with her drink, a vodka and tonic, her staple. She had been drinking more and eating less lately: she would have to watch herself. 'I hear you lost your job. What happened?'

He had been hoping she would not bring that up. He looked at his own drink, a beer. 'Business was down. They say the economy is growing, but that's bullshit. Are you getting more customers?'

'Yes,' she said. 'I'm thinking of opening up another salon.'

'I've been looking at going into the nursery business,' he said tentatively.

She didn't laugh, as he had been afraid she might. But she did say, 'What are you gunna use for money?'

'I've got a bit saved. And I think the bank'll listen to me.'

'You owe me three months on the mortgage, your share.'

Jesus, why did she always have to harp on about money? 'I'll cover that.'

'How?'

'Don't worry – I told you I'd cover it!' He was trying to hold on to his temper. Over at the bar Charlene was looking at him, talking all the while to the three or four men at the bar. She waved to him and he nodded back. 'Let's talk about us, hon – not money –'

Norma had looked back over her shoulder. 'You still got a thing for her?'

'Who?'

'Charlene, the freewheeling bike.'

'For Crissake, Norma – cut it out! I never had a *thing* for her – Jesus, it was just one night! You were away, I dunno where –'

'I was up at Gosford, taking care of my mother who was sick with pneumonia –' She stopped abruptly, as if suddenly exhausted by the argument. She stared at her glass, twirled it round again with those fingers that had been so clever at finding their way round his body. Then she said, her voice so low that he had to lean forward to hear her, 'Go, Ron. It's over. I don't want to see you again. Ever.'

'Hon –'

'Please go. Don't make a scene – just *go*.'

All at once in the huge room there was one of those silences that are magnified by the number of those present. Two hundred people had abruptly stopped talking; even Charlene, at the bar, who never stopped. The poker machines were motionless: no symbols fell, no bell rang. The garish lights, an electrician's nightmare, seemed brighter, more eye-burning. Heads turned to see

13

what had caused the silence; but there was nothing to be seen. It had just happened, like the closing of a book.

Ron stood up. There was an aridness in Norma's voice that all of a sudden opened up a desert before him.

'Goodbye,' he said and walked the long walk to the wide front doors. Norma didn't turn her head to watch him, which was a pity. He had never known the meaning of dignity, but tonight he accomplished it, even if he was unaware of it. His back was straight, his pace steady.

Come to think of it, Charlene would say later, he looked cold-blooded. Which would be damning, but was wrong.

3

He was a tall lean man with a bony face that stopped just short of being handsome. He had thick dark hair with already a touch of grey at the temples; he would be grey-haired by the time he was forty-five, thirteen years away. He moved with an unhurried easy grace, as if he knew he was destined for a long life and minutes and seconds saved did not matter. He wore a blue button-down shirt, a purple-and-green striped tie, a brown tweed jacket and grey slacks. He had a habit of standing with his right hand in his jacket pocket, rather like 1930s British actors in late-night movies. He was noticeable, though not by intent.

He was on his way back from Katoomba, where, due

14

to the bungling of the locals, he had had to work longer than he had planned. He had come down from the Blue Mountains and was on the freeway heading for the city when his bladder began to assert itself. He was coming into the outskirts of the suburbs and began to look for a place to pull off the freeway. A curving exit opened up ahead and he took the Mitsubishi Magna up it and brought the car to a halt. He got out, relieved himself, felt the relief of a long piss, one of the unlisted small joys of life. He was about to get back into the car when he saw the big neon-lit building about a couple of hundred metres along the crossroad. All at once he felt thirsty and hungry. Later he would remember, with sour humour, that the whole tragic night had begun with an urge to piss.

He drove into the car park of the club; it looked large enough to take at least a thousand cars, but tonight there were less than two hundred. He knew of it, it was famous, the first of the clubs that had started back in the fifties. It had drawn the local residents together, given them a haven and distraction from the sterile suburbs in which they lived; it had provided what the urban planners had not thought of, a focus. It was wealthy, had voting power with the other clubs, and it spread money where it was needed in the district. A sign by the wide front doors told him: All Visitors Welcome.

He walked in, was overwhelmed by the size of the huge room. He was accustomed to smaller places, had grown up in a three-bedroom semi-detached in Collaroy and size, especially interiors, still impressed him. There were a fair number of people in the room, most of them lined up before the banks of poker machines that sat, with smug faces, like creatures from outer space waiting for the suckers to pay homage. One woman wore a long black glove on the hand that pumped her machine; he wondered if she drew it on like a surgeon about to operate. He was not a gambler, never had been, and he wondered what other strangers like himself, coming in, thought of the machines and their brazen look.

He walked up to the bar. 'Can I get something to eat without going to the restaurant?' He could see a restaurant up on a mezzanine floor. 'A sandwich or something?'

The barmaid had the sort of smile that she gave to everyone, whether she was favouring them or disappointing them. 'I can get you some sandwiches from the kitchen.'

'Thanks. And a beer. You have a Heineken, by any chance?' He had a pleasant voice, every word distinct.

'We have everything. You name it, we've got it, definitely. You moved in around here or just visiting?'

'Just visiting.'

'I'm Charlene, the oldest inhabitant. I was a teenager when I started here.'

He hoped she wasn't going to tell him her life's history. She was in her mid-forties, he guessed, bright, bouncy and unembarrassed by her openness: you got what you saw. Her hair was a blonde dome, some

16

hairdresser's self-monument. One would not have been surprised to find an autograph on the wearer's forehead. But she was efficient and he could see why she had lasted so long. Members, he was sure, would say she was a pillar of the club.

She brought him his beer and sandwiches. 'It's ham-and-avocado salad. Nice – I had one m'self for supper. You'll have to take it to a table. We don't allow 'em lining up here at the bar to eat. You know what men are like. Let 'em near a bar and they think it's their mother's tit, if you'll forgive the expression.'

'Of course.' He couldn't remember his mother's tit, but was sure he hadn't hung round it after he'd left babyhood. He had been one of five children and his mother, deserted by their father, had never had the time to coddle any of them.

He took his right hand out of his pocket to pick up the beer and the sandwiches and only then was it apparent why he kept the hand hidden. It was crippled, a twist of claws. He grasped the sandwich plate, took the beer in his left hand and went across to a table some distance from the bar. He sat down and only then noticed the woman three tables away from him. She looked at him without interest, then got up, went to the bar and brought back a drink. She was an attractive woman, everywhere but in her face: pain was there and anger and those emotions were never attractive. He had seen them before, in his work.

He watched her while he ate and drank, taking his time. It had been a long, hard, full day and now he was enjoying the relaxation, no matter how short it might be. The woman interested him: what had brought the pain and anger to her face? In profile they were less obvious; he shifted his chair so that she remained in profile to him. The more he looked at her, the more he became interested in her. There was a sensuality to her that he had missed at first: something in the line of her body, the way she moved when she raised her glass to her lips. But she paid him no attention and at last he decided it was time to go. He had at least another three-quarter of an hour's drive to home.

He stood up, went across and paid the barmaid. 'Thanks. I'm refreshed.'

'Half your luck. I'm done in. I'm not as young as I used to be. But don't tell anyone.' She gave him the smile. He liked her friendliness, but wondered why she played the part she had created for herself. When she got home, did she take off the front and throw it aside like a dirty brassiere?

'I never tell on a lady,' he said, smiled at her and left.

Out in the car park he was about to get into the Magna when he saw the woman moving unsteadily towards a grey Volvo. He paused, watching her. She stopped by the car, opened her handbag, took out her keys and dropped them. He heard her swear, then she leaned on the side of the car and slowly slid down, her free hand groping for the keys on the ground. He shut the door of the Magna and moved across to her.

'Can I help?'

She looked up at him. 'I've dropped my keys.' She stood up, slowly, still leaning on the car. They were close and he could smell the liquor on her breath. 'I think the night air's got to me.'

He found the keys, but didn't hand them to her. 'Do you live far from here?'

She waved vaguely. 'About five minutes. I dunno – I'm not much good at distances. I'm not much good at closeness, either.' She giggled.

'I think I'd better drive you home. Or get you a cab.'

'No cab. You go back in there, ring for cab and someone's gunna ask you if it's for me again. No thanks.' She was still leaning against her car, but with her back to it now. She looked carefully at him, as if making a decision on him; then she nodded back at the club. 'I saw you looking at me in there. Why?'

'I often look at attractive women.'

If she had giggled he would have walked away. But she just nodded, as if she knew that was the most natural thing in the world for men to do. He wondered how much experience of men she had had, but guessed she would be able to handle them.

'What's your name?'

'Fred.'

'Fred what?'

'Just Fred. What's yours?'

'Norma. Just Norma.' Then she straightened up, stepped away from the car. 'Drive me home, Fred.'

She gave him directions and it was indeed only five

minutes' drive. She said nothing during the five minutes, just sat side on looking at him. He could smell her perfume; and something else? Did desire have a perfume? When he slowed, looking for her street, she spoke at last. 'The next street on the right. They all look alike around here. It's the egali – something or other look.'

'Egalitarian.'

'That's it. One of my clients said it – she's a teacher, a real bolshie. I'm a hairdresser. What do you do, Fred?'

He could see something was building here. He would go along with it, she attracted him, but he was still cautious. If this was going to be a one-night stand, that was all it was going to be. 'I'm an adviser.'

'I could do with some advice.' She continued to look at him, then she smiled to herself, shrugged and said, 'How are you gunna get back to your own car?'

'I'll walk.'

'It's a long walk. You want me to ring for a cab?' She opened the car door, got out. 'Come in.'

He was not a floater, someone who picked up women like fish; he had always been steady, almost careful in his courting. This, though, wasn't courting; nothing in this, if anything happened, would remain in the memory of either of them as anything of consequence. He was not inexperienced in women; he recognized he was being invited inside for more than a phone call for a cab. He got out of the car, already big in his trousers, and followed her in through the front gate and up the narrow path.

'Don't step on the garden. It used to be my husband's pride and joy. It's gone to pot now.'

He paused in his step. 'Where is he?'

She stopped and looked back at him. 'Don't worry. He's looking after someone else's garden somewhere. We're finished,' she said, fumbling with the front door key. He wasn't sure whether there was pain or anger in her voice, as there had been in her face at the club. 'Finished. Bugger!'

She had dropped her keys again. He found them, put a key in the door and opened it. They were close together; he could smell the perfume and the heat of her. But he was not going to kiss her on the doorstep. 'After you, Norma.'

He followed her into the house, closed the door behind him. She turned back, gave him the direct look again. 'Do you wanna call a cab?'

'Not yet.'

She came into his arms as easily as if they were old lovers. There was no frantic tearing at each other; she led him towards the main bedroom, again as if they were old lovers. Only when they were undressing, on opposite sides of the bed, did she notice his claw.

'Is that your loving hand?'

She said it with a smile and he wasn't offended; but all at once he was embarrassed by it. As he had been with other women. 'No.'

'How'd it happen?'

But he just shook his head, fell on the bed and pulled her down on him. Later, he would not remember the

21

next half-hour. Drunkenness seemed to overtake her: the drunkenness of sex, the delayed effect of the drinks she had had at the club: he would never know. She tore at him as if she hated him; but wouldn't let go. At last he struggled free, fell back from her.

She grabbed at him again. 'Yes!'

'No – I can't –'

'What's the matter? Your dick crippled like your hand?'

That shocked him, he hadn't expected that sort of cruelty; he was equally shocked when he hit her. Anger is the most primitive emotion, the least civilized attribute of man. It comes from the oldest and deepest part of the brain, is always there; the last emotion left in a paralysed brain is anger. Later, he would remember that psychiatrists had put that opinion in court.

She rose up in the bed, hit him in the face with her fist; the fist turned into a claw, tore at him. He put up his left hand, tried to push her chin up and away. The hand slipped to her throat as she clawed at him again. She was babbling incoherently; she hit him in the eye and he swore with pain. Then his grip tightened on her throat.

He was shocked when she fell on him, pushing his left arm back into him. His fist opened and he slid his hand away from her throat. He pushed her off him, slipped to one side and lifted himself to look at her.

Then tentatively, like a lover's hand, he put his left hand on her throat again. There was no pulse.

*　　*　　*

22

Ron Glaze couldn't take no for an answer: it was the salesman in him.

After he had left the club he had gone to McDonald's and stuffed himself with two Big Macs; unhappiness made him hungry. You'll never grow up, his mother had told him; but hadn't spoiled him by turning him into a mummy's boy. When McDonald's told him they wanted to close down for the night he had gone out and sat on a bench in the mall. People passed him, some that he knew; they said *Hi*, and he nodded back at them. Some of them looked back at him curiously, but none of them came back to speak to him. He sat there for almost an hour, then he got up and wandered up the main street, stood on the pavement and looked across at Wisden's Car Sales, at the cars standing there in long rows, the floodlights reflected in the windscreens like malevolent smiles. Oh shit, he said aloud and began to cry.

That was when he decided to go back home and try again. When he saw the Volvo parked out front by the kerb, he wondered if she had had too much to drink. Whenever she did, she would never pull the car into the side driveway and up under the carport. Once she had done that and had driven off the path and ruined a whole row of azaleas in bloom. He had nearly killed her, he was so bloody angry.

He paused halfway up the front path and looked

around him. Even in the moonlight the garden looked a mess; it was as if she had let it go, to spite him. He would start repairing it tomorrow. Rebuild the garden and their marriage.

He had parked his car behind the Volvo. The two of them together, one behind the other, were a reminder of happier times. She was a careless driver, even when sober, but tonight she had parked the Volvo neatly. Right in the gutter, not like a woman's usual parking, a short walk from the kerb. He grinned at the thought, a car salesman's joke. His mood was lighter as he let himself quietly into the house.

The light was off in the hallway; she had gone to bed. But why wouldn't she have? It was two o'bloodyclock in the morning. He headed in the darkness, with the sureness of long practice, for the bedroom. If she had had too much to drink, she would be dead to the world; he knew what the vodka and tonics could do to her. They could make her sexually wild, but afterwards she would be as dead as a log. He would get into bed beside her, go to sleep and in the morning she would turn to him and sleepily feel for him, as she always did. Or always had.

He was approaching the bed when he tripped on her clothes on the floor. He fell on the bed, across her. She didn't stir nor gasp: nothing. He felt the nakedness of her, ran his hand up over her thigh and hip: no movement, nothing. He sat up, kneeling on the bed.

'Norma – hon –'

Then, suddenly afraid, he stood up, crossed to the

doorway and switched on the ceiling light. Norma lay on the bed naked, legs wide apart, her head twisted to one side as if she were trying to avoid looking at him. The bed was a mess, the sheet and single blanket halfway to the floor.

'Hon – for Chrissakes –'

Then, back beside the bed, he saw the marks on her throat and the big eyes, luminous no more, staring at the end of her world.

That was when he started to run, though it was almost five minutes before he actually moved other than to sit beside her, stroking her head and weeping.

5

'Why'd you call us?' asked Malone.

'We're stretched. We're short three detectives, two sick and one suspended – he's under investigation.' The local detective-sergeant, Jeff Backer, didn't elaborate on why one of his men was under investigation; you protected your own, particularly against other cops. 'We're handling four homicides. This one came up, the obvious suspect's shot through. We could be weeks finding him.'

'So you expect us to go looking for him?'

'You're the experts, aren't you?' There was no real friction; this was trade talk. Malone had not previously met Backer, but he had immediately liked him. 'It looks to me like open-and-shut. All we have to do is wait till Ron Glaze gives himself up. Unless he's gone somewhere and done himself in.'

'Has he any form? Belting her, stuff like that?'

'Nothing we've heard of. Out here it's not uncommon, but the women don't report it.'

'Even less so in the eastern suburbs.'

'They have more money there to hide the bruises.' Backer was a local through and through.

Malone, easing himself back into work after the Noosa holiday, had come out here to get away from the paperwork that had accumulated on his desk in his absence. Normally a case as straightforward as this one would not have attracted the Homicide chief; two junior detectives would have been sent. Malone had brought one of them with him, Andy Graham; Andy, in whom enthusiasm ran like a fever, would do all the legwork without complaint. Malone felt relaxed, glad he had picked an open-and-shut case to begin with.

The house was still roped off by Crime Scene tapes when Malone and Graham arrived, but the Physical Evidence team had gone and now there were only Backer and two uniformed men on the scene. Malone had noted that the house was neat and well kept: no peeling paint, no dump of cartons and newspapers on the front verandah. The garden was a gardener's plot, crammed with shrubs, but it had been allowed to grow wild. The lawn was a thick carpet that needed a mowing. Inside the house the neatness fell apart.

'The wife was okay as a housekeeper, so the neighbours say, but since her and her husband broke up three months ago, she sorta slipped. She's got her own hairdressing business and she was negotiating to lease another one over in Penrith. Seems she got sorta sloppy about the house. The husband was a dead-keen gardener, when he wasn't selling cars, but once he'd gone she let the weeds take over.'

'Who found her body?'

'That's it. A guy phoned our duty desk six o'clock this morning, said there was a dead woman at this address. Then he hung up.'

'Glaze?'

'Who else?'

'Whose is that Volvo out the front?'

'Hers.'

'Any prints?'

'They've got some out in the kitchen, on the fridge door and on a Coke bottle and a glass. But the guy from Fingerprints said he was puzzled – there's not a dab anywhere in the car, the front seat, the wheel, the dash. All wiped clean. Same in here –' He led Malone into the main bedroom. 'The bedhead, the side table, the door – all wiped clean.'

'Mrs Glaze might've been sloppy, but hubby wasn't. That what you're saying?'

'I'm not saying anything. I'm just telling you what we've come up with.' Backer was in his forties, over-weight, bald; he had a thick black moustache and tired dark eyes. Malone recognized the type: the good cop worn, like an old tyre, by too much roadwork. Who could still be shocked by the occasional brutal crime or the murder of a child, but not by this straightforward domestic. 'Unless it was someone else killed her.'

'Any suspect? She have any boyfriends?'

'Not as far as we know. For the moment my money's on Ron Glaze.'

They had come back to the living room. It was comfortably furnished, looked lived-in; but it was the sort of furniture bought by a couple who had other things to think of. The prints on the walls were of castles, cathedrals, mosques: someone's escape? There was a photo of Norma Glaze on the television set in one corner, the only photo in the room. None of Ron Glaze. There were two rows of Condensed Books volumes on a small bookshelf and beneath them two heaps of magazines: beauty magazines and gardening ones. Somehow, perhaps because of the break-up of the marriage, it was all as sterile as a hospital waiting-room.

'What's your guy doing?' said Backer.

'Andy?' Malone looked over his shoulder at Graham, who had gone into the bedroom. 'Just looking. If there's anything that the PE people missed, he'll find it. Did you see the body?'

'Yeah, I was here when the pathologist arrived. He told me nothing, they never do. Strangled, that was all he'd say – I could see that for m'self.'

'I'll call in at the morgue on the way back. Anything, Andy?'

Graham had come back into the living room. He was a big young man and his restlessness seemed to make him bigger, his bulk changing shape as you looked at him.

'Nothing, boss. The usual stuff in the bedroom drawers – the PE guys left 'em, not worth taking. Women's stuff, a box of condoms that was open –'

'She wasn't using the Pill?'

Backer said, 'I've talked to a coupla the neighbours. Ron evidently played around – that was why she kicked him out. A guy plays around these days, HIV and all that, maybe his wife doesn't trust his dick any more.'

'When I was young, condoms were for stopping pregnancies. Then they tell me, sales fell right away when the Pill came in. Now the condom is back as armour-plating. What goes around comes around. When do you reckon they'll bring back the chastity belt?' Malone shook his head at the constancy of sex and the others nodded. Then he said, 'You said the Glazes were at the Golden West Club last night – together. You talked to anyone there?'

'Just the manager. Only him and the cleaners were there this morning. He said he saw her last night, but not him.'

'We'll call in there. You want to come?'

Backer shook his head. 'Later. I've got stuff back at the station I gotta attend to. I told you, four homicides. Things are getting worse.'

'You think they'll get better?' It was Malone's turn to shake the head. Cops rarely, if ever, felt optimistic about the future. 'Pigs will fly.'

'You talk to whoever's there, call in and tell me on your way back to town. And thanks for coming.' It was laconic, but sincere. 'This is another country for you.'

'It's educational,' said Malone, but he would be glad to get back to *town*. He was neither a snob nor a silvertail, but out here he would have to learn a whole new approach. It was not Bosnia nor Belfast, but over the past thirty years a new culture, a new mindset, had developed out here.

Summer was fading, but there was still heat in the morning. In the bright sunshine a tall tibouchina tree was a frozen purple explosion at the end of the street. A few other trees had been planted, but none of them had colour: the tibouchina stood out like a landmark. Malone wondered what Ron Glaze, the gardener, had thought of it.

In the unmarked Homicide car, with Andy Graham at the wheel, Malone said, 'You think Sergeant Backer has made up his mind about this one?'

'I think so.' Graham nodded emphatically; all his movements were emphatic, as if he were afraid that he would not make his indelible mark on the world. 'It's natural, isn't it?'

'How?'

'The easy suspect. I did a bit of door-knocking while you were talking to him. A woman over the road said she'd seen the husband drive up around two o'clock – she recognized his car, said she hadn't seen it around, not since they'd broken up. She saw him get outa the car, stand for a while in the garden, then he went into the house. She'd got up to go to the bathroom –'

'What would we do without neighbours getting up and going to the bathroom?'

Graham grinned; even his grin was emphatic. 'Yeah. Well, she didn't exactly see him go into the house – she said she had to hurry to the bathroom –'

'She told you that? She had to hurry? You've got a way with women, Andy.'

They drew into the car park of the social club, almost deserted at this hour. Out of the glare and the heat, the inside of the club was cool and almost dark, except for the banks of poker machines, which were either never turned off or had just been switched on. The cavernous room seemed twice as large with no one in it. They asked for the manager, but he had gone to the bank.

'He'll be gone about half an hour,' said the woman behind the bar. 'You're police from Sydney, are you? It's another country, I tell my husband. Twenty-five miles and it's another country. I can't remember when I last went to town – that was what we used to call it. Town. Now we've got everything we want out here. Almost.'

'Were you working here last night?' asked Malone. 'I'll have a light beer. We both will.'

'Nothing strong while on duty, eh? Some of the local guys . . . Well, no tales outa school. I'm Charlene, incidentally. My husband says there's a St Charlene, though the Catholics don't recognize her. As a saint, I mean. He says she's the patron saint of deaf mutes, but I think he's having a go at me.'

She laughed. It was probably the way she made her way through life, Malone thought: laughing at herself before others did. She was garrulous; she probably talked to her husband while giving him oral sex, which

31

wouldn't add to his joy. But she was also observant, a detective's joy: 'Yeah, they were in here last night. Things weren't too good between 'em.'

'You could hear them arguing?'

She put the beers down in front of Malone and Graham. 'No, no. But I could *see* 'em. I been working here – well, never mind. A long time. I don't have to *hear* things. Not when a husband and wife are arguing. I've seen more barneys than you've seen murders – no, that's a horrible thing to say. But I see 'em – you can't hear much, not on busy nights, but you *read* 'em. You just look at them and you see it, you know? You married?'

Malone nodded. 'But I never argue with my wife in public.'

She laughed again. 'If you did, I'd be able to tell. You could be on the other side of this room –' she waved, to Ultima Thule. Or Town – 'I'd be able to tell. Things were very cool, definitely, between the Glazes.'

'No bust-up? Ron didn't get up and storm out, nothing like that?'

She shook her head; the dome of hair didn't move. 'Nothing like it. He looked, I dunno, sorta cold-blooded. Ron could be like that at times.'

'Was he popular here at the club?' asked Graham.

'Oh yes. He was a car salesman – they're born popular, aren't they? Everybody's friend. Especially the women's. Ron was a Wandering Dick, if you'll forgive the expression.'

'Of course,' said Malone politely. 'Did he have any special lady friends here at the club?'

'None of 'em special.' She was busy polishing the beer taps.

'What about Mrs Glaze?'

'Nah, never.' She looked at the beer taps, as if they might spout some memory. She shook her head. 'No, not Norma. Not here at the club, anyway. She put all her energy into her salon – she was a hairdresser, you know that?'

Malone, trying to avoid looking at the dome of hair, couldn't stop himself from asking, 'Did you go to her?'

'Me? Nah. But she used to do a lotta the women here. She was very popular, very good, always up with the latest styles. She said she was the Lillian Frank of the West.'

Malone looked at Graham. 'You know who Lillian Frank is?'

Graham sipped his beer. 'Never heard of her. What band is she with?'

Charlene laughed; she had been laughing at men's jokes for – well, never mind. Too long. 'Big Melbourne hairdresser. Always in the news, all dolled up to the nines on Melbourne Cup Day – you must of seen her? Norma wasn't like that – I mean, all dolled up. She just wanted to be the biggest hairdresser out this way.'

'Would she have been?'

'I dunno. I don't think so. Money seemed to be their trouble, never enough of it.'

'She told you that?'

She was polishing the beer taps again. 'No, Ron. He

33

was a great one for confiding, you know? A salesman all the time.'

'But he could be cold-blooded, you said.' Malone finished his beer, stood up. 'Ron sounds as if he could be quite a mixture.'

'Yes.' She stopped polishing the beer taps, looked steadily at the two detectives. 'I'm just surprised he turned out to be a murderer.'

'People often are,' said Malone.

'Are you?'

'Never . . . Did Mrs Glaze stay on after her husband walked out? When she left, did she go with someone, someone from the club?'

'No. She went out on her own, a bit unsteady on the legs.' Barmaids and barmen had eagle eyes; armies, Malone thought, should recruit them. 'I called after her if she wanted a taxi, but she didn't hear me.'

'Anyone follow her?'

She shook her head. 'I dunno. I went downstairs to the cellar. You think someone might of been eyeing her? Nah, I don't think so. The men around here left Norma alone, most of 'em were Ron's mates. He was everybody's mate.'

'No strangers in that night? I see you have a sign: Visitors Welcome.'

'Oh, there were half a dozen or so. But none of 'em went near Norma.'

Malone paid for the beers. 'Thanks, Charlene. What's your surname?' And Graham had taken out his notebook. 'Colnby? C-O-L-N-B-Y?'

'You gunna be coming back?'

'Probably, when we catch up with Ron. If you think of anything else, call me.' He gave her his card.

'Scobie Malone – you Irish?'

'Just enough to make me interesting.'

She laughed. 'Come again. All visitors welcome.'

Out in the car park Malone looked up. The day had changed abruptly. A nor'-easter had struggled in from the coast, from *Town*, and the sky was racing towards the Blue Mountains, no longer blue up close but grey and green and scarred with development. Malone lived in Randwick, a seaside suburb, and he hated the thought of having to live out here. The Westies in the western suburbs always got the rough end of the pineapple: weatherwise, economically, socially. They always got the wrong winds, the worst cold, the worst heat. There were areas here as arid as the drawing boards from which they had been lifted; the original planners had never understood the meaning of *community*. The suburbs were not slums or ghettos. Houses stood on their own small plots and they all had gardens of a sort, some luxuriant, some just weeds. There were shopping malls, cinemas, clubs, a rugby league team whose players would have been gods if the voters had believed in gods. Those that believed in gods or God, the post-World War II immigrants, had long ago learned that gods and God had no influence with politicians or bureaucrats. The population was mixed, an ethnic stew, and their voices, multilingual, were as loud in protest as those from elsewhere. But when the crunch came, when the

35

pineapple was up-ended, who got the rough end? Malone looked back at the club. For all its indoor garishness, its temptation to gamble, it drew the locals together.

'Would you like to live out here, Andy?'

'I grew up here. I went to Mount Druitt High.'

'How'd you find it?'

'I felt like murder sometimes.' Graham was very still, very sober. 'I'd go down to the beaches, Bondi, Coogee, and I'd look at all of them who lived there and I'd want to murder the bastards.'

'You changed your mind since you joined the Service and got to know one of the bastards from the beaches? Me.'

Graham relaxed, his silhouette shivering again. 'It takes all sorts to make a world, doesn't it?'

'I wonder what sort of world Ron Glaze wanted?'

6

On their way back to Homicide, having paid their call on Jeff Backer and given him what little they had learned from Mrs Colnby, Malone and Graham diverted to the morgue in Glebe. Here in this inner suburb the breeze was cooler, as if it might have blown through the morgue before getting to the street. The two detectives entered the nondescript building from the rear; it had the look of a warehouse, which in a way it was. They were told that Dr Clements was in the Murder Room.

They went down through the long main room where

blue-gowned attendants, like bored priests, were administering pathology last rites to half a dozen corpses. Malone, though a man with a strong stomach, kept his eyes on the far end of the room. Out of the corner of his eye he saw something red-and-yellow and slimy, like something from a fisherman's net, dropped on one of the scales between the stainless steel tables at which the technicians worked. Behind him he heard Graham strangle something between a cough and a burp, but he didn't look back. Blue honeycombs of insect killers hung from the ceiling and a dozen air-conditioners did their best to strain the clogged air.

Romy Clements, in gown, apron and gloves, was working on the body of Norma Glaze. 'Not feeling well today, Andy?'

'I'd rather of stayed outside.'

Romy smiled at Malone. 'You notice how all the really big men are weak-stomached? Russ is the same . . . Well, here she is. Mrs Norma Dorothy Glaze – maiden name Compton. Born 22 May 1963. Death by strangulation.' She pointed to the purple fingermarks on the dead woman's throat. 'He was a strong man, whoever he was. He throttled her with one hand, his left.'

Malone looked at the corpse; there was an obsceneness to the naked dead. No matter how beautiful a woman might have been, or how handsome a man, in death the beauty, in Malone's eyes, was gone. Nothing showed but flesh, waiting to rot, and hair waiting to fall off the skull. He dreaded the day he would have to look on the corpse of someone he loved.

'She bruised at all?'

'Quite a lot. Breasts, ribs, on her jaw. Scratches, too. There's bruises, too, on the inside of the thighs, around the vagina.'

'There'd been intercourse?'

'I'd say so. I don't think it was rape, though.'

'Probably not. At the moment the main suspect is the husband. They were separated.'

'There's no semen, so you can't do a DNA.'

'We found a box of condoms,' said Graham, eye-level about three feet above the corpse. 'A box of a dozen – a couple had been used. We didn't find them, they'd probably been washed down the toilet.'

'If he used a condom, twice, then it doesn't suggest rape.'

'Looks like they had a fight,' said Malone, 'and it got out of hand.'

Romy pulled a sheet up over Norma Glaze, wrenched off her rubber gloves. 'She's booked for a more detailed autopsy this afternoon. If the husband is left-handed, I'd say he is your man. But I'm not a detective.'

'I'll bet Russ is glad,' said Malone.

She took off her gown. She was a good-looking woman, dark-haired and broad-cheeked. There was a composure to her that Malone always admired. Her father had been a serial killer; her career and her relationship with Russ Clements had been almost ruined by the scandal. But she, and Russ, had weathered it and Malone had a protective affection for them both.

'You should get him,' she said. 'Husbands who kill

their wives never seem to escape the wedding ring. Old German saying.'

7

That was Tuesday, 29 March 1994.

Enquiries confirmed that Ron Glaze was indeed left-handed in everything but his handshake.

'He had a strong handshake,' said the manager of the car salesyard where he had worked. 'The sort that made a customer believe in him. I was sorry to let him go, but that's the way things have been. I can't believe he killed Norma, no way.'

An ASM was put out for Ronald Glaze. His car was found two days later in a car park in Newcastle, 160 kilometres north of Sydney. Across the Hunter River from the car park the pipes of the BHP steelworks belched smoke, visual music to the Novocastrians. The Big Australian was still making money; *downsizing* was something that happened only to Americans, a word from another language. On 1 April a man's body was fished out of the river. At first it was thought to be Ron Glaze, which would have left everything simple and uncomplicated. Unfortunately it was another man, another murder, this time by the wife and her lover.

Ron Glaze disappeared and the Glaze murder case was moved to the back-burner of the computer files.

Part Two

March–May 1998

Chapter Two

1

Downsizing had hit Newcastle; the Big Australian was now not-so-big. There was a new government in Canberra, advised by economic rationalists; Thatcherism had taken root in Australia like rabbits and cod and other imports. The Asian economic house of cards had collapsed and the Australian voters were only now beginning to realize the shine might wear off the immediate future. Violence had increased, especially in the streets. The shine, it seemed, had worn off everything.

'Inspector Malone? This is Detective-Constable Mungle. Wally Mungle. Collamundra. Remember? Eight years ago, the Hardstaff case.'

'Wally – what can I do for you?' Had Amanda Hardstaff, the woman who had walked away from a bungled murder, finally decided to confess?

'Last night, on that Channel 15 programme, *Wanted for Questioning*, they ran a piece about a guy named

Ron Glaze, with his photo. Killed his wife four years ago. You still on that?'

'Only remotely, Wally.'

'I think he's living here in Collamundra.'

Twenty-five years in the Service and a cop can still feel the adrenaline suddenly surge. 'You're sure?'

'Pretty sure. I can't be certain, but I think I'd take a bet on it. He's bald now and put on weight, but I think he's the same bloke. He came into town about two, maybe three years ago. He runs a nursery, lives with the woman whose husband owned it. She's a widow.'

'Glaze was supposed to be a keen gardener, but I dunno that he could run a nursery. Still . . . You keeping an eye on him?'

'Without letting him know, yes. It's not easy – our establishment out here isn't what it used to be. There's been cutbacks, you know what it's like. I'm the only detective now. Sometimes I'm running around like a blue-arsed fly, other times . . .'

'It's a long way for me to send someone, Wally, just on the off-chance. Can you pick him up, put him through the grinder?'

'This is a bush town, Inspector. Another thing, I'm still the Abo cop for some of 'em around here. I pick him up and I'm wrong, he's not this Glaze bloke, I'm in the shithouse.'

'Who's in charge there now?' He frowned, trying to remember names: 'Inspector Narvo?'

'No, he's the area super now. Inspector Gombrich is boss now.' There was a pause, like a high jumper

44

measuring a jump; then: 'He and me don't always see eye to eye.'

Malone took his own pause; he knew, as well as anyone, the minefield in the Service. At last, measuring his own jump, he said, 'Put me through to Inspector Gombrich.'

'Yes, sir. Putting you through now.' There was no mistaking the reluctance in Mungle's voice.

I'm putting him in the shithouse, thought Malone; but it could not be helped. He remembered his arrival in Collamundra eight years ago, when he and Clements had been as welcome as nightsoil carters on a hot morning.

'Inspector Gombrich.' The voice was flat and harsh.

'This is Inspector Malone, Scobie Malone. Homicide and Serial Offenders Unit, Sydney –' Gombrich had the sort of voice that asked for identification, with papers.

'I know who you are. Constable Mungle filled me in before he phoned you. I don't agree with his suspicions –'

'Inspector –' Malone couldn't remember when he had been so formal with someone of equal rank – 'half our homicides begin with nothing more than suspicion. All I ask is that you question this man –'

'Roger Gibson is a personal friend.'

'Gibson – that's his name?' *R.G.* It was remarkable the number of times fugitives chose their original initials. As if afraid that a monogram, on a handkerchief or wallet, might give them away.

'Yes. I've been here twelve months, we play golf together, his wife and my wife are friends –'

'He's married?'

'All right –' the exasperation was like static on the line – 'his *partner*. They're a happily married couple, even if they're not married. I think Constable Mungle has made a mistake and we'll just forget it –'

'Inspector Gombrich –' Malone could see the road-blocks building up; at the same time he could feel his temper rising – 'this is *our* case – I can't just forget it, not till I'm sure that Mr Gibson is not Ron Glaze. I'll come out there –' he heard himself say; normally he would have sent a couple of junior officers. 'I'll come out and talk to Mr Gibson – Have you spoken to him?'

'Of course not!' The voice was even harsher.

'Then don't,' said Malone, a certain harshness in his own voice. 'I want him there when I arrive. I'll be coming with the authority of Chief Superintendent Random –'

'Are you threatening me?'

'No. I'm just sticking to police procedure. When can I catch a plane to Collamundra?'

There was a long silence, then Gombrich said, 'There's a plane leaves Kingsford Smith at twelve, Hazelton Airlines. It's usually booked solid,' he added and the harshness curdled with relish.

'Someone's going to be unlucky,' said Malone. 'But not me.'

He hung up and beckoned Russ Clements through the

glass wall of his office. The big man came in, slumped down in his favourite position, the couch beneath the window. For a while he had been going to a gym and had lost some weight, but lately he had begun to spread again. He was not *fat*, there was still muscle and bone there, but he was generously overlaid. Malone sometimes wondered, though he would never have mentioned it, if Romy, a gourmet cook, had lapsed back into Teutonic recipes. Clements had the sort of stomach that welcomed dumplings.

'You've got that shit-on-the-liver look again. Who is it this time?'

Malone filled him in. 'I'm going out to Collamundra. How's our slate today?'

'Two cases, that's all. I'll give you time off for twenty-four hours.' Clements was the Field Supervisor, the man who dealt out the assignments. 'Collamundra, eh? Narelle Potter, remember? I wonder if she still runs the Mail Coach Hotel?'

'You're a married man now. I'm not going to look up one of your one-night stands. Get me on the plane, there's one at noon.'

'You think this could be that guy Glaze?'

'I don't know. But Wally Mungle has shoved his neck out and I've got to back him. I'll be back tonight, with or without.'

There was a spare seat on the Hazelton Airlines plane and no one had to be offloaded for the Police Service. Malone sat next to a cotton farmer who had obviously fortified himself for the flight before boarding. He was

47

short and big-bellied, with a mop of yellow hair and a yellow moustache. He was also drunkenly direct: 'You on business?'

Malone nodded. 'Just looking.'

'What sort?'

Malone flitted down a list of businesses. Oil drilling, coal mining, brothel keeping . . . 'Fast food.'

'We've got a McDonald's and a Pizza Hut, we don't want any more. You're not Kentucky Fried Chicken or Hungry Jack's?' He was built like a man who frequented all four.

Malone shook his head. 'Shirley's Sausage Rolls. A new concept.'

'A new one, eh? That's the way the world's going, right? Fast food. Pretty soon we won't sit down to eat. Sausage rolls, eh? Well, at least that's *Australian*. Bloody pizzas. I *ask* you.'

The plane came in over the cotton fields, white lakes stretching away to the horizon, harvesters sitting in the middle of them like glass-cabined houseboats. Memory came flooding back. The Japanese cotton farm manager under the spikes of a module feeder; the resentment of the locals towards the two cops from Sydney, the outsiders; the climax with the arrest of the district's most prominent landowner, the bush aristocrat, Chester Hardstaff. That had been a complex, threatening case with the real murderer, Hardstaff's daughter, walking away unchallenged. Compared to that case, the Glaze–Gibson matter would be wrapped up, one way or the other, in the next hour.

48

When he stepped out of the plane on to the tarmac Malone felt the heat hit him like a soft physical blow. El Niño, reaching out all the way from the Peruvian and Chilean coasts, had had its effect here on the western plains. Further west, beyond the cotton belt, wheat and sheep farmers watched the cracks widen daily in the soil of their paddocks. Things were tough enough out here without a cop arriving from Sydney to kick up more dirt.

Wally Mungle was waiting for him in an unmarked car. 'You haven't changed, Inspector.'

Mungle had. He was still slight, still seemingly too small for his suit, but the years had doubled in his dark-coffee face. Somewhere back in his lineage was a white man; there was a hint of blue in the young detective's eyes. The eyes were sad, sadder than Malone remembered, and the cheeks were already showing lines.

'How're things? You had kids – how are they?'

'Fine. Neither of them wants to be a cop . . .' Then he looked sideways at Malone as he took the car out on to the main road to town. 'This bloke Roger Gibson. I'm sure he's the one you're looking for.'

'It's going to upset Inspector Gombrich, if he is. You still in the shithouse?'

'With the door shut and no paper,' said Wally Mungle.

'I'd better see him first. How are things around here?'

'You mean the locals? There's no money in wool any more – most of the sheep cockies have gone into cotton. There's still wheat, but even they are beginning to think there's more money in cotton. Water's the trouble.

49

The blokes downstream, still in wheat or wool, they're complaining they're not getting enough water. Irrigation takes most of it.'

'I've read about it. You country people fight each other, you forget how much you hate us city folk.'

Mungle looked sideways at him, grinned thinly. 'You wait till you pick up Roger Gibson and charge him.'

They went in past the avenue of silky oaks that was the entrance to the town, past the two used-car lots, then came to the roundabout at the eastern end of the main street. Malone suddenly remembered the war memorial, the bronze figure of the World War I Anzac, bayonet at the ready to repel the invaders from the coast, from the city.

'He's still there. Looks as if he could do with a polish.'

'He doesn't mean much any more,' said Mungle.

'Did he ever mean much to you?'

'No.' Mungle swung the car into the yard behind the police station. 'He didn't go away to fight for any of our mob, us Abos. But don't quote me.'

He went to get out of the car, but Malone put a hand on his arm. 'Wally, when I go out to pick up this feller Gibson, I think you'd better not come with me.'

Mungle's gaze was direct. 'I'm not gunna get anywhere in the Service by dodging issues.'

'How far are you going to get by going looking for them?'

'I dunno. But if Gibson is the man you've been

looking for, then I want the credit for picking him up. All the other blokes here at the station look in at that TV programme – none of them picked him.'

'Including Inspector Gombrich?'

'Including him.'

Malone offered no further argument. *Don't start playing the do-gooder, chum.* Wally Mungle had chosen his own path.

As they went into the station Malone saw two uniformed men stop by a marked car and look back at himself and Mungle. Their stare was almost readable: *Why don't you mind your own business?*

The station was a one-storeyed Victorian stone building built to last, to withstand everything, including prejudice; the white ants were inside it. It was backed by a 1950s' addition, a two-storeyed brick building as characterless as a butter-box. Gombrich's office was in the front section: high-ceilinged, cold-looking. Malone felt the chill as soon as he walked into the room; the heat beyond the big window was an illusion. But at least the man behind the big table-desk was polite. He rose, though he did not put out his hand.

'Inspector Malone –' No welcome, nice to see you. 'Leave us for a few minutes, Constable.'

'Yes, sir.' Mungle turned at once and went out, not looking at Malone.

The two inspectors gazed at each other for a few moments, then Gombrich sat down and gestured for Malone to do the same. 'I think you've come a long way for no purpose.'

'It happens. If I'm wrong –' Malone shrugged, waiting for the other man to develop the argument.

Gombrich was tall, overweight, with a shock of greying curly hair and a mismatch of features: a blue and a grey eye, a fine handsome nose and loose cheeks and a double-chin. From the voice on the phone Malone had expected an austere man: cold, bony, a human rule-book. Instead, he looked as if, away from this room, he might enjoy life and company. In the locker room of the golf club, on the walk between the seventeenth and nineteenth holes he would be telling jokes, even perhaps ones about dumb cops.

There were no jokes now: 'Roger Gibson came to this town three years ago. He got a job as a casual salesman at one of the car lots – Ron Harvey says he's the best salesman he's ever had, but to keep him on full-time would have meant putting off someone else. He couldn't do that, not in this town – you keep your old hands. Except if you work for a bank.' Malone then guessed Gombrich was a long-time bush cop. The closing down of bank branches in country towns was a treason that would never be forgiven. 'Then Roger went to work for Ollie McBride, he owned the nursery on the edge of town. Ollie was killed in a car accident about six months later. Roger ran the business – he just took over and made it even better than it had been under Ollie. Then about a year ago he and Ollie's widow, Roma, became – partners. He's only been here three years, but he's one of the most respected men in town. He told me he had at last found his niche

52

in life. He's in Rotary, he's on the committee of the golf club –'

Malone held up a hand. 'I don't doubt any of that. Look, Sam – mind if I call you by your first name?' The name had been on the door. Not the usual first initials, but spelled right out: Inspector Samuel Gombrich.

'Go ahead.' Coldly, as if he had been asked if he minded being called Boofhead.

'Sam, I'll go out to the nursery and if this feller can convince me he's not Ron Glaze, then okay, I'll catch the seven o'clock plane back to Sydney and nobody'll be the wiser.'

'Everyone here in the station knows why you're here.'

'Then put a lid on them if I'm wrong. If they talk, they'll be the ones putting the mark on Mr Gibson. Do you want to come out to the nursery with me?'

Gombrich for the first time looked uncertain. He had a habit, Malone remarked, of looking past one: as if each of the oddly matched eyes, the blue and the grey, had its own direction. Then they appeared to focus, glared at Malone. 'No.'

'Then can I take Constable Mungle? Or would you rather I took someone else? I have to have someone local – this is your turf.'

'Take Mungle – it's his pigeon.'

Malone stood up. 'Will it still be his pigeon if he's right? If Mr Gibson is Ron Glaze?'

Gombrich hadn't risen; he just looked up at Malone. 'Let's hope he's dead wrong.'

McBride's Nursery was on the western edge of town, across the wide road from the railway siding and the wheat silos. Here was where the country spread out, flat and limitless, to the edge of the world; the sky was, as Malone remembered it, vast and uncaring. There had been much talk this past year of El Niño, but it was only an occasional visitor. The locals had known for 150 years which way to look for trouble and, after prayer, for help. The nursery, here on the edge of the plains, was a faint green shout of defiance.

Ollie McBride, or someone, had planted trees round it: silky oak, cypress pine, kurrajong and a red river gum that looked lost without its companions along a river-bank. Its three acres, within a high wire fence, bloomed greenly, like a last oasis.

On the way out Malone had asked Wally Mungle about the town and the people he had met, no matter how fleetingly, on the murder case eight years ago.

'Chess Hardstaff and Sean Carmody and Fred Strayhorn, they're all dead. They were all old men, even then. Chess Hardstaff died in prison. While he was there he still thought he was king of the castle and they let him get away with it.'

Malone remembered the old man, stiff with pride and ego and the dignity of another age. But who had murdered his wife for sleeping with another man, had got away with it but taken the blame for the later murder that his daughter had committed.

'They brought him home and he was buried with full honours by some of the locals, almost like a State funeral. Being a murderer was just incidental alongside the number of Germans he shot down during the war.'

'You're cynical about us whites, Wally. What about Narelle Potter – she still run the Mail Coach Hotel?'

Mungle nodded. 'Still. She's married now and doesn't play around like she used to. Roger Gibson, when he first came to town, went out with her a coupla times – that was before she married. She still raises the colour bar, though. One of us has one too many, out he goes or she calls the cops. Whitey can get blind paralytic and she just leaves him to his mates.'

Malone asked no more questions: they had drawn up at the gates of the nursery. He got out, suddenly apprehensive for Wally Mungle. Why couldn't it have been one of the white officers who had recognized Ron Glaze on the TV programme? 'You can stay in the car, Wally.'

'No, I brought you all the way out here from Sydney –' He got out of the car. In the reflected glare from the whiteness of the car his colour seemed to pale. 'If I'm wrong, then I'll wear it.'

The March heat pressed down on them, pushing them into their sharp-edged shadows as they went in through the gates. From among the rows of shrubs and plants a man approached them, his left hand grasping the handle of a box of green shoots.

'G'day, Wally. You brought a friend for some horticultural advice?'

'Not exactly, Roger.' The bush friendliness of first names; except that this time there was a knife in the napkin of informality: 'This is Inspector Malone, from Sydney. He wants to ask you some questions. Not horticultural ones.'

Ease off, Wally. Malone looked around, then said, 'Could we go somewhere private, Mr Gibson?'

Gibson all at once was stockstill, his shadow a heavy base. He was wearing a khaki shirt and shorts, workman's boots and short socks, a battered stockman's hat. In the shade of the hat his eyes suddenly narrowed, as if he had only just become aware of the glare. 'What's it about?'

'It's about you,' said Malone. 'I have reason to believe you are Ronald Glaze.'

It was a moment before Gibson frowned; but Malone noted the hesitation. 'Who?'

'Let's go somewhere more private.' Two couples were looking at shrubs in the rows behind Gibson; over by a greenhouse a youth was stacking pots in the back of a Ford utility truck. All three had paused, had recognized Wally Mungle and were wondering who was the stranger with him. 'We don't want to make a production of this.'

Gibson didn't move for a long moment; he stared at Mungle, but the latter was seemingly interested in the youth by the truck. A magpie fluttered down, began to pick amongst the plants. The woman would-be buyer shooed it away and it went off with a protest.

Then Gibson said abruptly, 'This way,' and led Malone and Mungle towards a weatherboard office to one side of the entrance gates.

Malone stopped at the doorway. 'That your man over there at the ute? Better tell him to look after your customers. This may take a little while.'

'What the hell is this –?' Gibson's voice was unexpectedly loud; unexpected to him, it seemed. The couple amongst the nursery rows turned and looked at him. He gave them a wide smile, a salesman's smile, and jerked a finger at the youth. 'Look after things, Darren. We've got some business –'

He led the way into the office. Malone nodded to Wally Mungle, who closed the door. Gibson switched on a window air-conditioner, then sat down at a big roll-top desk and gestured for the two detectives to take chairs. He seemed to be gathering something into himself: front, confidence, whatever.

'Who sent you out here?' The salesman's smile was gone: Gibson was selling nothing in here. Except, maybe, himself.

Malone wondered who was responsible for the neatness of the office. There appeared to be a place for everything and everything in its place. Horticultural charts hung on the walls; there was a long shelf of gardening books. Two computers stood on a side table, each with a half-completed message on its face. Oddly enough there was not a pot plant or a flower-box anywhere in the small room. After the greenery of the nursery outside, the office looked as dry as a brown lawn.

Malone opened the office wallet he had brought with him, took out the photo of Ron Glaze that had been used on the TV programme. He looked at it, then at Gibson. Then he passed the photo to the other man. 'Recognize him?'

Gibson studied the photo, then shook his head. 'No.'

'I think it's you. We found it in your wife's wardrobe –'

'My wife? Which wife is that?'

Nice try. 'Mrs Norma Glaze. This, we'd say, was taken four or five years ago, maybe six. The photographer in Mount Druitt wasn't sure. More hair and less weight, but I think it's you.'

Gibson had taken off his hat as he came into the office. He was bald, except for a thin brush of grey-speckled blond hair along the temples. He looked at the photo again, then at Wally Mungle. 'What d'you think, Wally? You think it looks like me?'

Mungle took his time, but didn't look away. 'I think it's you, Roger.'

Gibson turned back to Malone. 'So what did this guy do?'

'Murdered your wife,' said Malone.

It took him a moment to laugh; but like all salesmen, he was a good actor. The laugh sounded genuine. 'Jesus! What wife? I've never been married. Except – well, my partner and I live together. My de facto, if you like, but I hate the bloody term.'

Malone sat back in his chair, looked at the photo again, looked at Gibson, then shook his head. 'It's you, Ron.'

'Bullshit!' The front was starting to break, he was getting angry now.

Malone was calm, unhurried. 'You came to Collamundra three years ago. Where were you before that?'

'Around.' Then the front was repaired. He suddenly looked more assured, settled back in his swivel chair as if ready for a chat about gardening. 'I was in the Northern Territory. At Katherine, then in Darwin.'

'Doing what?'

'Selling.'

'Cars? They said you were a good car salesman.'

He ignored that. 'No, computers.' He gestured at the two computers on the nearby table. He gestured with his left hand; Malone noticed that he had very big hands. They were labourer's hands and for the first time Malone had a moment of doubt. 'The hardware and the software. It was easy territory. The Territorians like to think they're up with the rest of the country. Ahead of it, in some respects. Beer drinking, for instance.' He smiled, the assurance growing.

'That's true,' said Wally Mungle. 'I checked with Roads and Traffic over at Cawndilla. We're in Cawndilla shire,' he told Malone. 'When he applied for his New South Wales licence, the computer showed he'd produced a Territory licence. They're very handy, computers.'

You haven't wasted any time this morning, thought Malone.

Gibson's face was stiff, the smile gone, as he looked at Mungle. 'You started all this, Wally?'

Mungle nodded.

'Why?'

'I recognized you last night on the TV programme, *Wanted For Questioning*.'

'You're out of your mind, Wally.'

'I don't think so, Roger.'

This was a local match; Malone was on the outside. He said nothing, waiting for Gibson to blow up. His anger would be greater at a local than at a stranger from out of town.

There was a knock at the door and it was opened. A woman stood there, indistinct for a moment against the yellow glare. Then she came in, closing the door behind her. 'Business? Am I intruding?'

Malone had kept his eye on Gibson. The anger at Mungle went out of the round face; it clouded for a moment, a shadow took all the life out of it. Then he recovered, stood up. 'No, come in, sweetheart. You know Wally Mungle. This is Inspector Malone, from Sydney.'

She was tall and lusty-figured and had a mane, one had to call it that, of golden hair. She was not beautiful, her face was too broad for that, but it was a face any man, or anyway most men, would look at twice. She wore a tan sleeveless shirt, a beige skirt and her arms, legs and face were deeply tanned. A woman, thought Malone chauvinistically, who wouldn't remain a widow too long.

Only her voice spoiled her: it was high, girlish, the voice from the back of the schoolroom: 'Have we done something wrong? Police from *Sydney*?'

Gibson opened his mouth, but Malone got in first: 'That's what we are trying to establish, Mrs – do I call you Mrs Gibson?'

'Yes,' said Gibson, getting in his word.

She had an eye or an ear or a nose for atmosphere. She recognized that some formality was called for; this inspector from *Sydney* was not here to buy a box of petunias. 'Mrs Gibson will do,' she said and her partner looked relieved.

'We have reason to believe –' the pedantry always coated Malone's tongue, but that was the way the Service wanted it – 'Mr Gibson is not who he claims to be. His real name is Ronald Glaze.'

She put out her hand to Gibson and he took it. She looked at him and he shook his head; that seemed to satisfy her, for she pressed his hand. Then she looked back at Malone. 'You're not here just because he's supposed to have changed his name. What's he supposed to have done?'

Malone waited, hoping that Gibson, maybe with a laugh, would tell her. He had at least a dozen times had to tell a wife or a partner that her man had been murdered; only once before had he had to tell her that he was a murderer. Gibson just stood beside his partner, saying nothing.

It was Wally Mungle who said, 'We're sorry, Roma, but he is accused of murdering his wife in Sydney four years ago.'

She turned on him, ignoring Malone, and said, 'You can't be serious!'

'I'm afraid we are,' said Malone, getting Mungle off the hook he had nailed for himself. Wally Mungle was getting out of hand; he was relishing this, getting his own back on his fellow cops who had sneered at his taking duty too seriously. He would talk to Mungle later.

'I'm taking him into town, to the station. The questioning may go on for some time. You may come to the station if you wish. You can have a lawyer present, Mr Glaze.'

'Gibson,' said Gibson. Now his partner was here he looked confident again. He'd get his strength from women, thought Malone, even though they were his weakness. 'Yes, I think I will get our lawyer. Go and get Trevor Waring, sweetheart – don't ring him, we'll keep it quiet till Inspector Malone has gone back to Sydney, then we can laugh about it . . . Something wrong, Inspector?'

'No. I happen to know Mr Waring, that's all.'

Gibson appeared slightly fazed, as if the ground ahead had become uneven. 'He's a friend?'

'Not exactly.' Trevor Waring had been the husband of a friend of Lisa Malone, but the marriage had split up five or six years ago. 'It's just a coincidence. He also acted for another man I arrested for murder. Man named Hardstaff.'

'Of course!' Roma Gibson looked at Malone with new interest: very acute interest. 'I was at a garden party at the Hardstaffs' –'

Malone nodded. 'The day we arrested Chester Hardstaff . . . Get Trevor, he's a good lawyer. Or he was.'

'He still is,' said Roma Gibson, kissed her partner and left, leaving the door open to the glare outside. It'll be nothing, thought Malone, to the glare when this case breaks. The Hardstaff case suddenly seemed like only yesterday. The glare then had been fiery, directed against himself and Russ Clements, who had been with him.

As he, Mungle and Gibson stepped out of the office a reminder was thrown at him like a brick. A woman in a yellow dress came down between the rows of shrubs. She pulled up sharply: recognition was instant. 'Inspector Malone?'

Perhaps it was the glare: Malone looked for other ghosts. Narelle Potter; the secretary of the local services club whose name he couldn't remember; Sean Carmody – ah, but he was dead. He blinked, became accustomed to the glare.

'Hello, Mrs Nothling.'

'Hardstaff.' It was a day for corrections. 'My husband and I –' She had a queenly air about her, always had had. 'We were divorced some years ago. Just after you left here.'

Amanda Nothling-Hardstaff had not changed. She was still attractive, still elegant despite the heat, still the arrogant aristocrat. They were a dying breed, the squattocracy, but she would be flying the banner till the last. She was a murderer, but if there was any shame in her it would never show. Her husband, Malone decided, would have been well rid of her.

'Some trouble, Roger? Inspector Malone is implacable.'

Implacable. Malone had been called many things, but

63

never that. He grinned at her and she gave him a knife of a smile in return.

Then she seemed to note the significance of Malone's attachment. 'You are still with Homicide?'

The first crack in the dam that was going to engulf Gibson. 'Yes. You have quite a memory.'

'Oh, I do, I do.' She looked at Gibson again. She was wearing dark glasses, but one knew that behind them the eyes had narrowed. 'Nothing serious, I hope?'

Gibson smiled, shook his head. 'They think I might've been a witness to something years ago, but I can't remember it. You want something, Amanda? Young Darren will look after you. Those liquidambars you ordered are due in a coupla weeks. Too hot to bring 'em out here right now. I'll see you Sunday. Tennis still on?'

'I remember your father's garden, Mrs Hardstaff,' said Malone as he and Mungle led Gibson towards the police car. 'That where you live now? Lucky you.'

It was a cheap shot, but he couldn't help it. He saw Wally Mungle glance at him; even Gibson turned his head. He ignored them both, opened the rear door of the car.

'Don't put your hand on top of my head and push me in,' said Gibson. 'I've seen it on TV – that's what you do to crims.'

'After you, Ron,' said Malone and stood back.

He got in beside Gibson. As the car drove away he looked back at Amanda Hardstaff some fifty yards away; in her yellow dress she seemed to shimmer in the glare, a fading memory from the past. He would take Gibson,

or Glaze, out of Collamundra this evening and hoped he
would never come back.

3

'This was not my idea, Roger,' said Inspector Gombrich.

'I know that, Sam. It'll all be over in half an hour.
Don't worry about it. I'm not.'

Malone had faced confidence before, but he was
impressed, though not believing, by Gibson's show of
it. 'Inspector, would you have someone book me two
seats on the seven o'clock plane?'

Gombrich chewed a lip, then nodded. 'I'll do that.
I'll bill your unit.'

'Of course. Now may we use your interview room?
There's a recorder there?'

'Yes, but no video. We don't run to that on our
budget.'

'What happens to the tape when this turns out to be
a farce?' asked Gibson.

'We sell it to *Comedy Commercials*.' Malone was
growing tired of Gibson; he wanted to nail him to the
wall as Glaze in the shortest possible time. 'You want
to sit in with me, Inspector?'

'No,' said Gombrich, already in retreat but doing his
best to hide it. 'Constable Mungle will assist.'

Malone looked at Mungle, who nodded. 'Glad to.'
Then he looked at Gibson and said, 'Nothing personal,
Roger.'

'Of course not,' said Gibson and gave him a wide smile, as if he were selling him a liquidambar. Or a low-mileage Holden Caprice driven only by an old lady.

The interview room was small; the crime waves in Collamundra were small. Gibson settled into a chair, looked around him. 'It's just like in *The Bill*, isn't it? Not crummy, like the room in *NYPD Blue*.'

'We're not on TV, Ron –'

'Roger.'

'Except you were on TV last night,' said Wally Mungle, setting up the tape recorder.

'What have you got against me, Wally?' Gibson was not aggressive; he genuinely wanted to know. 'I'm not anti-Abo, you know that Darren, works for me, he's part-Abo – or should I say half-indigenous?'

'Lay off, Roger. I've got nothing against you personally – I'm just doing my job.'

Gibson considered that; then, salesman-like, said, 'Make me a better offer.'

Then Roma Gibson arrived with Trevor Waring. The latter had changed since Malone had seen him last. He was in his early fifties and middle-age spread had wrapped itself round him; he was at least 15 kilos heavier, most of it round his middle. He had lost hair and volume of voice: Malone remembered a voice that had been middling loud. Now it was thin, as if middle-age spread was choking it in his throat.

'Hullo, Scobie.' He put out a plump hand. 'A nice surprise.'

'A surprise, Trevor, but it may not be nice. Would

66

you mind waiting outside, Mrs Gibson? It's pretty crowded –'

'Yes, I would mind. I want to be here to hear whatever ridiculous things you are going to say to Roger.'

Malone hated being crowded; the room was far too small. 'I'm sorry, Mrs Gibson –'

'Get Inspector Gombrich, Wally,' she said.

Mungle stood his ground. 'I can't do that. This is Inspector Malone's case.'

She then looked at Waring, who shrugged. 'That's the way it is, Roma. I'll take care of it. Roger will be out of here in no time.'

For a moment it seemed she would not budge; then she leaned towards Gibson and kissed him on the cheek. 'I'll be waiting, love.'

When the door closed behind her, Waring sat down, as if standing tired him, and looked up at Malone. 'How serious is it, Scobie?'

'Very.' Gibson had got to his feet when his partner had come in; he was still standing. 'Sit down, Mr Glaze –'

'Gibson.' He wasn't yielding an inch or a name.

'Have it your way. Trevor, this is what happened four years ago –'

He gave a quick summary, moving his gaze from one man to the other, watching their reactions. There was none from Gibson, but Waring a couple of times frowned, though he said nothing. Malone opened the office wallet and took out three large photos.

'That's your client, taken five or six years ago. Less weight, more hair –'

'The reverse of me,' said Waring, but it didn't sound like a joke.

'Now you mention it –' Then Malone laid out the second photo. 'This is Norma Glaze, taken about the same time – when they were happily married.' He glanced at Gibson, but there was no reaction. 'A good-looking woman. Don't you think so?' He swung the photo round, so that it was directly in front of Gibson. 'You remember her, Ron?'

Gibson glanced at the photo, then lifted his gaze directly back at Malone. 'How can I? I've never seen her before.'

Lying is part of salesmanship: Malone had been sold too many lies not to be cynical. Gibson, or Glaze, would sell the lie right down till the customer walked out of the yard.

'Then maybe you remember this?'

It was a close-up of Norma Glaze in death. The bruise on her jaw, the fingermarks on her throat, dark smudges that made her only a distant twin of the woman in the other photo. Gibson continued to stare at the detectives, first at Mungle, then at Malone. It was a long beat before he turned his gaze downwards. His big hands were on the table and there was no mistaking the sudden tightening of the fingers. It was the only giveaway. When he lifted his head and looked back at Malone his face was composed, his voice steady. 'Poor woman.'

'Yes,' said Malone.

'Scobie –' Waring shifted his bulk in his chair; he seemed to have trouble with his weight, as if it were new to him. 'Those photos prove nothing.'

'They will, Trev . . . Righto, let's go back to the beginning. What was your history before you came to Collamundra, Roger? I'll call you Roger for the time being, but don't read too much into it.'

'I won't.' Gibson leaned back in his chair; all at once he looked the most comfortable of all four men. 'I was born in New Zealand, in Dunedin in the south. I went to England when I was twenty, came to Australia six years ago –'

'How long were you in England?'

'Nine, ten years.'

'You don't have a New Zealand accent or an English one. All that time before you came here and you have a dinky-di Aussie accent. What d'you reckon, Constable?'

'Indigenous,' said Mungle and for the first time all day gave a full-mouthed smile.

'Are you an expert on accents, Scobie?' said Waring.

'Yes,' lied Malone. 'It's a hobby I picked up from my wife Lisa. You remember her?'

'Of course,' said Waring and shifted again in his chair.

'We'll check with Dunedin, birth records, that sort of thing. You have a passport?'

Gibson was very still in his chair. 'No. Someone stole it – I never bothered to apply for a new one.'

'Never mind, the New Zealand passport office will

have a record of it. We've used them before.' Lying again. 'What year did you first apply for it?'

'I dunno. Around 1982, 83.'

He's bluffing because he thinks I'm bluffing. He turned to Mungle. 'Could you get me some fingerprint sheets, Wally?'

Mungle stood up, but Waring held up a restraining hand. 'What do we need those for?'

'We have prints of his from their house. In the kitchen, Roger, on the handle of the fridge door. On a Coke bottle and a glass. Was that before or after you'd killed her?' He didn't give Gibson time to reply, but nodded to Wally Mungle. 'Get the sheets, bring in the dab pad.'

Mungle went out of the room. Gibson and Waring looked at each other, but said nothing. Then Malone, casually, said, 'When we get back to Sydney, Roger, we'll have your mother and sister identify you. They'll know you. They're both still alive, I think.'

There was a sudden silence, the sort of silence that one sometimes finds in music: not the end but the beginning of something. Malone waited: he had become an expert in silences, if not in accents.

Then Gibson sighed, a shudder of sound that came up through his body. He leaned forward, said softly, 'I didn't kill her.'

Malone felt relief course slowly through him; he had won. There was satisfaction, but it was not malicious. He didn't believe Glaze's claim, but the salesmanship was over. Glaze might go on lying, but he would be lying as his true self, not Roger Gibson. Gibson was dead, a shell discarded.

'Roger –' Waring was genuinely shocked; then he recovered. 'Don't say anything more –'

'I have to, Trev. Okay, I'm Ron Glaze. That's my wife –' He gestured at the photos, but didn't look at them. 'But I did not kill her. I went back to our house that night – she was dead when I got there. Lying on the bed – naked . . . I sat there, I dunno how long, twenty minutes, half an hour, then I left –'

'Why?' said Malone. 'Why didn't you call the police?'

'I did. I called 'em about daybreak, told 'em where she was . . . Then I took off. I panicked. We'd had an argument up at the club – people saw us, they knew we'd been living apart . . . I just wanted to get away. I sat in my car for, I dunno, two or three hours before I called the police. I just wanted to get away – what was there to stay for? She was dead –'

'When you went back to the house, what were you going to do?'

Glaze looked down at his clasped hands that appeared to be trying to strangle each other. 'If she kicked me out again, I was going to kill her and then kill myself. That was why I got outa there. Someone else had done what I was gunna do if she'd said no. Only thing different was I'd have topped myself as well.'

There was a downbeat silence this time; then Trevor Waring said, 'I think that's a reasonable explanation, don't you, Scobie?'

Nice try, Trev, but you're not as naïve as that.

71

'No, Trev, I don't . . . Ronald Glaze, I am arresting you for the murder of your wife Norma. Anything you may say . . .'

4

'I'd like to see Roma. Alone.'

'Five minutes, Ron. Don't try anything stupid.'

'Such as?'

Malone had seen average, placid men turn desperate; but he didn't think Glaze would be like that. He was a born salesman: hope was his diet. 'Five minutes. Leave the door open.'

Now that he had admitted his true identity, Glaze appeared almost relaxed. But not quite; the big hands were still restless. He looked at Waring. 'You disappointed, Trev?'

'Only for you, Roger,' said Waring and sounded sincere. 'Let's hope Roma can take it.'

Malone went out, followed by Waring. He gestured towards the interrogation room and Roma Gibson looked at him enquiringly. 'You're letting him go? I told you –'

'Roger has something to tell you, Roma,' said Waring.

She frowned, looked hard at the two of them, then went by them with a rush and into the interview room. Wally Mungle came back with sheets and a pad, pulled up sharply. 'He's confessed?'

'That he's Ron Glaze, yes. But not that he killed her.'

They were in the area behind the front counter. Two uniformed men, a middle-aged sergeant and a younger man, looked up from their desks. They stared at Malone, Mungle and Waring, as alert as pointer dogs; then they turned their heads. Gombrich had come out of his office.

'Well?'

'He's admitted he's the man we're after,' said Malone. 'He's denying he killed his wife. I'm charging him, nonetheless. Can we get the preliminary paperwork done?' He looked at his watch. 'I want to catch that plane. Have we got two seats?'

'You're going to take him in as he is?'

'No. If it's okay with you Constable Mungle can go out with his wife and bring in some gear for him. We'll hold him here till it's time to go out to the airport.'

'What if she wants to go down to Sydney with him?'

'That's okay, if there's a spare seat on the plane.'

'No, I got you the last two.'

'Leave it like that. She can come down tomorrow.'

The sergeant at his desk looked up at Mungle. 'You were right, Wally. Pleased?'

He was a bush cop, lean and hard and dry; his opinions would be the same. Mungle was not going to have an easy time of it; but he was not backing down. 'No, Jack. Just doing my job, that was all. Like you do yours.'

Before the sergeant could reply, Gombrich stepped in: 'It's done, that's the end of it.'

73

'Not the end,' said the sergeant, not giving up. 'Just the beginning.'

'That's how all homicide arrests start,' said Malone. He was watching that his tongue did not get away from him, but he was angry for Wally Mungle's sake. 'Ron Glaze will have plenty of time to argue.'

'Ron Glaze – who's he?' said the sergeant, but he knew he had lost the argument.

'Will you want Wally to come down to Sydney?' asked Gombrich. He was less formal now: he, too, knew he had lost the argument.

'Not for the charging. But for the committal and trial, probably.' He looked at the three locals: the inspector, the sergeant, the constable at his desk. Wally Mungle stood apart, identified by more than just being in plainclothes. 'I've been in Homicide more years than I care to count. Most murders, I get a certain satisfaction when we clean them up, bring in and convict the buggers responsible. I never get any satisfaction out of a domestic. I'm not going to get any satisfaction out of this one if we nail Ron Glaze. But someone – and it's us – has to do something for his wife. She's dead.'

For a moment nobody spoke; then Gombrich said, 'Fair enough,' and Malone knew he had won a point. For Wally Mungle, he hoped.

Then Roma Gibson and Glaze came in from the interview room. Not knowing the circumstances of her first marriage, but giving her the benefit of the doubt, Malone recognized that Roma Gibson had just had her life shattered for the second time. But there were no tears;

74

or if there were she had left them in the interrogation room. She was no longer aggressive, but she had already built defences.

'I'm coming with you.'

Malone said nothing, but glanced at Gombrich; the latter picked up the ball, reluctantly. 'The plane's full, Roma. There's a wait-list.'

She turned to Malone. 'When will Roger be charged? Where?'

He was still *Roger*: she wasn't giving him up to a dead woman. 'He'll be held at Surry Hills police station, in Police Centre, tonight. Then he'll go before a magistrate tomorrow morning, probably down at Liverpool Street. You know Sydney?'

'Yes.' She kissed her partner on the cheek, pressed his hand. It was for his benefit, not Malone's. She loves him, thought the latter. 'I'll drive down tonight. We'll be on our way home tomorrow night.'

He smiled at her, hugged her, then looked at Malone, who said, 'I wouldn't bank on it, Ron.'

5

While waiting to go out to the Collamundra airport Malone rang Mount Druitt and asked for Sergeant Backer. But Backer was no longer in the Service; he had joined a private security firm working for the Olympics. 'It's Senior Sergeant Hulbert here.'

Malone explained what he had in mind. 'You fellers

can take over, be there tomorrow morning and take all the credit.'

'Thanks all the same, but we just don't have the staff. You found him, you take the gold medal. It's all in the Olympic spirit.' He was another cop who, like Malone, was not looking forward to the events of 2000. 'Many thanks.'

'Up you,' said Malone and hung up.

Next morning, back in Sydney, Glaze was taken before a magistrate in the Liverpool Street court. Malone went down to the court with Andy Graham, just to tie his own ribbon bow on the case. By the time Glaze came to committal and trial, Andy Graham and someone from under-staffed Mount Druitt could present the evidence. This morning everything was over in a matter of minutes. Glaze's lawyer, briefed by Trevor Waring by phone, had not had time to prepare much argument.

After the hearing Malone made a mistake in taking a short cut through to the yard where the unmarked Homicide car was parked. Glaze was waiting in the hallway, accompanied by a court official, before being taken out to the van that would take him out to Long Bay gaol. Roma Gibson was there, her presence apparently tolerated by the court official, a young woman.

'Why did you oppose giving me bail?' Glaze was as nervous as an *NYPD Blue* cameraman; his eyes were everywhere, looking for something to focus on. All of a sudden he was falling apart. 'Jesus, *why*?'

'Ron, you pissed off once. Give you bail and you'd do it again.'

76

'Where will he be sent?' asked Roma Gibson. She was not as distraught as her partner, but one could see the effort she was making to hold herself together. 'For how long?'

'Long Bay, or maybe Silverwater. I dunno how long. We'll have the case prepared for the DPP –'

'The who?'

'Director of Public Prosecutions. They'll fit it into the court schedules. It could take three, four months, probably longer, before the committal, then there'll be the trial. It's out of our hands now.'

'Jesus!' Glaze threw up his manacled hands, looked around for escape.

'You don't care any more, do you?' said Roma Gibson.

'Mrs Gibson –' He drew a long sigh of patience; he had been down this road so many times. 'Have Trevor Waring get Ron –'

'Roger.'

'Whoever. Have Trevor get him a good barrister. That's more important than worrying about whether I care or not.'

'What do you do in the meantime?'

Doesn't this woman ever let go? But he had seen all this before, too: the thrown net, the drawing in of a cop as a hated relative. 'I go on to other cases. There are four or five homicides a day in this city – not much compared to other cities overseas. But we're kept busy.'

He walked past them out into the yard. The heat hit him at once, the glare blinded him; he took out his dark glasses, which he rarely wore, and put them on. He stood for a moment, getting himself together. He must be getting old; the net was growing tighter. Yet this was an uncomplicated case, at least for the police. He would put it out of his mind till he had to present the papers for the case to the DPP.

Andy Graham was waiting for him. 'Get in quick, boss. There's a girl from Channel 15 wanting to interview you. She says their show put us on to Glaze.'

'Let her talk to him, then. Maybe he'll sell them his story – they'll buy anyone with an open mouth.' He got into the car, slammed the door as he saw the girl, a cameraman and a sound man approaching. 'Get us outa here! Run over 'em, if you have to!'

Graham grinned. 'Nothing would gimme greater pleasure. But I don't think we have justifiable homicide, do we?'

Malone smiled wryly. 'You're developing a sour sense of humour, Andy.'

'It helps, doesn't it?' He would be a cop all his working life; another twenty-five years stretched ahead of him down the track. 'I've watched you and Russ. No offence.'

Chapter Three

1

Ronald Glaze's arraignment got only five lines, narrow single column, in the News Briefs in the next day's papers. Even Channel 15 did not run an item on him in its evening news on the day. Apart from political and economic stories and more scandal out of Washington, the big news was the kidnapping and demand for ransom of Lucybelle Vanheusen.

'Who is Lucybelle Vanheusen?' asked Malone at breakfast.

'She's that brat in the McDonald's commercials,' said Tom.

'And in the Toyota ads,' said Maureen.

'And in the Coca-Cola ads,' said Claire.

Malone groaned, remembering the moppet with enough red hair to have played a grown-up role in *Days of Our Lives*. 'I know her now.'

'Don't say it,' said Lisa.

'What?'

'That you hope the kidnappers don't give her back.'

Malone nodded; but he had been on the verge of being callously unfunny. 'I remember Dad used to say when he was growing up he couldn't stand Shirley Temple. She used to do dances up and down a staircase with some black dancer and Dad always wished she'd fall and break a leg. But I'm sorry about this kid. How much are they asking as the ransom?'

'A dollar ninety-five,' said Tom and jerked his head back as his mother swung the back of her hand at him. He grinned, but said, 'Sorry.'

Breakfast was the one meal that Malone insisted they all had together. All three were at university. Claire was doing Law and, already a lawyer, was advising her father on points that didn't interest him; her only good point, he would say, was that so far she wasn't charging him. Maureen was doing Communications and forever telling him he didn't know how to use the media. Tom had just started Commerce and after a month's study already knew more than Dr Greenspan, George Soros and the economic rationalists down in Canberra. They left the house each morning and were free souls; Tom, who liked home cooking, was home for dinner more frequently than his sisters. Lisa, still the boss in the house, insisted that there was a family dinner at least one night a week. The glue that held them together was stretched more than it used to be, but it was still holding.

'What's the percentage of kidnap victims who are returned unharmed?' asked Maureen.

Malone shrugged. 'I don't think anyone's ever done a survey on it. Kidnapping isn't a primary industry in this country.' But it would develop as more and more wealth was accumulated and the gap between rich and poor grew and violence became a way of life. 'Who are her parents?'

'How much don't you know?' Maureen was appalled at her father's ignorance. 'Her mum and dad are in the social pages every Sunday – they're on all the freeloader lists. He's the designer –'

'Of what?'

Maureen rolled her eyes, at which she was very good. 'Clothes. He's Sydney's Versace, only he's straight. Mum Vanheusen does nothing but promote little Lucybelle.'

'If he's so successful as a designer, why do they need to exploit the kid?' He was remembering Lucybelle more clearly now. She was in TV commercials as frequently as a certain popular blue cattle dog and Elle MacPherson.

'The mum was a model who never got as far as she hoped,' said Claire. 'Maybe she's hoping little Lucybelle will be the next – who'd you say Grandpa didn't like?'

It was Malone's turn to roll his eyes, at which he was not at all good. 'You lot know nothing about history, do you? You think everything started with the Beatles.'

'The who?' said Tom.

Later, Lisa walked out with Malone to the garage. She paused and looked around the garden; this was her green anchor, burned now by the long summer. She loved their house, though it was no more than a turn-of-the-century Federation model; the houses had become fashionable

81

again over the last five or six years, a reaching back to a history that property-owners never bothered to read. But it was the garden that held her; it was a calendar marked with azalea, camellia, lobelia, gardenia. The camellia had been a bush when they had first moved into the house; now it was a tree. Each evening, as she held the hose, she liked to think that she was spraying the garden with love. A thought she kept to herself: Malone and the children were not garden lovers.

'What are you looking at?'

'Nothing. It'll soon be time for pruning – you can buy me a new set of secateurs for my birthday.'

'I'll buy you a lawn-mower, too. How're you fixed for shovels and rakes?'

She hit him, loving him more than the garden. She got into the Ford Fairlane beside him. She worked as the Olympics public relations officer for the City Council and each morning he drove her into work before heading back to Strawberry Hills and his own office. He didn't enjoy the drive, but it was an opportunity for the two of them to discuss their own, and not the children's, affairs.

'That man you brought down from Collamundra –' Usually she waited for him to broach discussion on a case, but he had said nothing since his return home late the night before last. 'Did he kill his wife?'

'He did it, all right.' He took the car out of their quiet North Randwick street into the morning traffic. 'He'll lie his head off, but he'll go down.'

'What about this little girl?'

'What about her?'

'If she's been murdered –'

'Don't think about it –'

'Of course I think about it! Right now most of the mothers in Sydney will be thinking about it. Look at the number of girls, youngsters and teenagers, who have disappeared – there's a list in the *Herald* this morning –'

'I never anticipate – it's not Homicide's job to *prevent* murder –'

'That's pretty cold-blooded, isn't it?'

He looked sideways at her; in this hour's traffic it was the only safe way to look. Road rage was becoming endemic; every car had a potential terrorist in it. 'No, it's – pragmatic. It's the only way I sleep at night.'

'I'll remember that next time your loving hand gets out of hand.' She squeezed his thigh. 'Keep your eye on the road, sailor.'

He shuddered with love for her. Terrorists closed in on either side of him, shouting abuse: 'Learn to fucking drive, you arsehole!'

Lisa smiled at the terrorist on her side, a *woman*, then looked at her husband. 'Be pragmatic. Don't answer back.'

He dropped her at Town Hall, drove back to Homicide and was greeted by Russ Clements: 'We've got another one. That kidnapped kiddy, they dropped her off a cliff at Clovelly.'

Malone was abruptly ashamed of his approach to the

kidnapping this morning; the jokes came back like bile. 'Who's handling it?'

'Waverley. They want us in on it. You wanna take it with one of the girls?'

Malone went out of his small office into the big room. Most of his staff of eighteen detectives were at their desks, waiting for the morning conference to begin. They were a mixed lot, like the population in general; the older ones with that faded look of hope that investigators wear, the younger ones with their enthusiasm still to be tarnished. Police investigation was like gold-fossicking: one searched for the gleam of a clue amongst the gravel.

'Russ will take the meeting this morning.' He explained where he was heading. 'You come with me, Sheryl.'

He made no comment on the grimace that flashed across her face; she would do her job, no matter how much she might dislike the circumstances of this one. Sheryl Dallen had been with Homicide and Serial Offenders a year now and her competency and commonsense had increased with each case. She was of medium height, solidly slim or slimly solid, depending on male prejudice; she was a fitness fanatic, the gym was her church. Her attractiveness lay in her healthy look and her laconic approach to life and death. She would not be fazed by what might come up in the Lucybelle Vanheusen murder.

Driving out to Waverley in the eastern suburbs, under the blue glass of a sky that was forecast to turn black with thunder by evening, Malone said, 'I know nothing about this little girl, Sheryl, or her parents. You know anything?'

'I know the mother, slightly. She goes to my gym.'

He made no remark about the coincidence; experience had taught him that life got kick-starts from coincidence. 'What's she like?'

'You mean how'll she stand up to this? She's strong, I think. She's full of herself, but these days women have to be.'

'Don't start sounding like my daughters. Does she talk to you at gym?'

Sheryl shook her head. Her shoulder-length brown hair was worn in a ponytail today because of the heat; the ponytail swung like a bird trying to burrow into her head. 'I don't think I've ever said more than two words to her – I've just observed her, knowing who she was. She's usually surrounded by guys.'

'Does her husband – what's his name?'

'Damien.'

'Damien Vanheusen – why wasn't I born with a name like that? Does he come to the gym?'

'Occasionally, but he's not a regular.'

'What about the little girl – did Mum bring her to the gym?'

'I don't think so. Evangelina –'

'Who?'

'She's half-Spanish, I think. She's usually called Lina. She would usually come to the gym at night, after the little girl would be in bed.' She was silent for a while, then she said, 'I don't think there are any other children. They're gunna be devastated, both of them.'

'Well, we've missed the initial shock. Someone else will have told them.'

'That's a relief.'

The Waverley police station was next door to the courthouse, neither of them obtrusive in the surroundings. This was a small suburb that hadn't changed in over a half-century or even more; the houses and flats were the dull statements of architects of the twenties, thirties and forties. Under an overhang of trees by the courthouse offenders and witnesses sheltered from the too-bright sun. The offenders had the hang-dog look of people wondering why they had committed the offences in the first place.

The patrol commander of the station was Superintendent Joe Vettori, a handsome, enthusiastic man who this morning showed no enthusiasm at all. 'G'day, Scobie. A bugger of a case, this one. I heard you've just wrapped up an old one?'

'You lose some, you win some, Joe. What about this one?'

'So far, no clues. Chris Gallup is at the Vanheusen house right now, he's in charge. We'll set up the incident room here, I'll give you as many guys as you want.' He smiled at Sheryl; he had an Italian eye. 'Nice to have you with us, Constable Dallen.'

'Thank you, sir,' said Sheryl. Outside in their car again she said, 'What's Sergeant Gallup like? I saw you make a face.'

Malone grinned. 'He's not an admirer of women, if that's what you're looking for. I've worked only once with him and he resented us being there. But you may charm him, like you did Superintendent Vettori.'

'One thing I like about working in Homicide. You're a cop first and last.'

'Don't you believe it. I've seen the fellers looking at you.' He glanced at her. 'I'm not flirting with you, Sheryl. But don't ever think gender is going to disappear from the Service. They'll whistle at your walk and put minus marks against you for promotion.'

'Do you think there'll ever be a woman Commissioner?'

'About the same time as there'll be a woman Prime Minister. You're in a man's country, Sheryl. But as Superintendent Vettori said, nice to have you with us.'

'I'm overwhelmed,' she said, but smiled to show it wasn't insubordination.

The Vanheusen house was in a cul-de-sac in Bellevue Hill, a long stone's throw from the estate of the country's richest man, a missie's throw from the western suburbs and the 40-foot plot of Ron Glaze. This was a small district in the eastern suburbs, where wealth hovered like a miasma and the mortgages, if any, were of a size that had banks genuflecting. Most of the houses stood on modest acreage, but Mercedes, Jaguars and the occasional Bentley let you know this was not welfare territory. Two high-fee private schools occupied most of the east side of the main road that climbed the hill; there were no shops, no corner grocery nor a newsagent. It was territory, Malone thought, that would have watered the mouths of Butch Cassidy and the Sundance Kid or the Kelly Gang. Burglars tried their luck around here, but it was hard work. Kidnapping was a new venture.

The Vanheusens had built recently; their house was a rarity in the area, a new one. It was built in a style that had become popular in the past few years: Tuscan villas were more numerous than around Firenze or Siena. Columns were everywhere, like fossilized tree-trunks or pillars stolen from a temple; romantics looked for a stray vestal virgin, but there were few in Bellevue Hill. All the Tuscan villas had porticos, like museum entrances. At the moment, with police and media cars crowding the turning circle of the cul-de-sac, one might have suspected there was an exhibition of some sort going on.

Sheryl parked their car at the entrance to the short street and she and Malone walked down. Malone was instantly recognized by the regular police reporters; it wasn't stardom or even celebrity, it was just familiarity. Cameras turned on him like weapons, tape recorders were thrust at him. One of the closest reporters to him, almost in his face, was the Channel 15 girl.

'You're taking charge, Inspector?' She was tall, with long blonde hair, big blue eyes and the cheekbones that always looked good on camera, no matter what the light. She had a light voice and the local habit amongst TV reporters of moving her head all the time she was talking: a bob here, a nod there, a shake elsewhere, as if every word had to be underlined. 'Anything to report yet? How soon can we expect the police to come up with something?'

Malone just gave her his No Comment smile and he and Sheryl pushed through the crush and went in the open door of the house past the young officer guarding it. The entrance hall wasn't large, but it was two-storeyed, rising above the curved stairway that led up to a mezzanine floor.

Senior Sergeant Chris Gallup was in the hallway talking to a slim grey-haired man. He looked over the man's shoulder and his eyes hardened. Here we go again, thought Malone: I'm on his turf.

'G'day.' Gallup's nod was perfunctory. 'I was told you'd be coming.'

'Just to help, Chris. This is Constable Dallen.'

Gallup gave her a perfunctory nod; he was not a ladies' man. 'This is Mr Vanheusen.'

He was prematurely grey; Malone guessed he was not much more than forty. His hair was cut Roman style; that is, Caesar's Rome. He had a thin handsome face, a small mouth under an incongruously dark moustache; he wore blue linen slacks and shirt and dark blue deck shoes. His small dark eyes were red-rimmed and he kept raising his thumb and pressing it against his teeth.

'You're from?' He had a deep voice that at other times might have been pleasant; now it was ragged, rough. A voice he might have grown up with and then discarded.

'Homicide,' said Malone, and Vanheusen winced as if something had been added to his shock and grief. 'Have you been able to tell Sergeant Gallup anything that would help us?'

Vanheusen shook his head and Gallup said, 'We've got the ransom note and that's all, it and the envelope.'

He appeared to have relaxed a bit, as if accepting Malone's conciliatory approach. He was as tall as Malone, balding, with close-cropped ginger hair along his temples. His face was bony, with eyes set deep amongst the bones; sometimes the eyes, too, could become bony.

'How'd it happen?'

'They got in from the garden at the back. The alarm system broke down a coupla days ago and they just forced open the grille doors into the living room. There are French doors and the grille.

'The child had a room of her own?'

'Across the hall from my wife's room,' said Vanheusen.

A two-bedroom marriage? But it was too soon to ask such a question. 'Have you talked to Mrs Vanheusen yet, Chris?'

'Do you have to?' said Vanheusen. 'Leave her alone –'

'No, it's all right, Damien.'

A woman, black hair drawn severely back, stood at the top of the curving stairway. She stood there for a long pause, then she came slowly down the stairs. Crumbs, thought Malone, she's making an entrance *now*?

Evangelina Vanheusen was a run-of-the-mill beauty; she would have been the sort of model one saw in furniture commercials or in swimsuits in game shows. She had style, but it was exaggerated. Real style, Lisa had told Malone, was never immediately apparent. Mrs Vanheusen was very much immediately apparent. 'I can talk to the woman officer – why, hello, don't I know you?'

'We go to the same gym,' said Sheryl.

'Well –' It was hard to tell whether she thought that was good news or bad news. She led them out of the hallway into a large living room that stretched all one side of the house; out through the French doors there were a pool and an ornamental garden. The room itself had all the bland character of a room designed by a professional decorator for clients he hadn't yet met. One guessed there must be personal items in the room, but they were on display, not there as part of the odds and ends of the owners' lives. Even the Robert Juniper painting above the fireplace looked as if it were on loan. The room was as impersonal as a bank vault, but with no coded lock.

'You didn't hear anything when the kidnapper or kidnappers went into your daughter's room?' asked Malone.

'I wasn't here,' said Vanheusen.

The silence was all angles; but Malone said, 'You were away for the night?'

'Yes.'

Vanheusen took his wife's hand and they sat down on a couch; then the three detectives were waved to chairs. Malone took a stiff-backed chair that put him a head-and-a-half above the level of the Vanheusens. These were bereaved parents, but (he didn't know why) they were not going to be easy to deal with.

'Were there any phone calls besides the ransom note?'

'There was one phone call,' said Lina Vanheusen. 'About an hour after the note arrived. Just asking if I'd read it, then she hung up.'

'She? It was a woman?'

'I think so.' She suddenly lost her poise, looked uncertain. She tightened her grip on her husband's hand. 'I don't know, maybe it was a man. It was a high voice, like a boy's before his voice breaks.'

'Disguised,' said Gallup. 'So it could be someone who knows you.'

'Possibly.' She nodded.

'How did you get the note?'

Vanheusen took over: 'Our housekeeper found it, shoved under the front door yesterday morning. She came home just as my wife discovered Lucybelle wasn't in her room. At first she thought Lucy might've got up and was downstairs here, in the kitchen, getting her own breakfast –'

'She was a bright child?' asked Gallup.

'Very,' said the mother.

Malone looked at Gallup. 'They've taken the note and envelope to Fingerprints?'

Gallup nodded. 'Both. It was done on a computer, just three or four lines. The usual stuff – the money they wanted, don't tell the police, wait for further instructions . . . They never gave any further instructions.'

Lina Vanheusen gave a choked sob and Vanheusen looked reproachfully at Gallup.

'How much did they ask for?' said Malone.

'Five hundred thousand,' said Vanheusen.

'I have to ask this – was that within your capacity to pay?'

'Yes,' said Vanheusen and didn't look modest about the admission.

'Then it could be someone who knows you? Or your financial status?'

'These days,' said Lina Vanheusen, 'everyone knows that sort of thing. Everybody's business is the media's business.'

Not mine. 'You've been to the morgue and identified your child?'

'I went.' Vanheusen pressed his wife's hand. 'Lina couldn't face it.'

'Your little girl, was she handled through an agent for the TV work she did? Was there any jealousy, I mean from the parents of other children?'

'What do you mean?' Lina Vanheusen raised her chin.

'What the inspector means –' Sheryl took up the bowling; she had learned the technique of two-man questioning – 'what he means is, isn't there a great deal of jealousy in the model game?'

'We read about it,' said Gallup, making it a three-man attack.

'Of course there's jealousy in the model business!' Lina spoke as if she had experienced it. 'But amongst the children – no!'

'I wasn't thinking of the children themselves,' said Malone. 'I was thinking of – well, aren't there some stage mothers in the game?'

93

'It's not a game!'

'Sorry. Business.'

'If there was, we never experienced any of it,' said Vanheusen, still holding his wife's hand. 'Lucy was popular with everyone –'

'You sometimes deal with the agency?'

'Well, no. Lina . . . Is that where you're going to start, investigating the other kids' mothers?'

Malone looked at Gallup. 'I'm not sure where we'll start, are you, Sergeant?'

Gallup might be bone-faced, but he was not bone-headed. 'We're not gunna go off half-cocked, Mr Vanheusen. You and your wife are well known – you're celebrities, you'll have a wide circle of friends, acquaintances – we'll be talking to all of them –'

'It's not going to bring back Lucy –'

That's a cliché, thought Malone; but like most clichés it was a truth, a sad truth. He stood up, nodded at the doors to the garden. 'That where they came in? Any prints, Chris?'

'PE found none. None on the door to Lucy's room. He or they wore gloves.'

'Then we'll start with the ransom note and the envelope, that's all we have. Unless there's another phone call . . .'

Lina looked up at him. 'Another? Why would they call again after – I mean, *now*?'

'I hope they don't, Mrs Vanheusen. But we may be dealing with someone awfully sick . . . We'll be in touch.'

94

The three detectives left the husband and wife still sitting on the couch, still hand in hand. Yet not close, thought Malone.

As they came into the hallway another woman was coming down the stairs. She wore a white apron, apparently starched, a navy blue skirt and a light blue shirt. She was heavily built, almost fat, had a broad square-jawed face and thick blonde hair pulled back in a bun.

'The housekeeper,' said Gallup. 'Mrs Certain.'

'Cer-TAIN,' said the housekeeper, a woman with no uncertainty about her.

'Mrs Certain,' said Malone, getting the pronunciation right, 'what can you tell us about what happened?'

'I've already told Sergeant Gallup everything. I was away for the night, visiting a friend –'

'We've checked,' said Gallup.

The look she gave him should have knocked him unconscious. 'You don't think I had anything to do with this awful –?'

'No, Mrs Certain, we don't,' said Malone. 'But we check everything – it's in our nature . . . The alarm system was out. What happened to it?'

'It just went – phut!'

'It had been cut,' said Gallup.

'I noticed it wasn't working just before I went out to visit my friend. I meant to call the security people – I forgot –' She put her hand to her mouth, all at once looked very uncertain. 'I remembered on my way back here yesterday morning – by then it was too late –'

'We're checking everybody who had access here,' said

Gallup. 'The poolman, the gardener – they're too obvious, but –'

'Righto, Mrs Certain, we may be in touch again . . .'

As they moved towards the front door Malone glanced back into the living room. The Vanheusens still sat hand in hand. But still not close, thought Malone.

The vultures flew in as soon as the three detectives stepped out of the front door. Questions were hurled, but police, like politicians, become Tefloned with experience. Gallup pushed his way through the crowd after Malone and Sheryl, got into their car with them. Sheryl backed out of the street, swung round and headed back towards Waverley. The front doors of all the houses in the cul-de-sac were closed, the curtains drawn. The house-fronts looked like disapproving matrons beside what was going on in front of the Tuscan villa.

'What d'you reckon, Chris?'

Gallup shook his head. 'Nothing at the moment. That busted alarm system – that looked a bit coincidental. As for Damien and Lina – they haven't been the happiest couple for some time.'

Malone looked over his shoulder at him. 'Where'd you get that?'

'My wife. She reads that little column in the *Sun-Herald* on Sundays, *Guess Who – Don't Sue*. She guesses who they're talking about and reckons she's right about 75 per cent of the time.' Then he added defensively, 'She's not a featherbrain, the wife. It's her Sunday relaxation, she says, her Sunday crossword puzzle.'

'My daughters count the teeth in the photos in the

96

social section. You've never seen such stupid smiling.'

'You two old fogies,' said Sheryl, 'should get out into the real world and find out what makes it go round.'

'What does?' said the two old fogies.

'Addiction. Not just with the young, even the middle-aged who should know better have it. A guy with a camera approaches them, it's like giving them a needle. They smile, mug, get the silly pose. But it sells, otherwise editors wouldn't run the pictures. It's no different from all the aristocracy who used to have their pictures painted – they just didn't smile, that was all.'

'Are we gunna find the kidnappers in those photos?' asked Gallup. 'Smiling like bloody jackals?'

2

Clements, as Supervisor, assigned Sheryl Dallen and John Kagal to do the legwork on the Vanheusen case. Malone went back to his paperwork, concentrating on the Glaze case, where everything (well, almost everything) followed as in a well-constructed sentence.

Next morning he went to the offices of the Director of Public Prosecutions. They were in a building opposite a one-time department store that now housed a complex of law courts. He paused for a moment and looked across the narrow street at the ex-store. It had been a proud item in its day, its exterior walls of tiles glistening like ice when it rained; it had been owned by a Catholic family and, such was the nature of the times, it had been a

Protestant who had said the building looked like a urinal turned inside out. In its present guise there were many crims who would have pissed on it with pleasure.

Yellow tiles, set in a frieze at first-floor level, spelled out what had once been available inside. Costumes, Corsets, Mourning: there was still scope for the last in the building. Malone dreamed of the day when the yellow tiles would spell out: Crime, Punishment. But, like a true cop, he guessed that public display of such slogans would only offend the civil libertarians.

He went into the DPP offices. The staff occupied two floors here in the City office; the place was alive with the sound of muted briefs. There were 300 lawyers on the establishment: 70 barristers and 230 solicitors spread through 11 offices around the State of New South Wales. The DPP himself was here and the senior Crown Prosecutor. Malone was shown into the office of the latter.

'Greetings, Scobie.' David Winkler was tall, wild-haired and untidy; he looked like a mad scientist temporarily without an experiment. But Malone had seen him in action; he could blow a defence out of court with explosive force. 'What recipe do we have today?'

'G'day, Dave. You still wanting to be a TV cook?'

'I've given up that ambition, old mate. There are more cooks on TV now than there are anchorpersons – most of them fatter than I am.' He patted an ample belly; then took the file Malone handed him. 'The Glaze case? How will we go?'

'Pretty well, I think. He's going to plead Not Guilty, but I think we have enough to nail him.'

'Is he a bad bastard?'

'I don't think so. It was probably an argument that got out of hand. But the wife's dead and he did it.'

'Fine. We can do with some easy ones. Life's getting more difficult, with judges and magistrates granting pleas you wouldn't believe.' He picked up the phone on his cluttered desk, pushed the wild hair away from his ear. 'Tim, can you come in for a moment?' He hung up. 'Have you met Tim Pierpont? Good chap, one of the best on our staff. He'll probably finish up here in my chair. But don't tell him. Ambitious lawyers, they're a pain. Usually finish up as judges.'

'Won't you?'

'Of course.' He had a big-toothed smile, which added to the mad look. 'Being a prosecutor is only half the fun. The other half is whacking them with ten years hard . . . Come in, Tim.'

He was a tall lean man with a bony face that stopped just short of being handsome. He had thick dark hair, grey along the temples, though Malone guessed he was still short of forty. He moved with an unhurried easy grace, as if he knew he was destined for a long life. He wore no jacket and his striped button-down shirt looked as if it had just been ironed. His right arm hung at his side and he put out his left hand for Malone's handshake.

'Nice to meet you. Dave's spoken of you.' Then he lifted his arm, showed the claw that was his hand. 'I never offer this first time up.'

'I'm surprised we haven't met before.'

99

'Dave's had me running around the State. I've done homicides, but not many.'

'He's a whiz on civil cases, fraud, stuff like that. But now we're educating him in the seamier side of life, eh, Tim?' Winkler handed him the file. 'Chap named Glaze. Scobie's been after him for four years. Says it's open-and-shut.'

Pierpont opened the folder, glanced at the pages; then looked up at Malone. 'Is it? Open-and-shut?'

Malone shrugged. 'There's always the chance . . . No, I don't think we can lose. We've started work on it again, we'll have all the evidence you want by the time we go to committal. At the moment he's doing a great job of being innocent, but they always do that, don't they?'

The two lawyers nodded and Winkler said, 'Well, you two work together and we'll chalk up another one to Justice or whatever they call it . . . Are you on this latest one, Scobie? The kiddy they threw off a cliff?' He uttered a loud cough of disgust. He was a happily married man with six children, all of whom were his favourites. 'Animals like that, that's when summary execution has its points.'

'I've always thought you looked like a mad scientist. But a mad lawyer?'

'We're worse, far worse. Aren't we, old chap?'

'Far, far worse,' said Pierpont and folded the claw into his other hand.

When Malone had gone, Tim Pierpont said, 'Do you really want me to do this one, if it's so open-and-shut?'

'Tim, old man –' Winkler sat back in his chair. 'You had a bad loss last week –' he held up a plump hand as Pierpont leaned forward – 'okay, *we* had a bad loss. You were up against that bastard Moloney, who'd lie to God if it meant getting his client off. You were up before Spokes J, who thinks he *is* God. We had everything stacked against us, once we got into that court.'

'We should have won –'

'That's what we always say, Tim. You've got at least one more case, maybe two, before that one comes up –' he nodded at the file. 'The next one or two are going to be tough, bloody tough, old chap. You – *we* – need a few open-and-shuts to clear our good name. Take it, Tim. Get one of the girls to handle the committal, then you can polish him off.'

Pierpont went home that evening by train. He believed in public transport and looked out from the train window at the motor traffic polluting the atmosphere. He was a conservationist who wanted to protect the planet against developers, timber companies, mining companies, everyone who, at the end of the day, as they all said, looked only at the bottom line and their own satisfaction. Now, suddenly, he was in another form of conservation: that of himself, Ginny and Fay.

Turramurra is a North Shore suburb, even though it is some kilometres from any shore. No matter: the term is a socio-economic one. It suggests private schools; more wealth, if bigger mortgages; and a hint of snobbery apparent only to those who live in other western or southern areas. Beyond Turramurra are Pymble and Wahroonga, the peaks of the North Shore; there are social mountaineers further down the line, ready with pitons, ropes and growing wealth aiming to climb higher. Wahroonga and Pymble look at each other much as Everest and Lhotse do; they share the same high social and financial weather. The real weather, for its part, appreciates the distinctions: when it rains, the heaviest downpour always drenches Turramurra. Just as a reminder . . .

Pierpont got out of the train, left the station and crossed the road to the top of the steep street that led down to his own side street. He stopped and looked west. Out there the setting sun was a boil under the skin of smoke from a bushfire; just the sort of angry, threatening scene to calm a worried eye. Out there, somewhere under the smoke, was the house where he had murdered Norma Glaze. At least fifty times in the past four years he had travelled west, going to courts in Katoomba and Blackheath, to conservation protest demonstrations; from the freeway he had seen the club where he had first observed Norma Glaze, where the whole damned mess had started. Nobody, not even the man himself, had prayed harder that Ron Glaze would never be caught.

He walked down the hill, sinking as he got closer to home. His street was lined with crepe myrtles, in

102

the last of their bloom; his footsteps were quiet as he walked through the soft rosy snow of the fallen flowers. He turned in at his gate.

Ginny and Fay were sitting on the front verandah, waiting for him as they always did on a summer evening. Fay leapt out of her small chair and rushed towards him. He swept her up in his arms, hugging her too tightly, wanting to weep; but he had never been able to weep. Not even on that dreadful night when he had gone home and fallen into bed with the awful realization that he had murdered someone.

'Had a good day?' Ginny was blonde and plumply pretty; she had put on weight after the birth of Fay, but he hadn't minded. She was three months pregnant again and they were hoping for a boy this time. He had met her, a law student in her final year, at a Law Society reception; there had been a vitality to her, an enthusiasm for life, that had been like a medicine for him after his own life had fallen apart. They had met a month after the murder and they had been married three months later. Like using one woman as the shut door against the memory of another: marriage on the rebound . . . 'I thought we'd eat outside. It's just Atlantic salmon and a salad.'

She was not a good cook, not even interested in being one, and he always looked forward to the summer when she didn't have to strain her imagination. She was not even a good housekeeper, always spending to the limit in her efforts to please him, but he loved her dearly. Her and Fay.

103

He had never imagined he could love a child so much; but, of course, they had been other people's children. Fay was a miniature of her mother, blonde and plumply pretty; but what endeared her to him was her sense of humour. Already, at three, it seemed that she knew what in life was funny.

'Mummy fell over today.' She laughed, a gurgling laugh too old for her years.

Ginny showed a skinned knee on the tanned leg beneath her blue shorts. 'Chasing her. She's going to be a wild one – you'd better start practising getting her out of trouble when she gets to her teens –'

'You hurt yourself?' He patted her stomach.

'No.' She kissed him. 'You look tired. So it wasn't a good day?'

He gestured as they went into the house. 'You know what it's like. Some days . . . I'll have a shower. See you in the garden.'

The house was an older one, solid brick with a red-tiled roof. Flying in over Sydney one saw houses like this, streets and streets of them, spread like a geometrical eczema over the face of the city. But they were not flaky like eczema; they were rooted solidly in their small gardens, many of them with the blue eye of a swimming pool. This one had been bought with money he had inherited from his parents; there was no mortgage on it. There was a Landrover Discovery in the garage, a fenced pool in the back yard and a garden that warmed his conservationist's heart, full of native shrubs and trees, except for the purple mound of the tibouchina tree at the very end of the garden. Everything was there to give one a promise for the future.

The shower did nothing to lighten his depression. He stood under the water and let it stream over him; to hell with saving water this evening. But there was no balm to it, no washing away of secrets. He had no idea what he was going to do. *Conscience is a moveable feast.* David Winkler had said that, referring to a recent case; but Dave was a cynic, had seen too many offenders walk away free. He stepped out of the shower, looked at himself in the bathroom mirror. He had the bedraggled look that water gives one. His image was not reassuring.

He dressed in shorts, polo shirt and sandals and went out to the only security he knew. Ginny: to whom he could never tell the truth.

4

'How's Amanda?' asked Malone.

Romy Clements' daughter was now two years old. 'Fine. She's got her father's constitution.'

'Better that than his looks.'

She smiled. 'I don't think I ever fell for Russ's looks.'

'Does she like the child-care centre?'

'How does one know? She's bright, but not bright enough yet to talk to me about it. I've got a guilty conscience each morning when I leave her there. Am I being a neglectful mother, more interested in my career than my child?'

'Don't ask me. All I know is how valuable you are here –' He gestured round her office. It was small and lined with books and files; yet it didn't look cluttered. Romy had some of Lisa's neatness about her. Was it a Northern European thing or had he and Clements married a couple of paragons? What was the point of asking them? They would only say Yes. 'What have you got on Lucybelle Vanheusen?'

Romy picked up a print-out. 'I won't give you the details on her body – the injuries are just too horrible. But –' she looked at him – 'she'd been drugged before they threw her off that cliff. At least they didn't toss her over screaming her head off. There was enough Diazepam in her to put her out.'

'Diazepam – what's that?'

'It's the ingredient in several sedatives – Valium, for instance.'

'You need a prescription?'

'Yes. It has a bitter taste, so most children don't like it. Lucybelle would have spat it out. Hence the chocolate –'

'Chocolate?'

'We found undigested chocolate in her stomach. They'd mixed the Diazepam in it and given it to her as a chocolate drink. She'd have been no worry to them when they put her in the plastic bag.'

'Considerate of them. But why kill her before they got an answer to the ransom note? They must've panicked or they were never interested in the money, anyway.'

'Was there anything on the plastic bag – fingerprints,

anything? It was pretty badly ripped, but we gave it to Physical Evidence.'

He shook his head. 'Nothing. They used gloves. I've only got one foot in the door of this case, but already it looks – *planned*. They didn't do this on the spur of the moment . . . Anyhow, thanks. Can I have a copy of that report?'

She handed him a file from her desk. 'Ready and waiting. Teutonic efficiency, isn't that what you rough-and-ready Aussies would call it?'

'I love you, Marlene.' He kissed her on the cheek.

'She was before my time. I'd rather be Claudia Schiffer.'

'Glamour, glamour – that's all you women are interested in.'

She waved a hand towards her door, to what was outside in the morgue. 'It's a contrast to what's out there . . . Didn't Schiffer come out here for Vanheusen, for one of his shows?'

'How would I know? I'll ask him.'

He drove out to Waverley through a polluted day; the horizon looked greasy, as if one could scrawl one's name on it with a finger. The bushfires had started again on the edge of the city; TV screens last night had blazed like thousands of fireplaces. Asthmatics had been told to stay indoors; heart patients likewise; respirators were working overtime. Insurance companies were having their own respiratory trouble: the damage bill was rising with the smoke. The Vanheusen kidnapping and murder were now a small item on the inside pages and already history on the TV screens. Yeltsin had sacked his Cabinet in Moscow and another woman had come out of the woodwork in Washington. Channel 15 did remember Lucybelle; or rather, temporarily forgot. It ran a commercial featuring her and was deluged with protests.

So Malone was surprised when he found the blonde girl from Channel 15 waiting for him outside the police station. She was in the shadow of a wall, but erupted into the sunlight, yellow hair a glare. 'Inspector!'

'No sackcloth and ashes? Or don't you TV people wear them?'

'That was a horrible booboo, but it was programming's fault. I'm here to try and make up for it.'

'You could've fooled me.' He looked for her cameraman, but there was no sign of him. 'Where's your Seeing Eye?'

'He's out the back having a leak. Mr Malone – *please.*' She was no older than Claire, if that; but ambition might age her quickly. She was going to be the next Jana Wendt, Diane Sawyer, maybe even Oprah Winfrey. 'Fill me in. The local cops here think they're the KGB.'

'I'll tell Sergeant Gallup that. He may lock you up in the Lubyanka.'

'The what?' She looked over her shoulder, as if it might be right behind her.

She'd have still been at school when the Soviet Union fell apart. 'A police joke. I'm sorry – what's your name?'

'Sharon Garibaldi.'

108

It wasn't a name that would roll off the tongue. 'Sharon, we're still in the starting blocks. We don't solve crimes in an hour, not like on TV. As soon as we've got something concrete, we'll let you know.' That was a lie; but if she was going to be a TV celebrity host, she would get used to the atmosphere. 'Just give me a little time.'

She relented. 'You're nice when you try.'

'So my wife tells me.'

He went into the station, to the incident room. The first photos were on the wall, the faint footprints of a crime; the flow chart was stagnant. John Kagal, Sheryl Dallen and Chris Gallup sat despondent; in a corner a young officer was eating a sandwich and drinking coffee, waiting to be called into action.

'I've got four blokes out,' said Gallup, offering Malone coffee. 'So far they've come up with bugger-all. They've interviewed every mother and father who's got a kid at the agency where Lucybelle worked out of. Nothing.'

'Unless some kid, one of the older ones, from the agency did it,' said the young officer in the corner and everyone turned and looked at him. He fumbled with the sandwich in his hand. 'It's just a thought. Those two kids in Arkansas –' he pronounced it Ar-kan-sas – 'the ones shot up their school, killed their school-mates. They were only – what? – eleven or twelve. There was that kid we had here last year in Sydney – ten years old and he had 87 charges listed against him.'

'He wasn't a kidnapper or a killer,' said Gallup. 'As for Arkansas –' he gave it the correct pronunciation in

109

a tone of voice that suggested *anything* could come out of Arkansas.

Malone handed him the morgue print-outs. 'What went wrong with these kidnappers? Did they argue, decide to throw the kid off the cliff, just go home and forget it?'

Gallup passed the print-outs to Sheryl and Kagal. The latter looked at them, then said, 'The Vanheusens have been separated for the past month. They were fighting over the kid.'

'Where'd you get that?'

'Kate's sister is a model. Gossip is a three-course meal for them.'

Kate Arletti was his live-in girl friend, an officer in the Fraud Squad. She had once worked for Malone in Homicide, but he didn't encourage office romances and she had been transferred to Fraud. Kagal was bisexual and Malone had not expected the romance to last; he had been wrong and for Kate's sake, he was glad he had been. He was a reluctant surrogate father to the women on his staff, something his wife and daughters joked about but about which they were secretly proud. They would have knee-capped him if he had not been.

'The kidnappers must've known about the bust-up.'

'Are you saying that in the parents' emotional state they'd have come through more quickly with the money? What d'you reckon, Sheryl?'

'I dunno. I don't have any children.'

'I have two,' said Gallup. 'They focus your mind when they're in trouble.' He didn't say what sort of trouble his children might be in. 'Maybe the kidnappers know the Vanheusens really well. Someone who's in a hole and needs money.'

'I think we should now start in on their friends –'

'A coupla Chris's guys are already on that,' said Sheryl. 'But I'll bet there's hundreds of them. Well, not friends – acquaintances. They're that sorta people.'

Malone rose. 'Righto, let's find some of them. Chris, you and Sheryl take the gym for a start. John and I'll visit Damien. Where will we find him?'

'He has two shops,' said Kagal. 'One in Double Bay, the other in the city, Castlereagh Street. His factory – or his design centre, as he calls it – is just down the road in Bondi Junction.'

'Bondi Junction? High fashion?'

Kagal grinned at him. 'You're improving. You're starting to sound snobbish.'

'Do your junior officers talk to you like that, Chris?'

'All the time. It's the new democracy,' said Gallup and looked over his shoulder at his junior officer, who raised a hand in agreement. 'Okay, Sheryl, let's go down and pump iron.'

'She does that three times a week,' said Malone. 'I'd watch her.'

The humour was shallow, but it had brought Gallup into the Homicide team; or rather, it had brought the Homicide team into Gallup's. The territorial imperative is strong in the animal kingdom, at top and bottom level. Malone had learned to live with it: when to give, when to take.

Malone and Kagal walked the ten minutes to Bondi Junction; it was easier, despite the heat, to do that than look for parking space. Traffic was taking over the city and suburbs like metal algae; drivers and passengers sat in their cars and looked out at the freedom of the strollers on the traffic bank. Still, they wouldn't give up their cars. They believed a car driver had independence. Kookaburras sat in trees and laughed, and over at Taronga Park Zoo a chimpanzee rolled around in mirth.

The Junction is a knit of stores, big and small, of cafés and restaurants, a cinema complex, some high-rise apartment blocks. Nothing is high-priced: this is where the battlers of the eastern suburbs come to shop. It is often a surprise to the western suburbs that there are battlers in the east.

The Vanheusen design centre, or factory as the battlers would have called it, was in a street off the main stem. As they approached it Kagal said, 'What do you think of fashion?'

'I read once that fashion is for sheep that like conmen as their shepherds. I agree with that.'

'I can believe it,' said Kagal, eyeing Malone's off-the-rack suit and his pork-pie hat, a protection against sun cancers.

'These shoes I'm wearing –' Malone lifted his feet in an exaggerated step; two women passers-by stopped in puzzlement – 'I've had for twenty-two years. Every five or six years they're in fashion.'

'When we get to talk to Damien, you think I'd better lead the conversation?'

'How much did that suit you're wearing cost?'

'It's a Hugo Boss. Eight hundred dollars.'

Malone wobbled his head. 'On a cop's pay?'

Kagal grinned. 'My grandmother left me a small private income. On condition I dressed well.'

The building was two-storeyed, with a lobby, offices and Vanheusen's studio on the ground floor and the workroom on the floor above. It had none of the class of the European fashion houses; it didn't even have the class of a suburban Tuscany villa. There was, however, a touch of restrained elegance about the brass plate beside the entrance. It just said *Vanheusen*, like a brass visiting card that everyone should know.

Vanheusen was in black skivvy, black jeans and black loafers with no socks. Somehow it did not suggest funeral garb; it was still a fashion statement. The funeral, anyway, was not till tomorrow.

He did not appear surprised to see the two detectives. 'Still nothing? God, how long is it going to take to get these bastards?'

Malone's tongue, as it often did, got away from him: 'How long does it take you to design a frock?'

'A frock? I don't design fucking *frocks*!' Then he got hold of himself, relaxed his thin frame. 'Sorry. I see your point. Everything takes a while, doesn't it?'

'I've just spent four years waiting to nail a man, but we got him. I promise you –' it was an empty promise, but sometimes they were necessary – 'we'll get these people much sooner than that.'

'Mr Vanheusen –' said Kagal.

'Damien.'

'Damien, how do you get on with your staff?'

'Here? Fine, no trouble at all. I have two assistants, a cutter, a business manager and two secretaries – they're all on this floor. Upstairs in the workroom there are – let me see – there are twelve, all women.'

'What do they do?' asked Malone.

'They make my top-of-the-range *frocks* –' He smiled, was much less tense now. 'My *collection.*'

'Why is it called that?' Malone was trying to put him further at ease; in case the questions got harder. 'I've heard of only art collections.'

'Fashion is an art.'

Kagal got in first before Malone put a foot wrong at the next hurdle: 'That's your entire output?'

'No, no.' He waved both hands, a little effeminately; but Malone was sure he wasn't homosexual. Unless he was bisexual, like Kagal. But then maybe effeminate gestures were part of the fashion scene, just like a belch and a fart were part of a football dressing-room. Everyone to his culture . . . 'Our middle-of-the-range is done outside –'

'By outworkers?' said Malone.

The hands stopped still in mid-air; he said coldly, 'I don't exploit anyone, Inspector. A dollar an hour, two dollars a garment – that's not my way. Are you suggesting that if I did exploit my workers, some of them might have been trying to get back at me?'

'I don't know, Damien. We're throwing a wide net.

We work by a process of elimination – I suppose you work like that?'

'Occasionally.' Now that he had met Malone for the second time, had a good look at him, Vanheusen knew he was dealing with a Philistine. 'Depends on the year. Sometimes I add, sometimes I take away. This year everything is simple.' Then he bit his lip, shut his eyes for just a moment. 'Well, no, it isn't, is it?'

'No, Damien, it isn't . . . The ransom note was printed by a computer on plain A4 paper – plain but slightly flecked, right, John?' Kagal nodded. 'How many computers do you have here? Here and in your shops?'

Vanheusen had to think, screwing up his face. 'Four here, one each in the shops, two at home. Eight. They're not all used for letters, stuff like that. I design on that one there –' he pointed to a computer on a nearby bench – 'and on one at home. Of course, it all begins here –' he tapped his head – 'with a pen and a piece of paper.'

'That's where the kidnap idea began,' said Malone. 'In someone else's head. Then they moved to a computer. That, we hope, may have been their mistake, their first –'

'What were their other ones?'

Killing Lucybelle; but he caught his tongue just in time. 'We're checking on those . . . They couldn't resist technology. In the old days they used to cut letters out of newspapers and paste them together.'

'Really?' said Vanheusen. 'I thought that happened only in movies.'

115

Malone grinned. 'I think that's where I saw it. I've never actually seen a kidnap note. For some reason we don't go in much for kidnapping, not even now we're multicultural.' There was the tongue again, politically incorrect this time. Kagal, the son of immigrant parents, just smiled. 'There are abductions, but they don't send kidnap notes.'

Kagal produced a folded sheet of paper from his pocket. 'This is a photocopy of the note, Damien. I'd like to type copies of it on all your computers here, then go to your shops. Would any of your outworkers have computers?'

'I wouldn't know. You'll have to ask Peter, our business manager. He's in his office –'

'I'll find him.'

Malone and Vanheusen were left alone. The designer picked up a crayon, drew some lines on a sheet of paper; they were aimless, those of a man who had lost his way. Malone said carefully, 'Were you living at home when your daughter went missing?'

Vanheusen frowned. There were just the two of them in the studio; it was a large airy room with a bank of high windows on the northern wall to catch the light. There was a large tilted desk, like an architect's; two long tables, benches along two of the walls. There were half a dozen body forms, grouped haphazardly like passers-by who had wandered in from the street and didn't know why. A green, red and yellow swirl of cloth writhed on a table like a python that had had its skin split; bolts of cloth stood along a wall like

116

dwarf Tuscany pillars. This, Malone guessed, was the designer's real home.

'No, I wasn't. Things have been a little strained between Lina and me – I moved out while we decided what we were going to do.'

'Going to do?'

'Divorce. But this – what's happened to Lucy –' he looked away for a moment, blinked – 'it's brought us together again. I hope for good.'

'Where did you move to?'

He looked back at Malone, hesitated. 'I moved in with one of our models, DeeDee Orion.'

'D.D. – initials? – O'Ryan? O-R-Y-A-N?' Malone was making a note.

'No, DeeDee, all one word. A capital D in the middle. Orion, same as the giant in Greek mythology.'

'She's big?' He grinned. 'Sorry, I'm not up on Greek mythology. Celtic mythology, yes, but fashion never seems to get around to the Irish. I can see Greek goddesses on the catwalk. But leprechauns? . . . You and DeeDee are more than friends?'

Vanheusen looked at him quizzically. 'I don't like the way this is going, Inspector.'

'I don't like it, either, Mr Vanheusen. But when you're cutting out your cloth –' he waved at the swirl of colour on the table – 'how do you know when you're with or against the bias?'

Again the quizzical look, a little sharper this time. 'You're not a dumb cop, are you?'

'I try not to be. Which is how I hope we can tell

you who took your daughter. I'd like to talk to Miss Orion.'

'She's not here. She's a freelance, not a house model. You'd have seen her, surely.'

'You wouldn't believe how ignorant I am about fashion and models.'

'Oh, I'd believe it.'

'So where does DeeDee live?'

'Do you have to bring her into it?' Malone gave him no answer, just looked at him; and he went on, 'Okay, she lives in Paddington.'

Malone wrote down the address he was given. 'Is there anyone in the fashion game comes from out west? You know, the Elle MacPherson of Mount Druitt, something like that?'

'I suppose some of them came from out there –' he spoke as if Mount Druitt was just east of the Simpson Desert – 'but they all seem to gravitate this way. You won't be too rough on her? Though I don't know why you have to talk to her at all –'

'We'll be talking to *everyone*, Mr Vanheusen.' They were formal now: no Damien. 'Got what you want, John?'

Kagal had come back into the studio. 'Enough. I'll go into your shops now, Damien. Then these copies will go to Forensic and we'll compare them with the original note. We may have some luck.'

'Anyone could use the computers.'

'Of course. But it narrows the field. It'll mean they aren't complete strangers to you.'

Vanheusen was leaning back against the table, as if needing its support; his hand was squeezing the tail of the python. 'Jesus Christ –'

'You okay?' said Malone.

Vanheusen nodded. 'Get it over quickly, will you?'

There was nothing for Malone to say; he just nodded. Outside in the street as they walked back to their car, he said, 'What d'you make of that?'

'Damien? He's worried, now we've brought it up, that he knows the kidnappers. Or rather, they know him. We may get nothing out of the computers, but it's a start.'

'Righto, you try his shops and their computers. Drop me off in Paddington, I'll see if DeeDee Orion is home. You know her?'

'I know *of* her. She's a dish. They're tipping her to be the next super-model.'

'Models come in models?'

'Wait till you see her. You want me to come back for you?'

'No, I'll catch a taxi. Or if she's such a knockout, an ambulance.'

DeeDee Orion lived in one of the wider streets of Paddington, a jigsaw area that had once been the home of the eastern suburbs battlers; terrace houses that had once housed large families, of seven, eight or ten, now were home to couples. Gentrification had trouble finding room for kids.

DeeDee Orion was indeed a beauty, not run-of-the-mill. When she opened the royal blue door with the highly polished brass knocker in the shape of a lion's head he felt he was about to step into an expensive commercial. Maybe for Pantene hair shampoo or a Patek Philipe watch. Nothing from K-Mart.

He introduced himself and she said, 'Oh yes, Damien rang. You're not to grill me, right?'

'Is that what he said? Cops don't grill, Miss Orion. Cooks do that.'

She smiled (beautiful teeth, all thirty-whatever of them) and opened the door wider. 'Come in, I'm alone.'

'You share with someone?' She obviously didn't live with her parents if Damien had been sleeping here. Or maybe she had parents with a broader outlook than his own. Lisa had told him to mind his own business about their children's sex life; she would attend to it. But she, too, would not allow the sleeping partners to be brought home.

'Two girls.'

'Models like yourself?'

'God, no! I need someone to keep my feet on the ground. No, one's a legal secretary, the other's a computer expert. Coffee?'

She led him through the narrow house. The front rooms were tastefully furnished and everything was neatly placed; why had he expected three girls to have their home looking like a brothel after a wild night? Chauvinism still lurked in parts of him like a skin rash.

They came into a kitchen that obviously had never been inhabited by seven or eight kids. It was right out of *House & Garden*, nothing out of place, no dirty dishes in the sink; someone around here was neat and tidy – maybe the legal secretary? Glass doors led out to a small back-yard patio where small, neatly trimmed trees stood in pots, like big-bottomed soldiers waiting to be inspected. Malone sat at a granite-topped table and watched DeeDee as she prepared coffee.

She had jet black hair that caught the light every time she turned her head; features that were perfect; large dark blue eyes; a full mouth. Yet there was no mystery to her, something else he always looked for in a woman, something Lisa had and still did have. What you saw was what you got had never interested him as an attraction.

'How do you feel about Lucybelle's death?'

'Ghastly. I never liked her, but I cried when Damien told me.'

'Why didn't you like her?'

Still at the coffee-pot she turned to look at him. 'I had nothing to do with the kidnapping.'

'I'm not accusing you of that. Why didn't you like her?'

'I'm not sure. I only saw her once or twice. On TV, sure, dozens of times. Too many times. She was precocious. But don't get me started. I'm not going to speak ill of the dead.'

'What's your relationship with Mr Vanheusen?'

'Damien. Mr Vanheusen sounds a hundred years old.'

He didn't ask the obvious question: *How much older is he than you*? He guessed there would be twenty to twenty-five years between them.

She set the coffee down, sat down opposite him. She was wearing a white skivvy with no brassiere under it, royal blue slacks and no jewellery, not even a watch. Where was Patek Philipe?

'What's my relationship with him? To be honest, I don't know.' Then she raised an eyebrow, a studied expression. 'Why am I being honest with you? Because you're a cop?'

'Could be. Or maybe it's because no one has asked you that? Your girlfriends?'

'We all mind our own business.' She nodded to herself; light moved across the hair like tiny lightning. 'He's a really sweet guy. And yes, I guess I was half in love with him. Or maybe all the way in love – for a while. Are you in love?'

'Very much. With my wife. And my two daughters and my son.'

'I'm not flirting with you.'

'I know that, DeeDee.' He sipped his coffee. He wondered how he would have responded to her when he was young and single. But he'd been another man then . . . 'Lucybelle. How did Damien feel towards her?'

'He adored her – and she adored him, he said. But God –' She shook her head emphatically; lightning struck again. She was now familiar to him: he had seen her in the Pantene commercials. 'I'd never have wanted to play mother to her.'

'Did he want you to?'

'It never came up. I think he knew how I felt –'

'How did Mrs Vanheusen feel about you and Damien? She knew, of course?'

'Of course. I don't know how she felt. I stayed away from her – if I saw her at a party or an opening, I'd just disappear. Damien said she didn't care – not about me in particular. They'd started to drift apart before – well, *before . . .*'

'Does she have a boyfriend?'

The eyebrow went up again; it was one of her few false expressions, perhaps her only one. 'You're a real gossip, aren't you?'

'No, I'm a cop. We collect gossip as evidence. Does she have a boyfriend?'

'I dunno. Maybe. According to Damien, her whole life was bound up in the little girl.'

'And his wasn't?'

'Well, no, he had his business to run. He's ambitious – he'd love to have his own stores right throughout the world, carrying nothing but his name. He can't make up his mind whether he'd rather be Giorgio Armani or Ralph Lauren.' She smiled at him. 'Who would you rather be?'

'Marks and Spencer. Or who's that other crowd – Benetton?'

'Seven thousand outlets throughout the world – you think big, don't you?' She smiled again, looking at him, and shook her head. But she didn't say what he knew she was thinking: *No one would know from looking at you.* 'I think he was pretty close to Lucybelle in his own way.'

'So he said? But you never saw him with the child?'

'No. I never wanted to get into that tangle. I'm not a child-lover, not yet. Maybe ten years' time, but not yet. I'm heading overseas next month, New York. I've signed with the Ford Agency. You've heard of them?'

'They sell cars?' He grinned, stood up. 'Thanks for the coffee and the gossip, DeeDee. Is that what you were christened?'

She grinned, too. 'Doris Dulcie O'Ryan. Whoever heard of a model named Doris Dulcie? Versace would've fainted.'

'And the surname?'

'O-R-Y-A-N. I'm Irish – or my dad is. He wants to disown me for changing the spelling. I went out once with a Greek guy – he said I'd got the pronunciation of Orion wrong. But it pleases my dad to think he's still hearing O'Ryan.'

'It would please my dad, too. Here's my card. If you think of any more gossip . . .'

She was suddenly very sober. 'Look, I'm really sorry about Lucybelle's death – really. And I'd never believe Damien had anything to do with it.'

'We're accusing no one so far, DeeDee. Like I said – I'm just gathering evidence.' He gestured at the card in her hand. 'Get in touch, if –'

'I'll do that.' Then the soberness was gone. She smiled, stood leaning against the front door, a model's pose, as he went out the front gate. 'Any time, Mr Malone.'

He laughed, then shook his head at the two elderly women who were passing. 'It's not what you think.'

'A likely story,' they said and went on their way laughing at the foolishness of middle-aged men and their seven-year itch.

I won't tell this to Lisa tonight, he thought. For fifteen minutes he had been on the verge of flirting with DeeDee Orion. There was no lust, but his eye hadn't lost the appeal of looking at a beautiful woman. He could understand why Damien Vanheusen, a man of his own age group, had come here.

He caught a taxi back to Strawberry Hills, driven by a Vietnamese who leaned forward over the steering wheel, peering up constantly at street signs. Finally he stopped and got out a street directory. Malone, in the back seat, leaned forward, 'How did you get a licence?'

'No worries, mate.'

'I am worried, *mate*. I'm a police officer and I want to get back to my office at Homicide to report seven homicides. You may be the eighth.'

The driver closed the directory. 'No worries, mate.'

He found Homicide without further trouble. Malone got out, counted out the exact fare. 'I never tip, mate, not even good drivers. Can you find your way back?'

'No worries, mate,' said the driver and drove off in the wrong direction.

Upstairs, Trevor Waring was waiting for Malone. 'I've just come from Long Bay, seeing our friend. Ron, Roger, whatever you want to call him.'

Malone took off his jacket, sat down. 'You look hot and bothered, Trev.'

'It's the heat, not the case.' He wore a tweed jacket, moleskins, a checked shirt with a woollen tie, R. M. Williams boots. His broad-brimmed Akubra was held against his ample belly. He looked more like a wool or cattle farmer than a lawyer. But just as worried as those farmers presently were with falling prices. The bush was no place to be, not these days. 'I'm off it, Scobie. Biddle, Brown and Cartwright are taking over.' They were one of the biggest law firms in the city. 'They've engaged Caradoc Evans to defend him.'

'The Doc? At five thousand a day? Who's financing this? Legal Aid?'

'You always liked your little joke, Scobie. No, it's Roma. His wife – or his *de facto*, if you like. She's got the money. I looked after her husband's estate. Her first husband.'

'We're going to nail him, Trev, Caradoc Evans or not. He did it.'

'I don't think so. Okay, he's a liar, he's lied about the last four years. But he's not a murderer.'

'He said he was going to kill her if she had refused to go back to him.'

'He also said he was going to top himself. They have a different mind-set when that's how they see things.'

Malone shook his head. 'I've met more murderers than you, Trev. Maybe that's what he thought he was going to do. But he did her in and then lost his nerve. He didn't have a gun in the house, no gas stove – it was an electric job. So how was he going to do it? No overdose of sleeping pills – there were none in the house. A razor? Yeah, there was a razor in the bathroom. He wouldn't have slit his throat – I don't think he'd have the guts to do that, it's one of the worst ways of suiciding. Slit his wrists? Watch his blood and his life drain away? You think he has the patience to do that?'

'There are a dozen ways of topping yourself, but he tried none of them. You're just talking to convince me I'm wrong, Scobie. But I'm not listening. Roger didn't do it.' He stood up. 'When will he go to committal?'

'Maybe a coupla months – I'll let you know. You know what the system's like – it's a bloody disgrace, but there it is. You can't hurry the law, it never gets out of second gear.'

'Innocent till proven guilty. It's a joke – he could be kept dangling for a coupla years.'

'No, not that long till the trial – we've got an open-and-shut case. You're wrong about him, Trev. You were wrong about Chester Hardstaff. He was a pillar of the community, you never let yourselves believe he killed his wife all those years before. You think Ron Glaze is a pillar – or his wife is.'

'Chester confessed. Roger hasn't, he's denied it.' He hesitated, then: 'I never believed Chester killed that Japanese cotton manager.'

'Neither did I. But he confessed. I know who did it and so do you.'

'And it doesn't worry you, that she's still free? Still a pillar of the community?'

'Of course it worries me. But after Chester confessed to both murders, we'd never have been able to build a case against Amanda. You've all turned a blind eye and she's taken advantage of it. She's a tough lady.'

'So's Roma Gibson.'

'She's taken his name? Why didn't they marry? Was he scared that one day we'd catch up with him? Did he ever tell her the truth about himself?'

'If he did, she's a bloody good actress. I don't know why they haven't married. But I'm sure she never knew he was Ron Glaze.'

Waring left and Malone looked at the pile of paperwork on his desk. Then Clements came in with more papers, put one down in front of Malone. 'The Commissioner is putting out a media release on picking up Glaze. Shows that his Service never gives up.'

'He'll take credit for riot control on Judgement Day.'

'I think I'll take a sickie that day. How're you going with the Vanheusen thing?'

'Up and down in the one spot so far. Here are John and Sheryl.'

Kagal and Sheryl Dallen had returned together. They came into Malone's office, sat down without being asked. *Am I too casual, too easy-going?* Malone asked himself. He had eased into authority without ever really wanting it. If it fitted him it was by natural accident.

'How was DeeDee?' asked Kagal and refrained from smirking. Otherwise he would have been told to stand up.

'Like you said, a dish. I want you to go there this

evening and talk to her two flatmates – check with them if Damien was there all night on the night of the kidnapping.' He had been distracted by DeeDee more than he had thought; he should have asked for the flatmates' business addresses and gone to see them. 'DeeDee herself is in the clear, I think. Or else she's a better actress than I give her credit for.'

'Models are not good actresses,' said Sheryl. 'I see them at the gym.'

'There, that's an unbiased view from a feminist. Righto, look into the other girls, John. Now what have you come up with?'

'We've tried all the computers,' said Kagal. 'Forensic now have the copies, from the shops and the gym and Damien's design centre.'

'What luck at the gym, Sheryl?'

'Mixed. The guys think Lina is great. The girls – well –' she shrugged – 'some like her, some don't. But I don't think any of them are her *enemies*. Certainly not child-killers.'

'The killing may have been an accident,' said Clements.

'The kid was drugged,' said Malone. 'Romy will tell you tonight. She didn't say the drug was enough to have killed the little girl. There would have been cardiac arrest or something like that. The injuries she sustained when she hit the rocks were what killed her.'

Kagal said, 'In the shop in Castlereagh Street I talked to the woman who manages it. It's all their up-market stuff there, they sell to the tourists, the Japanese and the Koreans. Or they did before the bottom fell out of Asia.'

'Whom do they sell to now?' Malone had a wife who, like all educated foreigners, knew the difference between *who* and *whom*.

'That's it – virtually nobody. Vanheusen is looking for a buyer.'

'For the shop?'

'For both his shops, plus the design centre. He wants to go to London, try his luck there. I gather it's not common knowledge, he's kept it quiet. But this woman has been with him ten years and I guess he owes her, so he told her.'

'They didn't mention it, neither him nor his wife. He's – what – in his mid-forties and he wants to sell up everything and try his luck in the big-time. Have they heard of him overseas?'

'They would of heard of him,' said Sheryl. 'But I agree with you – it's a bit late for him to try breaking in. It can happen when you're young – it has with Collette Dinnigan – but when you're getting on –'

'Watch it,' said Malone. 'Book her, Russ.'

Sheryl smiled, unabashed. 'Experience counts with cops. But it has nothing to do with creativity. I think he's taking a gamble and I wonder why.'

'Perhaps we should ask Mrs Vanheusen what she thinks of the gamble.'

Chapter Four

⌒〰⌒

1

Miriam Zigler was a nice Jewish girl whose plain face was made attractive by its liveliness; her mouth, her eyes, her small round cheeks were as animated as a rock video. She was a damn good solicitor, would eventually be a barrister and one day might even be the DPP. Her one fault was her generosity of spirit.

'This guy Glaze – he made one mistake –'

'His one mistake was murder,' said Pierpont.

'I know, I know. But from this –' She tapped the file on her lap. She had a good figure, but sometimes it was impossible to find her lap. She dressed as if her clothes had been thrown at her in a strong wind; she wore cardigans, winter and summer, woollen or cotton, that hung on her like limp banners. 'From this he's been a pillar of the community for the past three years –'

'Is that what it says? A pillar of the community?' He

knew what it said, he had read the preliminary report a dozen times.

'It's in quotes, as if the cop who wrote this was being sarcastic. But he has been, hasn't he?'

'I don't know, Mim. Cops don't go looking for good character when they're putting in a prelim report on a murder, you know that.'

'He's pleading Not Guilty and he's spending money to prove it. Caradoc Evans –' She laughed, ran a hand through her dark curls. 'When I was a student I used to go and watch him. He was like a bald Richard Burton – that rolling voice, those gestures. That was what I was going to be – a five thousand dollar a day criminal lawyer, as theatrical as all hell.'

'What happened?' He had never had those dreams.

'I was stricken with a terrible disease – public service.' Her face was still a moment, plain but honest. 'Like you.'

He knew she liked him; perhaps even more than that. It made him uncomfortable; he was wary of all women but Ginny. Had been since the other woman . . . 'Is there a cure for it?'

Her face was active again; as if she had been waiting for another reaction from him and now was trying not to show her disappointment. 'Maybe. Let me know if there is. So when is the committal?'

He and David Winkler had often discussed the State court schedules. They were a disgrace, more tightly packed than a commuter train. It was not unusual for two years to pass between arrest and trial; if an offender

132

after all that time was declared Not Guilty, the State owed him nothing. There were constant calls for more judges, more courts, but, like health care, justice was always short-changed. In the system you were guilty till proved innocent. There's not enough money, said the government, while another $50 or $100 million went into the maw of the Olympics. A non-supporter of the 2000 Olympics, he would volunteer to prosecute anyone who fell from grace on the Games committees.

Miriam said, 'I haven't got a firm date yet –'

'There are likely to be two cancellations, the offenders have died. We'll try and grab one of them, jump the queue. Maybe a couple of months at the outside.'

She stood up; the cotton cardigan fell almost to her knees. 'You're not wildly enthusiastic about this one, are you?'

No. 'What makes you say that?'

'You don't seem to have any interest in it.'

Oh, I have an interest in it. 'I'm tired, that's all. Are you interested in it?'

Her face was plain. 'I could be.'

2

There were no developments in the Vanheusen case over the next few hours. Fingerprints reported they could find nothing on the ransom note or the envelope in which it had been delivered.

'They wore gloves,' said Clements. 'So are we dealing with professionals?'

'If they're professionals,' said Malone, 'why would they toss the kid off the cliff? They didn't wait at all to find out if the Vanheusens would deliver the money. No, whoever it was was being smart – they'd seen it on TV or read it in a detective novel. Crims are better educated today, thanks to TV. Somewhere along the line our friends would have forgotten something. We just have to find that.'

'Why are you Irish always so bloody optimistic?'

'We're not optimistic. We just know how bloody dumb the rest of the world is.'

Late that afternoon, Friday, Malone got a call from Forensic. 'Inspector Malone? This is Senior-Sergeant Alex Hurley – Document Examination Section. I think we may have something for you on the Vanheusen case.'

On his way out Malone passed Clements at his desk. 'The Irish may be right again.'

He and Sheryl Dallen drove over to Police Centre in Surry Hills. It is a fortress-like building and looks as if it has been designed to withstand rocket attacks from crazed criminals. It houses the local police station and, above it, several floors of technical services. The Document Examination Section was on the fifth level.

Its layout was spacious; there was none of the cramped quarters of *NYPD Blue* or *The Bill*. Crims would have been indignant at the money spent on catching them. The equipment was the best available; all round the room technology was lying in wait for human error. Which almost invariably obliged.

Hurley had spent twelve years on the beat before finding his niche in paper. But he had none of the dryness of paper; he was a plump jovial man who now traced crims without having to get out of breath. He knew how many ways there were of leaving a footprint.

'The paper is flecked,' he said. 'Not a common item, but there's enough of it about. No watermark, so we could be ringing around a dozen suppliers and they'd have a coupla hundred clients. No matter!' He had a small theatrical way with him, as if in the course of studying paper he had come across a lot of theatre scripts. Of which many, he would have told you, were frauds. 'We have an indentation. We put it through ESDA –'

Malone and Sheryl waited: experts always elaborated, never left you ignorant. Not if you were patient.

'Our Electro Static Detection Apparatus. In here.' He led them into a side room. 'Here we have a bronze plate. I put the note on it –' He took the ransom note out of its plastic envelope like a magician pulling a rabbit out of a hat. He laid it on the bronze top of a flat box. Then he overlaid it with a thin plastic sheet. 'This is what we call glad-wrapping it. I start a fan –' he flicked a switch – 'A vacuum is created. Now for our glass beads –'

He filled a small cup with a fine sand of tiny dark beads. He poured the cup on to the plastic sheet, tilted the bronze plate and the sand of beads fell off into a narrow side trough. On the ransom note there was now the faint outline of a scrawled word: *Powerobics*.

'The kidnappers took this sheet from a packet, probably a newly opened one. Someone with a biro had scrawled that word on the outside of the packet, judging by the faintness of it – if it had been on the previous page or two, the indentation would have been stronger.' He beamed at them; his experience and equipment had been proven. He knew as well as anyone that expertise is a suspicious quality. 'Powerobics. Something from a gym?'

Malone looked at Sheryl, another expert.

'It's a make of treadmill,' she said. 'There are four or five of them at Mode Gym. Where I go and Mrs Vanheusen goes.'

Hurley blew the last of the bead dust off the plastic sheet. He had not finished, the curtain still had to come down. Malone waited patiently, though he could feel the stir of adrenaline again.

'Look at the note. Here –' Hurley transferred it to another machine, fiddled with a knob and the note, magnified, came up on a small screen above the machine. 'We're practically certain this came out of a bubble-jet printer, probably a Canon BJ-210. The letter is sprayed on to the paper through a jet – they're called ink-jet printers. If a jet is partially blocked – as these two are –' he pointed to two letters: E and F – 'you get this slight sprayed effect. It's accentuated here because the kidnappers chose to write the note in upper case. On what we've got here, I think it's a fair bet that the ransom note came from someone at Mode Gym.'

'What about the envelope?'

'Nothing on that. But it was a saliva-activated adhesive, not a self-adhesive one, so if you could get a buccal swab from a suspect's mouth –'

'We'll try, but don't hold your breath. If a suspect says no, we can't hold a gun at his head, no matter how much we'd like to.'

'Try for it. A little spit can be very incriminating.'

'We'll try . . . Thanks, Alex. We now know where to start looking. I'll let you know if and when we get the bastards.'

'Killing a kiddy like that!' Hurley shook his head in disgust. 'You wonder what sorta mongrels they are.' He looked around him, no longer jovial or theatrical. 'Being here I don't have to put up with the ugly shitty side . . . Well, good luck.'

Back in their car Sheryl said, 'Mode Gym?'

'Where else?' He never got excited, but clues were an elixir. 'Let's go and talk to your sweaty friends.'

'Not my *friends*, not if they're kidnappers and murderers.' She sounded prim, but drove as if she were mad. Malone, a poor passenger even if he had been in a dog-cart, held on to the floorboards with his toes clenched in his 22-year-old shoes.

Mode gymnasium was in a side street in Double Bay, the fashionable and expensive area five kilometres east of the city's central business district. Here, modesty and a tight wallet and Fletcher Jones suits were alien; luxury here was an appetite usually taken with a cappuccino. It was Sydney's closest approach to Middle Europe and the older immigrants from *Mittel Europa*, those who

137

had made it, came here to recapture the past in accented conversation. The young came to look and be looked at. The expensive shops waited, traps set.

The gym was set back from the street in a small open-air arcade. It was double-fronted; the gold pillars on either side of the front door suggested you were entering a temple. Malone looked at it quizzically. 'Do they ever let any flab inside these doors?'

'All sorts are welcome, so long as their chequebooks are fat. Let's talk to Justin, the owner.'

'Your chequebook is fat?'

'It's my Christmas present from Dad every year.'

Homicide seemed to be full of doting parents, intent on keeping their offspring fit and well dressed. Con Malone would not have bought him a skipping-rope and Brigid thought the front rack in a St Vincent de Paul shop was *haute couture*.

This late in the day the eager-to-be-fit housewives had gone home to their appreciative husbands. But there were still half a dozen young women, figures sculpted by the machines around them. An old man in a white singlet and black gym trousers trudged to nowhere on a treadmill; skin hung on his arms like Spanish moss; he looked puzzled as well as exhausted, as if wondering why, so late, he had arrived on this road. A few younger men, sleek as seals, exercised in front of mirrors, their reflections mirroring their satisfaction with themselves.

'It's the slack hour. Things pick up again pretty soon, guys on their way home from work.'

Justin Belgrave was a good-looking man who had solved his falling hair problem by shaving his skull; a faint shadow of fuzz was a reminder of how far the problem had gone. His shoulders started just below his ears and ran down to his elbows; or so it seemed to Malone, who was ridiculously square-shouldered. He was dressed in a blue singlet that covered his pectorals tantalizingly and tight gym trousers. He was affable but wary when Sheryl told him they were on official police business.

'Jesus, this is just incredible – I can't believe someone from here –' He looked around him, but the mirrors told him nothing. 'Yes, we've got two computers here, with printers. One outside at the reception desk and another one in my office. Yes, they're both Canons – I dunno whether they're the model you named. I'll call Tiffany in –'

Justin, Tiffany: Malone wondered if anyone here was called Mick or Alby. Or Fatty.

Tiffany was the ideal front for the gym: blonde hair, vacuum-packed body, a neon-bright smile. 'Oh no, no one could get near my computer or printer. A guy once tried it, he had the most incredible gall, he thought membership bought him all privileges – he wanted to use my front desk as a branch of his office. I threw him out –'

'She's a kung-fu expert,' said her boss admiringly.

'When I'm not out front, like now, I lock the computer and printer. What's this about, anyway? *Not* the Lucybelle – ohmigod, it's incredible!' She wilted in her body-stocking. 'You think someone here –?'

'We don't think anything just yet, Tiffany,' said Sheryl. 'We're just making enquiries. Just checking.'

'Maybe we could look at your computer and printer, Mr Belgrave?' said Malone.

'Sure, sure. Tiffany, love – don't mention this to anyone, okay? We don't want to frighten the pets.'

'Of course not. No way.' It would be difficult; one could see the news trying to burst its way out of the body-stocking. 'I just can't believe – it's absolutely incredible –'

Belgrave led the way into a small office at the rear of the gym. On the way Malone paused by an exercise treadmill. 'This is a Powerobic?'

'I have four of them, that make. You exercise?'

'I walk around Randwick racecourse every morning, five Ks. That's enough for me, that and four sets of doubles Saturday afternoon. Sheryl keeps fit enough for the rest of us in Homicide.'

'Homicide? That's a word I didn't expect to hear around here. Well, there they are, the computer and the keyboard and the printer. I use it, mostly planning programmes for new clients.'

Sheryl sat down, took a sheet of paper from a packet on the desk, held it up to the light. 'Flecked.'

'It's new,' said Belgrave. 'I got a coupla reams a, I dunno, a week ago. The fancy notepaper is out front, with Tiffany. I only noticed that was different when I opened the packet. The ransom note was on *that*?'

Sheryl took out a scribbled copy of the ransom note. She typed it out, expertly, checked what had come up on the computer screen, then sat back and waited till the printer had done its job. She peered at the typed message, then nodded at Malone.

'Looks the same to me. Can we borrow the machines, Justin? Forensic will look at them, then return them to you. Just a coupla days, no more.'

Belgrave didn't protest, just frowned and ran his hand over his skull, as if hoping for revived roots. 'Jesus, this isn't real –'

'I'm afraid it is,' said Malone.

'But Christ Almighty, if it gets out – what's it gunna do for my business? Things are incredibly tough now –' Then he shut up, waved a hand in the air loosely and limply, as if his wrist had been broken. 'Forget I said that.'

'Justin –' Sheryl had disconnected the machines – 'how well do you know Mrs Vanheusen?'

Where did she get that one from? But Malone showed no surprise, was fascinated by Belgrave's reaction. His pectorals vibrated like tiny earth tremors, his neck seemed to swell. 'What's that supposed to mean?'

'Nothing,' said Sheryl. 'Not if you don't want it to.'

'I know her only as a client. An incredibly dedicated one – she's so incredibly fit –'

'For a woman of her age?' said Malone blandly.

'That's nasty –'

'It wasn't meant to be.'

Belgrave stared at him, then abruptly looked at the machines. 'If you're gunna take those, shouldn't you have a warrant?'

'We can get one,' said Malone. 'But that might cause a commotion, get you talked about. You don't want that, do you? That might be incredibly embarrassing. Would you mind helping Constable Dallen carry those out to our car? I have a bad back.'

'I thought you said you walked five Ks every morning?' He was surly now.

'I do. I'd be bedridden if I didn't. We'd like a list of all your clients. I suppose Tiffany can give us those?'

Once in the car Malone said, 'Whatever happened to the laconic Aussie?'

Sheryl was sharp. 'You mean the incredible this, the incredibly that? It's a buzz word. Nobody can be interviewed on TV or in the papers without using it.'

'Haven't any of them ever read any history? Nothing is incredible except coming back from the grave . . . What made you ask about him and Mrs Vanheusen?'

'I dunno – just intuition. It suddenly came to me that he was always her personal trainer – he would be, well, *familiar* with her –'

'You don't miss much, do you?'

'In a gym, when you're up close and sweaty –'

'Like you said, I must get out into the real world. In the meantime send those machines to Forensic, see if we can be incredibly lucky.'

Malone took the weekend off, played tennis on Saturday, went to Mass on Sunday, was a family man. Several times he stopped to look at his children, wondered what his reaction would be if one of them was kidnapped and murdered. And each time jerked the thought away, like a physical action.

'What's the matter with you?' Lisa, truly wifely, had an eagle eye.

'Why?'

'You're not developing Parkinson's disease, are you?' She looked unworried; she spread oil on herself as she lay beside the pool. She was fortunate: she tanned beautifully and seemed impervious to sun cancers. He, on the other hand, wore a hat and sat under the umbrella. 'That's twice I've seen you twitch.'

'I hadn't noticed. It must be nerves. Married life.'

'You've never suffered from them before.' She paused in her oiling, looked at him with concern. 'Are you? Something getting you down?'

'I think I need a holiday.'

'You're not thinking about a holiday, you're thinking about work.' She went back to oiling her legs.

He studied her, aware that she knew he was looking at her; in animal territory there is no closer awareness than between man and wife. 'I was thinking about the kids.'

'I know.' She wiped her hands, looked at him. Reflections from the pool rippled on her face like brushstrokes on the smooth skin. Oh Christ, he thought, I'm lucky! 'I know. I've seen it two or three times. As if you hadn't looked at them in a long time.'

'We're losing them, you know that? They haven't moved out yet, but they're on their way.'

'That's the way it goes. Families don't stay in a time-warp. Brigid is a stranger to you now, not like the mother she was to you when you were little. You've told me that.'

'I hope Tom and I don't ever grow that far apart. Nor the girls.'

'You won't,' she said and put her hand, still a little oily, on his thigh.

'A little higher,' he said oilily.

She gave him her Dutch smile: like a Dutch shout, it shared the pleasure and the price. 'Not in front of the children,' she said as Claire, Maureen and Tom, with their Sunday friends, came out of the house.

Saturday morning Lucybelle Vanheusen's funeral had been held. Cops and cameras were there, the cops unobtrusive, the cameras as obtrusive as cannons. Everyone in fashion, the anybodys and the nobodys, seemed to be there. Most wore black or some sombre colour; most of them also wore their best camera expression. Several children, fellow models of Lucybelle, were there, their mothers hovering over them with an eye always on the cameras. No one knew whom McDonalds, Toyota and Coca-Cola would be looking for next season. Time and advertising marched on.

Monday morning Malone went to work knowing the

144

load would be increased. There had been four homicides over the weekend; all four, he guessed, would bring a call from the local detectives for Homicide help. Clements had already received the calls; he handed out the assignments at the morning conference. Then he followed Malone into the latter's office, sat down this time in a chair instead of his usual place on the couch beneath the window.

'A woman from DPP rang first thing this morning. She's heard that Ron Glaze will be applying for Legal Aid.'

Malone raised an eyebrow. 'He's skint? What happened to his expensive solicitors and Doc Evans?'

Clements hunched his shoulders. 'I dunno. We can't go out to Long Bay and ask him. You think it's worth a call to Trevor Waring?'

'Why should we bother?' Then he shook his head. 'But maybe it's a ploy. They're trying it, some of them. If they can't get the best defence, then they plead they're not going to get a fair trial. I don't trust Mr Glaze. I'll try Wally Mungle first.'

He opened his notebook, then dialled Collamundra and was put through to Detective Constable Mungle without giving his name. 'G'day, Wally. How's the atmosphere out there? The shit still flying?'

'No-o,' Mungle admitted grudgingly. *Don't play the martyr*, *Wally*: but Malone kept that to himself. He was sympathetic to most Aboriginal causes, but some activists worked the angles too hard and spoiled what sympathy they had achieved. He hoped Wally Mungle was not going to develop into one of those.

'They're still not convinced Roger – Ron killed his wife, but they're admitting we did the right thing in picking him up.'

Then Malone explained the reason for the call. 'Have you heard anything out there?'

There was silence for a long moment, then Mungle said, 'Apparently Ron has been in someone else's bed – I mean before we picked him up. Roma Gibson found out about it and she's wiped him. Cut off his funds.'

'You know who it was?'

Again the silence; then: 'Amanda Hardstaff.'

Malone didn't know whether to laugh or fall off his chair. '*Amanda*?'

Clements straightened up; Malone shook his head.

'Who knows about it?'

'It's all over town, like a dust storm.'

'How's she taking it?'

'She's gone down to Palm Beach, she has a summer place. From what I hear, sleeping around is a social habit down there.'

'Wally, you're starting to sound like a bush Methodist. Let me know if there are any other developments.'

'Such as?'

'Whether Mrs Gibson is likely to come back into the picture.'

He hung up and Clements said, '*Amanda*?'

'Your child's namesake is not only a pillar of the community and a murderer, she sleeps with other women's partners. Ron Glaze wasn't only delivering liquidambars to her. You should have called your Amanda something else. Tiffany, for instance.'

'Tiffany? Where'd you get that one from? It was Romy who wanted to call her Amanda – she likes that old song. I didn't feel like dragging up an old murder case. If I did that, went back all the years I've been in the Service, I'd have had to call her just Number One. So what's with Amanda Hardstaff?'

Malone explained the situation at Collamundra. 'Roma, his partner, has cut off all his funds – evidently she's always had the money. He lived with her, but he also *worked* for her. I remember –' His mind went back four years. He did not have an exceptional memory, but it worked: like a lottery barrel from which the marbles were never emptied. 'There was a woman behind the bar at the Golden West, Mrs Idunno – Charlene. Yeah, Charlene. She said Ron was a Wandering Dick. I guess he couldn't resist it, even out at Collamundra. I wonder if he's asked Amanda if she'll come up with the funds?'

'Do you think she will?'

'I'll be surprised if she does. She came to court every day her dad was on trial, but she never once went into the box for him.'

'He'd of seen to that,' said Clements. 'He was cold-blooded.'

'So is she, I think. If she didn't stand up for Dad, she's not going to stand up for Ron.'

'I'm beginning to feel sorry for the poor bugger, I dunno why.'

'Lisa and Romy and my girls would know why. You're a male chauvinist. Let him stew, they'd say.'

Clements heaved himself out of his chair. 'Why do people kill?' Then: 'Why do I ask?'

'Exactly,' said Malone.

Half an hour later Sheryl Dallen came into his room. 'I just got a call from Sergeant Hurley – his report's on its way over. The kidnap note was typed on Justin's machine.'

'So whom do we go and talk to? Justin or Evangelina?'

'You love those names, don't you?'

'The first killer I ever arrested was named Duggie Brown. He killed his mum and dad with an axe.'

'What were their names?'

'Aggie and Bert. Let's go and talk to Evangelina.'

Summer had wrapped itself in cloud; rain hung like muslin on the horizon. The humidity, the car's radio said, was 77 per cent; out on the pavement pedestrians stood in shimmers of sweat. It was not a good day for good temper.

Without sunshine the Tuscan villa looked out of place in the cul-de-sac. The Georgian house on one side and the mock-Tudor on the other looked more at home under the greyness. Architectural multiculturism has been the vogue for over a hundred years, has been accepted more than the human equation. The odd thing was that a Murcutt Australian house would have looked foreign in this street.

The media horde had gone, the crime scene tapes had been removed. But a police car stood in the driveway, behind a blue Mercedes. A young officer got out of the police car as Malone and Sheryl walked up to the front door.

'Mrs Vanheusen asked for police protection, sir.'

'Threats?'

'So she says, sir.' His tone was bland; he wasn't paid enough to have an opinion.

'Why can't she get a private security guard?' But it was none of his business. 'Anyone inside with her?'

The young officer nodded at the Saab. 'A Lady Derry. She got here about ten minutes ago. I backed out to let her in. You know her, sir?'

'Only by repute.'

The young officer grinned. 'That's the way I know most of 'em around here. Only by repute.'

'She's a regular at Mode Gym,' said Sheryl.

The constable went back to his car and Sheryl pressed the doorbell. The door was opened almost immediately by Lady Derry. Malone had never seen her in person, but he recognized her at once. She was a leader of what Claire and Maureen called the Freeloaders Club; she was on every invitation list; she would, Maureen claimed, go to the opening of a garage sale. Her husband, much older than she, had been a prominent industrialist; he had died, it was said, in preference to going to another opening. She was close to sixty, but skilful use of scalpel and make-up made her look younger. In the doorway her voice had the edge of a scalpel.

'Yes?'

Malone produced his badge, introduced himself and Sheryl. 'We'd like to talk to Mrs Vanheusen.'

'Oh, do come in.' She melted, was instantly charming.

149

She had a round, pleasant face with a friendly smile; her figure might have been plump but for the efforts of Justin Belgrave. Malone, nastily but influenced by his daughters, wondered if she was on the free list at the gymnasium. 'You have some news? This way, we're having coffee. I'll get extra cups. Lina, darling, it's the police –'

As if they were window cleaners or meter readers from the gas company. Malone and Sheryl Dallen went on into the living room, while Lady Derry went to the kitchen. Lina Vanheusen rose from a deep chair as the two detectives came in, looked at them expectantly.

'You've found something?'

'Not much, Mrs Vanheusen. The young officer outside said you had received threats – when was that? How?'

'Sunday night – a phone call.'

Malone looked at Sheryl, who said, 'The phone tap was removed Friday night. There'd been nothing . . .'

Bugger. 'What did they say?'

'It was the same man, with the high voice. He just said, "I hope you've learned your lesson," then hung up.'

'What lesson would that be?'

'I don't know.' She was visibly stiffening. 'Is that all you've come to ask about?'

'No. We're pretty certain that the ransom note came from someone who had access to a computer and printer at the Mode Gym.'

The stiffening melted. She had no pose this morning;

150

she was all true self. She sat down again, a half-collapse. Her dark hair was worn loose; she ran a thin hand through it. 'The gym? From there?'

'I'm afraid so. Someone who knew you, whom you probably know.'

Lady Derry came in with more cups, sat down in front of a coffee table, played hostess. 'Good news, darling?'

Malone remembered now some of the Sunday social pages his girls had shown him: Patricia Derry was always laughing, the life of the party. Her teeth had been counted innumerable times by Maureen. But she was not insensitive to atmosphere: 'Bad news?' She looked at Malone and Sheryl. 'Damn! When is it going to stop?'

When is what going to stop? Malone let that one slide, took the coffee she handed him. Here in this beautifully but impersonally furnished room he felt a certain unreality. Tragedy needed darkness, neglect; even the immaculate garden beyond the French doors was suddenly bathed in sunlight, though only for a moment. The only harshness in the room was the Robert Juniper (he didn't know the artist) above the mantelpiece: a sunbaked hill, stark trees, drought eating away at the countryside. There were no photos. He couldn't remember if there had been any in the room on his previous visit, but there were none now. Not even of the child Lucybelle.

Lady Derry was still smiling; then he saw that it was not a smile, it was a grimace. He sipped his coffee, waited for Lina Vanheusen to rejoin them.

She had left them, no doubt of that: like someone sunk in lost memory. She was picking at a thread in the dark blue cotton dress she wore; then she saw that she had worked the thread loose and that brought her back. She looked at the two detectives, from one to the other and back again. Then settled on Sheryl.

'Who could it be? You go there. Do you suspect anyone? God – people I've thought of as *friends*!'

Lady Derry closed her lips over her teeth, looked at Malone. He told her what they had told Lina. 'It's a start. It need not necessarily be a friend. We could be looking at three or four hundred people.'

'Nobody has that many friends,' said Patricia Derry and sounded oddly bitter. 'One can't trust anyone these days.'

Malone put down his cup. 'Can we have a word outside, Lina?'

It was the first time he had called her by her given name. It was part of the old police ploy: I'm your friend, I'm on your side.

For a moment it looked as if she was going to refuse; he was not her friend, she would choose her own. Then she stood up and led him out into the garden. They sat at a table beside the pool, under a blue-striped umbrella. She put on dark glasses and instantly, as they always did, they became a mask. There were glasses in his pocket, but he rarely wore them. Eyes were not only a giveaway, they were a weapon.

'How well do you know Justin Belgrave?'

152

A small frown appeared above the glasses; Dior, Klein, Versace hadn't covered enough territory. 'What does that mean?'

'It was meant as a straightforward question. But if you want to add to it –?'

'Why do you ask?' The stiffening was coming back.

'Because the impression is that you're a favoured client.'

'Who told you that? Her?' She jerked her head at the open doors to the living room. 'Is that why she comes to the gym? Doing undercover work or whatever it is?'

He gave her a sour smile, all she deserved. 'Mrs Vanheusen, you know better than that. The computer and printer on which the ransom note was typed came from Justin's own office.'

'You're suspecting *him?*' She pulled the glasses down her nose as if they obstructed her view of him. 'Oh, for God's sake! He's – he's –' She floundered, pushed the glasses back up her nose. '*Why?*'

He was patient: 'I haven't said we suspect him of anything. Why are you jumping to conclusions?'

A 747 flew over, its sound an invisible avalanche. It was obviously off course. Flight paths never entered Bellevue Hill, this was sacrosanct country. Pilots knew a no-go area when silver guns were held at their heads. The plane that had just gone over was from Garuda, taking the shortest course home because of the falling rupiah.

Lina Vanheusen waited till silence fell back on the garden; she was in no hurry to answer his question. He

153

waited, too, then repeated the question: 'Why are you jumping to conclusions?'

'Am I doing that?'

He was patient; it was like separating the flesh of a nectarine from its stone. 'I think you are.'

'You're wrong.' He waited, just looking at her; after a long pause she went on, 'I know Justin well, if that's what you're asking.'

He took a chance: 'You're more than just friends, Lina.'

'What has he told you?'

'Nothing. Other than that he obviously thinks a lot of you.'

She smiled at that, nodded as if pleased. 'What sort of questions do you police ask?'

'The sort I'm asking now. We know you and your husband were living apart before –' He gestured; it was enough. 'I've been to see Miss Orion.'

'She told you about Justin and me? Shit!' She snatched off her glasses; he waited for them to break in the claws of her hands. 'That young bitch – she –'

'She what?'

She put the glasses back on, taking her time, fixing them as if they needed focusing. 'She's playing with him.'

'Does he know that?'

'Of course he doesn't! He falls for every young bit of arse that twitches itself at him. You know what it's like – you're about his age –'

He gave her another sour smile. 'Don't let's get

154

sidetracked, Lina. My seven-year-itch still has to arrive. What about you and Justin? Who's doing the playing there?'

She took the glasses off again, stared at him: the eyes were a weapon. 'Find out!'

'Oh, we'll do that, I promise you. In the meantime we'll keep our eye on the main target – finding out who killed young Lucybelle.'

Chapter Five

1

Tim Pierpont was dismayed when Miriam Zigler told him that Ronald Glaze was applying for Legal Aid. When he had learned that Biddle, Brown and Cartwright had engaged Caradoc Evans to defend Glaze, he had felt a certain hope. Some cases are not easy to lose; against Evans one could look good in losing. Or at least as if one had tried one's best.

'We landed that cancellation,' said Miriam. 'We go to committal Thursday week.'

'How did you manage it?' *Why was she so eager*?

'A quid pro quo,' she said, but didn't elaborate. The ways of the legal system are labyrinthine, otherwise lawyers would not be necessary.

'You're in a hurry on this one.'

She nodded emphatically; her face was alive this morning. 'He's a bastard. He murders his wife, he sleeps around – if he gets off, who's to say he won't go out and do it again?'

'Sleep around?'

'Yes, that. Then find someone he can't get rid of – some women are like that –'

She wouldn't be.

'– he kills her, too.'

'You've got all this on him just from the papers? Come on, Mim. Wait till we see the guy. Okay, he sleeps around but that doesn't say he's a serial killer, or likely to be.'

'You men always defend each other.' Her face was suddenly plain.

In this case, yes. 'Not me. I just don't make up my mind before the case begins. There are exceptions –' He thought of several horrifyingly brutal killings for which, privately, he had wished for the death penalty. He had seen the look on the faces of the relatives of the murdered, seen their wish more plain than his own. 'We'll push this case as hard as we can on the evidence, Mim. But don't spoil our chances with prejudice.'

'Would you rather give the case to someone else?' She could sometimes sound petulant, which fitted oddly with her otherwise generous spirit. He wondered if he would ever really understand women.

'No, I wouldn't,' he said firmly. 'Build it as strong as you can, but don't start judging the bastard before we've even seen him.'

'So you think he might be a bastard?' Her face came alive again with amusement.

157

He smiled in return, though he had no humour in him. 'He could be. We've all got a bit of bastard in us, according to you feminists.'

'Is Virginia a feminist?'

'I've never asked her.'

'Coward. Oh, we've got Mrs Indelli for the committal – she's a feminist.'

She went out with another smile and left him thinking: *Sure, I'm a coward.* He would strive, heroically, to avoid sending Ronald Glaze to prison. But he was not going in his place.

That evening he and Ginny offloaded Fay on Ginny's mother and went to see *Titanic*. He sat unmoved all through it, admiring the special effects, the very gigantism of everything, but was totally untouched. He was a movie fan, almost a cineaste, but tonight he was an iceberg.

When they came out Ginny said, 'You didn't enjoy it, did you?'

'I kept thinking about the two Irishmen on the iceberg. They weren't in the movie.'

'What two Irishmen?'

'The ones who were shipwrecked there. One of them stands up and yells, "Holy Jasus, Mick, we're saved! It's the *Titanic*!"'

She dug him in the ribs. 'You've been waiting all night to tell that joke . . . What's the matter, hon?'

He started up the Discovery, headed up Pacific Highway. 'What would you say if I went into private practice?'

She turned her head. 'You've always said it would never give you the variety you get with the DPP.'

'Maybe I've had too much variety.'

'Is it a case you've got coming up?' She was not without antennae.

'None in particular. I start one next week –' A fraud case: no blood, no death, just simple greed. 'The woman will go down, she'll probably get three years.'

'Is that what's upsetting you? Prosecuting a woman? You feel sorry for her?'

'I've prosecuted a couple of dozen women. If they've done the crime, they do the time – I don't worry about their gender. No, this woman deserves whatever she'll get. It's just . . .' He turned off down the hill that led to their street.

'It's just what?'

'Well, I could make more money in private practice. I could go in as a partner – there are a coupla firms would take me in –'

'You want to make more money?' He had pulled the 4WD into their driveway, but she made no attempt to get out. 'I don't want it, Tim, not if it means seeing less of you, you working harder. I've heard what it's like. Janette and Belinda –' two friends married to law partners – 'they say Bob and Ross are working sixty, seventy hours a week, often the weekends. The money's great, but they wonder what's happened to their lives.'

'I thought Janette loved the His and Hers BMWs.'

'You see? You judge women on externals.' Then she

leaned across and kissed him. 'Do whatever you want, darling. But don't go chasing money for me.'

He got out, looked up at the sardonic moon; a flying fox flew across it, dark and evil looking. Suddenly he started to laugh, dry as a sob.

'What are you laughing at?' said Ginny from the front door.

'Those Irishmen on the iceberg.'

2

'Start with Justin and Tiffany,' Malone had said. 'Though I can't believe Justin would be dumb enough to type a ransom note on his own computer. Get a full list of his clients, their names and addresses. See if any of them has got a score against him. Or her.'

Tuesday morning John Kagal came into his office. 'Eleven of the gym's clients have got form. Hold-ups, assault and battery, drugs. All clean now, the last one two years ago. But . . .'

'There's always a but.' It was the main punctuation in a police investigation.

'Mr Belgrave is in deep shit. Half a million might, just might, get him out of trouble.'

'What's his problem?'

'He's been planning for the past six months to start up a chain of gyms, half a dozen of them spread around Sydney. Taking Double Bay chic to the western suburbs, Hurstville, places like that.'

'There's chic in a gym? Go on.'

'His partner was an Indonesian, claimed to have family connections to Soeharto –'

'Nice connection.'

'Hasn't helped. The Indonesian's pulled out, his rupiahs couldn't buy an exercise bike, and Justin's been left holding the bag. His bank is asking him to run uphill backwards.'

'Does he have any form?'

Kagal produced a print-out; one of these days, thought Malone, he's going to produce a corrected version of the Old Testament. 'His real name is Ernesto Buccini. Born in Melbourne of Italian parents April 1962. He was up for false pretences in 1982, got off on a bond. 1984, he got nine months for passing dud cheques. He came to Sydney –' he folded the print-out – 'about ten years ago. He started Mode Gym in 1994, that was when he became Justin Belgrave.'

'No violent form?'

'No. But when they're desperate . . .'

'I'm not arguing against you, John. I've sent a copy of the ransom note down to Canberra, to the Criminal Intelligence people, asking them to do a profile. They'll want more, so give it to them when they ask.'

'In the meantime?'

'Bring Justin in for a cuppa tea. Before you pick him up, talk to Tiffany on the front desk there.'

'I've done that –'

Of course. Why didn't I know that?

'She only came back to the gym on Friday. She'd

161

been to New Zealand with her boyfriend for two weeks. She gave me places where they stayed and I checked. The night of the kidnapping they were bungee-jumping in Queenstown.'

'You check on the boyfriend?'

'He's a senior constable out at Marrickville.' Kagal grinned. 'Tiffany couldn't be cleaner.'

'Have a talk with her, anyway. Ask her how close her boss and Mrs Vanheusen were.'

Kagal left and Malone, reluctantly, turned to the pile of paperwork on his desk. Reports, like coat-hangers, breed and multiply: he was convinced of that. Someone, some-where, is always waiting for *his* copy of what he doesn't need to know. It is called the bureaucratic imperative.

It was another hour before Kagal returned with Justin Belgrave. The latter came in wearing a white T-shirt over tight gym trousers; he rippled with indignation. Kagal took him into an interrogation room and Malone got up and followed them.

'What the hell's this all about? I've got a business to run –'

'We won't keep you any longer than necessary, Mr Belgrave. Would you like some coffee?'

'Shove your coffee! Jesus, I told you all I knew –'

Malone and Kagal both sat down and after a moment Belgrave sat down on the other side of the table from them. He stared at them, then gestured at the video recorder. 'Are you going to use that?'

'Not unless you want us to,' said Malone. 'You're familiar with our procedure?'

162

'What does that mean?'

'We know your police record –'

'Jesus, that was, I dunno, fourteen, fifteen years ago! You guys've never heard the expression, turning over a new leaf? I've been on the straight and narrow ever since then –'

'We're not disputing that, Justin. You may not believe it, but cops are delighted when you turn over a new leaf. That's one more we don't have to worry about.'

'So why am I here?'

'You're in debt up to your armpits,' said Kagal and repeated what he had told Malone an hour before.

'Jesus Christ, you really do dig up dirt, don't you? How'd you get that?'

Kagal ignored the question. 'We've got confirmation from our Forensic section that the ransom note was printed on that Canon printer in your office. Half a million would get the bank off your back for a while –'

Belgrave held up a hand. 'Now hold on! Am I supposed to have kidnapped the kid and murdered her? You're outa your incredible fucking minds – you –' He was abruptly lost for words; he looked around the room as if notes might be scrawled on the walls. 'Would I be dumb enough to use my own machine? I may be muscle-bound, but I'm not *thick*!'

'We'll concede that,' said Malone. 'It did strike us as dumb. But you have to admit – it doesn't look good, does it? The note comes from your machine asking for half a million, you're in debt for more than that – why didn't you ask for a million? The Vanheusens could pay that.'

Belgrave sat for a while; one could see him getting himself under control. It was almost as if it were a physical exercise; the muscles were re-arranged, the hands placed on the table, fingers extended. 'Look, I'm in a hole, a fucking big hole, financially. It's just incredible how everything's fallen apart. The fucking Asian business . . .' He shook his head, as if the Asians were to blame for his situation. 'I'm gunna lose the gym, everything I've built up. But I'm not a killer, not of anyone, least of all little kids –'

'Did you know Lucybelle?'

'Her mother brought her to the gym once or twice, but no, I didn't know her. I never took much notice of her –'

'You're Italian,' said Kagal, 'and you're not a child-lover?'

'You're Australian – do you love fucking kangaroos?'

'Are you using that as an adjective or a verb?' asked Malone.

Belgrave looked at him, then caught the joke. He suddenly laughed, weakly, and sat back in his chair. There was quiet for a long moment, then Malone said casually, 'How well do you know Mrs Vanheusen?'

Belgrave didn't move, yet all at once the muscles were carved in stone. 'I've already been asked that. The answer's the same – she's a client.'

'No, she's more than that, Justin. You and her are an item, have been for the past month or more. Ever since Mr Vanheusen left home to go and live with DeeDee Orion.'

'You're a real gossip column, aren't you?'

'The gossip columns made your gym, didn't they? They'll undo you, too, when they hear about your debts. Come on, tell us about Mrs Vanheusen.'

Belgrave looked at the two detectives in turn. Then he looked away, biting his lower lip. When he looked back his voice was abruptly rougher. Not just the words but the voice itself, that of a kid, of years back, from a back street gang: 'Where is this gunna lead? My whole fucking life is falling apart –'

'Did Lina know that?' asked Malone, almost gently, not leaning forward.

'Yeah, I told her. But I wasn't asking her for help – she's got enough to put up with – there was Damien walking out on her, then this – what happened to her kid – Jesus!'

'Justin, if you know her as well as we suspect you do, you may also know someone from your gym who's been spending time with her, giving her more attention than usual –'

'One of my staff? Forget it. Okay, for the past, I dunno, five, six weeks, she's spent all her time in the gym with me. She'd stay behind after we closed down –'

'Who'd be looking after Lucybelle?'

'Her housekeeper.'

'Did the housekeeper ever come to the gym?'

'Are you kidding? She's built like a brick shithouse. She was a joke, a good-natured joke, with the Vanheusens, him and her. There'd be parties there, the place full of

165

models and health fanatics, and Louise, the housekeeper, would come in, all hundred kilos of her –'

'We get the picture. You've been to the Vanheusen house?'

'A coupla times. Before – well, no. Before and after Damien left.'

'Does Damien know about you and Lina?'

'I dunno. Look, between me and Lina, it wasn't serious – not for me. I was, I dunno, just –'

There was a knock on the door: it was Sheryl Dallen. 'There's a fax from Canberra, sir. I think you should see it.'

Malone got up and went out to the main room, took the fax Sheryl handed him. 'It's from the BCI, just a preliminary profile based on what we sent them. There'll be more.'

Malone read the profile: *It is impossible to determine whether there is one or more persons involved in the kidnapping. It could be that there are two or more involved and that the murder of the victim occurred because of disagreement, perhaps violent, between the kidnappers. They are not professional criminals. On the other hand, if there is only one kidnapper involved he could be someone who knew the child, who persuaded it to remain quiet while the abduction was taking place. Feeding the child the barbiturates was necessary to quieten it before putting it in the garbage bag. But it also suggests that if he knew the child, he couldn't bring himself to throw it off the cliff while the child was still conscious. He would be reasonably strong, but not abnormally so. If there is only one kidnapper, then, in view of the killing so soon after abduction, we suggest that money was not the only reason for the abduction. More to follow.*

More followed at once. The phone rang in his office and he went in to answer it. 'Scobie? It's Tilly.'

'Tilly Orbost? Where are you – Sydney or Brisbane?'

'Canberra. I'm down here on a month's secondment. Can I help on the Vanheusen case?'

'We need it, Tilly.'

'I've talked to the Director. Get your boss to fax him a formal application. I can come up tomorrow for two days.'

Tilly Orbost was a chief inspector in the Queensland Police Service. She had done the FBI course in Washington in Criminal Investigative Analysis, had come back for a year's duty in the BCI in Canberra and during that period had worked with Malone on a previous case. He could not think of anyone who could be more helpful, except, of course, a confessed criminal.

'I'll talk to Greg Random right away. I'll pick you up at the airport tomorrow. And thanks, Tilly.'

'Don't thank me too soon.'

He hung up, rang Greg Random, the chief superintendent in charge of Homicide and Serial Offenders Unit. 'We need her, Greg. Otherwise I think we may finish up going round in circles.'

'Okay, it's done.' His drawl belied the efficiency with which he worked. His men always got what they asked for, within reason. 'How are you going on that case?'

'Like on a treadmill in a gym.'

'Never gone in for that sort of stuff, m'self. People who exercise haven't got enough to do.' He was bony and lean and, like the bush cop he had once been, moved at the pace of the seasons. 'Oh, congratulations on that Glaze case. Looks like you got yourself a winner there.'

'I'm hoping. Thanks, Greg.'

He went back to the interrogation room. 'Righto, Mr Belgrave, you can go. You've been very helpful.'

Kagal looked surprised, but said nothing. Belgrave was not surprised, just still indignant. 'How do I get back to Double Bay? Do you pay for the cab?'

Malone grinned. 'You win. We'll take you back – you want a marked or an unmarked car?'

He fidgeted under his T-shirt. 'Unmarked. Am I unmarked, too?'

'Virginal, Mr Belgrave. Pristine. Get him a car and a driver, John, then see me in my office.'

Five minutes later Kagal and Sheryl Dallen came into Malone's office. Clements was there, lolling on his throne beneath the window. Beyond the window all the cloud had gone and the sky was a blue page. An unusual visitor, a sky-writer, was tossing his plane across the page: I LOVE YOU, BR . . . Then his pen ran out of smoke.

'Belgrave's in the clear?' asked Kagal.

'Yep. We're bringing in the BCI. Tilly Orbost is coming up tomorrow. We're going to start looking closer to home.'

'The housekeeper or the parents?' said Sheryl.

'The parents.'

'Shit!' Clements was forty-two years old and had been a parent for only two years; he had started late but had proved a natural. 'Killing your own kid! I remember seeing the smug little brat on TV and she used to turn my stomach – but *killing* her! They've gotta be sick.'

'Maybe they are. We'll bring them in tomorrow, after Tilly gets here.'

'Can she talk to them? I can remember when she worked with us on the gay bashings, she said they try to avoid the victims.'

'A fine point. What do you do when they're both victims and offenders?'

3

Next morning Malone got up at his usual time, went for his usual 5-kilometre walk round Randwick racecourse. A wind had sprung up during the night from the south and the humidity had gone, but autumn was still late. Everything in the early morning had the definition of a lino-cut. The huge stands were like cliff-faces; the sun came over the eastern hill and threw them into relief. The horses galloping by were all muscle: an equine gymnasium without the mirrors or the vanity. A 747 went over, the first of the day's disturbances; a jockey doing trackwork rose up in his stirrups and shook a fist at it. Malone stopped and applauded him and the jockey saluted him with his whip. Airlines should use only gliders, they told each other.

At breakfast he told Lisa, 'You'd better catch a cab into work this morning. I'm going to the airport to pick up another woman.'

'Oh migod, they're breaking up!' said Maureen.

'Who's going to get me?' asked Tom. 'What's the best offer?'

'A dollar ninety-five,' said his mother.

'I'll take care of the division of the spoils,' said Claire.

'Bloody vultures,' Malone said to Lisa. 'You want to move out?'

'Why not? You want to bring the other woman?'

Driving out to the airport he wondered what the Vanheusens would think of the Malone family life. Would the absence of pizazz, or whatever they called it, bore them? What sort of glue had held them together until they had begun to break up? Had it been the little girl Lucybelle or had she been the cause of the break-up? Which one, if either of them, had killed the child?

He pulled his car in behind two Commonwealth cars waiting to pick up MPs or bureaucrats from Canberra. Instantly a genie of a security officer appeared out of nowhere; rub a vacant parking space and they are there. 'You'll have to move that, sir –'

Malone produced his badge. 'I'm picking up the head of the Federal Police.' He gestured at the Commonwealth cars. 'Who are these for?'

'Foreign Affairs –'

'Public servants? Let 'em catch a bus.' He walked on into the terminal in time to meet Tilly Orbost.

She hadn't changed in the two years since he had seen her. She was tall, still slim; the big black eyes had lost none of their shine. She had, as she described it herself, a good deal of the tar-brush in her; but only an arrant racist would have remarked on it. There was just a faint sprinkle of grey in the black curls, but that could have been by design; Malone could never fathom what women did with their hair. She gave him a big smile and a warm handshake as they met.

'How's life in Brisbane?'

'The men have got used to me. I'm in line for superintendent.'

'I'd heard things were beginning to be civilized up there.'

Queensland was known as the Deep North by New South Wales and Victoria; the contempt north of the border for the southern states was complementary. Some day soon the nation would be a republic, beginning the new century with a new start, but the States would always be shoving and jabbing and rubbing against each other in the national scrum.

As they got into Malone's car the security guard approached. 'Head of the Federal Police?'

'She's his girlfriend,' said Malone. 'I'm taking her into protective custody. Did the public servants catch a bus?'

'You kidding?'

In the car Malone explained the exchange. Then he

171

told Tilly about the Vanheusen case. 'We may be barking up the wrong tree, but I've just got a feeling.'

'Child abuse is becoming a bit endemic. It's only a step from there to murdering them.'

'There's no evidence there was any child abuse. Evidently she was Mummy and Daddy's little darling. She was popular with other kids and their mums, the stage mothers at the model agency.'

'She was on her way to being the nation's little darling. The commercials she did ran in Queensland. The *Courier-Mail* ran the story of the kidnapping and killing on its front page. I liked her. There was a freshness about her, you couldn't help liking her. What did you think of her?'

Everyone to his or her taste. 'I always get up and go to the fridge or the loo when the commercials are on . . . How's your own life?'

'You mean my love life? It's okay, Scobie. Better than that. I'm living with a man, a lawyer. We're happy.'

'Good.' He liked her and was happy for her.

He had debated whether to invite Sergeant Gallup in for the interview with the Vanheusens, but decided against it. Gallup would probably resent it when he was presented with whatever came out of the interview; that was the nature of the business. But Malone had learned that crowding a suspect only muddied the questioning. A suspect, too often, saw safety in the numbers against him.

Clements who, two years ago, had been suspicious of criminal profiling, greeted Tilly as an old friend.

'We've got a headache with this one, Tilly. Scobie needs someone to hold his hand.'

'I thought you always did that?'

'People were starting to talk.' He grinned. 'Welcome back.'

Malone and Tilly waited in the interview room till John Kagal and Sheryl Dallen brought in the Vanheusens. The latter stood close together, holding hands; they were going to stand or fall together. They were both dressed casually, but in black; this was their week of mourning. Malone felt a curious mix of sympathy and contempt for them.

Damien looked more Roman than ever; but Caesar wary of Brutus. Lina had her hair drawn back under a black velvet band; she was severe looking, a flamenco dancer before the music had begun. They looked around the interview room, then at the video recorder.

Damien Vanheusen frowned; he knew the purpose of the recorder. 'We're going to be *interrogated*?'

Malone introduced Tilly, then closed the door of the room, enclosing just the four of them. 'Sit down, please.'

The couple stood perfectly still, still holding hands. 'Do we need our lawyer?' said Vanheusen.

'That's up to you, Mr Vanheusen. Do you think you'll need one?'

'Sit down, Damien.' Lina Vanheusen took her hand out of her husband's, sat down at the table. 'This won't take long. We don't need any lawyer.'

Vanheusen hesitated; he was angry, not afraid. Then

he sat down, jerking his chair away from the table as if about to throw it against the wall. Malone and Tilly sat opposite them: the old tableau. Television had made common a ceremony that had once been secret. Lina Vanheusen lifted her chin, ran a smoothing hand over her hair, as if the recorder was beaming this scene out to a dozen channels.

Vanheusen gestured at the recorder. 'You going to use that?'

'Not unless you want us to. Relax, Damien. We're not charging you with anything.'

Lina was watching Tilly, but saying nothing. She was very composed, as much so as Tilly.

Then Malone said, 'Do you use barbiturates?'

The question was blunt, unexpected. Vanheusen frowned, his face growing a fishnet of lines. 'Barbiturates?'

'Sleeping tablets, for instance. Or Valium, stuff like that. You must be under a lot of pressure, getting out new frocks – sorry, a new collection – what, twice a year?'

A faint smile flickered on Tilly Orbost's face at the mention of 'new frocks', but Lina Vanheusen looked as if Malone had uttered an obscenity.

She hadn't taken her eyes off Tilly. 'Who did you say you were?'

'I didn't,' said Tilly.

'Then what are you doing here? *Chief* Inspector – are you his boss?'

Tilly and Malone exchanged looks; their smiles were

too secret to be observed. Then she looked back at Lisa: 'I'm here to look at the feminine side of things.'

'Which are?'

'You,' said Tilly bluntly. 'To repeat Inspector Malone's question, do either of you use barbiturates?'

Vanheusen was observing the small exchange between his wife and Tilly. He appeared less angry now, but there was still tension in him. He's suddenly looking older, thought Malone.

'We both use them,' said Lina. 'Not habitually, but as he said –' she nodded at Malone – 'there are pressures at times. Ours is – was a busy life.'

'Was?' said Malone. 'It's slowed down for you since the separation?'

'It has for me.' She didn't look at her husband.

'Because of those pressures, were there any disagreements over Lucybelle?'

Neither party looked at the other. 'No,' said Vanheusen. 'But what have barbiturates got to do with her?'

'The autopsy showed a considerable amount in her stomach.'

Lina made a gulping noise and Vanheusen slapped a hand on the table. 'Jesus God! They did that to her?'

'The barbiturates had been mixed with a chocolate drink.'

'Poor Lucy –' Lina shook her head; a strand of hair came loose from the velvet band.

Tilly said, 'You said there was no disagreement between you over her. Neither of you felt that her career was being pushed too hard?'

175

'She loved what she was doing. She wasn't being pushed, as you call it. It was all a big game to her.' Lina bit her lip, looked as if she might burst into tears.

'What were your plans for her?'

'Plans?' Vanheusen frowned again, the dark moustache moved on his upper lip like a caterpillar trying to get traction. 'Christ, she was only five years old! Have you got kids? Were you planning things for them when they were five years old?'

'No,' said Malone.

'Did you have plans for her, Mrs Vanheusen?' Tilly's pressure was soft but persistent.

'No, I didn't.' She pushed back the strand of hair, anchored it again under the velvet band. She was composed again, hands together and still on the table. 'It's as my husband says – it was not a planned thing. It was like letting her play a game.'

'You're not getting anywhere, are you, tracking down these bastards?' Vanheusen was abruptly aggressive.

'We've made progress,' said Malone. 'We know the ransom note was typed on a computer at the Mode Gym, in Mr Belgrave's private office. So the field has narrowed a little.'

'On *his* computer?' Vanheusen looked at his wife. 'Jesus, not him!'

'Do you think it could be Justin?' Malone said to Lina. 'You didn't tell your husband we suspected Justin?'

'No. Because I just don't believe he would do it.'

'You didn't fucking tell me *anything*!' Vanheusen got up, spun round, almost walked into the wall behind him.

He put a hand on it, leaned on it, his back to his wife and the two detectives. Then he turned round, but did not resume his seat. His voice was hoarse, rough. 'Are you gunna bring him in and charge him?'

'No,' said Malone, sitting back in his chair. 'We only charge people when we have absolutely solid evidence against them.'

'Christ, how much evidence do you have to have?'

'Quite a lot, Damien. You have no idea the demolition job defence counsel can do on shaky evidence.' He stood up. 'We'll have solid evidence soon. Thank you for coming in. You any further questions, Chief Inspector?'

'No,' said Tilly Orbost, rising. The two detectives, both tall, made the Vanheusens look small and vulnerable. 'Not at the moment.'

Lina looked up at her. 'You still haven't told us who you are.'

'I'm with the Bureau of Criminal Intelligence, from Canberra. We're helping Inspector Malone. No effort is being spared to find the kidnappers, Mrs Vanheusen.' No mention of criminal profiling.

Lina stood up, reached for her husband's hand again. He hesitated, then gave it to her. 'Just find these people,' she said. 'That's all we ask.'

'We'll do our best,' said Malone.

When they had gone Malone took Tilly into his office. He beckoned in Clements, Kagal and Sheryl; the room was crowded. He was glad he had not invited Chris Gallup to come to Homicide.

'They didn't look happy,' said Kagal.

'They're still getting over the loss of the kiddy –'

'No, I mean, not happy at being called in here. What did you get out of them?'

Malone looked at Tilly. 'What's your opinion?'

Tilly settled herself in her chair. Two years ago the official side of her had been confident, the human side a little uncertain. The mixed blood in her, the skeins of Fijian, Aboriginal and white Australian twisted together in stages of history, had made her defensive; but there had been no uncertainty about her police skills, she had come back with top marks from the FBI course. Today she was all confidence.

Up to a point: 'You know as well as I do that profiling is not an exact science. We're dealing with human nature and you can't put that in a test-tube and analyse it perfectly. So first, what have you come up with?' She looked at Kagal and Sheryl. 'Inspector Malone told me you'd gone to the Vanheusen home while we've had them in here.'

'The housekeeper was co-operative,' said Kagal. 'She's as distressed as the parents over the little girl's murder. I'm not sure, but she could have been a surrogate mother to Lucybelle.'

'Definitely,' said Sheryl. 'I talked to her – she's genuine, even if a bit hard to know at first. She let us have the run of the house. I took the bathroom and the living rooms, John the kitchen and bedrooms. There were no barbiturates in the medicine chest in the bathroom, but the housekeeper remembered throwing out an empty bottle with the garbage the morning after the kidnapping. On our way back we checked with the chemist in Double Bay, where the Vanheusens buy their stuff. He gave Mrs Vanheusen a full bottle of Valium last week.'

'In the kitchen,' said Kagal, 'there was a half-full tin of powdered chocolate. The housekeeper said she often gave the little girl a drink of chocolate made on milk. She's Swiss, it was Nestlé's.'

'It's not looking good for them,' said Clements, not lolling this time but sitting up straight on the couch beside Sheryl.

'I found nothing in the bedrooms,' said Kagal, 'but the housekeeper produced a thin gold chain that she said Lucybelle always wore, never took off. She said it was in Mrs Vanheusen's bedside table.'

'No,' said Sheryl. 'It was in *his* bedside table.'

Kagal checked his notes. 'Right. Sorry, boss. I'm getting a bit too exercised about this case –'

'Who isn't?' said Malone. It was unusual for Kagal to make mistakes, to show any emotional upheaval, but there was always a first time. For himself he had tried to be as dispassionate as possible, to keep out of his mind any image of the shattered body of the little girl, but the defences were trembling.

'I think you should concentrate on these two,' said Tilly. 'The gold chain – perhaps he or she, whichever one it was –'

'Or both?' said Clements.

She nodded. 'Or both. Perhaps they wanted a reminder

179

of the child. It happens. The parent in them, no matter what they've done to their child, can't let go. The disposal of the body – I don't know the area, but from what you sent me it's not an isolated place, is it?'

'No,' said Kagal. 'It's not well lit, but occasionally smoodging couples park there.'

'The little girl was found at eight thirty in the morning by a rock fisherman,' said Malone. 'The ME's report said she had been dead five or six hours at the most. So we say two, two thirty. Would couples still be there at that hour?'

'Don't look at me,' said Sheryl. 'I don't smoodge, as you call it, in the back seat of cars.'

'Consciously or unconsciously,' said Tilly, 'he or she could have been looking for someone to stop them, stop them throwing the child over the cliff.'

'So if we're picking one or the other,' said Malone, 'who will it be? Mother or father?'

'It could be either. Mother love is supposed to be the stronger, but a father can love a child just as strongly. There have been half a dozen cases in the past year or two where the father has killed his children for love of them, thought they had no future in this world.'

'So you won't place a bet on which one?' said Clements.

'Not at this stage, no. The husband gets worked up more than the wife, but it could be an act. They're both theatrical.'

Malone stood up, closing the meeting. 'Righto, we look at both of them. We'll start with the house. The

180

French doors to the living room were jemmied with something. I'm sure Chris Gallup's men or the PE team looked for whatever it was, a chisel or a tyre lever or something. But look again, go through the house and the garage or their cars. Tell Chris we'd also like surveillance on the Vanheusens. I'll see him tomorrow. Don't mention Inspector Orbost – I'll introduce him to her tomorrow.'

Kagal got the message. 'Sure, she'll arrive tomorrow.'

Tilly looked at Malone. 'What's going on?'

'It's Sergeant Gallup's party. You know the drill, or is it different up in Queensland?'

She grinned. 'It's even worse.'

When only he, Tilly and Clements were left in his office, Malone said, 'I want you to have dinner with Russ and his wife and Lisa and me.'

'I'll be delighted.'

'Watch yourself. Cops' wives are the real experts in analysis.'

'Amen,' said Clements.

4

'I was over at the zoo the other day,' said Clements, 'showing Amanda the chimpanzee. Then I heard them talking, the chimps. There was purple hair and pink hair and ear-rings and nose-rings and necklaces and bracelets and tattoos – and that was outside the cage. And one chimp said to the other, "That's evolution? Shall we throw them some bananas?" And they did and then they swung up into a tree, laughing their heads off. I think there must be better prospects in life than being laughed at by chimps.'

'He's antediluvian,' Romy told Tilly. 'It's a male thing in the Police Service. You must have noticed it.'

'All the time,' said Tilly.

'They think it's endearing of them,' said Lisa, 'revealing old values to their deadhead kids. What did Amanda do?'

'She gave him a razzberry,' said Romy. 'Two-year-olds do that so well.'

'So do eighteen, twenty and twenty-two-year-olds.'

Malone listened to the after-dinner chat with warm, relaxed amusement. The three women had got on well together at once; Romy had cooked an excellent dinner and Clements produced three top bottles of 1987 Hunter reds that, he said, 'had been overlooked in evidence' in a ten-year-old case. Now they were sitting out on the front verandah of the Clements' house in Drummoyne looking at the moon grinning at itself in the still waters of Iron Cove. The night was warm, still humid, and there was an air of lethargy to them all.

'I think I might invite those chimps home to dinner one night,' he said.

'Over my dead body,' said Lisa. 'And Claire's and Maureen's and Tom's.'

Then Malone's pager beeped. 'Bugger!'

He got up and went into the house. He dialled John Kagal, who was on call this evening. 'What is it, John?'

'Surveillance has fallen down. Our mate Damien has shot through.'

Chapter Six

1

'That cul-de-sac was the trouble, sir. We couldn't park there – they'd have woken up to us right away. We parked round the corner in the street that forms a T-junction with their street. We could see their house clearly. At eight twenty Mrs Vanheusen came out, got into her car, a BMW, and drove off. Constable Kilkenny followed her and I stayed behind, just hanging around. Someone must of thought I was a prowler – the next thing I know there's a patrol car from here drawing up alongside me. Talk about comedy –'

'It wasn't comedy, Constable, it was a bloody cock-up.'

'Yes, sir.' His name was Stafford, a junior constable; he was big and dark-haired with a deep tan that now looked like red ochre with his embarrassment.

'Where did Mrs Vanheusen go?' Malone looked at

the second officer, a bullet-headed man in his thirties with a habit of opening his mouth, then closing it to click his teeth.

He went through the action now. 'To the Mode Gym, sir. To see the guy who runs it, Belgrave.'

'How long did she stay there?'

'About an hour. When she came out she looked pretty ropable – he came to the door of the gym, but she yelled something at him, then got into her car and drove back home.'

'You followed her?'

'Yes, sir. When I got there, Phil – Constable Stafford – told me that Vanheusen had flown the coop.'

'How did he get away?' Malone looked back at Stafford.

'The garage door just shot up and he came out in his Range Rover, flat out. He must of seen me when our patrol car came along –' Stafford could not have looked more sheepish. 'I'm sorry, sir. Like you say, it was a cock-up.'

'We've put out an ASM,' said Gallup. 'He won't get far, not in a four-wheel drive.' 4WDs were the bane of all other drivers; Highway Patrol cars particularly targeted them. 'We'll have him by daylight.'

'Not if he goes bush, finds some hide-out. Does he have a property somewhere out of Sydney?'

'Not as far as we know. He never takes the Range Rover out of the city. He's the sort has hand-crafted mud on the tyres.'

'With a bull-bar?'

185

'What else? Protection against feral pedestrians galloping out of the scrub along Oxford Street.'

It was midnight in the incident room at Waverley. Malone had come here from the Clements'; Russ had volunteered to take Lisa home and Tilly Orbost to her hotel. Gallup had already blasted his two men before Malone's arrival; Malone had contributed his own muted blast. But recrimination never advanced a subject: it was a tenet Malone never argued with.

He looked at his watch. 'Is someone keeping an eye on Mrs Vanheusen?'

Gallup nodded. 'She won't shoot through. If she does, our guys will be on her tail all the way.'

'Let her sleep.' He hadn't mentioned Tilly Orbost and the interrogation of the Vanheusens. 'We'll talk to her first thing in the morning, I'll meet you there at eight thirty. Maybe by then Damien will be home again. Have you checked he's not staying with his girlfriend DeeDee?'

'We checked – he's not there.'

'Get a warrant and put a phone tap on her. He may be looking for company.'

Gallup motioned for Stafford and Capote, the bullet-headed constable, to leave the room. That left Malone and himself alone in the gallery of the crime: the photos, the diagrams, the list of names like subscribers to a fund. 'You think Vanheusen kidnapped and killed the little girl?'

'I don't know, Chris. Either him or his wife.'

'That's a pretty cold-blooded thing for a mother to do,

the way it was done. They usually smother the kid or cut its throat, they do it while they're outa their minds. But I guess it takes all kinds . . .'

Malone grinned, but felt no humour. 'Chris, you know as well as I do – if it didn't take all kinds, our job would be a pushover. I'll see you in the morning at the Vanheusens.'

He went home, dog-tired. 'That's what I am,' he told Lisa. 'Why are dogs more tired than humans?'

'Why are we going to discuss that at one o'clock in the morning? I'm tired, too. Woman-tired.'

'I love you – on alternate days.'

'Go to sleep.'

He skipped his usual morning walk, left Lisa to catch a taxi to work and drove over to Bellevue Hill through a morning that at last had an autumn tinge to it, faint but welcome. Gallup was waiting for him.

'How are you, Chris?'

'Dog-tired. And depressed. I was looking at *Millennium* last night on TV when I was called out. How do these guys solve everything in fifty minutes? And look so bloody pleased with themselves when it's all over?'

'My thoughts entirely, Chris. But cheer up. You'll be pleased with yourself when this is all over.'

'No, I won't. The little girl will still be dead.'

Malone looked at him, saw a side that he hadn't suspected. He said nothing, just nodded. Then as they were about to walk up the front path to the Vanheusen villa he stopped. 'Anything, a chisel or something, in the garage?'

187

'They found nothing. In either of the cars, hers and his – zilch. If Mr or Mrs jemmied those doors, they got rid of the tool.'

'They could've thrown it over the cliff with the kiddy.'

'I'll have the rocks searched. But I'm not putting money on finding it.'

Malone rang the bell and the front door was opened by the housekeeper. 'Morning, Mrs Certain.' He was meticulous about the pronunciation. He wanted her kept on side. 'We'd like to talk to Mrs Vanheusen. And then you.'

She looked wan, almost weightless despite her bulk; her blue eyes were dull. 'I can't stay here. I'll have to leave –'

'Not yet, Mrs Certain,' Malone said gently. 'Would you make Sergeant Gallup and me some coffee while we talk to Mrs Vanheusen? Then I'll come out to the kitchen and talk to you.'

'She's not out of bed yet – she's still asleep –'

'Then we'll talk to you now.'

She hesitated, then closed the door and led them through the house to the kitchen. It was out of *House & Garden*; but Mrs Certain had put her stamp on it. It was *lived* in, though Malone wondered how often the Vanheusens came in here.

She made them coffee – 'We Swiss make the best coffee in the world. We and the Dutch. The rest –' Her plump fingers wiped away the rest of the world's coffee-makers.

'My wife is Dutch. She would agree with you.'

Malone and Gallup sat at the big table; she sat down opposite them, but didn't take coffee. 'You obviously like cooking. What's it like cooking for a couple who are so keen on being fit and slim?'

'Don't try to put me at ease, Inspector. Ask me what you want to ask me.'

She wasn't abrasive, just matter-of-fact. Malone had met very few Swiss, but his general impression of them was that they were a matter-of-fact nation. But multiculturism here in Australia had taught him history often miswrote character. He was still reading Mrs Certain.

'Do you know where Mr Vanheusen has gone?'

She shook her blonde head. 'He didn't speak to me. He came downstairs, he was carrying a bag, one of those sack things you carry on a strap over your shoulder –'

'The sort you take on a plane?' said Gallup.

'I suppose so. Yes, he took it with him whenever he'd fly anywhere.'

Malone sipped his coffee; it was excellent. She pushed a pastry towards him and he took one. She was relaxing a little. 'Lucy loved those. It upset her mother when I gave her one –'

'You were close to Lucy?'

She nodded, bit her lip.

He didn't pursue that line, went back to her boss. 'Mr Vanheusen didn't tell you where he was going?'

'Nothing. He was angry. Very angry. He could get like that sometimes – be frightening –'

'What made him angry last night?'

She hesitated: she was a good servant, you didn't broadcast to strangers. Then she said quietly, the words dragging out of her: 'They had a terrible row, he and Mrs Vanheusen. I was in my room –' she nodded towards a narrow hallway that led to two doorways – 'my room and my bathroom are down there. I could hear them upstairs – the bedroom windows were open . . .' She paused, broke off a piece of pastry and nibbled at it. 'They argued a lot. But nothing like last night.'

'Could you hear what was said?'

'What's going on here?' Lina Vanheusen, in a yellow silk dressing-gown, stood in the kitchen doorway.

'Morning,' said Malone, rising. 'We were just having coffee with Mrs Certain –'

'You were questioning her about me! Have you got a warrant to come in here and question my staff?'

'We don't need a warrant for that, Mrs Vanheusen. We were told you were still asleep – we were waiting to question *you* –'

'I'll have coffee, just coffee, in the living room, Louise.' She turned and walked away, not even looking at Malone.

'I'll stay and talk to Mrs Certain,' said Gallup and held up his cup. 'I'm enjoying this.'

Malone waited for Mrs Certain to refill his own cup, then he carried it out into the main hallway and into the living room. The house was spacious, only adding to the emptiness of its atmosphere. He tried to imagine the little girl Lucybelle in it, but couldn't. There was nothing in sight, a doll, a pet, a schoolbag, to suggest that a child had ever lived here. It was the parents' house.

Lina Vanheusen was standing at the French doors looking out into the garden and the pool. The morning sun bounced back from the blue mirror of the pool and the yellow silk dressing-gown seemed to take on a greenish hue in its folds. Was it imagination, he wondered, or was her complexion slightly greenish, too?

She turned, stared at him, then sat down as Mrs Certain brought in a tray with a coffee-pot and a cup and saucer on it. A small plate held one of the pastries.

'I told you I wanted only coffee.'

'I know.' The housekeeper spoke as she might to a small child; to Lucybelle perhaps? 'But you need more than that. I'll cook a decent lunch.'

'Never mind,' said Lina, but the housekeeper was walking out, her broad back shut against argument.

'Help!' said Lina and Malone wasn't sure whether it was a cry for assistance or a comment on what one had to put up with these days in the way of staff. Then she composed herself again and looked up at him. 'Well?'

He sat down. 'We're looking for your husband. He's disappeared. It doesn't look good.'

A plane roared overhead; the house sounded as if it might fall down around them. Then as the sound died away she said, 'Bloody planes! It used to be quiet and peaceful here.'

'When was that?'

191

She had been about to pour herself some coffee; she paused with the pot held above the cup. 'What does that mean?'

'You ask that a lot, don't you? What does that mean? I don't think I need an answer. It was quiet and peaceful here before Lucybelle, right?'

She poured the coffee, added cream. She was unruffled, as smooth now as the cream. 'What makes you say that?'

He shrugged, too much: he almost spilled his coffee. 'I've seen it happen. A child suddenly mucks up a life-style.'

She reached for the pastry, bit into it. Her dark hair was worn loose this morning. A thick lock had fallen down over her face and she seemed to be looking at him round a corner.

'Who wanted the child?' he asked casually, sipping at his coffee. 'You or Damien?'

She took her time. Finished the mouthful of pastry, pushed back the lock of hair, took a sip at her coffee. Then: 'I did.'

He changed tack, nodded at the French doors. 'It was pretty inconvenient, the alarm system breaking down the day before they took Lucybelle.'

'Life's been like that – inconvenient, as you call it.' She stopped, wiped her eyes with her finger.

'Why didn't you call in the security people right away?'

'Louise was supposed to call them.'

'She told one of my officers that you had told her to

192

wait till she came back – she was away for a day and a night.'

'Well, I made a mistake. One I'll regret for the rest of my life. They couldn't have got in, otherwise –'

'They could have. Alarm systems can easily be broken, if you know how . . . Do you know where Damien has disappeared to?'

'No.'

'What was the row about last night?'

The chin came up. 'Row? Who's been talking? That bloody Louise!'

Protect the housekeeper. 'We had a man outside last night – you should've shut the windows.'

'What was he doing there?'

'A couple of days ago you asked for police protection.'

'And it was refused. I'm under surveillance, aren't I?'

He ignored that. 'What was the row about?'

She poured herself more coffee. Offered the pot to him, but he shook his head. One could almost count the metronome of her pauses. At last: 'About that girl, DeeDee.'

'He's not with her. We checked.'

She shrugged, careless now. 'Then I don't know where he is.'

'Do you think he kidnapped Lucybelle?' *And killed her*?

Her fingers tightened on her cup: barely discernible, but he caught it. 'I won't think about that – it's too horrible.'

'It is. A father killing his only child like that.'

She put down the coffee cup. 'Do you think he killed her?'

'We've narrowed down the suspects.' He stood up. 'You had a row last night with Justin Belgrave. What was that about?'

She looked up at him; her dark eyes had tiny knives of light in them. 'Am I one of the suspects?'

'We'll let you know, Lina. Sergeant Gallup and I will see ourselves out.'

He had learned to be a good performer: always leaving them wondering what the next question would be. Out in the hallway he called to Gallup, then let himself out the front door and waited outside. Gallup came out, the housekeeper closing the door behind him.

'That was a bit sudden. What happened with Mrs Nibs?'

Malone looked up the short street, quiet as a deserted stage set. The surveillance car was just visible beyond the corner of the T-junction.

'Tell your fellers they're out of a job if they lose her. She's the one.'

2

'Not necessarily,' said Tilly Orbost. 'We don't know if she was the one who wanted the child. It could have been him. I want to know a lot more about both of them before I point the finger.'

194

Malone had invited Gallup into Homicide to meet Tilly Orbost. There was no mention that she had arrived the previous day. Gallup knew of the Bureau of Criminal Intelligence and its work in investigative analysis and he was not wary of it. He seemed impressed, in more ways than one, with Tilly.

'I've got Constable Dallen working on that,' said Clements, one of the four in Malone's office. Sitting beside Gallup on the couch, both of them looking up at Tilly in the higher chair opposite Malone. 'They're both celebrities –' He held up his hands, fingers crooked in quote symbols. 'We'll get the surface stuff with no trouble. Underneath?' He dropped his hands, spread them. 'That may take a little time.'

'Why has Vanheusen disappeared?' asked Gallup. 'His Range Rover has been found, out at the airport. We've checked the manifest of every plane that went out last night after ten o'clock, but his name wasn't on any of them. He wouldn't have to produce identification to buy a domestic ticket.'

'Wouldn't someone have recognized him?' asked Tilly. 'You said he's a celebrity.'

'Celebrities are a dime a dozen – they invent themselves, them and a paparazzo or two.' Clements had a low opinion of them.

'Depends who was on the airline desk,' said Gallup. 'Say it's an older guy, someone like Russ here –'

'Thanks,' said Clements.

Gallup grinned. He's becoming more relaxed, thought Malone, fitting into the team. Or letting us fit into *his* team. 'Russ, do you follow the fashion news? Neither do I. He might of been cunning enough to pick someone like that. We've got Immigration on the lookout for him, but he could of caught a plane to anywhere in Australia. Then what does he do? Shave off that lairy haircut of his and his moustache, find out where he can buy a passport. And –' he made a spitting noise with closed lips – 'he's gone.'

'Is Damien Vanheusen his real name?' asked Clements. 'If he had another name, maybe he has a passport in that one. Are people born with names like Damien Vanheusen?'

'They are these days,' said Malone. 'He wouldn't have a shaven head in an earlier passport. That fashion's only come in since the gays decided to save money on haircuts.'

Tilly smiled. 'A nest of homophobes.'

The men all smiled in return, safe in their own estimation of their tolerance.

'Righto, it's a late fashion. He's been Damien Vanheusen for at least the last ten years, we know that. He could've shaved off his mo and worn a cap when he bought his ticket.'

'He didn't use a credit card,' said Clements. 'Seven people paid cash on the various counters. Three to Melbourne, two to Brisbane, one to Cairns, one to Perth. But no one remembers what any of the cash customers looked like.'

Malone pondered a while, then asked, 'Would he have shot through because he's scared of her?'

'You may be right,' said Tilly. 'But from what you've told us, if you bring her in you're not going to break her in twenty-four hours. She'll stall and you'll have to let her go.'

Malone sat back in his chair, knowing she was right. He had met Lina Vanheusen only four times, but her armour was as apparent as if it were an iron body-stocking. Women were the weaker sex; except when it came to being questioned. The maze of their evasions, lies, lost memory and general bloody-mindedness had defeated him more times than he cared to count. But he was not going to tell that to Tilly, a woman.

'We've just picked up a bloke who went missing for four years,' he told her. 'I hope we're not going to have the same run with Damien.'

'I think you'll need the two of them together,' said Tilly. 'See who breaks first.'

'So we're agreed it's one or the other?'

She hesitated, then nodded. 'Remember I told you about Occam's Razor? What can be done with fewer assumptions is done in vain with more.'

Clements looked at Gallup. 'Do you get the feeling that the intellectual air around here has got rarified all of a sudden?'

'I haven't a clue what they're talking about,' said Gallup. 'But I'm impressed.'

'It just means,' said Tilly, 'we stick with the fewer assumptions on this one. We won't ignore the bloody obvious – Mr and Mrs Vanheusen.'

'Occam was a fourteenth-century philosopher,' said Malone.

'And the bloody obvious is a philosophy?' said Gallup. 'I must be ready for my Ph.D.'

Then Tilly left to fly back to Canberra; as more background on the Vanheusens came in it would be faxed to her. The surveillance on Lina would be intensified: a tool of pressure. Surveillance had already begun on DeeDee Orion. The search for Damien Vanheusen would continue. Plod, plod, plod would be the pace: nothing had to be solved before the next commercial.

Over the next two days Sheryl Dallen and John Kagal brought in more information on the Vanheusens. Malone looked at it, then it was faxed to Tilly Orbost. He sat at his desk while Clements put more paper on it. There were three more homicides within twenty-four hours: a tow-truck driver, a battered wife finally killing her husband, a Vietnamese drug dealer. The incidence of violent killings was rising. Malone occasionally lifted his head and looked across at the opposite wing of the building, where Fraud lived. No blood, no gore: just clean healthy greed. But he knew he would be unhappy over there.

The weekend came and went. Mrs Vanheusen had visitors: Lady Derry, a few other well-known socialites, a bevy of gay designers. No Justin Belgrave. There were no sightings of Damien Vanheusen: Roman haircut or shaven head, he had disappeared. Saturday night Malone and Lisa went to see *Titanic*. Malone fell asleep just before the ship hit the iceberg, came awake as the ship's orchestra played 'Nearer My God to Thee'.

'They're playing your song,' whispered Lisa. 'You've been dead to the world.'

Going home he asked, 'Were the two Irishmen on the iceberg?'

'Oh no, not that old joke! Yes, they were. One of them was named Malone.'

'My great-uncle Seamus.'

When they got home they stood in the front garden before going into the house. The night was heavy with humidity; the gardenias' fragrance was thick. The sky was clouded, but no rain was promised. It had been the sultriest summer for years and the only good thing was that the promised bushfires had been kept at bay. But out there, beyond the black battlements of the houses there was still –

'What are you thinking about?'

'Murder,' he said without thinking. Then he squeezed her arm. 'I'm worn out. I think I'll retire.'

'Retire to bed or retire from work?'

'From work.'

'And sacrifice half your superannuation? You won't, you know. Not while I'm running the bank.'

'You Dutch. Always counting the pennies. I'm surprised Rembrandt ever made a living.' He kissed the back of her neck as she opened the front door. 'I'm too tired for the usual. Mind?'

They made love as often as they could, always when the children were out of the house. Stifled cries of passion are a health hazard.

'What's the point? Tom's already home.'

199

They went into the living room, where Tom was watching a late programme on an athletics meet. 'I've just been perving on these women sprinters. It's better than going to the beach.'

Malone slumped down in a chair while Lisa went out to make iced tea. 'One of these days you're going to shock your mum.'

'Mum? Nothing ever shocks her. Anyway, she knows I'm not a perv. I'm just a healthy lad with healthy appetites. Didn't you perv at girls when you were my age?'

He remembered the bikinis of his youth, but changed the subject: 'How'd you go today?'

Tom played second grade for Randwick and was a promising fast bowler. 'None for too much. One of the Balmain buggers belted me all over the paddock. It was what you oldies call a learning experience.'

'You bowled too short?'

'Didn't matter what I bowled – short, up to him, yorkers, whatever. He just belted me. Me and everyone else. I'd have done better to have gone and watched the girls run in their nice tight shorts. You had a good week?'

No, I feel I've been belted all over the paddock. The callousness in the murder of Lucybelle had begun to weigh on him. He was not a natural lover of children. He could raise no enthusiasm for infants; they all looked as if they already knew too much about him. The Anklebiters Coalition, which already had a member in parliament under another name, was a party he would never vote for. As W. C. Fields once said, Any man who hates kids can't be all bad. He didn't hate kids, but he was no cheerleader for them. But he loved his own children, would use any weapon to protect them. Which he would have done if he had been there in time to prevent Lucybelle's murder. 'We're making progress.'

'On the Lucybelle murder? I always thought she was a pain, but what sort of bastard would do that to her? Chucking her over a cliff!'

'The world is full of all sorts of bastards. Just tread carefully when you're out amongst them.'

'What sort of advice did Pa give you when you were my age?'

'To beware of capitalist bastards.'

'Did you take any notice of him?'

'No. I was too busy looking at girls in their bikinis.'

Lisa came back with the iced tea. 'What are you two talking about?'

'World affairs,' said Tom, got up, kissed his mother, winked at his father and went to bed.

Malone took the iced tea, sipped it. 'How lucky can we be?'

'Just be grateful,' said Lisa. 'I'm not in the habit of talking to God, but occasionally I give him a nod for what He's given us.'

Sunday Lisa and Malone went to nine o'clock Mass. Tom and the girls were now left to choose their own time and their own wishes. Maureen had become a rebel against the Church and the Pope because of the attitude against women; Claire and Tom were ambivalent, though both were convinced the Church needed to change. Their attitudes didn't disappoint their parents;

both Malone and Lisa believed that force-fed religion only choked the mind. Claire, Maureen and Tom would find their own way in their own time.

It was another hot sultry day. The sermon was on papal infallibility. The old Irish priest, still up to his knees in the bogs of Irish Catholicism, droned on. Malone began to doze, wondering why it had taken the Church eighteen centuries to discover the Pope was infallible. God, looking more than ever like a Jewish grandfather, leaned down and whispered in his ear, 'Don't ask.'

Lisa nudged him. 'You're snoring.'

He blinked his way out of his doze. 'I was listening to God.'

'What did He say?'

'Don't ask.'

'He said that? Typical!'

Heat lay on the day like an invisible pall; Malone spent half the day in the pool. At odd moments work slipped into his mind: where was Damien Vanheusen, was Lina struggling with conscience? But that was for Monday. He had his own life to live, even if it, too often, came only in episodes.

Monday the weather changed. Rain scudded up from the south; autumn was a whisper on the wind. When Tilly Orbost phoned from Canberra he thought the seasons were about to change.

'Don't build your hopes,' she said. 'I've gone over everything you've sent me on the Vanheusens. Two of my colleagues sat in with me. We're agreed the kidnapping and the murder was done by someone in the Vanheusen house.'

'I've eliminated the housekeeper.'

'So have we. You've checked everyone who comes to the house – tradesmen, the pool cleaner, the gardener. They're out. So that leaves Mr and Mrs. But we're not sure which one.'

He had read what had been sent down to the BCI in Canberra. 'Tilly, I still think it's her. The mother.'

'Scobie –' She was a police inspector, but still managed to sound like a woman: all patience with a dumb man. He felt the ghostly crack of Lisa's hand across the back of his head at his thought. 'Damien has been a troubled character all his life. Troubled by ambition. He had four separate business partners before he made good on his own – he double-crossed all four of them because he wanted to be *the* one. He had a dozen live-in women before he married Lina. Two of them took out Apprehended Violence orders against him. He's calculating – he uses people. And he was going off to London without Lina or the child.'

'So why would he kill the child?'

'He wanted to leave Lina with nothing. That's the sort of guy he is.'

'Righto, he's a bastard.'

'He's worse than that, Scobie. He's an absolute shit. We're all agreed on that down here.'

'All three of you being women?'

She laughed. 'Who else?'

He looked out the window. Rain smeared the glass;

down in the park across the road the wind surfed through the trees. What was the weather like where Damien, the absolute shit, was hiding? Or –

'Do you think conscience has caught up with him and he's gone somewhere and done himself in?'

'Could be, but I doubt it. He's theatrical – he would have left a note somewhere. He wouldn't go out quietly.'

'Righto, you've built a case against him. What about Lina?'

'Just as bad. Just as ambitious, except that she never got anywhere. But she married him and that was something of an achievement. Twelve years ago, before her marriage, she was under psychiatric treatment for a period of nine months. Married Damien in 1988, had two miscarriages in the first two years –'

'Where did you get all this? That wasn't in what we sent you.'

'Don't ask.'

Analysts and God: partners in obfuscation.

'What did you say?'

'Nothing. Don't ask. Go on.'

'I didn't get back to you immediately because we were chasing this up . . . She was thirty-eight when she had Lucybelle. The child was five, going on six. That makes Lina forty-four or thereabouts, getting within sight of the menopause.'

'Sheryl Dallen interviewed Lina's doctor, but he wouldn't play ball. Doctor-patient confidentiality.'

'If she's in the middle of the menopause – and my guess is, she is – that, plus the stress of the break-up with Damien, could have tipped her over the edge . . . The consensus here, Scobie, is that either one could have killed Lucybelle. For different reasons.'

'Just to clear things up, you don't think we have to look beyond these two?'

'No. Get them together, see who breaks first.'

'Easier said than done.'

He hung up, went out to the main room, sat down opposite Clements and gave him Tilly's report. The big man sat back in his chair, unimpressed.

'Okay, we'll do what she suggests. Get 'em together and play one against the other. But does she suggest how we're gunna collar Damien?' He flicked a finger at the reports on his desk. 'So far we've drawn a blank. If he's the killer, I wouldn't be surprised if he's gone somewhere and topped himself.'

'Tilly doesn't think so. She thinks he's too theatrical to go out without big-noting himself in some way. Why would he go to all the trouble of driving out to the airport, ditching the Range Rover and catching a plane somewhere?' He was arguing against his own argument of a few minutes before; but borrowed arguments are like borrowed garments, worn if they fit. 'He could've driven out to the same cliff where he tossed Lucybelle and jumped over. That would be a big-note that wouldn't need a note. Unless –'

'Unless what?'

'Unless he didn't catch a plane to anywhere. What if he's still around Sydney, keeping an eye on Lina? If she's going to be the next one he does?'

205

'Last time you had an opinion, your money was on her as the killer.'

Malone nodded, slumped wearily. 'I think Tilly has told me more than I wanted to know about Damien.'

'There needn't necessarily be one obvious, there can be two. Clements' revision on Occam's Razor . . . You going to Glaze's committal?'

'When's that?'

Clements' exasperation showed. 'I put a note on your desk on Friday. What the hell's the matter with you? It's Thursday, Liverpool Street. They got a cancellation or something. A DPP solicitor named Miriam Zigler is handling it.'

'I'll go. Has Glaze got Legal Aid or has Mrs Gibson come to the rescue again?'

'Legal Aid was refused, they didn't believe he had no money of his own. But he's drummed up money from somewhere.'

'Amanda Hardstaff?'

'Your guess is as good as mine. Whoever's come up with the cash, he can't afford Caradoc Evans. He's got Billy Thrump.'

'He should save his money.' Thrump was an old hack who had tried swimming through grog to success, but found the tide too strong. He was at his best between ten and twelve in the morning, before thirst got at him; one caught glimpses of what he might have been, the occasional flash of a vein of wit that had petered out. After lunch he just took up room in the court. 'I'm beginning to feel sorry for our mate Ron.'

'Don't.'

'Have we suggested calling Amanda as a witness? He might've told her something in bed.' He looked out the windows of the big room. 'I think I'll give myself a break. I'll take Sheryl and we'll go down and talk to Amanda. That is, if she's still at Palm Beach.'

He went back to his own office, called Wally Mungle at Collamundra. 'How're things, Wally?'

'Dry. We had a few spots of rain, but not enough.'

'That wasn't what I meant.'

'I know. It's dry around the office, too. I'm outa the shithouse, but only just. There's still a Roger Gibson fan club out here.'

'Even after the Amanda Hardstaff affair?'

'It's a men's club here at the station.' He had lowered his voice.

'Is she back there at Collamundra?'

'No. Far's I know, she's still down at Palm Beach. Keeping outa sight till his committal's over. How d'you reckon he'll go?'

'He'll go to trial, Wally. Take care.'

3

Palm Beach is the most northern of Sydney's beaches, some 30 kilometres from the city. It is, as the gossip columnists describe it, the summer playground of the social set, has been since the 1920s. It has none of the mansions or estates of its Florida namesake; most of the houses are modest and on small lots. Its tiny shopping centre is devoted mostly to feeding the floating population, either over the counter or at table. There are no fashionable boutiques. Gucci, Armani, Versace, if they were there, would be selling to each other to cover their overheads. During World War II, when the Japanese shelled Sydney harbour from a submarine, the whole of the small Palm Beach peninsula could have been bought for £15,000; today modest blocks bring half a million to a million dollars. But laid-back, barefoot casualness is the order of the summer season.

The Hardstaff house was one of the older ones, built of sandstone and with a magnificent view up past the headland to the open water of Broken Bay. It was a symbol of old money, of wool and wheat and cattle, when it had been the real money of the country. But now the half-acre of garden had run wild, the lawn was a tangle of foot-high weeds; Ron Glaze, or Roger Gibson, would have attacked it with relish. The house itself, with its wide dark verandahs and the peeling paint of its woodwork, had a glum look.

Amanda Hardstaff opened the big front door to Malone's knock. 'Hello, Mrs Hardstaff. May Constable Dallen and I come in?'

If there was any surprise it did not show. 'Have I any choice?' She stood aside while they walked into the dark hallway. She closed the front door and led them through the house to a cluttered living room where at least the windows were open and sun shone in. 'You've come a long way – for what?'

'May we sit down?'

She waved them to armchairs, sat opposite them. The chairs were deep and slack, worn down by almost a century of bums. This room had been *lived in*, but now it appeared as if it might all fade away, be just an image in memory.

'Are you going to Ron Glaze's committal hearing?'

'No.'

'You're not interested in what might happen to him?'

'I didn't say that.'

'Are you helping him with his defence costs?'

'Is that any business of yours?' She looked at Sheryl. 'Have you any questions?'

'I think Inspector Malone is doing well enough.'

Amanda looked back at Malone. 'You have her well trained. Yes, I'm helping Roger with his defence costs. The woman he's been living with left him high and dry.'

'She wasn't going to do that till she found out about you.'

'*C'est la vie*. She didn't trust Roger enough – he would always go back to her. He loved her.'

'But not you?'

She laughed. She was still a handsome woman and, though the house around her had been allowed to head for ruin, there was nothing ruined about her. She wore white slacks and a pink, figured silk shirt; she was out of place in this shabby old room. She lifted her hand to her dark hair and a thick gold bracelet glinted like a tiny ripple of sunlight.

'It was an affair. But why should I explain to you?'

'You don't have to, Amanda – we're broad-minded. You're lending him money because you think he's innocent of murdering his wife?'

'I *know* he's innocent.'

'How do you know? There's something called post-coital blues – sometimes the lovers let slip things.'

She looked at him with cynical amusement, then at Sheryl. 'Do you suffer from post-coital blues?'

'I'm a virgin,' said Sheryl.

Amanda laughed, a genuine sound, putting no cork on her amusement. Malone, keeping a straight face, said, 'What did Ron tell you about his wife?'

'Post-coitally? Nothing. But I *know* men, Mr Malone –' She smiled at Sheryl. 'I lost my virginity at fourteen. I made one mistake with Ron – I went to bed with a local man. But I liked him, he can be very charming –' She looked back at Malone, the smile gone now. 'He is not a murderer, couldn't be.'

She'd know, thought Malone: she was one and so was her father. 'What makes you so sure?'

She didn't answer, just looked at him: *you know as well as I do how I know.*

He went on, 'I've met many more murderers than you, Amanda. They're all different . . .'

'Are you staying down here so that you can go to the committal?' asked Sheryl.

'No, I'm not going. Is my name going to be mentioned?'

'No,' said Malone. 'Unless Ron brings it up. But you're not in our submission to the DPP.'

210

She didn't ask what DPP stood for: she knew. 'Roger will be acquitted. Now is that all? I have to go out.'

At the front door Malone turned. 'What would you have done if Ron had told you who he was and what he had done?'

'Post-coitally, you mean?' She smiled. 'I'm not a kiss-and-tell lover. Do virgins kiss and tell?'

'You think *Sixty Minutes* is interested in virgins?' said Sheryl.

Standing on the verandah Malone looked north. 'Beautiful view.'

'I used to stand on the verandah at Noongulli and admire the view.' Amanda Hardstaff was suddenly sober, sad: a different woman. 'My great-great-grandparents settled there in 1845. There wasn't a better property in the whole of the State. Now it looks like a desert – no rain, no grass, hand-feeding the stock. If there's no rain in the next six months, I may have to sell. Then I'll come here to live and, maybe, admire *that* view.'

'It's a pity Ron will still be doing time.' Malone couldn't help the touch of malice. 'He could come and fix up the garden.'

'I don't think so, Inspector.' Her expression changed again; the amused expression was back. 'Roger will go back to Roma, if she'll have him. And she will.'

That night *Wanted for Questioning* ran a short piece on Damien Vanheusen. Calls came in from eight different locations, from places as far apart as Kalgoorlie in Western Australia and Rockhampton in Queensland; Caesars were loose in the goldmines and the canefields. Constable Capote, from Waverley, thanked the callers and said further developments would be aired next week.

Tuesday Lina Vanheusen was visited by Justin Belgrave who, according to Constable Stafford, who was on surveillance, arrived looking harassed and left looking harassed. Lady Derry called with a food basket – 'Meals on Mercedes', as Constable Stafford reported. Lina did not leave the house Tuesday or Wednesday. The media had disappeared, gone scavenging to another spot.

Thursday the rains came to Sydney: 190 millimetres in twenty-four hours. More than had fallen in the year up till then; but none of it fell west of the mountains, the plains were still bone dry. Malone wondered how Amanda Hardstaff, sitting in the lonely house at Palm Beach, the view to the north obscured by torrential rain, felt about the downpour. And wondered, too, if she was giving a thought to Ron Glaze.

He and Andy Graham went down to the Liverpool Street court, at several points fording flooded streets, dodging pedestrians rushing blindly under their umbrellas, cursing 4WD drivers who drove as if their vehicles were ferries.

The magistrate was a woman, Mrs Anastasia Indelli:

not a good omen for a man accused of murdering his wife. Malone had seen her before; she was formidable but fair. She was a cracked fashion plate, not one to have been seen on a Vanheusen or any other catwalk; she was also soaked, which didn't improve her appearance or her mood. She had a voice that needed the thick walls of the old Victorian courthouse to contain it. Glaze, Malone felt, was already doomed.

He had seen Miriam Zigler once or twice in court, but had never spoken to her. She approached him now as he and Graham sat in the police box.

'Do you want to be called, Inspector?'

'Not unless you need me. You've got everything there you'll need.' He nodded at the file she held.

She was alive with eagerness this morning. 'Unless he pleads temporary insanity, we'll be out of here in half an hour.'

'You're up against Billy Thrump. If he's sober he could talk for an hour. Good luck.'

The courtroom was almost half-full; more people than Malone had expected had braved the rain. He glanced idly over the crowd, wondering if Roma Gibson had come down from Collamundra. There was no sign of her. Then he saw a woman fluttering her hand at him from the far side of the court. He frowned, peered at her; she looked vaguely familiar. Then he remembered her from four years ago – Charlene? The beehive hairdo was gone, but there was no mistaking her. She was sitting with two other women, one about her own age and the other an older, grey-haired woman. Charlene Colnby

213

fluttered her hand again at him and he ducked his head in reply.

'His mother and sister,' said Andy Graham. 'The other woman's Mrs Colnby, works at the local club.'

'Still?' But why did he ask? The club was probably her life; he didn't sneer at the thought. The herd instinct was natural; it was why the clubs thrived. He sometimes wondered why he had been born without that instinct. And yet – what was the Police Service but another herd with that instinct? Why had the mobile phone been invented but for the fact that someone recognized the commercial prospects of the herd instinct? What was the Internet but a rush of lemmings to be together? 'Is she going to give evidence for him?'

'I don't know. You know what Thrump is like – he'd subpoena the Virgin Mary if he thought she'd help.'

'You're not a Catholic.'

'The girlfriend is. She's trying to convert me. I tell her I'll join if I can vote who'll be Pope. Here comes Thrump.'

Thrump came in, all swagger and bonhomie, last night's whisky or wine or whatever still tickling him. Unlike most *bons vivants*, his indulgence did not show in his weight; he was of average build and his clothes hung on him as on a hanger. He had a shock of iron-grey hair that rose up in a coxcomb and a genuine smile of excellent false teeth. Only in his eyes and his thin cheeks were the tell-tale pink signs. He bowed to the magistrate as if she were royalty and she gave him a royal dismissal in reply.

'Sit down, Mr Thrump,' she said, waving a hand as if the Bench were a royal carriage. 'You're late.'

'The weather, Your Worship. I think the Second Flood is upon us. Soon we shall be called two by two to the Ark –'

'Not lawyers, Mr Thrump. Not lawyers two by two – hordes of you. Now let's get down to business . . .'

Then Glaze was brought in. The weeks in prison had done him well; he had lost weight, looked tanned and very fit. He glanced around the courtroom, smiled at his mother and sister and Mrs Colnby; then saw Malone and gave him a smile. He looked as confident as a man who had just been acquitted.

As proceedings began Tim Pierpont slid into the seat beside Malone. 'He looks confident.'

'He's a car salesman. They're born looking like that.'

Pierpont leaned forward, both hands resting on the back of the seat in front of him. 'He'll be committed. You chaps did a good job. Mim Zigler, my assistant, thinks we can't lose.'

Malone looked sideways at him. 'You don't sound too confident.'

Pierpont returned the look. 'How many times have you thought you had an odds-on favourite and lost?'

Malone nodded, experienced in sour knowledge. 'Too many times.'

Pierpont raised his claw hand, rubbed it against his cheek. 'Are you working on the Vanheusen case?'

'We've lost one of our two prime suspects.'

'You'd narrowed it down to two?'

'The mother and the father – but it's still just a guess. The father's shot through, just like he did –' he nodded at Glaze across the court, now looking a little less confident as Miriam Zigler painted bars round him. 'I hope we don't take four years to pick him up, like we did with Glaze.'

'The mother and the father?' Pierpont screwed up his face. 'How could they do that to their own child?'

'That's what all the fathers in Homicide are asking. But it's a pointless question. It happens all the time.'

Pierpont stared across the court; it was impossible to tell what he was looking at or if he was looking at anything at all. Miriam Zigler was still putting her points with precision and Mrs Indelli was listening with interest and, it sometimes seemed, with sympathy. Twice Thrump rose up to object, but she put him down abruptly. She had a way of moving one hand that was like a slap across the face.

Then Pierpont stood up. 'I'll see you at the trial. I'll be prosecuting Glaze.'

'Maybe I'll see you before then. When I bring you the papers on Mr or Mrs Vanheusen. Or both. Take care.'

'I'll try to,' said Pierpont and left.

Glaze was committed for trial just before lunch. Thrump argued eloquently but to no avail; the case against his client was too strong. Glaze, no longer confident, looked wildly around the courtroom, as if some sort of evidence might fall off the walls. There was a cry from his sister, but his mother sat up straight and stiff, seemingly unmoved, as if she had arrived without hope and everything had gone as she had expected. Glaze stopped looking around the court, then stared across at Malone and abruptly shouted, 'You're wrong, you bastard! Dead wrong!'

'Let's go,' said Malone and turned his back on the prisoner and, with Andy Graham, walked out of the court. They stopped in a doorway, pondering whether to brave the rain which was still pouring down. They were both wearing raincoats and Malone his hat, but they hesitated at running through a waterfall.

Then Charlene Colnby was standing beside them. 'Inspector – remember me? From the Golden West?'

Malone waved Graham on and the latter, after a moment's hesitation, then plunged into the rain like a hippo.

'Of course, Mrs Colnby. You've been following the case all this time?'

She was wearing designer glasses, which evidently she had put on to follow the court proceedings more closely. 'I'm a friend of Ron's sister, Gloria. He doesn't like you, does he? I mean, picking him up after all those years. Do you really think he did it, I mean, killed Norma?'

'I'm not the judge, Mrs Colnby. My job was just to bring him in.'

'Oh, I see your point. I'm not criticizing – a policeman's job is not an easy one. But –' Her new hairstyle had reduced her height by five or six inches; she was quite small, smaller than he remembered her. 'Who was that guy in the box with you?'

'Constable Graham.'

'No, not that one who's just left us. The other one.'

'Why?'

'He was at the club the night Norma was murdered.'

Malone showed no expression; he wished the sun were out so that he could put on dark glasses. 'You're sure, Charlene?'

'I remember faces. But what I most remember was his hand – you know, that claw? I served him at the bar – I can't remember what – and I saw his hand. I seen it just then, when he was sitting with you – he had it on the back of the seat in front of him. Then he scratched his face with it –'

He was remembering her more clearly now: how observant she had been about the Glazes that night. 'Why didn't you mention him when we interviewed you that next morning?'

'You didn't ask me. All you wanted to know was how Ron and Norma were the night before. Ron had disappeared and you were interested only in him.' He wasn't sure, but that could have been true. 'Why would I mention him? We had – still have – people come in all the time. That's what the sign outside the club says – Visitors Welcome. Who is he?'

Caution was called for: 'He's just someone works with the courts. You didn't see him talk to Norma at all?'

She shook her head; the new flat hairstyle didn't move. 'No, I don't think so. I'd of noticed, I'm sure –' She would have, he was certain of that. 'No, definitely.'

'Well, I'll talk to him.' The rain had eased; he wanted

218

to escape and could not say why. 'But I'm sure it was just coincidence. He probably won't remember back that far.'

'Why wouldn't he remember? He's in the club and next morning he hears on the news or reads it in his newspaper, a woman who was at the club has been murdered. Why wouldn't he remember?'

An observer, an analyst: she should be in the Service. 'I'll talk to him.'

'Why wouldn't he mention it to *you*? He's sitting there beside you and he doesn't say anything?'

'Charlene, leave it with me.'

'Is he a mate of yours?'

'Charlene –' He almost took the dark glasses out of his pocket. 'What are you getting at?'

'I'm just asking – is he a mate of yours? Another cop?'

'No, Charlene, he isn't. I hardly know him. He's a Crown Prosecutor. He'll be prosecuting when Ron Glaze goes to trial.'

'Well –' she dropped her glasses down her nose, looking at him over the top of them: as if she didn't need them to look at him closely – 'that'll be another coincidence, won't it?'

'Why are you so concerned? Coming all the way to town, on a day like this, just for the committal –'

'I've changed my mind. I don't think Ron killed Norma.'

'Why didn't he say something when I gave him the first papers on the case?'

All day Thursday Clements had been in court giving evidence on another case; it was Friday lunch-time before Malone could get him alone. 'Come and have a sandwich with me.'

'Where?'

'Anywhere but here.'

Clements, big and clumsy but a perceptive buffalo, asked no more questions. They bought sandwiches and fruit and drove into the city and out along Mrs Macquarie's Chair. Most of the rain had gone, leaving wreckage and flooded streets in the suburbs, but clouds still were massed in the south like troops readying for the second assault. Clements parked the unmarked car in a No Parking zone and he and Malone got out and sat on a seat in the soft-edged shade of a big ficus tree.

Elizabeth Macquarie, the wife of the fifth Governor of the colony, used to sit here on this outcrop on the southern shore of the harbour, pining for England and home. Up to a few months before, Asian tourists came here in busloads, photographing each other against the silhouette of the Opera House across the small cove to the west. Weekends, brides and grooms fluttered in like pigeons and penguins to be photographed against the same backdrop. The ghost of Mrs Macquarie shifted uncomfortably in her invisible chair and England was further away than ever.

'Are you saying he had something to do with the

murder?' Clements chewed on a salmon-salad sandwich. Romy had told him he had to lose weight.

'I don't know.' Malone knew he sounded despairing. 'He's left-handed – his right hand is practically useless and his left hand should be extra strong. I looked up the copy of the autopsy – she was strangled with one hand, the *left* hand.'

'But why?' Then Clements saw Malone's look and went on, 'Okay, I'm playing devil's advocate. But you know what you're trying to suggest? That a Crown Prosecutor could be prosecuting a guy for a murder he himself did? You're stretching it, mate.'

'I haven't yet stretched it as far as it might go. Do you still have your mole in the DPP? You've got them everywhere else.'

'What do you want?'

'Find out if Pierpont lived out that way four years ago. If not, find out if he was on a case that day somewhere out there. Penrith, Katoomba, Blackheath – he could've called in at the club on his way home.'

A sixty-seat tourist bus pulled up and four passengers, all Japanese, got out. They photographed each other, photographed the Opera House, photographed the car parked in the No Parking zone, smiled at each other at the cheeky rebellion of the natives and got back into the bus. The ghost shifted again in her chair.

Malone bit into a peach. The peaches had been excellent this summer; a few small pleasures were left in life; but this one was floury. Then two cars drew up; three photographers and a transvestite got out. The

221

transvestite, in a sequined dress and under a purple punk hairdo that made him/her look seven-foot tall, pranced up and down for the cameras. Six weeks before had been Mardi Gras and the transvestites had been in season, strutting up and down Oxford Street like peacocks that had forgotten their gender. Malone had been amused by them, guessing that many of them were often amused at themselves. In season and in their own domain one took hardly any notice of them; this one was out of place and looked as if he/she knew it. The camera-snapping finished, the transvestite and the photographers got into their cars and drove away, photographed by the Japanese tourists hanging out of the bus windows. The two trying-not-to-be-homophobes looked at each other.

'I'd like to see you like that,' said Malone.

'Camp is where the small talent lives,' said Clements. 'I'd rather have no talent than camp it.'

'Do you have any talent?' But Malone smiled as he said it. Clements' talent, thoroughness, could never be photographed.

'You're sure you want to go on with this Pierpont business?'

'If we don't there could be trouble. I've got the feeling Mrs Colnby isn't going to let this rest. Find out where he came from that night four years ago and we'll take it from there.'

'*You'll* take it from there. I'm not taking on the DPP.'

The weekend passed without incident. Lina Vanheusen

went shopping with Lady Derry; Damien Vanheusen was still missing; DeeDee Orion went out with three different men Friday, Saturday and Sunday nights. Monday, Clements' DPP mole, whoever he or she was, produced. Clements came into Malone's office with his notebook.

'Four years ago, Pierpont was single, lived in Balmain. He's married now, has a little girl and his wife is expecting again. On the day of the murder he was on a case at Katoomba, assault-and-battery.' He sat down. 'He could of stayed in Katoomba, had dinner there. Then decided to stop off at the Golden West on his way home, try his luck on the pokies.'

'Is he a gambler?' Clements shrugged and Malone went on, 'You're coming around to my way of thinking?'

'Reluctantly. Have you thought of the stink it's gunna cause. We charge a Crown Prosecutor with murder? It's been done, in that book by the American Scott What'shisname and in the movie. But for us to do it? After we've spent four years chasing another guy and charging him? Who's gunna be patting us on the back after that sorta shemozzle?'

'So what are you suggesting?' Malone couldn't help his sarcasm. 'We keep our suspicions to ourselves and let Glaze take the rap?'

'Don't be sarcastic, mate. I know we're in a bugger of a hole. We have no evidence that he killed Norma Glaze. We could be dead wrong. It could be just coincidence that he was there at the club that night and that he's left-handed. The world would stop running if there was no coincidence.'

'You're starting to sound like Greg Random. All bloody philosophy from Welsh poets.'

'Talk to Greg. Don't ask me to advise you. I'm your junior – I'm pulling rank the other way.'

He got up and went back out to his own desk. Malone sat tapping a pen on his desk like a prisoner sending a message; but there was no answer. He looked out the window but there was no message there, except a discouraging one; the rain was pelting down again, flooding gutters. At last he picked up the phone and called his boss in the Crime Agency.

'You busy?'

'Up and down like a lavatory seat at a beer party.'

Malone grinned to himself. My lovable, dry, flat Aussie. None of your *incredibly busy* or *fantastically busy* of the moderns.

'Greg, can I come and see you?'

'Trouble?'

'I think so.'

'The Vanheusen case?'

'No, the Glaze case.'

Random, finger to the wind like the farmer's son he had once been, asked no more questions. 'I'll be waiting.'

Malone went across to Police Centre in Surry Hills, driving as cautiously through the rain as a latecomer trying to catch up with the Ark. Cars were stalled; pedestrians, skirts and trouser-legs held high, waded

224

through small lakes. A Toyota Landcruiser swept by, its driver sitting up as smug as Noah.

'Get wet?' said Random, grinning as widely as he ever allowed himself to. He was not a dour man, just one economical with expression.

Malone took off his raincoat and hat, put them on the floor and sat down. Random, grey-haired and lean, sat behind his desk, which he hated. His feet still itched for a detective's beat; instead he trod amongst shoals of paper. He had just been added to the police Olympics security team as an adviser, but he expected no excitement there, at least not till 2000.

Malone explained the situation to him. 'Pierpont could be the killer, but how'm I going to prove it? All the evidence points to Glaze.'

'Pierpont will be prosecuting? If he suspects you're on to him, he could nail Glaze to the wall. Do you still think Glaze did it?'

Malone threw up his hands. 'Greg, I dunno. Up till I went down to the committal, yes, I was convinced he'd done it. But then Mrs Colnby came along –'

'If Pierpont is your man, your trail is stone cold, it's four years old. Where do you find someone who saw him and Mrs Glaze together? Do you want to go and put it to him that he's your killer?'

'It might work –'

'Balls it might. You'll have to do better than that. Try some Chinese torture – a dropped hint every so often that you know something. But then are you Irish any good at dropping hints that aren't like sledgehammer blows?'

'I like coming to see you. You fill me with confidence. What sort of advice are you going to give on the Olympics?'

'Run upwind from the torch. You do the same. That way you won't get burnt.' He took out the pipe that Malone had never seen him light. It was a prop, something to fill his hands when he could not grasp a slippery subject. 'Watch it, Scobie. Stick close to Mrs Colnby. She could make things awkward for us.'

Us: Random never left his men and women out on their own like shags on a rock. 'I'll keep you posted.'

6

Tuesday morning there was a call: 'Inspector Malone? This is Sergeant Glover, Telephone Intercept Unit. We've got a trace – well, half a trace – on Vanheusen. He's just called his girlfriend DeeDee Orion. He called from a public phone somewhere on the Gold Coast, he wants her to join him.'

'Did he say where?'

'The usual place, he said. *Their* place was the way he phrased it.'

'Is she going to join him?'

'It was hard to tell – she hung up on him. She sounded pretty pissed off.'

'Righto, keep tapped in on her. We'll follow it up.' He hung up, dialled the two officers on surveillance of DeeDee. 'Where is she now?'

'We're outside a photographic studio in Neutral Bay.' Twenty minutes away, on the other side of the harbour.

'Stay there, don't let her leave before we get there.' He hung up, picked up his hat and went out to the main room. 'Righto Sheryl, we're going to talk to DeeDee Orion.'

The day was fine. Some of yesterday's rain had fallen west of the mountains, out on the plains; maybe Noongulli would be saved for the Hardstaffs for another century and a half. He hoped so: not for Amanda but for heritage and history. The nation was too young to be losing what history it had.

As they drove over the bridge Malone filled Sheryl in; but only on the Vanheusen case, not the Glaze situation. 'When Damien shot through, did you check if he had any hideaways? A farm somewhere or a weekender at some beach?'

'They have a farm up outside Bowral and a house at Whale Beach – the local police are keeping an eye on those, but so far he hasn't showed.'

'Nothing up on the Gold Coast?'

'Nothing we could trace.'

Neutral Bay is a mix of solid old homes, flats and low-rise office blocks; it also has a ribbon of restaurants along its main stem. The office blocks house a collection of advertising agencies and attendant suppliers.

The photographic studio was in a small two-storeyed building where a silk-screen printer had operated in the thirties. The photographer was either a sentimentalist or a fan of old-time film stars. The small lobby downstairs and the stairs that led up to the working floor were lined with old silk-screen posters. Clark Gable smiled at Claudette Colbert; Hardy, as usual, was exasperated with Laurel; Garbo looked every inch the Queen Christina. Malone, a late-night movie fan, paused on the stairs.

'They don't make them like that any more.'

Sheryl was unimpressed. 'They wouldn't get a job today.'

He shook his head at the ignorance and taste of the young.

They went up into the studio where, against a huge roll of white paper, DeeDee Orion was posed in a bright red evening dress, black hair swirled down over one eye. The hair, the gown and the white background were a stark contrast.

'Beautiful! Terrific! Great! Incredible!' The photographer was not a laconic admirer, either of the model or his own genius. Then he turned and saw the two detectives. 'Who the fuck are you?'

Malone held up his badge. 'We'd like to talk to Miss Orion if you could spare her for a few minutes.'

'Can't it wait? We'll be finished in half an hour.' He was a plump young man with dark glasses on top of his head where his hair had once been. He looked as exasperated as Oliver Hardy on the stairs. 'Get some coffee, Geraldo –'

Malone put a hand on the arm of Geraldo, a thin black youth, as he went past. 'Not for us, Geraldo. But maybe Mr Photographer would like one while we talk to Miss Orion.'

'Mr Photographer!' said the photographer. 'Jesus!' Malone waited patiently, then the photographer threw up his hands. 'Okay, ten minutes, everyone. Will that be long enough?' He glared at Malone.

'We'll try. But in police work we're not used to working to a stop watch.'

DeeDee Orion had watched all this without moving from her pose; which, Malone guessed, was a pose within a pose. She was afraid, not the confident girl who had stood in the doorway of the Paddington terrace and told him, *Any time, Mr Malone*. Then she relaxed, stepped out of the backdrop and motioned to some chairs under a far window.

'Sorry to butt in and upset your man,' said Malone.

'Forget it. Tommy likes to play-act the temperamental one – but that's all it is, play-acting. He's sweet, really.'

'I'll apologize on the way out. Nice dress.'

She looked down at it, as if examining it closely for the first time. 'It's one of Damien's new collection. Ironic, eh?'

'At least it's wearable, not like some of that English stuff I saw in *Good Living* the other day.'

'He reads *Good Living*?' DeeDee asked Sheryl.

'Not out in the open,' said Sheryl. 'Where's Damien?'

DeeDee had smiled a couple of times, but the smiles were fleeting, as if borrowed only for the moment. Now she put on the model's mask: 'I haven't the faintest idea.'

'Come on, DeeDee. He spoke to you from the Gold Coast this morning.'

'I'll have to get out of this.'

She slipped out of the dress; she wore only a pair of briefs. Sheryl looked at Malone and grinned. He said, 'Nice weather we're having.'

'Do bare boobs embarrass you?' DeeDee pulled on a robe.

'Not as much as their owner telling lies. We've had a tap on your phone ever since Damien disappeared.'

She bridled, pushing back her hair with a savage flick of her hand. 'You bastards! And you expect me to help you?'

'You'd better, DeeDee. Otherwise we can take you in and hold you for twenty-four hours. It won't be pleasant and your friend Tommy might be upset, losing you . . . You hung up on Damien this morning. You don't want to go and join him?'

She hesitated, then shook her head. The hair fell down again and she pushed it back. 'No.'

'There'd be no future in it, DeeDee. You had a place where you used to go together. Where is it?'

'What happens to him if I tell you?'

'We'll bring him back for questioning.'

'Questioning on what? Not the murder of –? Oh Christ! You can't think he did it!'

'That's what we want to ask him. And why he disappeared all of a sudden. Maybe he's got a perfectly good reason. But we won't know till we talk to him. Where can we find him?'

Again the hesitation; again the sweeping back of the hair. Then: 'He has a flat in Surfers –' She gave the address. 'It's in my name.'

'DeeDee Orion?'

This time the smile wasn't borrowed; now she had committed herself she seemed more relaxed. 'No, Dulcie O'Ryan. My real name.'

'Thanks, Dulcie. I'm sorry, but Constable Dallen is going to have to stay with you till we pick up Damien. We can't have you changing your mind and phoning him.'

'Okay.' She was not angry, just resigned. 'I wouldn't go with him. It's over. He won't come to terms with that. I'd better get back to work –' She slipped out of the robe, pulled on the dress. Her breasts were as good as Malone had seen in a long time. He wondered if Garbo had ever exposed hers to a photographer. 'I'm leaving for New York next week.'

'Good luck, DeeDee. And thanks for the look.'

'What does he mean?' said DeeDee, all innocence.

'He's full of surprises,' said Sheryl.

On the stairs Malone passed Tommy, the photographer. 'I'm sorry we cut into your time.' Then he gestured at the posters on the wall. 'I wonder if Garbo ever bared her tits?'

'No way.' Tommy was agreeable now, no sign of temperament. 'She'd have had no mystery if she'd done that.'

'They don't make 'em like her any more.'

'You said it.' He went on up the stairs, said back over

231

his shoulder, 'Some day it may all come back. But you can't teach a woman mystery, can you?'

Malone paused on the bottom stair. 'I wouldn't want to. I'd know the answers then.'

Tommy looked down at him. 'Did you learn that as a cop?'

'There's no mystery for cops. Only unsolved crimes.'

Tommy thought about that, then nodded. 'Good luck with Damien.'

'How'd you know we were here because of him?'

'I saw the piece about him on *Wanted for Questioning*. You used one of my photos.'

Chapter Seven

1

Damien Vanheusen was picked up by the Queensland police at 11.45 a.m. Chris Gallup sent two of his men up to Surfers Paradise and the Queensland police handed Vanheusen over without argument. No police service likes to play host to another's suspects; it is one of the few aspects of States' rights that is piously observed. Vanheusen himself offered no argument against being taken back to Sydney. Indeed, said one of the escorting officers, he seemed almost relieved to be caught.

He was brought straight from the airport to Homicide and arrived there at 8.15 p.m. Malone had not gone home for dinner. He had phoned Lisa and then, free of *her* surveillance, sent out for two pies, chips, a light beer and a chocolate eclair. Clements joined him with a similar order. When Vanheusen was brought in by Chris Gallup, the two Homicide men were well fed and in the mood for questioning.

Vanheusen had shaved off his moustache, but not his hair. The Roman style was gone and it was parted on the side; Caesar had left the Senate and gone to the suburbs. He looked anonymous, untalented, a man who couldn't design a plain handkerchief.

He was taken into the interview room. Malone and Gallup sat opposite him across the table; Clements, to one side, reversed a chair and straddled it. Malone pointed to the video recorder.

'We're going to tape this, Damien. I have to warn you, anything you say will be recorded and used in evidence. Do you understand?'

'I've done nothing but disappear for a few days. Go ahead, run the tape.'

'You don't want your lawyer?' It was all routine, but it had to be asked.

Vanheusen shook his head; a short forelock fell down, he was halfway to being Roman again. 'I told you, I've done nothing.'

'Why did you disappear?'

'I wanted to think. Things were piling up –'

'What things?'

'Pressure from you people, you cops. The situation with my wife. The grief over –' He stopped for a moment; then said, 'Everything.'

'Did you kill Lucybelle?' Gallup was blunt but not aggressive.

'Christ, no! I know that's what you think, but Jesus – no!'

'Do you know who did?' said Malone quietly.

234

Vanheusen had locked his hands together on the table; he looked at them as if they were cuffed. 'No, I don't.'

'But you suspect someone?'

There was no answer; then Gallup said, 'Where were you the night Lucybelle was kidnapped? You said you were with your girlfriend DeeDee. We've checked, Damien. You weren't – not that night.'

Vanheusen looked at the recorder. 'Can you turn that off for a moment?'

Malone flicked the switch. 'Go ahead.'

'I – I spent the night with Pat Derry.'

'Lady Derry?'

He nodded; and Clements said, 'You get around, don't you?'

'You mean I'm a shit?'

'If you like,' said Clements.

'Damien –' Malone took his time. 'Have you been having an affair with Lady Derry? As well as with DeeDee?'

'No. The other night – it just happened. Okay, a coupla years ago we had a weekend together. But the other night – I went there because she's a family friend –'

'And one thing led to another,' said Clements. 'As they do between family friends.'

Lay off, Russ. But Malone said nothing. The good cop–bad cop routine had its points. Gallup, still blunt but not as unsympathetic as Clements, said, 'Does your wife know about Lady Derry?'

'No.'

'She'll corroborate your story, that you were with her on that night?'

'I think she will – if you don't tell my wife. You'll probably find it hard to believe, but she's Lina's best friend. Lina needs her –'

'Round and round the merry-go-round.' Clements stood up, disgust plain on his big face; he was a good actor. His own morality was not stainless, but since his marriage to Romy he had been as faithful as a hidebound chaplain. He had, however, to be part of the machine that ground or rubbed the truth out of Vanheusen. 'Why should we believe you, Damien? Eh?'

Vanheusen looked up at him. He had unlocked his hands and one of them had nervously ruffled his hair; the Roman fringe had crept down again. He looked more tired than afraid now. Which was a better target in interrogation.

'Because I'm telling the truth. Okay, I'm a shit, if that's what you want to believe. But I'm telling the truth. I had nothing to do with my daughter's death.'

Yes, you did, Damien, even if it was involuntarily. Malone switched on the recorder, said, 'Will you do a saliva test for us?'

'A what?' His brow creased. 'Saliva? What for?'

'A DNA test. We'll compare it with the saliva residue on the ransom envelope. It could clear you, Damien, we'd cross you off our list of suspects.'

'How many suspects have you got?'

'Several,' said Gallup.

Vanheusen looked at him, then at Malone, then at

236

Clements now standing against the wall. Malone suddenly saw the defeat in his face. *He knows we know.*

'Okay,' said Vanheusen and seemed to shrink. 'You've got to get to the truth, I guess.' Then he blinked, seemed to realize what he had said and added, 'About me.'

'That's all we want from you,' said Clements, coming off the wall and giving him a sympathetic pat on the shoulder. 'Come with me and we'll get a doctor to come in and you can give him a swab.'

'Why do we need a doctor?'

'It's procedure, Damien.' Clements was all solicitous now. 'We've got you agreeing to give the swab on video, but just in case you change your mind . . . We'll have a doc here in twenty minutes, he'll take the swab, it goes to the Police Clinical Forensic Medicine Unit, they pass it on to the Forensic Biology Section of the Department of Health.' He smiled, now the really good cop. 'It's bureaucracy, Damien, but it protects you if you're in the clear. We'll know within twenty-four hours that you've been telling the truth. The doc will take a blood sample, too, just to make sure we're not loading you. You'll be in the clear this time tomorrow.'

Vanheusen locked his hands together again, stared at them, then looked at Malone. 'You know who did it, don't you?'

'Yes, Damien. That's why you disappeared, right?'

He nodded, opened his hands, put his face in them and began to sob.

When Malone got home that night Lisa said, 'Problems?'

He kissed her. 'I don't think so. We made progress tonight.'

She led him out to the kitchen, made him tea and toast. 'What did you have for dinner tonight?'

'A salad sandwich and an apple.'

'You're lying. I smelled meat pie on your breath when you kissed me.'

'You want me to take a DNA test?' He loved her, every nook and cranny of her.

'So you picked up Damien Vanheusen. Is he the killer?'

'I'll tell you tomorrow night.'

Then Claire, Maureen and Tom came in, sat around the table and stared at him. Tom said, 'How'd he take it, Mum?'

'I haven't asked him yet.'

'Asked me what? I want this video'd.'

'Not asked – *told* you,' said Maureen with a Communications student's direct approach; not for her the subliminal attack. 'We've decided to buy a second car. Mum needs it.'

'So do you,' he said and his three kids nodded. 'What sort would you like?'

'I'd like a BMW, Tom would like a Porsche and Claire would like a Lexus 400. But we're realistic –'

'You had me worried for a moment.'

'We'll take a Ford Laser or something like that.'

'What colour's the Ford Laser?'

'Dutch blue,' said Lisa. 'That's what they called it.'

'They saw you coming. Righto, Mum runs the bank. Have we got enough money on hand to pay cash, interest accounts or whatever? No loan finance.' He hated loan financing, which made him unpatriotic in the eyes of banks and finance companies.

All four car buyers looked at each other. 'There must be something wrong with him,' said Tom. 'He didn't have a reason for not spending money. I've been reading about guys like him in Economics. They're on the hard Labour left.'

'He's getting more conservative every day,' Malone told his son's mother. 'I'll put Dad on to him.'

'Then it's all settled?' said Claire. 'We can buy the car tomorrow?'

Later in bed Lisa said, 'There's something wrong with you, as Tom said. You do have a problem, don't you?'

'Do you have problems at Town Hall?'

'All the time. If I stay on Olympic public relations I'm going to have problems for the next two or three years.'

'Do I ask you about them?'

'Don't get shirty with me.' She kneed him in the groin and he grunted. 'What's your problem?'

They were close together, face to face; which is too close for serious talk. He lay back on his pillow, took his time; then told her of Ron Glaze and Tim

239

Pierpont and Damien and Lisa Vanheusen. She listened in silence. He turned his head and looked at her when he had finished.

'Have you got problems like that?'

'No. We don't have life and death problems at Town Hall. Throats are cut and people stabbed in the back, but only symbolically.'

'You're sounding like a media release. You left out "at the end of the day".'

'You never mention a cut throat in a media release. It's called "a resignation for personal reasons". Or "he has decided to pursue other interests". What are you going to do?'

'I'd like to pursue other interests.'

Damien Vanheusen was still being held, but if he was released tomorrow would he go home and discuss things like this with his wife? Had Tim Pierpont discussed his crime with his wife?

'With Vanheusen I'll wait till the DNA test clears him. Then we'll tackle his wife . . . Pierpont? I dunno. Greg Random suggested water torture. But how do I do that? I never see him. Do I ring him up, whisper in his ear?'

'What about this woman, the barmaid from the club?'

'She could be a problem, too. If she starts talking –' He reached across and switched off the bedside lamp. 'You're a comfort, darl.'

'So are you.' She kissed him. 'Old Moneybags.'

Next morning he drove out to the Golden West Club. The big car park was virtually empty; somehow it suggested that the big clubhouse was hollow. He wished it was, that it had been. That Norma Glaze and Tim Pierpont had never met in it, that no sign, *All Visitors Welcome*, had been there beside the big doors.

He went up into the club. Charlene Colnby was there on day duty; so was Sharon Garibaldi from Channel 15. They were sitting at a table in the hugely empty room, the poker machines silent, the only sound that of a vacuum cleaner somewhere at the far end of the room. The two women looked up in surprise as he sat down between them.

'I didn't expect to see you, Sharon.'

'I didn't expect to see *you*,' said Charlene Colnby.

'What does Sharon want?'

Sharon Garibaldi, head moving as if she were reading from an autocue, said, 'I saw Mrs Colnby talking to you yesterday morning at the committal. I thought she might have some background on Ron Glaze. He shouted at you across the court.'

'I'm sure Mrs Colnby does have some background on Mr Glaze. But Charlene –' He looked at her. She was not yet in working order, wore no make-up, looked older and – worried? 'You can lay yourself open to contempt of court if you start talking to the media before the trial.' He wasn't sure if that was totally correct, but he was sure he knew more than either of the two women. 'If you want to say something, I'll suggest you're called as a witness when the trial starts. Fair enough?'

'I haven't said anything yet,' said Charlene. 'Miss Garibaldi only just got here. I haven't even offered her a cuppa coffee.' She gestured at the empty table.

'Then we won't keep you, Sharon. If there are any further developments, I'll let you know. You know where to reach me.' He didn't want her going to the police media bureau; he wanted to keep his hands on the reins, loose as they were. He stood up, pulled back her chair but did it politely, every inch the gentleman cop. 'I have to have a word with Mrs Colnby.'

Sharon Garibaldi stood up. She was unruffled, she was used to having chairs pulled from under her, doors shut in her face. 'You got Damien Vanheusen. Is he going to be charged?'

'You'll be the first I'll let know.'

'Is that a policeman's promise?'

'Better than a politician's promise.'

'What isn't?' She gave him a small-screen smile and departed.

He looked around the room, at the banks of poker machines arrayed like temple guardians, sentries that frisked you not on your way in but before you left. 'You play the pokies, Charlene?'

'I used to.'

'Ever win anything worthwhile?'

'If I did, you think I'd still be working behind the bar?' She no longer had the bounce she had had four years ago. But she was as direct: 'Are you doing anything about that guy I pointed out to you?'

'We're working on it. It's not as straightforward as you think, Charlene. You remember him from four years ago? One sighting? A lot of people wouldn't believe that, not on a jury.'

'I told you – I don't forget faces. And other things.'
She held up her right hand, turned her fingers into a
claw. 'He was here that night, definitely.'

'Could it have been another night? The night before,
the night after?'

'You think I'm trying to make things easier for Ron
Glaze, don't you?'

'You are, aren't you? But I'm not saying you're
making all this up. I'm just saying you could've got
your nights mixed.'

She shook her head. 'No way. That was the last night
I saw Norma alive. It was the last night I saw Ron till I
saw him in court yesterday. I saved all the newspapers
the next day on the murder. Two reporters interviewed
me, I got that much –' she held up two fingers half
an inch apart. 'A TV reporter interviewed me, but I
finished up on, waddyacallit? The cutting-room floor.
I remember the night, all right.'

'Did anyone else see him? Have you discussed this
with anyone else?'

She looked away, then back at him. 'Yes. A coupla
women.'

He shook his head in mock annoyance. 'Charlene,
I told you – don't talk about it to anyone. *Anyone* . . .
These women, were they friends of Ron? You said
he was a Wandering Dick. If you'll forgive the
expression.'

She smiled, then was sober. 'Did I say that? You see,
you remember.'

'I have my notes.' He tapped the old notebook he

had unearthed from a bottom drawer. The past is not another country, not for a cop. 'Were they friends of his?'

She hesitated, then said, 'Yes. All three of us, if you really wanna know.'

He held up a hand. 'Charlene, I'm not here to judge you and how it was between you and Ron. I'm really trying to see if we might've been wrong about him. But all I have to go on is your memory of seeing him here in the club that night, that he's left-handed like Ron, that he might've followed Norma outside –'

'Left-handed. You see, that gives you a hint, don't it? Norma was strangled by a man using his left hand –'

'How do you know that?'

'I told you, I've saved everything was in the papers. The coroner's inquest said that was how she died –'

'When did you start believing Ron didn't murder his wife?'

She was quiet a moment, looking towards the far end of the huge room. The vacuum cleaner had been switched off; the room was silent. She looked back at Malone. 'I told you I hadn't seen him till I saw him in court. That's not right. I went to visit him with his sister at Long Bay. I – I really wanted to see for myself if I'd made a mistake when – when I went to bed with him. Ron was always a salesman, he could sell you anything – yeah, including himself.' She paused, as if remembering a particular sale. 'But he wasn't selling anything, not out there at the gaol. He's scared, they're too tough for him there. He was, you know, his real self. His sister and me, we asked for the truth and we got it. That was when I started believing him.'

The doors had been opened; a few members had begun to drift in. Most of them were elderly, greyheads looking for company. A plump white-haired woman stopped by a poker machine, patted it as if it were a friend; she put a coin in the slot, pushed a button. She waited, looked at the combination that had come up on the machine, tut-tutted, patted it again and moved on.

'That's her favourite pokie,' said Charlene Colnby. 'Like a pet. Do you play them?'

'I'm not a clubman, Charlene.' He stood up, put away his notebook. 'I'm lucky so far. I'm not lonely.'

'Lucky you,' she said.

'I'll be in touch. But do me and yourself a favour – don't talk to anyone about the man who was here that night. Leave him to me.'

'You told me he's a Crown Prosecutor.'

'He is. I also told you he's the one who'll be prosecuting Ron Glaze.'

She winced, as if he had hit her. She thought about what he had told her, then she looked up at him. 'Then Ron is stone cold dead.'

'Not necessarily. Leave the man to me. And don't talk to anyone about him. *Anyone*. Not even the two women who were friends of his. You understand?'

'I'm not dumb,' she said, bridling a little.

'No, that's what I want you to be. Not a word to anyone.'

He left her then, wondering how he was going to put the word to Tim Pierpont.

3

'Basically at the end of the day –' said the Prime Minister.

'Basically at the end of the day –' said the Premier.

'Basically at the end of the day –' said the business leader.

'Basically at the end of the day –' said the union official.

'Basically at the end of the day –' said six economists, five bureaucrats, four educationists, three farmers, two medicos and one housewife.

'Basically at the end of the day,' said Con Malone on the phone, 'I gotta be there.'

'Where, Dad?'

'On the picket line, at the demo.'

A national waterfront strike had broken out and was spreading into other industries. Uncertainty about the immediate, even the long-term future was a gathering dark cloud. Down on the wharves violence simmered, rhetoric flew like trapped eagles. Police had been called in, but so far the Service was doing a good job of being impartial.

'You gunna be there?'

'Where, on the wharves? Dad, I'm with Homicide.

We see a demonstration, we run for our lives. It's too dangerous.'

'I'm going down there. It did me heart good to see all them pictures on TV. It was just like the good old days.'

'Dad, the good old days are gone forever.' It was a mantra that sons told their fathers generation after generation. That Tom, already, was telling him.

'You on the side of the gov'ment?' Even over the phone Malone could see the fists coming up.

'No, I'm not on either side. I think the government's been hamfisted, but your blokes won't face up to the facts of life. There's got to be reform, Dad, or the country goes down the gurgler.'

'The country's going to the dogs anyway under this gov'ment.'

'Things are worse in Russia. Even the *Daily Worker* would admit that. Go down to the wharves, Dad, but just yell and shake your fist when the cameras are on you. Don't get into any fights with the police or the scabs. I've got enough problems of my own without having to worry about you.'

'What sorta problems?' Con sounded as if personal problems couldn't be compared with industrial problems.

'Just problems.' *Perhaps if I went on strike I might solve them? Fat chance.* 'Have you still got my cricket bat?'

'I'm taking it down to the wharves with me.'

'Oh Christ!' He sighed, at which he was becoming adept. 'Righto, Dad, enjoy yourself. Just don't get arrested.'

'Look for me on TV –'

Malone hung up in his father's ear as Lisa, dressed for the office, came down the hallway. 'I heard you mention problems.'

'Dad. He's going down to the wharves to turn the clock back.'

'Let him enjoy himself, so long as he doesn't get hurt. The adrenaline will probably take a few years off him. Or a week or two.'

'Mum will worry.'

'When we gave that party for their golden wedding, she told me she had stopped worrying about your father a year after they were married.'

His mother had never confided in him any worries or fears about his father. Would it have been different if he had been a daughter? The white picket fence that was supposed to surround the ideal family home had surrounded three separate hearts in the Malone house.

'She realized,' Lisa was saying, 'she was never going to change him, so she gave up and just waited for him to come home safe each day. Like I do with you.'

'You're a coupla suffering saints, aren't you?'

'We think so. Now you go and solve your problems and I'll go and solve mine.' They were in the front garden now; the new Ford Laser stood in the driveway. 'Having the new car is convenient, but I miss our chats on the way to work. I just talk to other drivers now, mostly abuse.'

He kissed her. 'Don't turn into a road rager.'

She kissed him back. 'I love you. You know something? We have more than a marriage. We still have a love affair.'

He kissed her again, the public-shy lover, right out there in the open.

He drove into Homicide, smiling at the road ragers who hurled abuse at him, went up to his office and Clements came in and laid Damien Vanheusen's DNA report on his desk. 'He's clean. So that leaves just Lina.'

Malone lay back in his chair. 'Do you think she'll give us a DNA test without a fight?'

'No.'

'So what do we do? That's the clincher, the saliva on the envelope. The rest is only suspicion.'

'We can bring her in again, keep at her. Maybe she'll cave in.'

'Maybe. But I doubt it.' Brief acquaintance with Lina Vanheusen had convinced him she was a woman who could build battlements.

'Let's bring Damien back up here. Maybe he'll give us the word on what she told him.'

'We don't know she told him anything. He could be guessing that she did it. We'll get the two of them together again, see what happens when we accuse her in front of him. He's been released?'

Clements nodded. 'He's gone back home.'

'Where we want him. Let's go.' Malone got up, reached for his jacket and hat.

'You want me?' Clements hadn't moved from his couch. 'I've got a pile of bloody paper –'

'Stick it on a nail in the dunny. I want you with me. Two senior men, maybe they'll get the idea that we're serious.'

They drove out to Bellevue Hill through another warm, cloudy day; the weather was as erratic as the people they were dealing with. They saluted the surveillance car, drove down the cul-de-sac and parked in the driveway of the Vanheusen house. A gardener was mowing the lawn of the house next door; he stopped and stared at them, recognized them as cops, nodded to himself and mowed on. A woman came out of a mock-Tudor house, got into the Jaguar in her driveway, stared at them, then backed out and drove slowly away, no doubt watching them in her driving-mirror. Malone pressed the bell of the Vanheusen front door.

It was opened by Mrs Certain. She showed no expression, neither welcoming nor hostile. She had the look of someone who had already left here, had broken her ties with the house.

'They're out by the pool.' *They*: as if her employers were strangers.

'You all right, Mrs Certain?' Malone asked.

She shrugged. 'I wish it were all over and done with.'

'You haven't remembered any more that would help us?'

'No. I'm trying not to remember Lucy. It is difficult.' She turned abruptly and left them standing in the hall.

The two detectives looked at each other. Clements said, 'I don't think you'll get any more out of her. Let's see if we have better luck out by the pool.'

They went through the house and out to the garden. The Vanheusens were sitting on either side of a garden table beneath a large umbrella, but they might have been sitting on either side of a wide street. Both of them were reading, he a newspaper and she a hardcover book. They looked up as Malone and Clements came out through the French doors, but neither said anything at first.

Then Vanheusen said, 'You announce yourselves now, do you?'

Both he and his wife were wearing dark glasses and nothing showed on Lina's face beneath the glasses. Damien's mouth showed only a sour tiredness.

'This won't take long,' said Malone as he and Clements pulled out chairs and sat down. There was little glare from the overcast sky and neither detective put on dark glasses. 'Has your husband told you, Lina, that we had him do a DNA test?'

'Yes.'

She closed her book and put it on the table. It was a novel by Edna O'Brien. Malone had never read her, but Lisa had told him her books lately were never happy ones. He had asked Lisa why she read the books and she told him O'Brien knew the pain that women could go through. He wondered now what Lina was looking for in the O'Brien pages.

'We're doing this to eliminate people from our list. Has he explained to you what needs to be done?'

'Yes.'

'So you will allow us to have a buccal swab taken?'

'No.'

'Why not?' asked Clements.

'I have the right to refuse, haven't I?' She ignored Clements, addressed herself to Malone.

'Yes, you have. But then we'd wonder why you refused.'

'Do you think I killed my daughter?'

'Yes.'

Her face was expressionless; there was no shock, no anger, nothing. Malone had a sudden image of looking at a skull, the dark glasses the eyeless sockets. Then she turned her head towards her husband. 'Did you plant that idea in their stupid heads?'

He was equally expressionless. 'No.'

There was absolute stillness in the garden. The pool was a pane of flat glass, the shrubs and flowers plastic. No sound came from outside: no lawn mower still working, no plane climbing towards faraway places, no child laughing.

'You refuse to take the DNA test?' said Malone.

'Yes.'

Malone stood up. 'Then we're taking you in for further questioning, Mrs Vanheusen. We'll hold you. Then we'll release you. Then we'll bring you in again. And again, if needs be. We call it water torture, the Chinese use it very effectively.'

He ignored Clements' sudden glance at him. Then the big man stood up. 'Do you want to bring something with you, Lina? Some clothes, toilet things?' He was the good cop now, solicitous. 'Overnight in a cell isn't comfortable.'

'And if I refuse to come with you?' She hadn't moved in her chair.

'Darling –' said Damien Vanheusen.

'Shut up!' She didn't look at him, but continued to stare at Clements, unafraid of him. 'If I refuse to move from here?'

'We'll send for a coupla young guys – we older men have to watch our backs – and they'll carry you out. Don't make a fuss, Lina. Bellevue Hill mightn't let you come back.'

'Go with them, darling –'

'Shut *up*!' Still she didn't look at him.

He's superfluous to her requirements, thought Malone. He's been offloaded, down-sized, no longer wanted. She's on her own and she's going to be bloody tough to shift.

Then Lady Derry came out into the garden. She was all smiles, bonhomie barging into the brambles. 'Am I intruding?'

'Not at all,' said Malone. 'We're just taking Mrs Vanheusen into Homicide for questioning.'

'They're not doing anything of the sort, Pat,' said Lina. 'Sit down. The police are leaving.'

Pat Derry hesitated, the smile suddenly gone, then she sat down on the chair vacated by Clements. All at once she was unsure of herself, all that party confidence gone in an atmosphere where there was no party at all. 'I think I *am* intruding. Am I, Damien?'

Vanheusen almost shuddered with the depth of his sigh. He took off the dark glasses and pinched the bridge of his nose. 'I don't think it matters, Pat. Lina seems to think the police can be told to go to hell. Maybe you can talk some sense into her.'

Malone and Clements were still standing, both silent. Pat Derry put a hand on Lina's arm. 'Can I help, darling?'

'No, darling, you can't.' Lina removed the hand from her arm as if she were taking off a bracelet. 'I'm perfectly okay.'

'You're not perfectly okay, Mrs Vanheusen.' Malone's voice was as formal as a bishop's; or a judge's. 'You are suspected of murder and we want to question you.'

'Oh shit!' said Lady Derry, unladylike. 'This is ridiculous! Murdering who? Her own child?'

Malone was watching Lina. Under the dark glasses the claypan of composure looked as if it might break. There was a tremor of emotion round the mouth, the jawline was more pronounced.

'Damien, can't you do something?' Pat Derry threw out a hand towards him.

'I've done something. I took the DNA test, just as they want Lina to do.'

He's abandoning her, thought Malone, just as she's cut

254

him loose. He's a shit, in a way he contributed towards the little girl's death, yet he's leaving her to us. Malone felt a sudden sour spasm of revulsion. *I should've gone down to the wharves with Dad.*

'Mrs Vanheusen,' he said quietly, 'you are only making it more difficult for yourself. Come in to Homicide, take the DNA test and you'll be back here within an hour.'

She abruptly stood up; her chair teetered as she pushed it back but didn't fall over. 'I'll come with you, but I won't take the test. You can put me in that cell,' she told Clements. 'Again and again.'

'And we will,' said Clements.

'Darling –' said Pat Derry, but said no more and didn't rise from her chair.

'I'll get you some things –' Damien Vanheusen turned towards the house.

'Never mind, I'll get them myself,' she said and almost ran into the house, calling for Mrs Certain.

Malone nodded to Clements. 'Better keep an eye on her.'

Clements went into the house. Vanheusen hadn't moved, as if he had been stopped in mid-stride by his wife's refusal to let him help her. Now he put his dark glasses back on and walked to the edge of the pool, stood there as if contemplating whether he should dive into it.

Then he turned back to Malone. 'What did you mean – better keep an eye on her? You think she'll commit suicide?'

'Oh Christ no!' Lady Derry straightened in her chair,

but didn't stand up, as if afraid that her legs wouldn't carry her.

Vanheusen shook his head. 'No, not Lina. She'll never take the easy way out. It is easy, isn't it?' he asked Malone.

'It is for some. I agree with you – it wouldn't be for your wife.'

'Is it true?' said Lady Derry. 'Did she kill Lucybelle?'

'We haven't charged her yet. If the DNA test proves negative, then we have no more against her than we have against anyone else. Has she talked to you about the child?'

Lady Derry frowned; then shook her head. 'Come to think of it – no. She's just been – *numb* about it all. Isn't that so, Damien?'

'What?' He had gone back to contemplating the pool. 'I wasn't listening.'

'Lina hasn't really talked about Lucybelle and what happened, not to me. Has she to you?'

'No,' he said, then looked at Malone. 'I'd better go and ring the lawyers. Someone should be there with her, shouldn't they?'

'I'll go with her,' said Lady Derry, rising at last.

'No,' said Malone. 'From now on she's going to need legal eagles more than she'll need friends.'

The legal eagle might have been sent by a casting agent. She was blonde and attractive, wore a dark suit with shoulders that suggested they could carry a million-dollar litigation or a murder defence and her black leather briefcase looked as if it might hold High Court secrets. Her name was Lydia Wilkox and she gave the impression she had little time for police officers, especially male ones.

There were three of them in the interview room: Malone, Clements and Chris Gallup. Malone, sticking to protocol, had invited Gallup into Homicide. After all, it was his men who were still the task force, still doing the legwork. The ones who never got to sit in on the interesting part, the interrogation.

'My client has the right to refuse to take this test,' said Ms Wilkox.

'Every right,' said Gallup. 'We don't dispute that. But why does she refuse? Health reasons?'

Neither of the two women answered that, so Malone, changing tack, said, 'We're going to charge you eventually, Lina. Your only hope is to take the DNA test and prove you had nothing to do with the kidnap note.'

'You're bluffing,' said Lydia Wilkox. She had the calm, almost unnatural air that lawyers took on, like a cloak, in these interrogations. Malone had seen it count-less times. They had nothing to lose, except a client.

'I don't think you know me, Miz Wilkox. I've charged – how many murderers, Russ?'

'Two hundred and eighteen, last count,' said Clements, lying like a pyramid salesman. 'You were wrong fourteen times, they were acquitted.'

Ms Wilkox smiled. 'Too glib, Sergeant. Try the other leg.'

Malone smiled, but at Lina Vanheusen. 'You have a good lawyer, Lina. But I'm still going to take my chances with you. The question is, will you take your chances?'

'Yes,' said Lina, speaking for the first time since the detectives had come into the room after she had conferred with her lawyer. 'Yes, I shall.'

There was silence for a moment, then Lydia Wilkox said, 'My client has called your bluff, Inspector.'

'I don't think so. What will she say when we call her husband to give evidence against her?'

He was watching Lina, but she showed no reaction. Her lawyer said, 'He was the one who called me in on this case. I don't believe he will give evidence against my client. He is her loving husband.'

'Is that what he is, Lina? Your loving husband, who'd moved out to sleep with DeeDee Orion?'

She had been sitting very still, expressionless; her face was like the face of a blind person. She sat in a sudden silence all her own. Her dark eyes were empty; or behind battlements of glass. She sat like that for almost a minute, then her eyes focused, she looked across the table at Malone, ignoring Gallup and Clements. He was the sole enemy.

'I am not taking the test. Lock me up.'

'Scobie, this is Jack Annabel.' A uniformed inspector whom Malone had known for twenty years. 'Can you come down to Day Street and take your old man off our hands?'

Malone groaned. 'What's he done?'

'We had to move him and forty others off the roadway, they were blocking the entrance to a wharf, stopping scab trucks from getting through.' There was no doubt where Annabel's sympathy lay in the dock strike. 'We brought them back here, gave them a lecture about law and order –' Malone could imagine the tongue in the cheek – 'then we released them without charging them. But your old man won't leave.'

'What's he doing?'

'He's got a cricket bat, waving it around, threatening to dent the skulls of my men. We don't want to charge him, Scobie. If we do that we'll have to charge the lot of them and the bloody place will be chock-a-block.'

'Righto, Jack,' said Malone wearily. 'I'll be down. Tell him if he clocks anyone with that bat, I'll do the same to him.'

'I wouldn't fancy your chances, mate. He's dangerous.'

Lina Vanheusen had been taken away by Chris Gallup and one of his men to Surry Hills station. She would be kept in the cells there, then released. Malone had threatened to pick her up again, but he doubted that he would. The water torture was not going to work on Lina Vanheusen.

He had a moment alone with Lydia Wilkox before she accompanied Lina to Surry Hills. 'Try and talk some sense into her, Lydia.'

'You think she kidnapped and killed the child?'

He nodded.

'Your sergeant said you'd been wrong before. Fourteen times, wasn't that the figure?'

'Fourteen acquittals.' He hadn't a clue how many acquittals there had been; though Irish, he never lingered over his losses. 'That didn't say we'd been wrong in all of them.'

'You have been wrong, though?'

'Yes.' *Don't ask when.*

'You may be wrong this time too, Inspector.'

Now he told Clements where he was going and the big man grinned 'This must be like Christmas for Con. Another big wharfie strike. Ask him while you're down there why, if the wharfies are so overworked, so many of them are overweight. Good luck, sport.' He held up a clenched fist, a familiar sight on television this past week.

'Up yours,' said Malone and gave him the middle finger salute. As he went out the door he saw Sheryl Dallen and Gail Lee smile at each other. He could read their unspoken thoughts: *There's the blokey culture for you.*

At Day Street station there was only one demonstrator still making a nuisance of himself. Con Malone was in the front section sitting on a chair below the counter, hands resting on the cricket bat as on a walking stick. He looked up as Malone came in, but didn't rise.

'What you doing here?'

'Relax, Dad. I'm the cavalry . . . Where's Inspector Annabel?' he asked the policewoman on the counter.

'He's gone back to the docks. He told me to give over Mr Malone to your charge.'

'Where are the forty other blokes who were brought in?'

'We let them go, sir.' She grinned. 'They're probably all back at the demo.'

'Where I should be,' said Con, still on his chair, still leaning on the cricket bat.

'No, Dad, your day is over. Figuratively and actually.'

'Don't try your fancy words on me –'

But Con knew the truth of it. It was there in the gullies of his face, in the sudden tiredness in the rheumy eyes. It happened to all old men: in sport, politics, the workplace. Malone felt an abrupt welling of affection and sympathy for his old man. Yet in it, as at the core of all sympathy, was the often unrecognized selfish wish: don't let it happen to me.

Con stood up, slowly. 'We're gunna win, y'know.'

'Maybe, Dad. There'll be court cases and court cases and in the end only the lawyers will win.'

'Those buggers ever go on strike?'

'You kidding?'

He drove his father back to Erskineville. The old

261

man was silent all the way, holding the cricket bat like a totem.

'Would you have used that?' Malone asked at one point.

Con shrugged, but said nothing. The past was suddenly gone; from now on even his memory would have trouble grasping it. All at once he looked lonely, as if he had been deserted.

When they drew up he made no attempt to move. 'Don't get out. You and Mum'll only be picking at me.'

Malone, more wearied even than his father, sat back in the corner of the seat. 'Dad, I've got enough problems of my own. I'm not going to add to them by arguing with you.'

Con looked sideways at him, a glimmer of sympathy in the still-shrewd eyes. 'They getting you down?'

'Yeah.'

'Maybe your day is over, too.' For a moment there was a smear of malice; then he grinned. 'You wanna talk about it?'

'I can't, Dad. I'd like to –' He put his hand on his father's shoulder; the first time he had done that in God knew how long. 'I warn witnesses about contempt of court.'

'You talk to Lisa about your problems?'

It was Malone's turn to grin. 'Of course. What would you choose – contempt of court or contempt of Mum? I've got two cases where pretty soon I'll be banging my head against a wall. You know the cases, you've read about them, but I can't discuss them with you. But sometimes I wish I had that –' He nodded at the cricket bat. 'There's a simple logic to what you were going to do with that today.'

Con looked straight ahead; two Wogs were crossing *his* street, but he didn't see them. 'No, I don't think I would of. It would of been like Mum's handbag she carries everywhere with her. What d'you call it?'

'All old ladies have it. Their comfort bag.'

'Yeah, that would of been it.' He held it up, grinning again. 'You want it?'

As he drove away Malone saw his mother open the front door. She stood there waiting for Con, on her face the mix of patience and exasperation that, he guessed, she had worn from the day after her wedding. He couldn't see whether she was holding her comfort bag.

Chapter Eight

1

Lina Vanheusen was released from the cells and called for by Pat Derry, her best friend and her husband's one-night lover. Chris Gallup arranged that she should be kept under surveillance, this time with no attempt to be discreet. The surveillance car was to be parked in the cul-de-sac, the officers in uniform. The aloof dignity was being challenged. Lina soon would be more unwelcome than land tax.

Malone, relieved of one problem for the moment, decided to tackle the other one head-on. He checked that Tim Pierpont was in the DPP offices for the day and made an appointment.

'What's it about, Scobie?'

'I've got more evidence. I want to discuss it with you.'

'The Glaze case?'

'What else?'

Malone decided to walk in to the DPP offices. It took him no more than twenty minutes, but that gave him time to marshal his approach. He was about to ask a Crown Prosecutor, no matter how circuitously, if he was a murderer. People passed him, some laughing at each other, others grim as if heading for suicide. A bag lady stood on a corner under a traffic light, her vehicle a pram loaded with other people's discards; she looked up at the traffic light, as if wondering which green light to follow, as if destinations meant something to her. She gave him a gap-toothed smile out of a face that looked as if it had been brushed with brown boot polish; he knew he had seen her somewhere but couldn't remember where. Then as he passed on he remembered: he had sat beside her on a bus when he had been on another case, where the options had been no less daunting than on this one. The more things change . . . Lisa had once quoted the French sentence to him and she hadn't needed to translate. He knew the truth of it.

He walked on, pushing his own vehicle of thoughts ahead of him. Would Pierpont blow up or give him a tired smile?

The prosecutor greeted him with a smile. 'Nice to see you, Scobie. Coffee?'

'Thanks, Tim, but I think I'd rather get down to what's brought me here.'

'Shoot.' Pierpont sat back, elbow on his chair-arm, his jaw resting on his claw hand.

Malone decided to be point-blank, but with a silencer; he said quietly, almost casually, 'Tim, why didn't you

265

tell me you were at the Golden West Club the night Norma Glaze was murdered?'

Pierpont didn't blink, didn't move. Then he looked back over Malone's shoulder. 'Dave, what can I do for you?'

David Winkler looked as if he had just emerged from a wind tunnel. His hair was awry, one sleeve was rolled up, the other hung loose, his tie was trying to flee over his shoulder. 'I wanted to ask – Scobie! How are you, old chap? Bringing us problems?'

'Not really, Dave. I'm just bringing Tim some more evidence in the Glaze case.'

'There always is, isn't there? More evidence than you need, more than you can use. Why do we have to complicate life with it? You're also on the Vanheusen case, aren't you? How's it going?'

Malone held up finger and thumb an inch apart. 'That close.'

'You got a suspect?'

'The mother, if we can get her to take a DNA test.'

'Hah! What did we do before we discovered DNA? If and when we get that one, would you like to take it, Tim?'

'I think I might,' said Pierpont, still relaxed in his chair, though his claw hand was no longer holding up his jaw. 'Put me on the list. What do you want, Dave?'

'It can wait, I'll come back later. Sorry to interrupt. Look after yourself, Scobie old chap. Keep bringing us more interesting cases. The cut-and-dried ones are a bore.' He dragged his tie from over his shoulder, looked at it as if he hadn't seen it before. 'Ghastly, isn't it? A present from my kids. Remember the flares and the haircuts we had in the seventies? The nineties are the decade of dreadful ties. Yours is tasteful, Scobie.'

'Anonymity,' said Malone. 'I dress for it all the time.'

'With a pork-pie hat? Cheerio, old chap!'

Then he was gone. Malone looked at the open doorway. 'Mind if we close it?' He got up, shut the door and sat down again. 'Why didn't you tell me you were at the club that night?'

'Because I wasn't there.' His phone rang and he reached for it.

'Tell 'em to call back,' said Malone. 'You're engaged.'

Pierpont stared at him, lifted the phone, then put it back in its cradle. Then he took it off again and laid it on the desk. 'I wasn't there, not on the night you're talking about.'

'You admit you've been there?'

'Just the once. I'd been up to one of the Blue Mountains courts, Katoomba or Blackheath, I can't remember which, and I stopped off there on my way back. It was a week or ten days before the murder. I can look up my court list, if you like.'

'I've done that. You were at Katoomba on the day of the murder.'

'Possibly. I was also there the week before, there or Blackheath.'

Malone felt a prick of doubt, but it didn't show. 'I have to admire you, Tim.'

'Why?'

'Most fellers would've denied ever going near the club. But I have to tell you, you've got your dates wrong. You've been identified. There were a dozen or more visitors the night of the murder – you were the only one who didn't sign the visitors book. Because you came in late and no one was on the door, it was a quiet night. That – and your hand, Tim. The witness is absolutely certain you were at the club on the night of the murder.

'They're wrong, whoever he or she is.'

'Actually, there are three.' He had to protect Charlene Colnby. 'Did you talk to Mrs Glaze out in the car park?'

'No.'

Malone sat still for a long moment, then said, 'Why aren't you flying off the handle, Tim, at what I might be suggesting?'

'I don't know what you might be suggesting.'

Malone smiled in admiration. 'You're good . . . I might be suggesting you had something to do with the murder. How does that strike you?'

'This is the moment I'm supposed to fly off the handle?' Pierpont shook his head. 'I don't react like that, Scobie. I'm not hot-tempered. Anyone will tell you that.'

'You might've been hot-tempered with Mrs Glaze.'

The claw stroked his cheek; he said nothing, waited for Malone to go on. But Malone had noticed the increasing tension in the prosecutor's other hand. Barely perceptible, but it was there.

'She was throttled by a left hand, no other marks. That was what put us on to Ron Glaze, that and he being her husband and separated from her.'

'So you've got your killer. Why do you want another one?'

'We're having our doubts now about Ron.'

The claw moved from the cheek to tap the file on Pierpont's desk. 'I got this out, to re-read it when you told me you were coming. There's none of your doubt in here.'

'We didn't know about you when that was prepared.'

There was a knock at the door and a secretary poked her head in. 'Tim, Judge Bilson is trying –' Then she saw the phone lying on the desk. 'Oh, you don't want to be interrupted?'

'Tell Bilson I'll call him back.' The secretary closed the door and Pierpont smiled without humour at Malone. 'Won't it be a coincidence if we get Bilson J. presiding at Glaze's trial? Maybe that's what he's calling me about. He was on the Family Court for a short time, but they moved him back. He was too tough on erring husbands.'

'What about erring wives? Did Norma invite you home?'

Pierpont was no longer smiling, with or without humour. The hand on his desk, the good hand, was tightly clenched. 'Isn't it about now you ask me if I'd like my lawyer present? Shall I call in Dave Winkler?'

The pauses between them now were part of the game: a serious game but nevertheless a game. 'Tim, call in

269

whom you like – but I don't think it will be Dave Winkler. I don't know you at all well. You may be a perfectly nice bloke who got himself involved in something he didn't expect. I've handled a dozen cases like that. The woman was as much to blame for her own murder as the man.'

'The feminists would chop your balls off for that suggestion.'

'Maybe. But feminists don't have the copyright on truth. Virtually all of them don't have my experience, either . . . Was that how it happened between you and Norma Glaze?'

'No. Because, as I've told you, I never met the woman.' He leaned forward, put the phone back in its cradle. 'If you think I had something to do with that murder, then withdraw the case against Mr Glaze.'

'You know I can't do that. It's out of our hands, it's all yours now.' Malone stood up. 'I came in here, Tim, not sure about you and Mrs Glaze. But now I am. You were there at the club that night and you went home with her. Ron Glaze didn't kill his wife. I think you did.'

Pierpont just looked up at him. 'On the flimsy evidence you have, if you bring it in here the DPP will throw it out. I'll see you in court when Ron Glaze goes on trial.'

'No,' said Malone. 'You'll see me before that.'

Tim Pierpont went home that evening in a depression as dark as a pocket. In the train a Turramurra neighbour, sitting across from him, wanted to discuss the docks strike, but he pleaded a bad migraine and turned to look out the window. He watched the sun go down in a wildfire of blazing cloud, but he saw none of the beauty of it. It just looked like the end of the world.

Going down the hill from the station, slipping occasionally on the last of the crepe myrtle snow, his neighbour caught up with him. 'You look pretty peaked, Tim.'

'I've had one or two migraines lately.' He had had them off and on for four years.

'You'll be okay for Saturday week?'

Pierpont stared at him blankly: Saturday was somewhere in the middle of the next century.

'The protest up at Springwood.' Tod Ulrich was a fellow conservationist. 'That new development they're planning. We've got to stop it.'

'Oh sure.' Who cared about conserving the landscape when his own had been devastated? 'Yeah, Ginny and I'll be there.'

'Our job's getting harder. The government doesn't back us.'

'Yeah, all the time.' He turned into his own street. 'See you Saturday.'

'Sure. Hope the headache clears up. Have a cuppa tea, a Bex and a nice lie-down.' Ulrich went off, grinning widely at the old joke. Poor humorists, unfortunately, are not an endangered species. No conservationist would lift a finger to save them.

Pierpont turned in at his gate. Now the evenings were cooler, Ginny and Fay no longer waited for him on the front verandah. He stood a moment staring at the house, at the closed front door; Ginny, who could be absent-minded, had forgotten to turn on the light in the hallway. The house, all of a sudden, looked deserted. *There's no one in it, no one to welcome me, no one I can confide in*!

Then the light went on, the door opened and Ginny was pushed aside as Fay rushed out to fling herself at him from the top of the three steps that led up to the verandah. She was fearless, had complete faith in him. *Oh Christ*; he wept inwardly. He gathered her to him, holding her tightly to protect her against the demons that surrounded him.

Ginny said, 'Sorry. I forgot the light. It's just been one of those days . . . You look tired.'

'One of those days,' he said. 'What's for dinner?'

'I got something from Pizza Hut,' she said apologetically. 'I just didn't feel up to cooking. I had morning sickness this afternoon.'

Pizza, his least favourite food after hamburger; but what did it matter since he had no appetite? He kissed her, put an arm round her while Fay struggled in behind him lugging his briefcase. 'Morning sickness in the afternoon?'

'You know me. If I can turn things upside down, I will.'

'Never mind, I'll get out a good bottle of shiraz. Though pizza deserves Grange Hermitage.'

Jesus, he thought, my jokes are as bad as Tod Ulrich's.

'Have your shower,' she said. 'Twenty minutes and everything will be ready.'

'What's for dessert?'

'Chocolate mousse.'

His least favourite dessert. Was God, in whom he didn't believe, laughing at him all through this day? Then Fay dropped his heavy briefcase on his instep and with her gurgling laugh looked up at him with satanic glee as he yelped.

He went into the bedroom, stripped off and went into the bathroom and stood under the shower. It was some minutes before he realized he couldn't tell the water from the tears streaming down his face.

3

'How'd you go?' asked Greg Random.

'I think the first round was a draw.' Malone was on the phone to his boss. 'He's cool and smart. I think I'm going to be pouring a lot of water before I wear him down. He's iron, not sandstone.'

'Do you think he did it?'

'Yes, I do. But he's never going to admit it.'

'So what about Glaze? He's the DPP's pigeon, but we can't let him go to gaol if he didn't do it. Can you talk to Dave Winkler?'

'How? If someone came to you and said Scobie Malone had committed a murder that someone else was on trial for, but he had only the flimsiest evidence that Malone was the killer, what would you do?'

Random was silent, sorting that one out in his mind. Malone knew him well: Random never jumped off a springboard till he was sure he was at the deep end of a pool. Then he said slowly, 'I'd make sure the other guy didn't go to gaol. Having said that, I haven't a clue at the moment how to go about it. As we get closer to Glaze's trial, I think we may have to go higher, as far as the Commissioner and the Minister and the Attorney-General –'

'Shit.' It was turning into a steeplechase. He could see the political hurdles that would suddenly be there, the inevitable inquiry that was always called for when politica got into police action.

'Exactly,' said Random. 'You'll need more evidence, Scobie, a lot more. In the meantime . . .'

'In the meantime I've got another headache, the Vanheusen woman. I think I may resign, get a job with the Olympics, chasing swimmers on steroids.'

'Stay where you are. You'd be swamped by FINA, IOC, AOC, SOCOG and all the rest of the alphabet. Stay with it, Scobie. We'll find a way out.'

'That's what the captain said when the *Titanic* went down.'

In the meantime . . . In the meantime there was Lina Vanheusen. Malone picked up the phone again and rang Gallup. 'Chris, get your men to bring in Mrs Vanheusen again. No, not here. Take her to Waverley. Clear everyone out of the incident room and have one of your men – not you – put her in there on her own so's she can have a look at what she did. Then bring her into your interview room – apologize if you have to, but only if she asks. Ask her if she wants Miz Wilcox – she probably will. I'll see you in twenty minutes. If she gets shirty about being put in the incident room with all those *horrible* photos, I may have to chide you.'

'I've never been *chided* before. Thanks.'

Malone drove out to Waverley through an afternoon tinged with autumn. Leaves drifted in gutters, shadows had a softer edge. His car radio told him the docks dispute had now moved from the chill air of the wharves to the hot air of the courts. Black-gowned lawyers were gathering like crows in a field of spilled grain; argument would wash backwards and forwards in a thick sea of words. Malone just hoped that Con would not head for the law courts with the cricket bat. Then, again, he grinned at the prospect.

When he arrived at Waverley police station Lina Vanheusen had already been taken to the interview room. 'How'd she react when you put her in front of the flow chart?'

'I had one of my guys observe her through a doorway at the end of the room – she didn't know he was there. There was no reaction from her. He said she stood in front of the flow chart and looked as

275

if she was in some bloody art gallery. She's a cold-blooded bitch.'

'That, or she thinks she did the little girl a favour. I think she's part way round the bend, but she'll never agree to us calling in a psychiatrist. We'll try it on her, but neither she nor her lawyer are going to say yes. Not at this stage.'

'She's asked for the lawyer – oh, here she is.'

Lydia Wilcox, dressed in a powder-blue suit today, strode in, guns blazing. 'This is bloody outrageous! What are you trying to do to my client?'

'Trying to get her to confess she killed her daughter. Hold it a minute –' as the lawyer went to protest. He was not sure that Ms Wilcox's attitude wasn't partly show; she still had to defend a client who so far hadn't shown much co-operation with anyone, including her. 'Miz Wilcox, Lina did it, no two ways about it. She may have been out of her mind when she did it, but the planning was cold-blooded. Breaking the alarm system, drugging the child so she wouldn't be any trouble . . . We won't object if you'd like to call in a psychiatrist, will we, Chris?'

'I think it'd be a good idea.' Gallup was learning to catch every ball Malone threw at him.

Lydia Wilcox put her guns away. 'You're suggesting there could be a temporary insanity plea? I don't think you're ever going to get that out of Lina.'

'If she recognizes the inevitable, she might.'

'I don't think she recognizes there is any inevitable. I've never dealt with such a self-contained client.'

'Self-contained? The shell could be thinner than we think.'

'You're absolutely sure she did it?'

'Certain.' *Just as I was about Ron Glaze*. But no doubt showed in his face.

'I'm as certain as Scobie,' said Gallup, who had no doubts.

'Tch, tch.' She considered the suggestion, then looked at both men. 'Let me have five minutes alone with her. I shan't make a deal with you now – I'd have to talk to counsel about it. That is, if she agrees. Which I doubt. You know what she's like. You probably know her better than I do now.'

'I don't think anyone knows her,' said Malone. 'Maybe not even herself.'

'What about Damien?' She said his name as if it were a disease. At least Lina had influenced her that far.

'I don't think he knows her – or anyway, understands her. Which, I guess, is the same thing between husband and wife. Good luck with her.' The chill had gone out of Ms Wilcox; he had convinced her that police were not the enemy. He had also recognized that they needed her on side. 'Five minutes, Lydia. More if you think you're getting somewhere with her.'

Ten minutes later Lydia Wilcox opened the door of the interview room and shook her head. 'My client wants to know how long this charade is going to go on.'

Malone and Gallup went into the room, sat down

opposite Lina Vanheusen. The room was stuffy, but Lina was doing her best to put a chill on it.

'It's going to go on for quite a while yet, Lina. Maybe Mrs Vanheusen would like a glass of water, Chris?'

Gallup looked startled that he should be a drinks waiter, but he got up and went out of the room.

'This can go on indefinitely, Lina, unless Miz Wilkox wants to get an order to stop us. But we can keep coming back at you on one pretext or another. We're great ones for pretexts. Ask Miz Wilkox or any lawyer. Right, Lydia?'

'All the time,' said Ms Wilkox, playing the game.

'Oh thanks, Chris –' Gallup had come back into the room with a glass of water. Malone took it and pushed it across the table towards Lina. 'Would you like an aspirin?'

'If I have a headache,' said Lina, 'it's only because of you.'

'We'll be giving you plenty more if you won't take the DNA test and clear yourself. Do you want an aspirin?'

Lina Vanheusen was feeling the strain. She looked tired, appeared even thinner than usual. But there was no surrender. 'The water will do. I should throw it in your face.'

Malone faced her. 'Do it, Lina, if it'll loosen you up.'

Beside him he felt Gallup ease himself slightly backwards so that he wouldn't be splashed. Lydia Wilkox frowned, as if to say, *You're goading her too far. I'll have to intervene.*

Lina's hand tightened on the glass. She stared at Malone and for a moment he was certain she would hurl the glass itself at him; his hands moved, ready to go up and protect his face. Then she drew in her breath, sucking it through her teeth, and raised the glass and drank.

When she put down the glass he reached for it. 'Thanks, Lina. There'll be saliva on the outer rim of the glass. Not much, but enough for the DNA test.'

'You bastard!'

'Every other inch, Lina. We often have to be.'

'You know you can't do that, Inspector.' He was surprised at how patient Lydia Wilkox sounded; or resigned. 'You're grandstanding.'

Of course he was. Forensic would not accept the sample without a doctor's certificate and he was not even sure that the rim of the glass would show any saliva. But: 'We can do what we like unofficially. We'll have it tested and it will prove we are right – that Lina killed her daughter Lucybelle. We won't produce it in court, but we'll have enough evidence to keep pestering you, Lina. Giving you a headache that will go on and on.'

'You haven't taped any of this,' said the lawyer, nodding at the video recorder. 'Why?'

'It's broke,' said Gallup, who had been this route before.

'But if my client decided to make a statement, it could be fixed in a jiffy?'

'Probably sooner,' said Gallup.

Then Lina Vanheusen abruptly said, 'I'll take the DNA test. Call the doctor. The police doctor, not my own.'

Somewhere deep inside her, Malone thought, she still has some shame.

4

'How's it going?' said Greg Random.

'Mrs Vanheusen took the DNA test.'

'What made her change her mind?'

'Search me. She could've been deaf and dumb for all we got out of her after she said she'd take the test. She didn't even speak to the doc when he came. The swab's gone off to the Forensic Biology Section. We just have to wait on them.'

Random was silent for a while; then he said, 'The other matter, Scobie. I took it to Charlie Hassett.'

Hassett was the Assistant Commissioner, Crime. Malone said carefully, 'You jumped the gun, Greg.'

'No, I didn't.' Random was patient, not tart. 'We're heading for what might be a serious situation. I filled him in on the Glaze case and what you think about Pierpont. He wants to see us at eleven. Pick me up.'

Random had not sounded irritated, but his abrupt finish to the call was enough. *Don't tell me how to run my show, Scobie*. Malone replaced the receiver, wondered why Random wanted to be picked up when he was only five minutes' walk from Police Headquarters.

He looked up as Clements came into his office with some papers

'You look as if someone just shat in your lap.'

Malone told him about Random's call. 'I think I'm going up to Headquarters to get my arse kicked. Or sent to Tibooburra.'

Tibooburra was the remotest posting in the State. If he finished up there, Clements would send him food parcels.

'It'll be worth it if they take the responsibility. I think you're in a no-win situation, sport. Let someone else carry the can.'

'You think it's going to be that easy?'

'No. But you're gunna have to be diplomatic or smarmy or whatever it is that's needed when you admit someone from HQ might have a better idea than yours. You'll never learn, will you?'

Malone handed back the papers Clements had given him. 'Take care of these, Sergeant.'

'I'll do that, *sir*. So long as you take my advice. Anyone will tell you that the nitty-gritty intelligence in the Service is always with the sergeants.' He patted Malone on the back as the latter passed him on his way out. 'Good luck, mate.'

Malone drove over to Police Central and picked up Random. The latter got into the car and said, 'We don't discuss it till we've seen Charlie, okay? We'll talk about the weather or the wharfies or Welsh poets –'

'Not Welsh poets. You're such a melancholy lot.'

'My mother, who was from the Valleys, told me we

had a lot to be melancholy about. You might have, too, if you don't accept whatever Charlie Hassett tells you. Don't be Irish and stubborn, Scobie. Listen to the voice of reason.'

'Yours or Charlie's?'

Random shook his head in despair. 'Why did St Patrick bother to drive the snakes out of Ireland?'

'He didn't. They left of their own accord. We'd talked them blind.'

'Well, keep your mouth shut while Charlie is talking to you.'

Police Headquarters stands on College Street, an appropriate address in the eyes of those in the Outback of the Service, which was everywhere in the rest of the State. It is a college of blue-suited cardinals; Commissioner Zanuch is looked upon as a fallible Pope. It is housed in a building as characterless as a silo. It is neighbour to one of the city's most prestigious private schools; stands across the road from Hyde Park, the city's green lung; and is half a block north of Oxford Street, the gay community's main artery. Earlier commissioners and assistant commissioners would have died of apoplexy had the gay community been so close in their day.

Charlie Hassett was an old school officer, but he had risen through the ranks on merit, not seniority. He wore his sleeves rolled up above his elbows and a scowl that suggested continual bad temper. He had used a sledgehammer in the old days and spoke nostalgically of those simpler, more direct approaches. But it was all a façade. Behind the gorilla stance there was an acute intelligence and a sympathy that he seemed embarrassed to show.

He walked up and down his office as he talked to Malone and Random. 'Holy Jesus, you buggers like stirring the pot!'

'Charlie, that's not true,' said Random calmly.

'Well, whether you meant to or not, the pot'll boil over if we take this any further. You've seen what the pollies down in Macquarie Street are on about – clean up the streets, wipe out violent crime, let's have law and bloody order! Jesus!' He hit his forehead with his open hand; it would have knocked out a lesser man. 'What the hell got into you, Scobie?'

'I didn't go looking for it, sir. This woman, the bar-maid at the club, she came to me –'

'She's the only one?'

Malone could see the gate ready to be shut. 'Yes, sir. I think she's probably mentioned it to one or two of her friends –'

'Bloody women!'

'Yes, sir.' Malone felt he had better agree for the moment. 'She's the only one who remembers him at the club that night.'

'And he claims he was there another night? Scobie, it's got more holes in it than a Macquarie Street promise. You've got one witness – *one* –' he held up a finger as thick as a mining peg. 'She didn't see him talking to the victim, she didn't see him follow her out to the car park. She's sure it was the night in question, but he says it was another night – and there's nothing in

283

the visitors book to substantiate what either of them's claiming.'

'I know all that, sir, but I'm sure Pierpont was the killer.'

'You're stubborn, aren't you?'

'He's Irish,' said Random.

'So am I – well, two generations back. Maybe that's enough to make me see reason – what're you grinning at?'

'I told him on the way here,' said Random, 'that yours would be the voice of reason.'

'And you better believe it! I can't take this to the Commissioner. And we sure as hell can't take it to the DPP. But –' He paused, moved round behind his desk, flopped down in his chair. He gazed at the two of them, then said, 'It's a problem, isn't it? What if Pierpont did do it? How long is it to Glaze's trial?'

'Two months, sir.'

'Then you'd better get your finger out if you want to prove your case. But you've gotta find more evidence before I let you go anywhere near the DPP. Understand?'

Malone chanced his tongue: 'What happens to Glaze?'

There was no hint of the gorilla now: 'Scobie, we've made mistakes before and we'll make them again. They're called miscarriages of justice. But justice isn't something decided on a gut feeling. It's based on evidence that we collect and check. You did all that and it all pointed to this bloke Glaze. You have a gut feeling about Pierpont, but nobody is going to listen to the rumbling in your stomach – it's not evidence. You've got two months to turn your gut feeling into evidence. Otherwise Glaze goes to trial and a jury decides. Not us.' Malone remained silent and Hassett said, 'You think I'm callous?'

'No, sir.'

He looked as if he was about to say something more, but Random got in first: 'He's listened to the voice of reason.'

'Get outa here,' said Assistant Commissioner Hassett, 'or I'll get my sledgehammer out of the closet.'

5

'Get on to your DPP mole,' Malone told Clements, 'and ask him or her to check if Pierpont was on a case at Katoomba or Blackheath the week before the Glaze murder.'

Clements sat back in his chair. The big room was empty, the other detectives at lunch; the computers were mute, phones and faxes silent. The emptiness of it all only emphasized the isolation of Malone's problem.

'He's gunna ask questions,' said the big man. 'He was curious when I got on to him last week, but I fobbed him off.'

'Righto, fair enough. So get on to Katoomba and Blackheath courts, ask them to check through their records if he prosecuted a case or cases during that week.' Malone thought a moment, then went on, 'Tell 'em we're checking an accusation that someone was wrongly accused that week.'

'If there were no murder cases that week, why would we be checking?'

'Why are you so bloody pedantic?'

'Because that's how we solve cases. Private eyes have flights of inspiration. Cops are pedantic.' He looked across at Malone with a mixture of sympathy and exasperation. Lately, in the comfort of a happy marriage and a growing child whom, against all his own expectations, he adored, he had begun to look for comfort in his job. There would be none of that in raising four-year-old spectres. 'Okay, leave it with me, I'll think of something. But I think you're on a loser, sport.'

'Why are you also so bloody discouraging?'

Clements stood up, blocking out the security entrance door, a bulwark against outside forces. 'Because I don't want you in trouble, that's why.'

Malone had been expecting something flippant; he had to change the words already on their way to his lips. Then he said, carefully, 'I know, Russ.'

Clements just nodded, then turned and went into the storage room; not to look for anything but knowing he had said enough and not wanting to spoil it. Malone looked after him. He and I are like Dad and me, he thought: afraid of display.

Clements came back to him next morning. 'I talked to Katoomba and Blackheath courts – I know the clerks up there.' He knew everybody; his network was a cross-hatch across the State; he had run his own Internet before

286

it ever got on to computers. 'Pierpont was at Blackheath the week before the murder, the Thursday. The case he prosecuted was over by midday.'

'Did your mate at Blackheath ask why we wanted the information?'

'I played a dead bat. You think he's gunna worry himself over a minor case four years ago? Cases are piling up like shit in a storm – he's not gunna worry himself about history. The thing is, if Pierpont sticks to his story that he called in at the Golden West on *that* night, the only time he was there, where was he between midday and ten o'clock at night?'

'I'll ask him. I'll give him a day or two to stew over what I've already said to him, then I'll go back.'

'Water torture. You're learning.'

That afternoon the results of Lina Vanheusen's DNA test came back. Sheryl Dallen brought it in to Malone and he saw at once, from the expression on her face, that it was bad news: 'She's in the clear, boss. Her saliva doesn't match that on the envelope.'

'Bugger!' He looked at the paper, then threw it on his desk. Anger and disappointment made him sour; he wanted to get up and rage up and down his office – no, the *big* office outside. Slam his fists on desks, toss computers across the room, turn over file cabinets – but that was what raging actors playing cops did in movies. He wasn't built that way; and for a moment wished that he was. Instead he looked across at Sheryl, said with tight restraint, 'Then why did she object so strongly to taking the test?'

'I dunno.' Sheryl herself looked ready to rage; she was as deeply immersed in the Vanheusen case as himself. 'She didn't strike me as a civil rights demonstrator. I don't think she cares two hoots for what goes on outside her own little circle. She hates us – maybe that was enough to make her uncooperative. She's not the first.'

He nodded resignedly. 'Call Miz Wilkox and tell her her client is in the clear. But only temporarily.'

'Miz Wilkox will tell us to back off permanently.'

'Maybe, maybe not. I think she agrees with us – that Lina killed her daughter.'

Sheryl produced her notebook. Lately he had noticed a certain restrained theatricality to her: the use of pauses, not laying everything on the table in a heap. He wondered if she had been spending too much time as partner to John Kagal. 'All is not lost,' she said and sounded like Kagal. 'I've come up with something that may explain Lina's state of mind – I mean, added to what else we know about her. I went to the agency that handled Lucybelle. They were pretty tight-lipped at first – they said Sharon Garibaldi, from Channel 15, had been nosing around there.'

'She's going to go a long way, that girl. To oblivion, I hope.'

'She's only doing her job –'

He looked pained. 'So are we, Sheryl. Anyone who gets in my way is a pain in the arse. That's the way I feel at the moment. Go on.'

She studied him; like a mother, he thought. 'Maybe you need a holiday.'

'Sheryl –' He was about to tick her off, pull his rank; then he realized she was not being impudent but solicitous. *Here I go again, afraid of display*. He relaxed, managed a smile. 'I'll think about it. Go on.'

She went back to her notebook; but he saw that he had hurt her. 'The agency finally came good when I told them that whatever they told me would not be used in evidence.'

You had no right to tell them that. But he wasn't going to hurt her again.

'They are protecting *their* clients, just like Miz Wilkox. Or rather they're protecting the advertising agencies' clients. The three or four big names that have been using Lucybelle in their TV commercials decided – individually, I gather – that she was over-exposed. I guess they saw it as a composite of a little girl admiring a Toyota while eating a Big Mac and drinking a Coke – it was too much.'

'It would be for me.'

She nodded; her mood was improving. 'Me, too. So the clients had all cancelled – they weren't going to use Lucybelle any more. The advertising agencies then decided they wouldn't use Lucybelle, not till she grew up. Five years old and she was a has-been.'

'And that put the kibosh on all Lina's plans.'

'Whatever they were. It could also explain her state of mind.'

'You think she was round the bend leading up to the murder?'

Sheryl nodded. She had grown up in the six years she

had been in the Service. She had not yet run the gamut of human nature, but she was slowly working her way along it, like a runner who had not realized how long a marathon could be. 'Her husband had been sleeping with another, younger woman. He was about to piss off to England, hopefully with the younger woman. A real dish, as you said.'

'Did I say that? I can't remember.'

She grinned; they were on an even keel again. 'Lina was about to be left with nothing. She'd have money, I guess, but without Damien and his label there, she'd be a nobody in no time. I dunno, maybe she thought that if they both lost the child, he'd be more sympathetic towards her.'

'You don't sound convinced. About him, I mean.'

'He's a bastard. If you'll forgive the language, he's a shit.' He was always careful of his language in front of the women who worked for him and she was aware, and respectful of, that. Amongst her friends four-letter words were a *lingua franca*, but she was still unsure how strait-laced her boss was. 'And that's just a woman's point of view.'

'The men on this case would agree with you.' He was silent for a moment; then: 'I couldn't stand that little girl in the commercials. But then I can't stand most kids on television. The only time I like 'em is when I see them on the *World's Funniest Home Videos* and they fall flat on their faces or run their bikes into a brick wall.'

'You'll make a great grandfather.'

'I know and I'm not looking forward to the future. The only thing that consoles me is that my nineteen-year-old son agrees with me all the way . . . But what I was going to say is that I now feel terribly sorry for young Lucybelle. She appears to have had the parents from hell. She might've been a case for the Department of Community Services, but who'd have reported it? Wealthy parents, TV commercials star – DOCS would've looked at it and said she had everything compared to the abused kids out amongst the battlers.'

Sheryl nodded in agreement. 'But we can't bring her back. So what do we do now?'

'We keep at Lina. Chinese torture.' She looked puzzled. 'Water on a stone, drop by drop. I'm practising it,' he said, but didn't explain on whom. 'You and John Kagal keep after her. You might try annoying Damien, too. He might blow up and put pressure on her.'

She stood up. 'That's one of the joys of this job. You can get to be cruel with a clear conscience.'

He smiled at her; they were on friendly terms again. 'The lion tamers felt that way about the Christians.'

He went home to the house in Randwick where, if cruelty ever entered, it would be cruelly belted with a cricket bat. Claire, Maureen and Tom were all home for dinner tonight; with autumn coming on Lisa was changing the menu. *Osso bucco*, diplomat pudding and a Hunter shiraz are one of the glues that hold a family together. Malone had never explained to his mother that he had left home because of corned beef and cabbage and prunes and custard.

291

'How'd it go today, Mum, with all the bigwigs?' asked Tom.

An Olympic delegation, led by the IOC chairman, was in town to see how much progress had been made towards 2000.

'The usual bowing and scraping,' said Maureen before her mother could reply. 'You'd think it was Jesus Christ and the Twelve Apostles.'

'J.C. and his delegation never had it so good,' said Claire.

'There's a big reception tonight,' said Maureen. 'The freeloaders will be meeting the freeloaders.'

'I was reading the other day,' said Tom, 'Australians are the greatest bunch of freeloaders since the mob at the Sermon on the Mount.'

'They'll never settle for loaves and fishes,' said Claire. 'Not unless it was smoked salmon.'

'President Samaranch offered me five seats in his private box at the opening ceremony,' said Lisa. 'Any takers?'

'Done,' said Tom. 'Where do we bow and scrape?'

Malone listened to the chat, relaxing in it as in a warm bath; his own problems had been left at the door. But later, in bed, Lisa said, 'You were quiet tonight.'

'We've got three good-looking kids. Would you have sold them to a TV commercial?'

'Lucybelle still on your mind? Getting nowhere with the case?'

'No, getting somewhere. But an inch at a time. Get your hand outa there.'

'I was examining it an inch at a time.' She kissed him, turned out the light. 'Cuddle into me, the nights are getting colder. I'm glad I have you to come home to.'

'Likewise. What did President Samaranch think of you?'

'He kissed my hand and gave me a gold medal.'

He hugged her to him. And then for no reason at all, he hoped his mother and father were cuddled into each other.

Next morning he rang the DPP offices, asked for Tim Pierpont. 'He's in court, Inspector.'

'Where?'

'Downing Centre, Court 3 on the fourth level. He'll be there all day. I'll tell him you called.'

'Do that.' Another drop on the stone. Then he decided to add to it. He called in Clements: 'I'm going up to have a look at Pierpont in court. I might have lunch with him.'

'Why don't you leave it? Let nature or justice or whatever take its course.'

'What would you do in my place?'

Clements considered a moment; then spread his hands. 'Same as you, probably. But I'm not in your place, thank Christ, so I can be objective. Good luck.'

The Downing Centre, the court complex, was in the ex-department store building opposite the DPP offices. Court 3 on the fourth level was crowded: half the criminal population of the city seemed to have turned up. In the dock were three crims Malone recognized:

two Lebanese and a Greek. For too long they had been allowed a loose rein by corrupt police in the King's Cross area, running brothels, strip shows and drugs. But now the broom was going through the Service and the three, along with lesser crims, had been picked up and charged. Long sentences lay ahead of them if the Crown Prosecution could nail them.

Malone sat down at the back of the court, next to a crim who recognized him and edged away. 'Relax, Jockey. I'm here as a sightseer. A tourist.'

Jockey Mailer had begun his career as an apprentice rider, pulling horses that the punters thought should win and the horses' connections thought otherwise. From there he had graduated to armed robbery, running two brothels and drug dealing. He had a bony, rather stupid face, like a knee with a nose, and at the moment was unhappy.

'You don't look happy, Jockey. Your stomach playing up with you?'

'Me stomach's okay. But things have changed, Mr Malone. You blokes have got serious.'

'You don't have any sympathy for those blokes in the dock, do you? They'd slice you up as soon as look at you.'

'I'm not worried about *them*. I'm like everyone else here –' He looked around the court. One face in four, it seemed, was an honest one; these spectators had made rubble of the Ten Commandments. He had been, like Malone, whispering; but now he lowered his voice so far Malone had to lean close to him. He was surprised to find Jockey wore some sort of cologne. 'Those guys go down, who takes over the trade?'

Malone leaned back. 'Jockey, you're not going to –?'

Mailer looked at him in horror; or a good facsimile of it. 'Jesus, no, not me! The bloody Viets'll come in – it was bad enough with them Wogs –' He wasn't as old as Con Malone but he had all the bigotry of earlier generations. 'What you gunna do about them? The slopeheads?'

'Until they start killing each other, or you, they're not my problem. I'm still with Homicide, Jockey.'

'Lucky you,' said Mailer and even his cologne seemed to turn sour.

Pierpont was putting the Crown case and putting it well. Malone was impressed. Pierpont knew how to play the witnesses, the defendants, the jury and the judge. His questions could be precise or seemingly rambling; but they all had an edge. The English of the three defendants obviously was not good; their expressions as they tried to follow the arguments was almost comical. Malone looked around the court at the other crims; some of them were enjoying the ordeal of the men in the dock. Crims usually do not attend the trials of their fellows, but this trial was a climax to the police clean-up and the crims were here to see which way the road, and the trade, were going. In a way it was almost like an auction and Malone knew, like most cops, that the police could never outbid the crims. The war would be fought but never won, despite the trumpet-calls of the law-and-order politicians.

At noon the judge adjourned the proceedings. Malone, patting Jockey Mailer comfortingly (or warningly) on the shoulder, got up and moved quickly after Pierpont as the latter headed out of the courtroom. 'Tim –'

Pierpont, still in wig and gown, turned; for a moment his eyes were stony, then he relaxed and smiled. 'More evidence on Glaze?'

'Not really. How about a coffee or lunch with me? My shout.'

'Sorry –'

'Afraid?'

People were passing close by; some of them, particularly the defence's lawyers, turned to look when they heard the word *afraid*. Pierpont took off his wig and gown, put out a hand as Miriam Zigler passed him. 'Mim, would you take these for me? Inspector Malone is taking me to lunch.'

She had an armful of files; he put the wig and gown on top of them. 'Have a nice lunch –'

She'd carry bricks for him, Malone thought. I wonder how he treats *her*?

As they walked out Pierpont said, 'Just a sandwich and coffee.'

'Just my strength.'

They were fortunate enough to find a vacant table on the terrace outside the building. The wind was coming from the south with some bite to it; but they were out of it, comfortable in the sun. Pierpont had his right hand in the pocket of his jacket. In a well-cut blue suit, white shirt and a Sydney University tie, he looked successful and at ease with himself and the man opposite him.

He put on dark glasses against the autumn sun. Or against me? Malone wondered. 'What's it about this time, Scobie?'

Their table was on the rim of the dozen or so that was the outdoor set-up. They could talk comfortably, but would have to watch their voices to avoid being overheard. 'We've done some checking, Tim. You prosecuted a case up at Blackheath on the Monday before the Glaze murder.'

'There! What did I tell you?' He smiled expansively, the problem was solved.

'That's only half the story. The case finished at midday. What did you do between then and walking into the Golden West at ten o'clock at night? You went Blue Mountains sightseeing?'

Pierpont waited till the waitress had given them their sandwiches and coffee and an automatic smile; when she had gone he said, 'I'm trying to remember, but I probably went bush-walking. It was around that time I got interested in conservation. Are you a conservationist?'

Malone thought a while. 'Only of my prejudices. It comes with middle age.'

'Admirable. We give up too much in the interests of political correctness.'

'Cut out the bullshit, Tim. You didn't go bush-walking till ten o'clock at night.'

Pierpont chewed on his sandwich, holding it with his left hand. His right hand was still hidden, as if it were some sort of evidence. 'I'm still trying to remember. There was a girl, a solicitor – I wasn't married then . . .' He chewed on the sandwich again, then swallowed. 'She came in from Bathurst – we used to meet, have – you know –'

'Would she remember your – you know – four years ago?'

'She might. But I'm not going to give you her name. It lasted only two or three months –'

Malone ate his own sandwich. 'You're good, Tim. You'd try and tell the Holy Ghost to get a body.'

'I'm not a Catholic. There are no ghosts in my scheme of things, holy or otherwise. Why did you choose to come along today. Were you interested in those goons on trial?'

'No. I just had a spare hour or two. I thought you and I might share a truth or two.'

'We're witty today, aren't we?'

'It's the company. Lawyers are supposed to be the wits in this country.'

'Probably. Our professional comics are so smug and self-satisfied.'

'Lawyers aren't?'

'Of course we are – we just disguise it better.'

'You could have fooled me.'

Pierpont wiped his mouth with a paper napkin. Then he abruptly looked sour, as if there had been something in the sandwich he hadn't liked.

Malone said nothing and after a long moment Pierpont said, 'Those bastards in there –' he jerked his head backwards – 'they are murderers. You should be in there arresting them for murder with intent. They know the crack and the rest of it they peddle, they know it can kill.'

'You know it doesn't work that way. Not like it did in your case –'

Pierpont looked around him, as if only now realizing how exposed they were. The street they looked out on, this tributary of the city, flowed by with all the cold unconcern of water. A courier cyclist in a speckled silver jacket was weaving his way upstream, against the flow of the one-way traffic, like a salmon going to spawn. Cars, trucks, buses were like slow-moving rocks; then suddenly the pace would pick up and they would tumble down the slope of the street. There were two lovers hand in hand; another couple arguing on a corner; groups at the tables nearby chattering like birds safe in their flock. Midday in a city that had its own problems. Pierpont looked back at Malone.

'It's bizarre. Who would believe what you and I are talking about? What you are accusing me of.'

'You want me to stand up and tell 'em?'

Pierpont considered a moment; then nodded. 'Yes. Go ahead.'

Malone stared at him; then gestured surrender. 'You know I don't have the evidence.'

'It would be that way in front of a jury. It's not only that, Scobie. I was not there on the night in question. Your witnesses have got it all wrong. The evidence you have against Glaze is as strong as I have back inside there.' Again the jerk of the head.

'You're going to nail those fellers?'

'Without a doubt. And they know it. I've already had two death threats from their mates.'

'You should increase your insurance.' Then Malone relented. 'Sorry. That's a poor joke.'

'Maybe not. Maybe I'll take your advice.' He drank his coffee. 'Did you ever read *Les Miserables* or see the show?'

'I read the book at school. I'm the dogged detective, that it?'

'Javert, yes.'

'He finished up jumping off a bridge, didn't he? I'm not going to do that, Tim, so don't keep your hopes up.'

Pierpont smiled, but the smiles seemed an effort now. Then he looked at his watch. 'Time I was getting back. I'd like to tell you something about conservation, Scobie. If you're doing nothing Saturday, why don't you come up to Springwood? We're demonstrating against a developer who wants to build a string of apartments and town villas along the top of the escarpment. It'll take the blue haze off the Blue Mountains. Interested?'

Malone was caught off-guard by the invitation. 'I'll think about it. I usually play tennis Saturdays or watch my boy play cricket or rugby.'

'That's all in the future for me. Watching my girl play netball or my unborn son play rugby for Gordon. Well, thanks for lunch. We'll be doing it again?'

'Probably.' *But the water has run off you today.*

'My shout next time.'

Malone watched him go. He walked with his right hand still in his pocket. Malone remembered images from old movies: upper-class Englishmen with their hands in their pockets, American Mafiosi with the same habit, brothers in style. As he disappeared into the court complex Pierpont looked back over his shoulder and smiled at someone. *Why am I starting to like him?* Malone wondered and tried to remember what the *Les Miserables* cop had felt about his quarry.

Jockey Mailer stopped by his table. 'You going back inside, Mr Malone?'

'No, Jockey. Go back inside, sit there and think about retiring. You're history now.'

'Bloody immigration, I'm dead against it, y'know what I mean?'

'That's the way it goes, Jockey. And we've still got the Russian Mafia and the Chechens to come.'

Jockey Mailer shook his head mournfully. 'Bloody country's going to the dogs. A bloke oughta take up arms.'

'Buy a cricket bat.'

6

Those in court that afternoon were surprised at the venom in Pierpont's cross-examination of defence witnesses. He was surprised himself; and embarrassed. He had always prided himself on the cool approach, the quiet sidling up that put the witness or the defendant off-guard. This afternoon he had all the subtlety of a demonstrator.

He was back in his office, tidying up his desk, when David Winkler blew in, dropped into a chair. He had a glass of whisky in one hand and he leaned forward and put another glass on the desk in front of Pierpont.

'A dram of Chivas Regal, Tim old chap. I think you may need it after what I've heard.'

'What've you heard? Who from?'

'Various sources, as they say. You flew off the handle this afternoon. Why?' He held up the hand without the glass. 'I'm not criticizing. I've flown off the handle myself in times past, roared like a bull, wanted to kick every arse in court, including the judge's. But you were out of character this afternoon, old chap. Why?'

Pierpont took a mouthful of whisky, let it drain slowly down his gullet. He was not a spirits man, but sometimes the spirit needed more than the comfort of wine. Whisky, they said, was to be savoured; it also gave him time to think. 'Those scum in the dock just got under my skin. One of them actually grinned at me. A pregnant fifteen-year-old kid died from an overdose supplied by one of those shits.'

'You have proof they were the actual ones supplied that dose? Come on, old chap. You're getting conservation mixed up with justice. A prosecution is not a demonstration.' It was the first time Winkler had ever mentioned Pierpont's out-of-the-office cause. 'You haven't lost us this case, but you could if you continue the way you went this afternoon. I've had three reports on it, Tim, all negative.' He raised his glass, finished his drink, stood up. 'That's the end of the lecture. You'll be your old self tomorrow. Cheers.'

He was gone; he blew in and out of offices as if a gale were behind him. Pierpont drank the rest of his whisky slowly, like a reluctant suicide. Then he shut his eyes against the tears.

Chapter Nine

1

'Would you like to go to a conservation demo Saturday?' Malone asked.

'Sure,' said Maureen, who went to demonstrations as if they were outdoor balls. Malone hadn't dared ask how she had managed to miss the docks demonstrations. 'Where?'

'I wasn't asking you, I was asking your mother.'

'Mum? When did she ever go to a demo?'

'I demonstrated against the sacking of the Whitlam government in my last year at university,' said Lisa. 'Will I have to let my hair be scraggly, wear torn jeans and carry a banner?'

'There!' exclaimed Maureen. 'I'll bet you never wore torn jeans in whenever it was.'

'No, I wore my twinset and pearls. Mr Whitlam himself came down the steps of Parliament House and kissed me. Mrs Whitlam wasn't too happy about it. I was a good sort in those days, a real dish.'

'Don't ever demonstrate outside the White House,' said Tom.

'Why would an arch-conservative like you,' said Claire, the lawyer, to her father, 'want to go to any sort of demo?'

'I'm not an arch-conservative. I'm just someone in the middle of the road wondering why all the parking spaces are taken up by people who won't listen to anyone else.'

'Listen to him!' said Maureen. 'He sounds like one of my Communications lecturers.'

'I've been listening to your mother since she started writing PR releases for the council's Olympic business.'

'Thank you,' said Lisa. 'I'll go with you Saturday. Do we take the crowd or do we go alone?'

'I'm playing rugby Saturday,' said Tom. 'It's the last of the trials.'

'I'm going to watch Tom,' said Maureen. 'There are some terrific-looking guys in his team. All with tight shorts.'

'I'm washing my hair,' said Claire, 'and doing my nails.'

'Every one a rebel,' said Malone with approval. 'Don't change. Stay in the middle of the road with your dear old dad.'

'And get knocked arse-over-charlie by a bus,' said Tom.

'We'll sue,' said the lawyer. 'More wine, Dad?'

Next morning Malone sat down at his desk and looked at the overnight computer print-outs. Three more murders, all in the suburbs: a hold-up at a bottle shop, a knifing at a dance, a domestic. All uncomplicated murders that would not trouble Homicide, would be looked after by local detectives. The newspapers, however, were full of stories of protest meetings throughout the State at the rising crime rate; country towns in particular were up in arms, even if only metaphorically. Still, those again were not Homicide's problem. Police Commissioner Zanuch and the politicians would have to handle that. Malone felt a small, if only temporary, comfort.

He looked up. Sheryl Dallen and a stranger stood in his doorway.

'Boss, this is Dr Fairbanks, from the Biology Section at Lidcombe. He has something I think'll interest you.'

Malone had spoken to Fairbanks on the phone but had never met him. He was a big man, middle-aged, with wavy hair and a thick salt-and-pepper moustache. He had a broken nose and scar tissue round his deep-set blue eyes; Malone guessed he might have been a boxer or a front-row forward in his university days. He was disarmingly direct, something Malone appreciated.

'I wish we'd woken up to this sooner –' He stopped. 'We're talking about the Vanheusen case.'

'What else? Go ahead, Doc.'

'Mrs Vanheusen's DNA test proved negative, okay?'

Malone grinned, shook his head. 'Not okay. You have no idea how disappointed we were when your report came in.'

306

Fairbanks nodded. 'I can guess . . . Anyhow, looking at it made us go back and have another look at the report on the ransom envelope. The saliva on that had a faint smear to it when we tested it – you could only pick it up with our procedure. As if whoever sealed the envelope had had something else in his or her mouth when they did it. We didn't think much of it – we should've, but we didn't. It was a cock-up and I've taken the blame for it – it happens maybe once in a thousand times, but it happens –'

Malone nodded sympathetically. Right now was not the time for him to be criticizing someone else's mistake.

'People often have other stuff in their mouth – a touch of drink, anything like that. We've looked at it again, analysed it – it was the faintest trace of chocolate –'

Malone sat up.

'You with me or ahead of me?'

'Ahead, I think. But go on.'

'Forensic at the morgue had done a routine blood test on the little girl. We sent for it – the p.m. report on the contents of her stomach . . .' He sat back, ran a hand through his thick hair. 'It's hard to believe. The little girl sealed her own ransom note.'

'What's hard to believe,' said Sheryl, 'is that a mother would be so heartless as to have her child do that.'

Malone said nothing, just looked at both of them. Fairbanks saw the look, sucked on his lips, then nodded. 'I know. Kids are treated like that every day in the week, by both parents. We're only just starting to admit it.'

'I don't like Mrs Vanheusen,' said Malone slowly, 'and I'd like to think she is heartless. But I'm beginning to think she was very much not right in the head the night she killed Lucybelle. If we can get her lawyer to persuade her to take an insanity plea, we can wrap this up. What d'you think, Doc?'

'Scobie, I'm not a psychiatrist. I deal with simple things like blood and tissue and bone. I sometimes think you have to be round the bend to deal with the human brain.'

'Try being a cop.'

'No way. It's much easier arguing with the dead than with the living.'

When Fairbanks had gone Malone called Sheryl back into his office. 'Get on to surveillance, find out where Lina is. I think it's time we picked her up.'

Sheryl was back in two minutes. 'She's at an Australian Fashion Week show with Lady Derry, at the Congress Hotel. Sitting two rows back from the catwalk.'

'Is that good or bad?'

'The overseas buyers and fashion writers, *Vogue*, people like that, get the front row. Damien has got some items in the show, so I guess he got her and Lady Derry the seats. Front-row seats are harder to get than front row at the Olympics.'

'Well, let's get down there. We'll stand at the back till it's over. We don't want to put on our own show.'

'Why not?' said Sheryl maliciously. 'While we're at it, let's pinch a dozen or so of those skinny models who don't have to diet. Oooh, I hate every scrawny bone in their bodies. Incidentally, it's DeeDee Orion's last stroll down the catwalk before she goes off to New York.'

'I didn't think she was scrawny.'

'I didn't think you'd noticed.'

Malone was enjoying working with Sheryl. He had worked with other women; as with other male cops, it had taken him some time to adjust to the company. But he felt comfortable with Sheryl.

This particular event of Fashion Week was being held in the ballroom of the Congress Hotel downtown in the city. When Malone and Sheryl arrived, they checked with the two surveillance officers who were at the front entrance to the ballroom.

'Stay here,' Malone told them. 'Constable Dallen and I are going inside.'

For some reason the fashion show was lit by the ballroom's huge chandelier. Such illumination, undoubtedly invented by a misogynist, is the most unflattering of lights. The faces in the audience were upturned to the models on the catwalk; the least unflattered were the few men amongst the sea of women. Even the models on the catwalk looked gaunter than usual. Everyone in the room appeared to be dressed in black, some with dandruff and loose hairs as accessories.

As Malone and Sheryl took up their places at the back of the room, DeeDee Orion was making her last appearance. She slunk down the catwalk with an animal sensuousness; Malone, blind to fashion and to what she was wearing, was impressed. Then he looked past DeeDee and saw Lina Vanheusen staring up at the model. If the light had been softer, more flattering, she might not have looked so ugly. Hatred disfigured her and he waited for her to rise up from her tiny chair and shriek abuse.

But DeeDee had completed her last walk and was disappearing through the opening at the end of the catwalk. It was only then that Malone realized she had been dressed as a bride, though not the sort he remembered; if ever she walked up the aisle as she had up the catwalk, the priest would forget his vow of celibacy and be forcibly held back by the altar boys. The audience stood up and the show was over. A few moments, then three designers, Damien Vanheusen one of them, came out and surrounded by the models paraded down the catwalk. The audience went into meltdown; some came close to swooning, including two of the men. The fashion writers could be seen searching in their mental grab-bags for new, or nearly new, superlatives. Words such as *lyrical*, *rapturous* and *heavenly* would splatter the fashion pages tomorrow.

The slob in the Fletcher Jones off-the-rack looked at Sheryl. 'We'll pick her up at the door. No fuss, keep it low-key.'

'If she co-operates. But did you see that look on her face? She's planning to murder DeeDee Orion.' She saw him frown and she nodded. 'Okay, she's not. But she'd like to. Oh, damn!' She had been following the movements of Lina Vanheusen and Lady Derry. 'They're going backstage.'

'So are we. We've hung around here long enough. I'm starting to swoon.'

They found a door guarded by two huge Tongan security guards. 'Sorry, you'll have to go out by that other door –'

Malone produced his badge, not flashing it, just palming it. 'We've got business back there.'

The guards looked at each other. 'Will you need us?'

'I don't think so. It's just routine questioning.'

'Not one of the models?'

'One of them your girlfriend?'

The Tongans exchanged smiles as brilliant as the chandelier but more friendly. 'They're too skinny for us. We like 'em about a hundred kilos, plenty of flesh to hang on to. No offence, miss.'

'None taken,' said Sheryl with her own smile. 'I'll look you up when I put on weight.'

The banquet room, where the collections were hung like old curtains and the models had changed, was large but not large enough; it seethed and sucked like a lake of well-dressed mud. The air was full of flying kisses; lips, not just women's, brushed Malone's cheeks four times before he got to his objective. There Lady Derry turned and kissed him before she realized who he was.

'Oh God, I've smooched the *police*!'

Several heads turned on the word *police*; the last to turn was Lina Vanheusen's. The look on her face was the same as that he had seen directed against DeeDee Orion; she hated him, could kill him. Then abruptly the

311

hatred was gone. Her face changed, was wan, sad. The war was over.

'Jesus!' said Damien Vanheusen behind Malone. 'What are you doing here today? *Here*, for Crissake!'

Only then did Malone realize, or admit, why he had chosen to come to this crowded, public place; he could quite easily have waited at Bellevue Hill for Lina to come home. It was mean-spiritedness, malice if you like, that had brought him here. He was tired of killers who denied their crimes, who thought life could go on as if nothing had happened. As if a woman dead in a house four years ago and a small child dead at the bottom of a cliff were no longer of any account.

But he couldn't admit that, not publicly. He said quietly, 'Could we go outside, Lina? We have to talk.'

2

The Blue Mountains, like all Australia's ranges, are molehills compared to those overseas; mountaineers who had scaled the Andes and the Himalayas would climb them in slippers. But there are cliff-faces and rock formations that have their attraction and every weekend hikers get lost in the tree-clogged gorges. The magnet for those who live there is the mountain air and the richness of the soil in the residents' gardens.

'So you've tied up the Vanheusen case?' said Pierpont.

He and Malone were sitting on a fallen log at the cliff-edge of the clearing, the scene of the demonstration. They were apart, did not have to lower their voices.

'Only as far as charging her and holding her. It'll go to arraignment – there's an insanity plea. It'll be in your hands when I give you all the evidence. The DPP's,' he added. 'You probably won't be there if and when it comes to trial.'

Pierpont smiled. 'Oh, I'll still be there.' Then he changed the subject, gestured around him. 'What d'you think? It's worth saving?'

The day, if not the scene, was worth conserving. A cloudless autumn sky, soft at the edges, stretched away to the distant city. The breeze, which might be a wind by nightfall, stroked the cheek rather than knifed at it. Far below the Nepean River was yellow-green from the recent rains; beyond it green merged into the dun-coloured housing estates of the outer suburbs. In the far distance, on the cold winter days to come, when the air would be sharp and clear, the high rise of the city would be there, like the ruins of a past civilization. Malone wondered why distant vistas always suggested to him the past rather than the present.

There were forty or fifty demonstrators, plus four uniformed police. There was no sign of any developer. The development so far was no more than a long cleared site and some survey pegs. There were four bulldozers lined up like army tanks at the back of the site; the demonstrators had hung insulting banners on them, but had made no attempt to interfere with the machines. There were no press photographers nor TV cameramen and the demonstration had rapidly wound down to a big picnic. There were half a dozen Rent-a-Crowd protestors, long-haired and ragged, who had arrived in a VW rust-bucket; they sat in a group aside from the others, not picnicking but smoking, drinking cask wine and looking sneeringly at their co-demonstrators. The latter had arrived in their corduroys, Timberland boots and 4WDs and were now opening their picnic baskets.

'I always thought conservationists were feral,' said Malone. 'Chaining themselves to trees, stuff like that.'

'What were you expecting? Crowds like we've seen on TV this week in Jakarta? We're just trying to toss out a developer, not a dictator like Soeharto.'

'I sometimes wonder what we'd do with someone like Soeharto. We're a pretty apathetic lot. But –' he waved a hand – 'I thought you'd be a bit more stirred up than this.'

'That's the forestry crowd, they go ape sometimes. I was like that once, at university – well, not *feral* but pretty angry. But now I can't take Ginny and Fay to things like that –' He waved a hand towards his wife and child sitting in the Discovery with Lisa. 'Picketing developments like this isn't going to stop global warming, but it helps stop ruining the landscape. Developers are ruining Sydney – look at what they've done to East Circular Quay, blocking out the Opera House. For economic rationalists at the end of the day, as they

314

chant, there's only the bottom line. It's the mantra, too, for developers. But there are better things in life than the bottom line, aren't there? I mean, at the end of the day?'

Malone looked sideways at him. 'Are you trying to get me on side?'

'As a conservationist?' Pierpont laughed; it sounded genuine. 'You'd have a conflict of interest, wouldn't you? Where would you draw the law-and-order line when things turned nasty?' He stood up. He wore corduroys, a Country Road sweater and Timberland boots. Beside him Malone, in his early-morning tracksuit and trainers, felt under-dressed. 'Come on, I think the women are ready to feed us.'

Malone held back a moment. 'You've not changed your mind?'

'About what?'

'What we talked about.'

'Ah, *that*? No. You're mistaken about the night I was there.' He looked down at the plain below them. Malone had been trying to pick out the Golden West Club somewhere there in the distance, but couldn't be sure he had found it. 'You and your witnesses are wrong, Scobie.'

'I don't think so, Tim.' They began to walk across towards Lisa and Ginny and young Fay, all of whom had now got out of the Discovery. 'Have you had any more threats from the mates of those drug dealers?'

'No. Maybe they were just hot air, I don't know. But

315

I took your advice – I'm taking out extra insurance. Just in case.'

'You didn't ask for police protection?'

'I reported it to Police Centre. They said they would look into it.'

'Did you mention me? I'm a threat, too.'

Pierpont seemed to manage a smile without effort. 'No, you're not, Scobie.'

He's either a cold-blooded sonofabitch or a nice bloke who made one fatal error and will never admit it. 'We'll see . . . You've got a nice-looking family.'

'I think so. Your wife is beautiful.'

'I'll tell her.'

Then young Fay came running towards them, stumbling over clods of earth, falling down laughing, picking herself up and flinging herself at her father. He caught her, swept her up and hugged as he spun with her. In that moment he looked at Malone and the latter saw the pain, the entreaty. Then he was laughing as he carried Fay under his arm towards the two women.

Jesus, thought Malone, did Damien ever embrace Lucybelle with love like that?

'Come on,' Lisa called. 'Time to eat.'

The two women, apparently, were already friends; Fay, too, had taken a liking to Lisa. It was a happy gathering; the picketing seemed incidental. Lisa had brought the Malones' own picnic lunch; which was just as well, Malone thought, as Ginny Pierpont's contribution seemed to be store-bought sandwiches in plastic wrap

316

and store-bought plain cake. Pierpont, however, did produce a good bottle of chardonnay.

'Chardonnay demonstrators,' he said. 'Those professionals over there have nothing but contempt for us. Still, we're all true believers.'

'At the end of the day,' said Malone.

Ginny was sitting in a folding chair while Pierpont fussed about her. She smiled up at him, love as plain on her face as a birthmark. She patted her stomach: 'A few more months, though, and you'll be demonstrating on your own. You can take Fay for support.'

'No way,' said Pierpont and pressed her shoulder. 'Did Scobie stick by you, Lisa, when you were pregnant?'

'I can't remember the first two,' said Lisa, chewing on a chicken leg, 'but he was up to his knees in a dirty murder when Tom was born. He was checking his notes while I was in labour.'

'Women's imagination,' said Malone.

'Of course,' said Pierpont. 'But we must always take it into account, mustn't we?'

He doesn't miss a trick, thought Malone. But Pierpont, getting a flask of coffee out of the Discovery, didn't look at him.

Going home Malone said, 'He thinks you are beautiful.'

She took it for granted. 'I think he's charming. But why did we come all the way up here today?'

'I think I was being given a lesson in conservation.'

'Environment or family?'

'You're not only beautiful, you're smart.'

She squeezed his thigh, but said nothing for a while. Then a mile or two further on she said, 'What are you going to do about his wife and children?'

He shook his head, not looking for an answer. Then over to their left from the freeway he saw the top of the big building, half-hidden by a low hill. 'That's where it started. The Golden West.'

Then it was gone from sight as they sped along. *If only the problem would drop out of sight as quickly as that . . .*

3

Monday morning Malone drove out to the Golden West Club, having first made sure that Charlene Colnby was on the daytime shift. The newspapers and the TV screens and serious radio were full of the Indonesian crisis; the stock market and the money offices and the government in Canberra hung on every despatch that came out of Jakarta. The rioting students and the riot police in their medieval helmets scratched nervous graphs on computer screens and for the first time in a generation army generals were sought out by local reporters for opinions.

But out here in the suburbs the fall of another dictator would wash over voters like a gentle swell in the tide of affairs in a wider world than their own. They knew corruption and cronyism, they saw it in councils and politics, but it was small-time, it would never bring down the system under which they lived. Out there in the fine autumn day life, and death, went on with barely a noticeable tremor.

Nobody, said Charlene, was talking about Indonesia at the club. 'All they're talking about is how many shares they're gunna get in the TAB stock market float. And how the Penrith team is doing in the comp. You think someone on the pension or a guy who brings home three hundred bucks a week and dunno if he's got enough to pay the rent, you think they're gunna be worried about Mr Soeharto?'

'That's why I'm here, Charlene. Something else to worry about.'

The club had just opened its doors and the first members were drifting in; a few young people but mostly older ones, their faces breaking into smiles as suddenly they were amongst company. Charlene, knowing Malone was coming, had put on her face, was ready for company.

'You're not getting anywhere, are you?'

'Charlene –' he wished she had another name: it was like reciting a product name – 'we've checked and re-checked. He was working up the Mountains the day of the murder, but he was also up there the Thursday before that. He says that night, the Thursday, was the night he called in here.'

'No way.' She shook her head almost savagely. 'I know when I saw him. The night Norma and Ron were here, sitting at this table where you and I are sitting now.'

He tilted his head. 'Come on, Charlene, you're stretching it. Four years ago and you remember it was *this* table they were sitting at?'

'Well –' She twisted her watch round her wrist, looked disappointed in herself. She hated to be wrong. 'Maybe not this one, but it was around here.'

'In court that's the sort of thing the defence lawyers pick on. They'd demolish you as a witness in five minutes.'

She looked hard at him. 'You're protecting him, aren't you?'

Maybe I'm protecting myself. He looked away at the trickle of members still coming in, their faces lighting up as if they had left all their troubles outside. He recognized the comfort of company. And wondered why outsiders so often criticized police for keeping their own company.

'No, I'm not,' he said, looking back at her. 'I'm just trying to show that if you point the finger in a court of law, you have the onus of proof on you, you have to have hard evidence. All you're offering me as evidence is that you remember a man, a left-handed man, who came into this club on what you're sure was the night Norma Glaze was murdered. The man in question admits to coming here, but not on that night. He is a Crown Prosecutor –'

'And I'm just a barmaid, that it?'

He did his best to look pained. 'Charlene, my dad was a wharfie, my mother a cleaner at my school. I don't draw social lines.'

'Sorry. I'm a bit het-up about all this – I *know* Ron

didn't kill his wife. Oh yeah –' she waved a dismissive hand – 'I know what I said the morning after. He looked cold-blooded, all that. But I've changed me mind. He didn't do it. You don't think he did it, either, do you?'

'I don't know. Why did he disappear?'

'He told me and his sister that – why. The bottom fell outa his life when he saw she was dead. I can understand that. I was in love like that, once –' She didn't elaborate. Some loves are best left undisturbed. 'He said he never looked at another woman till he got to that place – Collamundra. His sister and me believed him.'

He had sold himself to them, made another sale; but maybe he had been telling the truth. 'Charlene, whatever he told you, all the evidence is against him and I can do nothing about it.'

'So Ron goes to gaol for God knows how long?'

'Unless you can come up with something solid that puts Mr Pierpont –' That was the first time he had named him. And instantly regretted it: somehow it linked him more personally to the Crown Prosecutor. 'Did you discuss anything with him? Something that was in the papers or on TV that day? The weather, anything –'

She shook her head. 'I can't think of anything. But I'll try –'

He knew that she would; all he could hope was that she would not rely on invention. He stood up, looked around him. Now the lunch crowd was beginning to filter in: more elderly folk, a group of young women, a couple of dozen businessmen. There was a buzz to the place and Malone saw how the club had become the hub that it was.

But Ron Glaze, he guessed, had gone from the thoughts of most of them; he was not irrelevant like Soeharto but they didn't have to think about him. He would come back, like a ghost, only when his trial would begin. In the meantime everyone had his own life to live.

'Don't forget, Charlene. What you suspect is between you and me.'

'I've told Ron's sister and she's told him. How you gunna handle that?'

People were flowing around them; she stood solidly amongst them, challenging him. All he could say was, 'Time will tell, Charlene.'

Which was the sort of evasion estranged couples indulged in.

Part Three

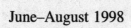

June–August 1998

Chapter Ten

1

'We'll arraign her,' said Miriam Zigler, 'and then you can plead how you like. You know the McNaghten Rules.'

Lydia Wilkox nodded, but Malone shook his head. 'I'm hazy on them. I've heard them quoted before, but I've forgotten the detail.'

They were in Miriam Zigler's office at the DPP. It was a small room that she shared with another junior advocate; the prosecution of the law can't afford the fancies of the defence of it. Books were everywhere, on shelves, on the floor, on Miriam's desk; she could have built a barricade against defence lawyers. Her desk was a shoal of papers, she herself looked as if she had gone aground on it.

Four weeks had passed since the arrest of Lina Vanheusen and she was still being held in Mulawa women's prison at Silverwater, an inner western suburb. Almost as if it were a penance, she had not asked for bail but accepted being remanded to Mulawa. Perhaps, Malone had thought, she could no longer tolerate the house where she had staged the murder of her child.

'McNaghten sets the law for insanity. Everyone is presumed to be sane and to possess a sufficient degree of reason to be responsible for his or her crime. Until the contrary is proven.'

Malone looked at Lydia Wilkox. 'Are you going to try to prove the contrary?'

'We'll give it a go, but it will depend on counsel.'

'Who've you got?'

'Henry Marble.'

Malone nodded. 'You've gone for the best.'

'My client can afford it.'

'Is Damien standing by her?'

Lydia looked first at Miriam Zigler; the women seemed to understand each other. They certainly seemed to understand Damien Vanheusen. Lydia looked back at Malone. 'He hasn't visited her at Mulawa or tried to get in touch with her. He rang me and said no expense was to be spared, but he hasn't put in an appearance.'

'Husbands,' said Miriam sourly and Lydia nodded.

'I'm one,' said Malone.

The two women looked at each other: *Shall we forgive him*? Then Miriam gave him a big smile, her face suddenly turning lively. 'We've got several here in the office – Tim Pierpont, for instance. All nice, loving blokes, just like you, I'm sure. But don't let's waste any compliments on Mr Vanheusen, not till we see him holding his wife's hand. If he becomes a witness for the defence . . .'

'We'll call him,' said Lydia. Within the power broker's suit she was much more relaxed now; she and Malone were no longer enemies. 'To show her state of mind leading up to the murder.'

Miriam pursed her lips. 'You can try your luck, Lydia, but you know what the Rules say. It must be clearly proved that at the time of committing the act the accused was labouring under such a defect of reason, from disease of the mind, as not to know the quality and nature of the act. Or, if she did know, she did not know what she was doing was wrong.' Somehow she managed to say it all as if she were not reciting; like a good Shakespearean actor. 'You'll argue that?'

'We'll try. Mr Marble will argue it much better than I can, sitting here.'

'Who's prosecuting the arraignment?' asked Malone.

'I'm doing the donkey-work,' said Miriam, 'but Tim will be the leader.'

'He'll do the trial, too?'

'If it gets that far. He's doing the Glaze case for you, isn't he?'

'Not for me.' Malone smiled to hide the double meaning in his own mind. 'When is the Glaze trial? You got a date yet?'

'First week in August. Tim's had me running around looking for cancellations on the lists, he seems eager to get on with it. I've swapped with one of my colleagues who wants *his* case put back to November. I'm a juggler, a wheeler-dealer, a poker player – I've learned to be an operator since I came here, something they never taught me at law school. I've swapped someone else's slot in the lists for the Vanheusen arraignment. I'm Jewish – I'm beginning to think I could have transferred the trial of Jesus Christ to another jurisdiction and saved all the bother.'

'You'd have never heard the end of it from St Paul,' said Malone.

Miriam looked at Lydia. They were a contrast: the one in her jumble-sale couture, the other a designer's model. Both, however, knew each other and they were long past judging on exterior. Neither wore kid gloves, but knew how to use them if necessary. The same with boxing gloves.

'You ever heard of him, Lydia? St Paul?'

'He was that misogynist, wasn't he?'

'You sound like my daughters,' said Malone.

The conference, like so many serious law conferences, ended on a light note. But Miriam said, 'You're not going to plead any unfitness to be tried, Lyddy?'

'No, she's fit to plead now. How she was at the time of the crime will be our case.'

She stood up, picked up her briefcase, the weapon of the peacetime warrior. Malone wondered how she handled her husband, if she had one, or her boyfriends; he was still wary of women who had broken through the glass ceiling, as Lydia Wilkox obviously had. She was an associate partner in one of the city's leading law firms; she would, in the eyes of many, be reckoned more successful than he. He didn't resent women's success, he was just careful of his approach to it. Prejudice is not like a snake's skin: it takes longer to shed. All smooth and confident, she left them.

'She and I were at law school together,' said Miriam Zigler. 'She was a ratbag, no one thought she'd ever amount to anything. Now look at her – yes, Tim?'

Pierpont was leaning against the door-jamb, right hand in his jacket pocket, all smooth and confident. 'Everything straightened out on the Vanheusen case? Hello, Scobie. You must be pleased, wrapping it up so quickly. No four-year wait.'

'I don't think it ever occurred to Lina to run away,' said Malone. 'Maybe it also never occurred to her that we'd pick her up and charge her. It happens.'

They were fencing again. Miriam sat a little bemused, like someone who had bought a ticket at a cinema complex and found it was for the wrong movie. It wasn't that the dialogue puzzled her, but that the actors seemed to be in a scene she had missed.

'We have to watch they don't make her a Mental Health charge. At the end of the day –' he smiled – 'we have to put her away.'

'Oh, we'll do that. How's your conservation demo going?'

'It's gone back to the Environment Court. We'll win.'

Malone couldn't resist it; he looked at Miriam. 'He's all confidence, isn't he?'

Her face was plain, no liveliness in it; she had the feeling they were talking past her. Malone all at once saw it, realized he was taking things too close to the edge. 'But if you DPP people don't have confidence, where would we be?'

'We just believe murderers should pay,' she said. 'Right, Tim?'

'Every time,' he said.

But he sounded un-confident, Malone remarked.

2

Charlene Colnby rang him. 'It's taken me a while, but I wasn't gunna give up. That man, what'shisname, couldn't have been at the club on the night he said he was.'

'Why not?'

'I dug out the club's booking list for that year –'

'How'd you get them, Charlene?'

'Don't worry, I didn't tell the manager why I wanted 'em. I said we were having an argument about when Julie Anthony came out here to sing.'

'Was she there that Thursday night?'

'No, it was –' it sounded like a triumphant pause – 'it was the Chippendales! The club was booked out that night, it was Ladies Only Night. No visitors were allowed, 'specially men.' Again the pause. 'So he couldn't have been in the club that night!'

Why didn't I think of digging up the club's booking list? But he knew why – *now.* He hadn't wanted to know.

'So what are you gunna do?' Charlene was sounding demanding.

'Charlene –' He tried to sound patient but not condescending, which isn't always easy.

'You're not gunna do anything, are you?' It seemed that she wanted no stone unturned or unthrown.

Women, thought Malone, not thinking of stones unturned but of weave unravelled. Surely she didn't expect him to unpick the Glaze case and start again? 'Tell me where to start unravelling –'

'Unravelling? What're you talking about?'

'Charlene –' it sounded like a mantra now, but not a sacred one – 'I've been to my senior officers –'

'Who? The Commissioner?'

'Charlene –' He would have to stop this, find something else: *My good woman*? But if ever that got back to Lisa and the girls they would kneecap him. 'Officers of my rank don't take their problems to the Commissioner.'

He sounded pompous in his own ears, but she didn't accuse him of it.

'So you admit you have a problem?'

You're part of it. 'Of course we have –'

'*We*? It's not my problem, it's the police's –'

'It's much wider than that. It's out of police hands now, it belongs to the DPP –'

'Who?'

He had had easier situations with probing defence counsels. 'The Director of Public Prosecutions. That's the way things work. Do you ever watch the TV programme *Law and Order*?'

'I never watch cop shows. On my nights off, I watch hospital programmes – *ER, Chicago Hope* –'

331

He couldn't resist it: 'Nice clean blood and gore?'

'Pull your head in, Mr Malone. You and I are gunna – what do they call it? – agree to disagree, right?' Then she hung up in his ear.

For the rest of the morning he was in a bad mood and it showed. Even Clements paid him only a short cursory visit. He was left alone to get the shit off his liver.

Midday he left the office, caught a cab into Town Hall, was fortunate enough to find a cab driver who knew where it was. He picked up Lisa and took her to their weekly lunch in the Queen Victoria Building.

'You look as if the Commissioner has just posted you to Tibooburra. You go on your own – I'm not coming.'

'Tibooburra would be a holiday resort right now.'

He looked out through the big window of the restaurant. It seemed that all the boutiques in the big galleried building were having their winter sales; 50 per cent off everything, another mantra. But the stores were empty: no Japanese, no Koreans, certainly no Indonesians looking for bargains. Everyone had their problems and they would just laugh at his. He didn't have to worry about the bottom line, not at the end of the day.

'Tell me about it. It's the Glaze case, isn't it?'

He told her, quietly, while they ate their light lunch, cocooned from the chatter around them. In general Lisa always tried for the big picture, being foreign and not Australian; when it came to her family, Scobie and the children, the frame was too large. She would always protect them: even, she told herself, against principle.

'You have no evidence at all against him, have you?' She meant Pierpont, but now she was back in politics, even if only council politics, she knew not to mention names. One never knew, even in the roar in a football stadium, when there was going to be a moment of silence.

'None. Just suspicion. And conviction,' he added.

'Not enough,' she said with wifely assurance. 'All we can do is pray that the other man doesn't have to pay.' Careful with how she phrased it: there had been a sudden drop in the circling chatter.

'Someone else will be paying?' said the waitress at her shoulder.

'Only my husband,' said Lisa and gave her the sort of smile she had come to see at Olympic funding parties.

When Malone got back to his office there was a note from Clements on his desk: *Lina Vanheusen tried to commit suicide this morning.*

3

'Mulawa told me she's okay.' Clements had been out to lunch with *his* wife; it was domesticity day. He came in half an hour after Malone and said, 'Somehow or other she got hold of some broken glass and cut her wrists. She'd lost a lot of blood and passed out, but they found her before she carked it. It might of been better in a way if they hadn't. Or does that sound callous?'

'No, not if you meant it the way I think you did.

Her life is going to be hell from now on, at least in her own mind.'

'She's going to go down. The next ten or fifteen years, she'll be doing time.' Then he said, almost as if talking round a corner: 'The same as Ron Glaze.'

'Quit being subtle. I'm up a creek there, with no paddle and a woman on the bank telling me I'm going the wrong way. She's right – I *think* – but I'm buggered if I know what to do. And you're no help.'

Clements sat down, not lolling on the couch this time but sitting opposite Malone. 'Okay, let me play devil's advocate again. You haven't got a skerrick of evidence against Pierpont, have you?'

'No. But I *know*. Look, PE went all over the bedroom and all over the wife's car. There wasn't a fingerprint anywhere in the bedroom and not a dab in the front seat of the car – none on the steering wheel, none on the dash or gear lever, none on the car doors. They'd been wiped clean, everything. In the kitchen there were Glaze's prints on the fridge and on a Coke bottle and a glass. Why would he miss those and wipe out all the other dabs?'

'Okay, try that one on a jury. Where do you reckon you'd get? That's the sort of defence Glaze's counsel is gunna use for his client. It won't get you anywhere trying to switch it to Pierpont.'

Malone was slumped and stumped. 'Like I said, you're a great bloody help.'

'I'm trying to stop you getting out on a limb, mate, that's all. I agree with you – Pierpont may have done it, probably did do it. You shouldn't have made such a good case against Glaze. Let it lay, forget it.'

Malone looked up at the big man as he stood up. 'You think I can?'

'No, but I can't think of a better idea.'

After Clements had gone back out to his desk Malone sat for ten minutes. He felt the frustration that is close to rage; but rage had never been one of his accomplishments. It had held him back as a cricketer, because fast bowlers are encouraged to be in a constant state of repressed rage; motivators, who have never bowled a fast ball in their lives, are hired to tell them that. His temperament, however, had never held him back as a cop. He had been angry, often, sometimes furious, but had never given in to rage. An old man, Sean Carmody, had once told him of a song that was his own philosophy: 'Happy is he who accepts what cannot be changed.' It was not a song he wanted to hum right now. He would have sung a dirge if he had known one.

At last he picked up the phone and called Miriam Zigler.

'I know,' she said. 'Corrective Services were on to me as soon as they knew. Don't let it upset you, Scobie. It's a ploy.'

'A plea?'

'No, a ploy. It's my Jewish accent.' She laughed; she was in good humour this afternoon. He wondered what songs she sang when things went wrong. 'She'll come into court with bandaged wrists and her counsel will make the most of it, but we'll just ignore it. Lydia

Wilkox has already called and asked for a delay, but I told her it wasn't on. Monday week, Scobie.'

'Will Tim be in court?'

'He will. She's going to trial in a wheelbarrow, even if we have to push it. How are you? You sound as if you've got the 'flu.'

'No, just a lump in my throat.'

'Not about *her*?' She sounded horrified.

He grinned; talking to her was a small tonic. 'I'll see you Monday week.'

Chapter Eleven

1

India had exploded its nuclear devices and Pakistan had replied with six of its own; it was like a children's game except that the world was in danger. Five thousand Afghan villagers died in an earthquake and 101 middle-class and wealthy Germans died in a train wreck; in Sydney churches prayers were said for the latter; God couldn't be asked to work overtime, not on a holiday weekend. A Federal election was in the air, like pollution; politicians were coughing abuse at each other and election promises at the voters. Beyond the law courts the world spun on its axis, spinning off earthquakes, tornadoes, famine. Murder was a page 4 or 5 item.

The Vanheusen arraignment was in a Downing Centre court before a magistrate, a sour-looking man whose heart might have been a lemon. He was notorious for handing down severe and lengthy sentences, which the Appeals Court, a softer-hearted bunch, invariably revoked. But the voters were starting to talk in flattering terms of the new Judge Jeffreys. That seventeenth-century hanging justice would have been welcomed back with open arms and a choice of nooses by a growing section of the voters. Things did not look good for Evangelina Vanheusen.

The courtroom was crowded, though this was not a trial. The media, from newspapers, television and radio, were out in force; there was no jury, so they were accommodated in the jury-box, which suited their image of themselves. The public section was also crowded; everyone wore black, not in mourning but because current fashion dictated it. All the major magazines were there, indignant at being excluded from the more comfortable seats in the jury-box. Lina's parents and a brother and sister were there. Malone, sitting in the police-box, was surprised when Sheryl Dallen pointed them out to him; he had somehow never imagined Lina as having *family*. Damien Vanheusen was also there and Lady Derry, sitting together. Missing were Mrs Certain and Justin Belgrave.

When the magistrate entered the court Sheryl stood up and left. She and Chris Gallup were to deliver the evidence, Malone having nominated her, and she would remain outside till called. Malone was saving himself, though he did not tell himself that, for the Glaze trial. His mind was slowing, as his bowling arm once had; or so he thought. He no longer cared about Lina Vanheusen, but did care about Ron Glaze.

Pierpont was on his feet presenting the Crown case. He looked towards Lina in the dock; she was dressed in a simple black dress with long sleeves that covered her wrists. She was thinner than ever, looked uninterested in where she was or what was going on. Malone had noticed that when she came into the dock she had looked towards her family, but had neither smiled nor even nodded. She was alone, resigned.

'We are not prepared to accept the defence's plea –' said Pierpont.

'What plea is that, Mr Marble?' asked the magistrate.

Henry Marble, in his university days, had been a rugby forward He had twisted testicles, chewed ears, gouged eyes; he knew the boundaries of sanity that sport allowed. He rose now, taking his time. He was thick-set, looking thicker still in his robe; he had a pugnacious face, like a bunch of knuckles; his wig rested on his mop of black hair like an abandoned nest. He was an actor and today he was going to pull out all the stops. Malone had seen it all before and knew how good Marble could be. Ham is a delectable dish, even if some religions and drama critics frown on it.

'Your worship, my client has been under great strain for months past. Prior, much prior –' he made it sound like fifty years ago – 'to the event that has brought us here today . . . We shall produce medical evidence –'

'As to what, Mr Marble?' The magistrate's expression seemed to be getting sourer.

'Her state of mind prior to the tragedy –'

'Mr Marble –' the magistrate was an impatient man. Given a free hand he could have cleared the crowded court lists in a month – 'how does your client plead?'

Marble didn't like being hurried. He took his time again, looking at the papers on the table in front of him as if he had not seen them before. At five thousand dollars a day, the minutes didn't count for much. At last he looked up at the bench. 'Not guilty, your worship.'

Biddle, the magistrate, looked down at Pierpont. 'You contest that, Mr Crown?'

'Yes, your worship. There has been no submission as to fitness to be tried. I'm not sure whether my learned friend is asking, if the accused goes to trial, that she should be considered as mentally ill at the time of the alleged crime.'

Biddle looked at Marble. 'Is that what you are asking, Mr Marble?'

'The Crown has stolen my thunder –'

'I haven't heard any loud clap.'

All the lawyers and court officials laughed politely; like a good audience they knew who the star was. Magistrates might only be supporting players to judges, but while in the spotlight they ran the show.

'It was just beyond the horizon of the court, your worship.' He was Marble by name and marble by nature: everything bounced off him like tennis balls.

Another giggle from the lawyers and the officials. They live in their own little world, thought Malone with a cop's cynical eye. But he noticed that Pierpont had neither laughed nor giggled.

340

Marble went on: 'My learned friend from the Crown is correct when he says there was no submission as to fitness to be tried. However –' again the long pause. *However*, practised by lawyers, is a word that trails a pause like a comet's train – 'there is a question as to the fitness of my client's mind at the time of the alleged offence.'

The magistrate looked down at Pierpont. 'Do you have any objection, Mr Crown?'

'No, your worship,' said Pierpont and looked and sounded weary.

Malone left the police-box; argument might go on for another half-hour. Out in the main lobby, threading his way through the throng waiting to be called to the other courts on this level, he suddenly found himself in front of Sharon Garibaldi. Or rather, she was in front of him.

'I saw you in the police-box, Inspector. You landed her at last.'

'Are we talking fish? That's not the way I work, Sharon.'

She was not ungracious; she had a lot to learn but she was willing. 'Sorry. But it's been a dirty case –' He made no comment, showed no expression, and she went on: 'Are you still on the Glaze case?'

'We're always on a case till it comes to trial.'

People milled around them, but no one was listening to them. Everyone here had his own case: defendants, lawyers, witnesses, litigants. The law, and the breaking of it, is a current that never stops.

'Will you be calling Mrs Colnby as a witness?'

Careful here, Malone. She's still hoping to get to Charlene. 'The police don't call anyone, Sharon. You know that. You'd better ask the Crown Prosecutor.' And knew at once he had said the wrong thing.

'I'll do that. Who's it going to be?'

'I haven't a clue.'

She smiled: it looked genuine rather than a TV baring of the perfectly capped teeth. 'Why do policemen always say, I haven't a clue?'

'I haven't a clue,' he said and gave her a genuine smile and left.

That afternoon he rang Pierpont. Sheryl Dallen had already come back to Homicide and reported to him, but he wanted an excuse to talk to Pierpont. 'How'd it go?'

'I noticed you left early.'

'You didn't need me, Tim.'

'No. They're going to plead diminished responsibility at the time of the crime. They're calling in the psychiatrists.'

'How do you rate her chances?'

'Fifty-fifty.' He sounded tired. 'I'm surprised at myself, but I'm beginning to feel sorry for her.'

'You're probably surprised at yourself for other reasons, too.' He waited for an answer to that, trying his own use of a pause; but Pierpont didn't bite. He went on: 'A reporter from Channel 15, Sharon Garibaldi, will be looking to talk to you about Mrs Colnby at the Glaze trial. I'd be careful of her, Tim.'

'I never talk to reporters, never ever. Are you feeling sorry for me, Scobie?'

'Actually, I am. For myself, too.'

2

Ronald Glaze went to trial on Monday, August 3.

'Are you going to court today?' Lisa asked.

'Not today. I'm not wanted till tomorrow – most of today will be spent challenging the jury and swearing them in. Thrump will try to choose as few women as he can and Pierpont –' he shrugged. 'I've given up on him. I dunno what he's going to do.'

'Why doesn't he retire himself from the case? Get the 'flu or something, there's enough of it around. If he murdered Mrs Glaze, he can't really want the husband to go to gaol.'

They were in the Fairlane on their way to Town Hall. Lisa had already become only part-time owner of the Laser; Claire had it this morning. The traffic was as thick as ever, drivers wore road rage like make-up. Malone kept to the middle lane, which was where he hoped to stay in the Glaze case.

'If he's not in court, he can't control the way things go.'

'You think that's what he's got in mind – to control everything?'

'I don't know.' He used a hundred-metre pause, pulled up at the traffic red: 'I should've gone to Dave Winkler, the DPP, at the start, let him work it out.'

She thought about that till Malone pulled the car into

the side entrance of Town Hall. She undid her seat belt, leaned across and kissed him. 'You know that would never have worked. Nobody in the whole system checks evidence like the DPP.'

'Where did you learn so much about evidence?'

'I'm married to a cop.' She got out of the car, leaned in again and nodded over her shoulder at her work-place. 'You should come in here for a week or two. We take no notice of evidence. If you scratch my back, I'll scratch yours. It's the bottom line.'

'Get outa here,' he said with love.

He drove back through the city to Strawberry Hills, where there are no hills and no strawberries have ever grown. It was an odd address for Homicide and first-time crims had often been misled when invited to Strawberry Hills. It was a joke the detectives loved to play.

As he did at the beginning of every week he checked on Lina Vanheusen. She was still being held in Mulawa on remand while psychiatrists searched for her state of mind on the night of Lucybelle's murder. Lina, it was reported, was doing nothing to help them or herself. She had closed her mind and herself, she was in retreat and no one, it seemed, could prise open the door. Malone was neither sorry nor angry to hear it. He had stepped out of Lina's life, had one foot in the door of another's. For the next week or two he would be walking on a floor as brittle as gelatine.

Tuesday he went up to Darlinghurst, to Court 7 in the Criminal Courts complex. It was a small court, the media and the public gallery regulars had better offerings in other courts; the Glaze case was four and a half years old, it would get maybe six column-inches on an inside page and nothing on tonight's TV news. If they only knew, thought Malone as he waited outside to be called . . .

The judge was not a character, as some tried to be. Cayley J. was a mild-mannered man, plump-faced and bespectacled under his wig; he looked like an aunt in a nineteenth-century cartoon. He wielded a loose rein and appreciated the wit of barristers because he had little of his own; but, and nobody knew how, his court was always run to his timing and his temperament. There would be no fireworks.

Malone took his place in the witness-box, took the oath and settled himself in his chair as Pierpont rose to question him. Malone had been in this situation more times than he bothered to count, but he never found it routine. The man, or woman, in the dock saw to that. Homicide, more than any other crime, produces a greater variety of characters.

'You took charge of this case –' Pierpont began. 'Why?'

What sort of question is that? 'Homicide, my section, was called in by the local detectives – they were under-staffed and at the time could not have done the investigation justice.'

Pierpont nodded. 'And you pursued the case over the next four years till you finally apprehended the accused living under an assumed name at –' he looked at his papers, though Malone guessed he was word-perfect in every detail – 'at Collamundra?'

'Yes.'

'Admirable work, Inspector.'

'Thank you.' *What's the bugger getting at*?

'Now could you run through the details that started you in pursuit of the accused?'

Malone took out the notes he had made from his old notebook of four and more years ago. 'Fingerprints, to begin with . . .'

Once or twice he lifted his eyes from the notes and looked across the court at Ron Glaze. The latter sat leaning forward in the dock; one could see the tension in him. He was tanned and healthy, probably fitter than he had been in twenty years. He looked ready for the biggest sale of his life, himself.

'All solid evidence,' said Pierpont, 'but the bird had flown?'

'May we dispense with the avian references, Mr Crown?' said the judge, surprising everyone with his attempt at wit, so much so that everyone forgot to laugh. He looked disappointed.

'Of course, your honour . . . When you finally caught up with the accused, Inspector, what happened?'

Malone described the day at Collamundra and the interview with – 'He was calling himself Roger Gibson. Then –'

'Then?'

'He admitted he was Ronald Glaze.'

'He also made another admission, didn't he?'

'Objection.' Billy Thrump came up out of his chair at the Bar table like a bird that had not flown in quite a while; his gown flew out at the back and his wig wobbled. 'My learned friend is leading the witness –'

'I withdraw the question,' said Pierpont. 'Inspector, did the accused say anything to you at the interview in Collamundra?'

'Objection!'

Judge Cayley looked down over his spectacles, looking more than ever like a period maiden aunt. 'Mr Thrump, it is going to be a long day. I'll allow the Crown to ask the question.'

'Inspector, could you tell us what was said by the accused?'

Malone knew what Pierpont was referring to: 'He said that when he came back to his house early that morning he was going to ask his wife for a reconciliation. If she refused, he was going to kill her, then kill himself.'

'Did you believe him?'

What sort of question is that? Malone waited for another objection from Thrump, but the defence counsel was leaning forward, head cocked as if looking for a second meaning behind the question. Malone hedged: 'At that point in an investigation I'm still gathering evidence.'

It was an evasive answer. Malone flicked a glance sideways at the jury-box. There were eight men and four women there; the men didn't move but two of the women scribbled a note on their pads. Then he looked across at Glaze, who stared at him a moment, then nodded. *He's beginning to realize I'm no longer the enemy.*

Pierpont was the enemy, in a double role. He wondered how much Glaze believed Charlene Colnby's suspicion and when he would burst out with his own accusation. Glaze was watching Pierpont closely, but so far he had masked his feelings.

'That is all for the moment, your honour,' said Pierpont unexpectedly and sat down.

Thrump was on his feet at once; pauses weren't in his vocabulary. 'The accused's wife was already dead when he came to the house at – he thinks it was between two and three o'clock in the morning. Is that correct, Inspector?'

'That was what he claimed.'

'The body was discovered next morning at eight fifteen when one of Mrs Glaze's assistants called at her house – I understand Mrs Glaze always gave her a lift to work – and when the medical examiner arrived at nine o'clock, his guess was that Mrs Glaze had been dead approximately eight or nine hours.'

'That's all it would be – a guess. As I understand it, the timing of a death can never be exact.'

Thrump had seen his mistake too late; he hurried on, covering Malone's last words: 'The estimate would not be *two* hours out. At midnight my client was seen in the Penrith mall by three separate witnesses. At two o'clock a neighbour saw my client arrive at his home.' He looked at the jury. The two women note-takers made another note. They're on Glaze's side, Malone thought, and felt a measure of relief. So far the other jury members, especially the men, looked either bored or as if they could have been listening to weather reports. Thrump looked at his own notes: 'Inspector, the fingerprints. The evidence states that my client's prints were on the fridge in the kitchen and on a Coca-Cola bottle. But in the bedroom, the scene of the crime, there were no prints at all – the room had been wiped clean. Same with the deceased's Volvo car – not a print anywhere in the front section of the car. Wiped clean.' He allowed himself a joke at his client's expense: 'Now we know my client was a car sales representative, but don't you think that was taking his trade to unusual lengths?'

Malone didn't laugh; nor did Glaze. 'Yes, we thought so.'

'All that wiping clean – what might it have suggested to you, Inspector? Perhaps the murderer knew what police would look for? Someone with a previous record, who knew the way police worked?'

We're getting into dangerous territory here. Malone looked for Charlene Colnby, was relieved she wasn't in court. 'No, that possibility didn't suggest itself to us.'

'But Mrs Glaze could have had another visitor that night?'

Malone avoided looking at Pierpont, but was aware of the latter looking at him. 'It's possible, yes.'

'But right from the start of the investigation you never considered that other possibility?'

'No.'

Thrump looked triumphantly at the jury; he was not one to hide his triumphs, no matter how small. The reaction, though dim and fleeting, was enough for Thrump to retire for the moment: 'That will be all, Inspector.'

'Mr Crown?' The judge looked down at Pierpont.

'No further questions, your honour.'

Malone left the witness box and moved across to the police box. The medical examiner and the fingerprints expert had preceded Malone; he was followed by Andy Graham and Wally Mungle. Thrump asked no questions of Graham but he wanted to question Mungle.

'Detective Constable, you knew of my client all the time he was in Collamundra – what sort of citizen was he?' He did allow himself a pause this time: 'From a policeman's point of view?'

'We had no complaints,' said Wally Mungle.

'No complaints? That was the extent of your impression of him? A member of Rotary, on the committee of the local golf club, a leading businessman in the town and all you can say about him was that you had no complaints?'

Mungle shifted uncomfortably. Don't start playing the poor Abo down from the bush, thought Malone, watching him closely. Thrump's tone had been superior when he asked the question, but that was endemic with lawyers in court. It had nothing to do with race superiority, it was a virus of education and profession.

'You did ask from a policeman's point of view,' said Mungle at last.

Malone almost gave him a fist of approval. *Good on you, son.*

'So I did –' Thrump retreated, without moving. 'Well,

let's change the point of view. As a member of the Collamundra community, how did you see my client?'

You don't know Collamundra, Malone thought. He's not a full member.

But Mungle was at ease now; he had come through the barbed wire. 'He was okay.'

'That all? Just okay.'

'We're more laconic in the bush. What d'you want me to say? He was fantastic?'

Watch it, Wally.

Judge Cayley said quietly, almost gently, 'No, Constable, we don't want you to exaggerate, though that's the modern fashion. Here in the city,' he added and smiled at Mungle.

The latter suddenly seemed to realize he had a friend in court. He smiled back at the judge, then turned back to Thrump. 'Mr Glaze was what I suppose you'd call a pillar of the community.'

Thrump nodded approvingly. 'He never showed any violence towards anyone?'

'No.'

'You had the opportunity to observe him over the extended period he was in Collamundra. Would you have taken him for a violent man, one capable of the crime he's been accused of?'

'No-o.'

Hul-lo, thought Malone. Wally, too, now has his doubts.

'Thank you, Detective Constable. That will be all.'

At the midday adjournment Malone went out to the

front of the courthouse. A small group of women stood to one side of the path, almost like a prayer group. Malone recognized Glaze's mother and sister and Charlene Colnby; it took him a moment or two longer to recognize Roma Gibson. The mane of golden hair had been cut short; she looked thinner, less lusty-figured. She turned her head and stared at him, but didn't smile or nod. For her he was still the enemy.

Then Charlene Colnby broke away from the group and came towards him. She had a quick walk, like a hen on its way to be fed; but he would feed her nothing. Not out here in the open.

'I haven't been in court, I'm being called as a witness.'

'Who by? The defence?'

She shook her head. She was wearing a brown woollen coat and a matching cap against the coldness of the day; she looked even smaller than when he had last seen her. 'No, that friend of yours.'

'Charlene –' He took her arm and led her aside, away from those still coming out of the courtroom. The other three women watched them, a prayer group putting a hex on him. He saw Sharon Garibaldi, but there was no sign of a television camera; she looked incomplete, he thought, like his mother without her handbag.

'Charlene, he's not my friend. He's the Crown Prosecutor. When you get into the box, that's all you have to remember.'

'Will you be going back into the box?' She made it sound like a coffin.

'No, I'm not expecting to be called again.'

'How's it going for Ron? His mum and his sister and that Mrs Gibson, they're not happy.'

'It's going all right for him. It's a long way from over.'

She looked at him with a barmaid's eye, than which there is nothing shrewder. 'You know something, don't you?'

'No, Charlene, I don't. I've got my fingers crossed, that's all.'

'No, you know Ron didn't murder Norma.'

'No, all I know is I don't know who did.'

'You're a liar, Mr Malone. But in a good cause. We're gunna get Ron off.'

Then Wally Mungle came out and Malone was glad to escape. He took Wally to lunch at a local café. 'What sort of food do you like?'

'You mean do I like bush tucker? Grilled wombat, something like that?'

'Pull your head in, Wally, or I'll pull rank. Just because one or two of the questions you got were city slicker ones . . .' He relaxed. 'Come on, Wally. Around this part of town you can have everything from Mexican to Yugoslav, but no steak and eggs or saveloys.'

'I like Thai. There's one opened up in Collamundra, the locals are rushing it. Even the Kooris.' He grinned and everything was all right between them.

The café was crowded, but no one from the court was present. The talk over their meal was roundabout and each of them seemed to know it. Mungle accepted that there was no rank at their table. He was relaxed, though here in the main stem of the gay belt he seemed to be having trouble from raising his eyebrows at some of those around him. Out in Collamundra men didn't hold hands across the table, unless in an arm-wrestle. It even occurred to Malone that they were possibly the only two straights in the café, but it didn't worry him. Two or three years ago it might have made him uncomfortable.

'Relax, Wally. This isn't Collamundra. How're things out there? I saw Mrs Gibson outside the court.'

'My wife says that women's talk is that she'll take Ron back if he's acquitted.'

'What about Amanda Hardstaff?'

'She's back at Noongulli since the rains came. Roma Gibson has just stopped supplying her with liquidambars or whatever it was she used to buy from Ron.'

Malone sipped his light beer, said casually, 'Do you think he'll be coming back to Collamundra?'

Wally toyed with his food, took his time: he, too, was learning the uses of pauses. 'Do you mean do I think he didn't do it? The murder?'

'Yes, I think that's what I mean.'

There was another long pause; then: 'I don't think he did it, even if you can't find another suspect.'

'How will you feel if he does go down?'

'Lousy. If I hadn't been such a bloody eager beaver and called you –'

'Wally –' Malone put down his beer – 'Wally, we all make mistakes. There isn't a cop with ten years' experience who hasn't made one major mistake. We're not bloody geniuses or miracle workers.'

'Do you think you've made a mistake this time?'

Malone took his own pause while he made sure he did not give too much away: 'Yes, I do.'

Wally Mungle considered that, then nodded understandingly. 'We may be lucky – and Ron, too. The Crown guy seems half-hearted about it.'

Oh, you're wasted out at Collamundra, Wally. But why would a bush cop be any less shrewd than a city one? Especially this one. 'Well, he's Ron's only hope. You want dessert?'

Wally Mungle left to catch a train back to Collamundra; police expenses as a witness did not run to plane fare. He would go home, sitting up all the way in second class; he had come down overnight. His visit to the city had been to spend two hours in a courtroom and an hour in a gay café. It wouldn't be much to talk about when he got back to Collamundra, not in the culture of the town's police station.

Malone went back to the court. Ron Glaze came back into the dock, smiled and gave a small wave to his mother and sister and Roma Gibson. He looked cheerful if not confident, as if he were waving to customers looking for a new car, ones who weren't sure if they had enough money to buy what they wanted.

Charlene Colnby was called as a witness in mid-afternoon. She was wearing her big coat, but had taken off the matching cap. Her hair, newly blonded, was worn in a style that Malone hadn't seen on her before. This was an occasion for her: for her or Ron? Malone wondered. As she sat down in the box she peered short-sightedly around her, then opened her handbag and put on her glasses. She wasn't nervous, she was taking her time: all the men could wait. She had dealt with drunks, she could deal with lawyers.

Judge Cayley, smiling slightly, looked down at her. 'Ready, Mrs Colnby?'

'Yes, your honour.' Then she looked at Pierpont as if to say, *I'm ready for you, too*.

'You were on duty at the Golden West on the night of the murder of Mrs Glaze? You work behind the bar there?'

'Yes, I'm the senior barmaid.' As if drawing a class distinction.

Pierpont caught it and smiled. 'I'm sure you got that position on experience. And that experience would have made you very observant, am I correct in saying that?'

'I don't miss much.' Staring straight at him as if there was no one else in the court.

Pierpont stared back. 'Tell us what you observed of Mr and Mrs Glaze that evening.'

Charlene Colnby adjusted her glasses, took her time: another user of pauses. 'Mrs Glaze was obviously unhappy –'

'Unhappy? How could you tell that? Did she confide in you?'

Another pause, lips tight: 'Women can tell when another woman is unhappy. Men can't.'

356

Pierpont looked at the judge, but the latter only nodded, gave another small smile. 'The witness is probably right, Mr Crown. But don't let's get into gender warfare.'

Cayley J. was excelling himself. The lawyers sat up, polishing their giggles.

'Proceed, Mrs Colnby,' said Pierpont.

'She had several drinks. Over the month or two before that night, she'd come to the club two or three nights a week, never stay long –'

'Would she join other members? Was her husband there those nights?'

'No, not that I remember. They had broken up and were keeping the break-up to themselves.'

'Who told you that?'

'Ron – Mr Glaze.' There was a single giggle from the Bar table, but Charlene Colnby cut it short with a glare. 'I never talked much with Norma – Mrs Glaze. We didn't get on – I dunno why –'

Of course you do, thought Malone. You'd had it off with Ron and she knew about it.

'She was drinking more than she used to before the break-up. One night we had to call a cab to take her home. She came in the next day and apologized. We didn't get on, but she was polite and she paid her debts – better than some men.' The men in court stared back at her, undented. 'She give me the money for the cab fare.'

'On the night of the murder, did you see the accused arrive?'

'Yes, I did. He said hullo to some people, to me too, then he went and sat down with his wife. But you could see there wasn't much going on between them –'

Malone, after many years and long experience, was still impressed by the memories of some witnesses. Or the manufactured memory . . .

'They weren't arguing, but – well, you know –'

'I'm sure we all do, Mrs Colnby, but tell us.'

'Well, it was – *chilly* between them. Then he got up and walked out, not looking at anyone –'

Pierpont looked at the paper in his hand. 'In your statement to Inspector Malone next morning you said the accused looked cold-blooded when he walked out. That's the word you used – cold-blooded?'

'I suppose so. I don't remember everything I said that morning –' the convenient memory at work – 'I was still in shock at what had happened.'

'You did say it, Mrs Colnby. *He looked cold-blooded –*' Pierpont read from his paper; then he looked up: 'And on the strength of the way you thought he looked, you instantly jumped to the conclusion that he had murdered his wife?'

Hold on, that's the sort of question the defence should ask. Malone sat up, looked up at the judge. Cayley J. leaned forward as if to question Pierpont, changed his mind and sat back. Malone glanced at the Bar table: everyone there was very still. Miriam Zigler was frowning, but not looking at Pierpont. In the jury-box one of the women was scribbling on her note-pad.

Charlene Colnby had been absorbing the question in

358

her own way; she straightened her glasses again, ran her lips up and down over her teeth. Then she said slowly, as if she wanted every word perfectly understood: 'No, I didn't. I never for a moment believed he had killed her.'

Pierpont looked again at the paper in his hand, chewed his lip, then nodded. 'Thank you, Mrs Colnby,' he said and sat down.

Thrump this time took longer to rise; he had been caught off-guard. At last he was on his feet, gathering his robe round him like a fusspot matron from a BBC period drama. He was equally theatrical: 'Splendid, Mrs Colnby! An unbiased view –' He glanced towards the jury, most of whom took no notice of him. This was their third day of duty, they had become inured to theatrics from the Bar table. They all had their eyes on Charlene Colnby who, for the moment at least, was the star. 'You have known my client for how many years?'

'Up till now, including the time he was missing?'

'Up till now.'

'Nine or ten years, maybe longer. Ever since he joined the club.'

'And have you ever known him to show any violence towards anyone?'

Charlene shook her head. 'Never.'

'Did you ever hear his wife mention any violence towards her?'

'Never.'

Malone had remarked it before: women can say *never* with more emphasis, with more honest effect, than men.

But why would Norma Glaze, who had *never* been close to Charlene, have confided such a personal matter? He looked towards the Bar to see if Pierpont had made a note, but the prosecutor was just sitting back in his chair, seemingly uninterested. Then Malone let the suspicion that had been rustling in his mind turn into conviction. Pierpont was trying to lose the case.

When Thrump was finished with Charlene, the prosecutor did not rise to cross-examine further. Malone saw Miriam Zigler, at the table, lean towards him and say something, but Pierpont just shook his head.

Two more witnesses were called, but the case was over; the feeling in the court was palpable. The judge left the bench, the jury filed out and the courtroom slowly emptied. Malone sat on in the police box, staring across at Pierpont, who was slowly gathering up his papers, nodding as if not hearing a word of the many Miriam Zigler was spitting at him.

Her voice rose for a moment: 'For Crissakes, Tim, what's the matter with you?'

Pierpont looked across the court at Malone. The two men's gaze was like a handshake; Malone recognized it as such. Then Pierpont turned abruptly and went out of the court, walking quickly, snatching off his wig as if he might throw it away. Miriam Zigler looked after him, picked up her own papers, then waited for Malone as the latter stood up slowly and came out of the police box.

'We've lost it, you know. Tim's let it go down the gurgler.'

All he could say was, 'You win some, you lose some.'

He did not go to the court next morning. At eleven thirty Andy Graham, whom he had sent, phoned him. 'The jury's just come back. Not guilty.'

Malone put down the phone, beckoned to Clements through the glass wall of his office. The big man came in, stood in the doorway. 'The jury's back in court?'

'Not guilty. Our problem's over.'

Clements heaved a sigh of relief, dropped down on the couch. 'So what do you do with Pierpont? Let up on him?'

'We've got Ron Glaze off.'

'Don't dodge the issue, mate. Ron Glaze's wife is still dead.'

Malone threw up his hands in exasperation. 'What's the matter with you? A week ago you were playing devil's advocate, asking me how much evidence I had, what jury would listen to me. I think this devil's advocate bit has gone to your head.'

'I'm only asking the question you'll be asking yourself in bed tonight. Or that Lisa will be asking you.'

Men will tell you that women are unpredictable; but not always. That night in bed Lisa asked the question Clements had said she would: 'Are you going to let up on Tim Pierpont?'

'Don't ask.'

She dug him in the ribs. 'Don't play smarty with me. What are you going to do?'

He rolled over on his back, stared up at the dark ceiling. 'I don't know.'

'I've been thinking since you told us about today's verdict.' The family had accepted the verdict without much comment; perhaps they had noticed his quiet mood. 'Mrs Glaze has been dead – what? – four and a half years. I know crimes should be paid for. But what about Ginny Pierpont and his little girl and the baby when it comes?'

'Do you think I haven't been thinking about that?'

Then he held her close to him. Wondered if in another bed Tim Pierpont was holding his wife just as closely.

Next morning he sat in his office and thought about Pierpont. Should he call him or not? What was there to say – *Congratulations*? Would Pierpont respond gracefully or tell him to get stuffed?

At last, because it was not in his nature to leave strings untied, he picked up the phone and called the DPP offices. Miriam Zigler came on to Pierpont's phone. 'He's not in this morning, Scobie. He went home yesterday right after the verdict was brought in. I don't know what was the matter with him during the trial – he wasn't with it. What did you think of the verdict?'

He hesitated. 'It was always going to be fifty-fifty.'

'I was more optimistic than that. We stuffed it.' It was her turn to hesitate: 'I'm worried about Tim. I'll tell him you called.' She sounded sour, let down, and he couldn't blame her.

He put down the phone, reached for the L–Z phone book and got Pierpont's home number. Even then he sat for another five minutes wary of the disquiet he felt. Then he rang the Turramurra number.

Ginny Pierpont answered. 'No, Tim's not here, Inspector – or do I call you Scobie?'

'Scobie will do. How is he? His office said he wasn't well.'

There was silence for a while; then: 'I'm worried, Scobie. He hasn't been himself these past few weeks. I've been trying to tell him to take time off. He's taken the Discovery and gone up to the Mountains to have another look at that development. He said he wanted to sit there and think. He loves the view from there.'

'Does he have a mobile?'

'Yes, he does. But he's forgotten it – he's left it here beside the phone.'

He didn't want to worry her: 'Righto, I'll call him tomorrow. You okay?'

'Just some morning sickness. Give my regards to Mrs Malone. Lisa.'

Malone put down the phone, let the disquiet bubble up in him. Then he got up, took his hat and jacket and went out to Clements.

'I'm going up to Springwood. But keep it to yourself.'

'I'll ride down in the lift with you.'

Out in the car park Clements said, 'What are you expecting him to do?'

'I dunno. Maybe he's just gone up there to think things out. Or –'

'Or to top himself? Don't use the siren or the red light getting there, mate. Don't kill yourself for him. Ring me when you get there and find him.'

4

He sat on the rock and looked out at the distant city. There had been overnight rain and the winter's day was as clear as French glass; he could have seen forever but for the tears in his eyes. He held his hands out in front of him and looked at them, the damaged one and the one that had done the damage. He tried to remember what had possessed him that terrible night four and a half years ago, but couldn't. He had been sitting here an hour, going through the dusty drawers of his mind, but it had been like sorting shredded papers.

He dropped his hands, automatically put the withered hand back in the pocket of his jacket. He was wearing his oldest jacket and a pair of faded jeans: he would die neither in style nor in fashion.

He stood up. He knew from experience in court that any death within twelve months of an insurance policy being taken out would be investigated painstakingly by the insurance company. He also knew from experience the contradictions in staging an accident. He would have to be careful in his apparent carelessness; there would be deliberation about what looked like desperation. He made slip-marks with his shoes right to the edge of the cliff; he went down on his knees in the mud, ran his fingers, even the claw, through it. Then he tore off a slim branch from the log resting on the edge of the cliff.

He took a deep breath, said a prayer. Then, clutching the branch, he went backwards off the cliff and down to the rocks far below. He was weeping with rage at himself, dying with anger.

Malone was half an hour too late. When he drove on to the edge of the clearing, two police officers stopped him. He showed them his badge and asked what had happened.

'An accident, sir. He went over the edge – some of our guys and the ambulance blokes are down below with the body. They're gunna take it out from there, not bring it back up here. You mind me asking, sir – were you supposed to meet him here?'

'He was trying to get me to join his conservation group. I was to meet him here, then we were going on up to Katoomba to look at what the government's proposing with the new national park.'

'Well, he's past all that now.' Then the officer gestured awkwardly. 'Sorry, sir, that sounded a bit callous – I didn't mean it like that.'

'No, you're right. He doesn't have to conserve anything any more.'

'They phoned up to say they'd found identification on him.' The officer tapped his mobile. 'Will you tell his wife? If he has one?'

'Yes, he's married, has a child and a pregnant wife –'

'Jesus!'

'I think it better if someone from his local station does that – he lived at Turramurra. I really don't know the wife, we weren't exactly friends. Just acquaintances.' He was cutting himself adrift, running away.

'Sure, we understand. We can get in touch with you if we need you?'

'Homicide will find me.'

He went back to Strawberry Hills, driving carefully, like a man finding his way out of territory where the maps had been unreliable.

Chapter Twelve

1

'Stop beating your breast.'

'I was sloppy. I took Occam's Razor and nearly cut my own throat. I accepted the bloody obvious and the obvious was wrong.'

Greg Random had come across from Police Centre, ostensibly on an administration check. He sat now in Malone's office with the door closed; to the staff out in the main room, with the exception of Clements, it looked as if Malone was being ticked off for some management error.

'You didn't shove him off the cliff. If it wasn't an accident then his own conscience sent him off.'

'It looked like an accident, thank Christ.'

'Don't try and change anybody's mind. You had no real proof that he ever killed that Glaze woman – you've got no proof that he committed suicide. Let the insurance company, if one's involved, make up its own mind. They don't need your suspicions on the matter.'

Malone said nothing. He had his suspicions, but, as Random had said, no evidence. He could not go back over that ground again.

'Why did he kill that woman?' Random took out his pipe, but as usual didn't light it or even fill it. 'Who knows? I think all of us have got the killer instinct in us somewhere – it's our animal nature. In most of us, thank Christ, it never comes to the surface. In him it did – and we'll never know why. But from now on stop looking like you crucified him. He made his own cross and bought his own nails.'

Malone nodded, sat slumped in his chair. 'Righto. Just don't quote any Welsh poets at me.'

'Rage, rage against the dying of the light . . .' Random smiled his thin smile; out in the main room everyone but Clements thought, everything's okay. 'We Welsh make the most of dying. All the best voices in the heavenly choir are Welsh.'

Malone gave him a weary smile. 'The Welsh and the Irish – we could've been contenders. Why weren't we?'

'Poets and singers can never beat the blokes with calculators. We always sing the bottom line on a low note.'

'At the end of the day. Go home, Greg. I'm cured.'

Next morning Malone went to Tim Pierpont's funeral at the Northern Suburbs crematorium. The chapel was packed: with family, friends, lawyers, conservationists.

Ginny Pierpont, looking stricken and lost, was there. Beside her was young Fay, with that bemused look that children wear when surrounded by drab, sad grown-ups. Miriam Zigler was there, sitting at the back of the chapel, weeping, as stricken as Ginny Pierpont. David Winkler spoke the eulogy and the dead man, a good man, went into the flames on a wave of praise and sorrow.

Later Malone and Winkler walked together down to their cars. It was another bright winter's day; looking west one could see the Blue Mountains; they were too far away to see the developer's scar. A magpie carolled in a tree, then sharpened its beak for the spring bombardment of humans.

'The irony of it is,' said Winkler, 'he took out a two million dollar insurance policy a couple of months ago. He'd received a death threat or two from some drug dealer's mates.'

'He told me about them.'

'They were empty threats. But –' Winkler opened the door of his car, a Jaguar that, like himself, looked in need of a paint job – 'at least the insurance will take care of Ginny and the children. Not that that's any compensation, not really.'

'No,' said Malone.

2

Time has gone backwards into history and memory has become a floating anchor, not always reliable. The eastern half of the globe is in recession; small wars are still being fought; famine has taken the life out of parts of Africa. The Four Horsemen never stop riding.

DeeDee Orion has already achieved almost supermodel status in New York. She has been featured on the covers of *Vogue*, *Harper's Bazaar*, *Vanity Fair* and *Architectural Review* (don't ask). She has been seen in the company of Lachlan Murdoch, Leonardo DiCaprio and someone who looked like Al Gore but turned out to be one of the many millionaires from Microsoft. For Doris Dulcie life is but a dream.

Justin Belgrave went bankrupt and has gone back to Melbourne, where he is working as a waiter in a restaurant where slimming and fitness is not the intention of the proprietor.

Damien Vanheusen has sold his shops but has kept his design centre, just in case. He has been in London, knocking on doors, but no one is opening them. He is thinking of changing his name to Damien Izziyaki.

Ron and Roma Glaze are happily married, surrounded by flowers. The nursery business, like most businesses in the country, isn't booming, but at least it is green.

Amanda Hardstaff is back at Noongulli. The rains have continued to come to the plains; Noongulli, too, is green once again and, if not yet profitable again, is at least salvageable. History there is safe for the time being.

Charlene Colnby's husband won $14,000 on a poker machine jackpot at the Golden West and he and Charlene are blowing it on an economy trip round the world. Charlene has so far not bothered Malone again. She has a new hairstyle.

And Lina Vanheusen? She is now in a minimum security correction centre, still under psychiatric care. She was deemed unfit to stand trial and spends her days in a locked mind. She will ultimately be released, but the psychiatric assessment is that her surroundings will mean nothing to her. She is dead with her daughter Lucybelle.

Homicide and Serial Offenders goes on: murder never stops.

3

'Your mum says her rosary, but I got me *Herald*.' Con Malone tapped his folded newspaper on the iron railings of the front verandah.

Malone and Lisa had come to Erskineville for dinner. It would be the same as dinner every month: roast lamb, three veggies, bread-and-butter pudding. Malone always brought a good red and his mother had at last accepted a half-glass, sipping it with caution and a certain reverence, as if it were communion wine. Lisa was now inside the house with Brigid, and Malone and his father were standing at the front gate watching the street lights come on. In this light, Malone thought, gentrification looked its best.

'Hegel –' Con pronounced it Heggel –' he said reading

your newspaper is the secular equivalent of your morning prayers.'

'Heggel? Who's he?'

'German smart-arse. One of me Party mates used to read bits of him when we'd stop for a smoke-o. Half the time I didn't know what he was talking about. But that's about it with smart-arses. Philosophers, I think you call 'em.'

'Don't knock philosophers. That's what cops have to be as we get older.'

Then Lisa called that dinner was ready. Son and father went into the house, the safe house, and closed the door.

'You still got my cricket bat?'

Kirribilli
December 1997 – June 1998

Five Ring Circus

Jon Cleary

As Sydney prepares for its grand role as host of the next Olympic Games, homicide detective Scobie Malone stumbles upon a scam that will do nothing for the city's image. Illicit deals are being struck and money from Hong Kong is being banked in large quantities. But whose money is it, and where is it really from?

A series of cold-blooded assassinations follow, as the ruthless individuals behind the conspiracy seek to eliminate anyone who poses a security risk. Meanwhile Scobie's investigation is frustrated at every turn by a wall of silence as vast as the Great Wall of China, making progress impossible . . . until he finds the cracks which will lead him to the unexpected truth.

'A first-class, well-written, entertaining thriller'

Adelaide Advertiser

'When the ruminants and the lucre-chasers are growing lichen on library shelves, Jon Cleary will continue to be read'
Los Angeles Times

0 00 651142 2

The Big Killing

Robert Wilson

Bruce Medway, go-between and fixer for traders in West Africa, smells trouble when a porn merchant asks him to deliver a video at a secret location. Things look up, though, when he's hired to act as minder to Ron Collins, a spoilt playboy looking for diamonds. Medway thinks this could be the answer to his cashflow crisis, but when the video delivery leads to a shootout and the discovery of a mutilated body, the prospect of retreating to his bolthole in Benin becomes increasingly attractive – especially as the manner of the victim's death is too similar to a current notorious political murder for comfort.

His obligations, though, keep him fixed in the Ivory Coast and he is soon caught up in a terrifying cycle of violence. But does it stem from the political upheavals in nearby Liberia, or from the cutthroat business of diamonds? Unless Medway can get to the bottom of the mystery, he knows that for the savage killer out there in the African night, he is the next target . . .

'A narrative distilled from pure protein: potent, fiercely imagined and not a little frightening'   *Literary Review*

ISBN 0 00 647986 3

A Different Turf

Jon Cleary

'The Malone stories come alive through their setting . . . Cleary's writing is seamless and his plots imaginative and mature'
Miami Herald

Homicide detective Scobie Malone returns to tackle one of his toughest cases yet: in the gay community of Sydney, where 'gay bashings' are a daily occurrence, the culprits are being eliminated, each shooting apparently carried out by a different person. Whoever they are, Malone soon realizes that he is dealing with an intelligent, highly dangerous killer. At the same time, this difficult case is causing tension within the force as prejudices of all kinds – race, creed, colour and sexual inclination – rear their ugly heads.

It's bad enough that the killer seems to be one step ahead, constantly protected by the gay network who are refusing to co-operate, but when Malone's own precious daughter has a near escape, his determination to crack the case and the killer's identity intensifies, while he tries to remain professional.

Tense, topical and compulsive, *A Different Turf* brings to the surface some important social issues as well as spinning an intriguing mystery, guaranteed to keep Scobie Malone's fans hooked.

0 00 649996 1